EARTH
Residents' Manual

EARTH
Residents' Manual

A Novel by
Arman Manoucheri

Published by Unified Ink Publishing, Bellevue, Washington

Front cover design by Shahrzad M., @artwithsherrymah
Interior book design by Mi Ae Lipe, whatnowdesign.com.

Printed in the United States of America.

To contact the author or order additional copies:
Arman Manoucheri
Email: arman22@msn.com

First Edition, 2021
ISBN: 978-1-7361123-0-4
Library of Congress Control Number: 2020922694

I dedicate this book to my mother and father—
you always made me proud to introduce you as my parents.

CONTENTS

You were born in my imagination
and will live in my belief

1

In the Time of Your Life, Live

In the high altitude across the bright blue sky of dawn, the whoosh of two jet engines ripped across the crisp air. Inside the luxurious private plane's cabin, all was calm, with only a quiet humming of the engines and a light tapping sound of fingers on a sliding tray.

In the jet's sleek, state-of-the-art cockpit, the captain and copilot sat side by side, monitoring their instruments and display screens.

"Our ETA is 30 minutes, Captain," announced the copilot.

In a voice that was deep but gentle, the captain made an announcement over the intercom to his only passenger in the cabin. "Good morning, Mr. Saint Clair. We will be arriving at the target area in 30 minutes. I will be out shortly to assist you with your parachute."

The only response from Saint Clair was the repetitious tapping of his fingers on the tray.

The copilot turned to the captain. "What is that sound?"

"Tapping," replied the captain. "He does that even when he sleeps. He's a restless soul."

Inside the elegant, plush cabin, Saint Clair lay reclined in his soft beige leather seat with his eyes closed. He was dozing lightly, but his right hand kept tapping the hard surface of the tray next to him. Awakened by the captain's voice, he pushed a button to move the back of his seat upright and glanced at his sport watch. He then pushed another button on his seat, and soon he faced the window.

Peering out with curiosity, he looked down. He could feel the jet slowly descending, and below lay a glorious, immense jungle so dense that no bare ground was visible as far as he could look with his naked eye. A solid velvet, emerald-green blanket of old forest carpeted the land.

Saint Clair had his jumpsuit on. It was nothing like a military outfit, but rather a high-tech–looking jumpsuit equipped with various apparatus.

Back in the cockpit, the copilot turned to the captain. "Shouldn't we be seeing a clearing on the ground by now?" he asked.

"No, it's just one spot in the middle of the dense jungle," replied the captain. "It's only about a dozen acres of cleared forest. That's the clearing where the heart of the village is. I have heard it referred to as the Emerald Island. Of course, it's not an island, but it would sure look like one from here in this ocean of trees."

"Is he really going to be able to land in that little village?" asked the copilot. "We don't exactly know the wind factor at that point."

"I have never done this without some survey, and I've already told him about the risks," said the captain. "Like I said, he called me in the middle of the night and told me we were doing this the next day."

"But why the rush? The village isn't going anywhere."

"No, but the man he is looking for is. He got some kind of intelligence report that this doctor guy has been in the village for a while now and is planning to move on. Once he heard that, he dropped everything and now here we are."

"What did he say when you told him about the risk of jumping out in this region?"

"He said you can't tiptoe in life so that you can safely arrive at death," said the captain, getting up from his chair. "I'm going to help him get ready now."

"He's a little crazy, huh?" said the copilot.

The captain chuckled. "Crazy is a term for poor people. When you're that rich, they just call you eccentric."

Back in the cabin, the captain asked Saint Clair, "Were you able to get some sleep?"

"Some," Saint Clair answered, "but mostly I just relaxed and imagined where I'll be later today."

The captain looked concerned. "I know it's pointless, but is there anything I can say to change your mind?"

Saint Clair smiled. "Yes, tell me he is not there."

"I have something that I wish you'd take with you," the captain said.

"What, a Power Bar?" Saint Clair asked.

"No. Well, kind of," said the captain. "This is my gun—please take it with you."

"A gun?" said Saint Clair, incredulously. "What would the villagers think if I land in the middle of their home with a gun on my side? It would look hostile, wouldn't you say? Besides, what would he think?"

"But it's a jungle down there."

Saint Clair shook his head. "I've made arrangements for a guide to meet me at the village in three days and escort me out to civilization, and he's already left the capital with all the supplies."

"But it's going to take him a few days to get to the village," the captain said.

"In the meantime," said Saint Clair, "I'm going to have to rely on the hospitality of the villagers and my Power Bars. Besides, I have my satellite phone and you to worry about me. I'm all set." He grinned.

The captain looked worried. "How do you know the natives are not hostile?"

"*He's* there, isn't he? He brought his wife, for God's sake."

"But he didn't jump out of a jet plane, sir," said the captain. "He probably had an envoy who carried him through the forest, and his biggest worry was perhaps the rough terrain and the mosquitoes."

Saint Clair chuckled. "Yes, that's pretty dull, isn't it? But, I didn't have the luxury of time like he did."

The Captain opened a compartment and pulled out a high-tech parachute that belonged to Saint Clair's jumpsuit.

Over the intercom, the copilot announced, "I can see it—the opening that is Emerald Island! It's beautiful. Like you said, it's like finding an island in a vast ocean. You'll see it on the right side of the plane in just a few minutes."

As Saint Clair put on his parachute, the captain checked all its gears and instruments. Then they both looked outside. Indeed, in this beautiful verdant ocean, one could see an undulating wave formed by the tops of thousands of ancient trees. Suddenly, a tiny island of cleared land appeared, along with several small groups of rooftops fashioned from wood and colorful clay tiles.

The plane circled several times and stabilized at 3,000 feet. Saint Clair strapped on his helmet and gave a thumbs-up sign to the captain. The bay door opened, and the captain unhooked a wire that had tethered Saint Clair to the inside of the plane. Holding Saint Clair back from the opening with an outstretched arm, the captain looked out and shouted, "No!"

He pressed on his earphone and instructed his copilot, "We're going to have to circle one more time."

He pushed Saint Clair back a little further from the opening and kept checking on the timing and angle. A few minutes later, he gestured to Saint Clair that he planned to signal on the count of three. Glancing at the opening one more time, he held up three fingers in the motion of counting 3-2-1.

"Now!" he yelled.

Without any hesitation, Saint Clair jumped out of the plane.

The air smacked his face and body in a swooping, stunning rush. A monstrous, buffeting wind pushed him toward the edge of the forest away from the clearing where the village lay, and he instinctively straightened his body to direct his fall. Everything was happening so fast as his mind attempted to process two separate thoughts—changing the direction of his fall and keeping track of his altitude so he would know when to pull his parachute open. Already he was so off-course that his last hope for a proper landing was a change of direction when he opened his chute. Pulling the release mechanism, he felt the parachute instantly balloon above him, catapulting him upward in a dizzying thrust.

A few moments later, a surreal peace overcame him as he began to descend again, much more slowly this time, and he could see the village getting closer and closer. The sharpness of the air hitting him had subsided, and he looked up to see his jet now a small speck circling way above him. He tried to take in the magnificent scenery, but the moment passed before he could truly enjoy it.

As the ground loomed closer, he was still moving too far to the edge where the forest met the village. He tried to maneuver the parachute ropes, but as he drifted past the last few feet of open land below him, he crash-landed among several tall, ancient trees on the very edge of the forest.

The crunching sound of his boots hitting the branches and snapping some of the smaller ones made his heart race even faster. He shouted out as his body kept dropping until several large branches ensnared the top of his parachute, jerking him to a stop. Breathless, with the wind knocked out of him, he found himself dangling about a hundred feet above the ground, bouncing up and down, his back to the jungle as he faced the village hundreds of yards away.

For a fleeting moment, Saint Clair felt relief, but anxiety soon set in. Looking around, he took stock of his predicament. His ropes looked secure enough that he was not going to fall, but climbing down would be no small task. Suddenly loud screeching pierced the air, and Saint Clair realized that his landing had agitated numerous monkeys who were now leaping branch to branch in the neighboring trees. They scolded and screamed at him, disturbing nearby birds and alerting them to the stranger in their midst.

Saint Clair turned his focus on the beautiful village in front of him, which stood peaceful and serene. In one corner stood a large cabin. In front of it, several people loaded three safari-type envoys of porters with human-carried chariots. Suddenly, he spotted a man and a woman dressed in safari clothes emerge from the large cabin and walk toward the chariots followed by a few natives.

"No, no, no!" mumbled Saint Clair. "They're leaving, they're leaving."

He began to yell as hard as he could. "Dr. Kamron! Dr. Kamron! Dr. Kamron!" The monkeys, already upset by Saint Clair's landing, suddenly grew alarmed by his shouting, and they too began screaming with him. Saint Clair hollered until his voice grew hoarse.

In the village, Dr. Kamron and his wife Elizabeth finished saying their goodbyes to their hostess. Dr. Kamron put one of his bags on the chariot and helped his wife get in. They heard the commotion of the monkeys and turned their heads toward the nearby forest with curiosity.

"I could swear they're calling your name," said Elizabeth as she looked at her husband with puzzlement. Then they boarded their chariot and the three envoys began to carry them away.

As Saint Clair watched them from above, he whispered doggedly, "I'll find you, Kamron, I'll find you."

In the village, the medicine man was staring at the edge of forest. Turning to one of the young men standing nearby, he slowly declared, "We have another guest."

—◦◦⋈◦◦—

2

To Catch a Giant

(Seven months later, halfway across the planet)

With every step, a unique harmony of sound arose between the orchestra of crickets, fountains, and the gravel as Dr. Kamron walked toward a pond. More than 100 fountains lined either side of this magnificent walkway. It was the first evening of summer, and he was dressed in a formal suit that Elizabeth had selected for him to wear for his appearance that evening.

When he reached the pond, he was stunned by the incredible reflection of the moon on the surface of the water. "Oh, Dr. Kamron!" Elizabeth hollered playfully as she walked toward him. "The car they sent for us is here."

Without turning his head, he told her to come closer. When she arrived next to him, he said, "Look at this reflection—it seems as if the light is coming from an underwater projector. Have you ever seen the moon this bright or this round? It's not even quite dusk yet."

She looked for a moment, and then raised her eyebrows, perplexed. She then started to fix his tie.

"Look, Elizabeth," he said, "the water in this pond is not moving even one bit."

He pointed at a butterfly that was resting on a leaf, which was also at a standstill. The butterfly had only a single wing that sported sparkling, silvery lines with underlying circles of multiple colors. The wing was upright, but it did not move at all.

"Do you see that beautiful insect?" asked Dr. Kamron, not taking his eyes off it for one moment.

"No. Where?" asked Elizabeth.

"Right there, look—I've never seen one like it anywhere!" exclaimed Dr. Kamron. "Those colors—what are they? It's so delicate. Look! An amazing insect with one wing."

Elizabeth smiled. As she adjusted her husband's tie, she said, "Are you finding another creature mysterious again?"

"I have never seen anything like this one. It's so thin. How can anything be so thin and still have anatomy? It has virtually no dimensions. In fact, it's made of only a wing, that's it! That one wing is its entire body and there are eyes on the tip of each side of it, as if they're painted on. They look like they're staring into your soul."

Dr. Kamron kept gazing at the insect, transfixed. "I can't get over these colors. I keep blinking just to figure out what color they are. Is that orange? Or silver? How can it be both at the same time? It's like it's from another world. I can't even register those colors in my brain."

"We must go, honey." Elizabeth whispered. "There must be a hundred people anticipating your arrival."

They walked away from the pond, but Dr. Kamron turned twice to take another look at the pond and the butterfly. He repeated to Elizabeth, "The water did not move at all. I have never seen nature at such a standstill."

"You say that as if it's a bad thing." Elizabeth said.

"No, honey, but I do wonder what this is in anticipation of," said her husband. "The nature of Earth is to balance herself; she likes to correct her every move no matter how perfect her manifestation is. She is like a superb painter that tears the canvas into pieces as soon as she completes a masterpiece."

They walked back to the front of the small mansion where they were staying. A gleaming, smoke-silver, classic town car awaited them.

"Good evening, Dr. Kamron," said a distinguished-looking man dressed in a formal chauffeur's outfit. He tipped his traditional driver's hat toward them.

Dr. Kamron nodded his head. "Good evening to you. And how is your evening so far?"

"Splendid, sir. In fact, it's an evening I have very much looked forward to for a long time."

"What is your name?"

"Adrian," he said, closing the door after Dr. and Mrs. Kamron entered the vehicle. As Adrian walked around the back of the car to go to the driver's side, he looked up to the sky and whispered with quiet gratitude, "Yes, finally." On his face was the triumphant joy of a fisherman who had just caught a giant fish in his net.

For about 10 minutes, Dr. and Mrs. Kamron remained immersed in conversation, and Adrian did not dare interrupt them. Dr. Kamron mentioned the butterfly to his wife again and how he couldn't get its image out of his mind.

Meanwhile, an old truck towing a trailer packed with exotic, aging animals traveled toward them in the opposite direction, less than a quarter of a mile away. At the right rear corner of the truck, a large white goose stood in a cage with its tail sticking out.

Suddenly, a sports car that was speeding recklessly swerved in front of their town car as it moved to pass them on the left. As Adrian reflexively maneuvered to the right to avoid a collision, a second sports car that was racing the first one used the shoulder to pass them on the right. Adrian swerved to the left, avoiding a second collision but violently pitching Dr. and Mrs. Kamron from side to side inside the vehicle. At that exact moment, Adrian came face to face with the truck from the opposite direction. Thinking fast, he steered the town car into the shoulder of the oncoming lane and missed the truck by a hair. They slowly drifted back into their lane, a single goose feather lodged into the edge of their rear bumper.

Once Adrian managed to resume driving normally, Dr. and Mrs. Kamron simultaneously sighed with enormous relief. Moments passed, and they gradually relaxed after the commotion. Nonetheless, Adrian's anxiety was building, not because of what had just happened but rather for the precious time that was passing. He had not even initiated his planned conversation and his time was running out.

"I am so sorry, folks," he said, a little breathlessly.

Dr. Kamron replied, "No, no. No apology, it wasn't your fault. We thank you for being so attentive in your driving and for saving us from certain disaster. I sometimes wish enlightenment were instinctual so that humans were born with at least a minimum amount of it. That would make this a much kinder, safer world, don't you think?"

"Sir, if I may say so, this planet is the home of the disenlightened," Adrian answered. "You're the one out of place here. It is you who should adjust and maneuver around the locals with caution, for safety."

Dr. Kamron smiled. "Huh, I never thought of it that way. I suppose you're right—we should. Is there a back entrance to the building where we can bypass the crowd when we arrive at the event?"

"I will find out, sir," Adrian replied. "Dr. Kamron, may I ask you a question?"

"Of course, Adrian."

"Frankly, I'm beside myself. I'm talking to the man who gave the world the holy grail sought by scientists for over a century—the unification of the twin pillars of physics: quantum mechanics and Einstein's theory of general relativity. Your discovery was simply amazing—a single explanation for both the large-scale force of gravity and the short-range force inside the atom. Sir, what did it for you?"

"What did it for me?" asked Dr. Kamron.

"I mean that usually something triggers a discovery. You know, like the eureka moment when the light goes on in our head. What was it in your case?"

"Well, do you really want a technical answer or what inspired me to study these subjects?" asked Dr. Kamron.

Adrian eagerly answered, "No sir, we can skip the inspiration stuff. The actual technical answer would be great, if you would, please."

"Well, let's see how I can simplify it."

"You don't have to, sir."

Dr. Kamron was quiet for a second, since he wasn't sure of Adrian's intellectual caliber, but he decided to reply with courtesy and continued. "Okay then, this is how it started. It is not a secret that I have always suspected that space-time itself has quantum properties. I was working on establishing the foaminess of space-time, and everything else followed from there."

"I understand."

"You do?" Dr. Kamron exclaimed, surprised. "It can get into some technical physics."

"Yes, sir, I do. Could you go on please, sort of sequentially if you would?"

"Well, like I said, I was working on the idea that quantum mechanics requires that space-time becomes fragmented and foamy at tiny scales. Now think of this space-time foam—these holes with their tiny hills and valleys offering a longer pathway to a small particle and then to a larger one that represents space as being flat and smooth."

Adrian interrupted, "I have already read this much in your published paper, but if I may, I am actually asking about your initial vision. Where did that come from? That amazing initial perspective that opened up the flow of information in your mind that led to this stunning, unifying discovery. How is it that the greatest minds of science failed to see what you saw? Where did that vision come from? Where was it that you were looking that they weren't?"

Dr. Kamron nodded. "Ah, Adrian, I understand what you're asking. Let's see ... at a younger age, I noticed a common pattern in the design of the visible world and invisible world, at least to the human eye. From the smallest to the largest, some characteristics remain the same. Just like electrons orbit around the nucleus of an atom, the Earth orbits around the sun in the same fashion. Although later I had a more accurate understanding of this, that initial vision was the first clue that shifted my thinking on to the right track—sort of like looking at things from a different angle."

"And then?"

"Then, based on that came the realization that the universe is the projection of the quantum world."

"Projection, as in mirror?"

"More like a prism, except one that is not operated by light but instead by sound."

"Sound?"

"By sound, I mean vibration."

"Of course, you mean frequencies!" said Adrian. "I understand. That's amazing. And are the formation of these frequencies random?"

"There is never anything random," answered Dr. Kamron. "To have anything random-based, you must have a program to base your random outcome on, which in essence makes it not be random."

"Then there is a process to the development of this universe?"

"No, there is no process in this universe."

Adrian grappled with this. "I don't understand ... how can there be no process? This universe is expanding and life is evolving."

Dr. Kamron patiently answered, "First of all, don't confuse the universe with life. I'm just talking about the universe here. It's going to take a lot more time to explain this. You should really read my new paper that is being published this year if you're interested in the comprehension of the universe as the shell versus the life within.

"But I can simply tell you this: The existence of this universe appears to us to have a process because we can observe it only from the inside. We're capable of seeing, visualizing, or calculating only a segment at a time, and thus it appears to have a process. In reality, there are no events in the universe. We think the universe is created only by a series of events that contribute to a process because we cannot envision the universe at its entirety, which is one single event. This is an event that's already occurred and we're just visiting it from inside each segment at a time."

"I don't understand, sir," said Adrian.

"The example I'm about to give you is so oversimplified that it takes away the true meaning of what I just said. But look, imagine a ruler 50 centimeters long. The ruler is already made, but you're such a small being—like a microorganism—who is capable of only observing and understanding writings on the ruler that signify a micromillimeter at a time. To you, the calculation of these micromillimeters amounts to understanding a process that the ruler represents as it increases in measurements. But there is no process because the ruler is already made—it was one event that already took place. From your perspective, however, you see only various evolving and expanding events. Segments are only visible to you depending on your viewpoint. If that doesn't help, then familiarize yourself with the concept of no beginning and no end."

Adrian exclaimed, "No beginning, no end? But everything must have a beginning, no?"

"Why's that?" said Dr. Kamron. "Beginnings and endings are simply human concepts. We just cannot imagine something that doesn't resemble our own concept of existence. Get over it. Oh and while you're at it, try to be unique and don't say, 'What about the big bang?' as everyone else does. The big bang is a localized phenomenon, of which we've had many in the past and will continue to have more to come. But perhaps it should have been called something else because yes, there was something big by human standards, but it didn't have a bang. It was simply the reproduction of an existing universe because these universes copy and duplicate themselves."

Dr. Kamron paused. "Okay, Adrian, does that help to answer your question?"

"No, sir—I mean yes, sir. May I inquire about something else?"

"Go ahead."

"When you gave your speech at Sorbonne University in Paris about three years ago, you said you were out of time to answer the last question from the audience. Would you mind if I asked you the same question now?"

"You were at the Sorbonne, Adrian?"

"Yes, sir."

"What are you doing here, if I may ask?"

"There is no short answer to that, except I'm just passing through, like yourself."

"But you work here, don't you?"

"No sir. I just got in last week from Boston."

"We were in Boston ourselves last week."

"I know. I was not as successful to cross paths with you there, or even at the Emerald Island."

Dr. Kamron looked shocked. "What were you doing at the Emerald Island?"

"Just hanging out, so to speak," answered Adrian.

Elizabeth moved closer to Dr. Kamron. She looked at Adrian and then at her husband with a suspicious expression on her face.

Dr. Kamron looked at his wife reassuringly. "You don't need to be alarmed, honey." He turned back to Adrian. "Who exactly are you, Adrian?"

"Please forgive me, sir," Adrian answered. "Let me introduce myself a little better. I am Adrian Saint Clair. I did my post-doctorate with Professor Bishop. I trust you're familiar with his work."

"Of course, but what is this all about?"

"Please don't be alarmed. As you've been unreachable by every means these last couple of years, this was the only way I could get one hour of direct communication with the great Dr. Kamron."

"What happened to the original driver? Is he okay?" Elizabeth asked.

Adrian replied, "I assure you I have not hurt anyone for this opportunity. The man is so well paid he probably does not need to work for several years. Frankly, if you would have kindly accepted my offer to make this trip on my private jet, it would have made things a little bit more dignified for me."

"Your private jet? What invitation, Adrian?"

"Didn't your publisher tell you about the offer to use a private jet for this trip?"

"Yes, I do recall him saying something, but I readily rejected the offer as I assumed it must have had some kind of endorsement attached to it," said Dr. Kamron.

"No, sir. I just wanted the opportunity to talk to you."

Elizabeth asked, "How does an academic afford a private jet?"

Dr. Kamron nodded in agreement. "Yes, Adrian, that's what I was wondering about."

"Sir, I know you don't have much interest in the business arena, but in the business world, the story of the sales of my genetically engineered wood company is common knowledge."

"Oh yes, I know who you are," said Elizabeth. "You're the man behind the Steel Tree. Tell us, Adrian, was it out of concern for the environment or did you hold a grudge against the lumber industry?"

"Neither. Like most inventions, I was aiming for something else and this was the byproduct of my failure."

"But didn't the lumber industry try to buy you out and suppress your invention like the oil companies do to new energy sources and inventions?" Elizabeth asked.

Adrian chuckled. "They tried and they even attempted to intimidate me, but I was too vain. I guess I wanted the notoriety too, so I sold it to a conscientious company with an agreement that they would actually produce it."

"Didn't you want to run the company yourself?" Dr. Kamron asked.

Elizabeth turned to her husband. "Honey, didn't you read anything about what he did with that deal? It was unheard of in the business world. He sold his invention to HomePro Center with the agreement that 50 percent of the net profit would go to world food and health organizations. HomePro jumped on the deal and changed their name to GreenPro, which you see in every town now. I think it was 10 years ago."

"I have no idea what you're referring to," replied Dr. Kamron.

Adrian chuckled. "How long have you folks been married?" he asked.

"Seven years," Elizabeth answered.

"And may I ask how long you've known each other?"

"Just about seven years," Elizabeth said. "He proposed to me on our first date."

"I think that's very cool," said Adrian. "It shows certainty of choice."

"Technically, it was our second date," Dr. Kamron corrected his wife.

"Honey, surely you remember HomePro?"

"Never heard of them."

"He's not kidding!" said Elizabeth, incredulous. "Can you believe this, Adrian? It's like someone saying they've never heard of the company names like McDonalds, Apple, or Twinmill!"

"I do believe him," Adrian replied.

"You do?" Elizabeth said, shaking her head. "Anyway, honey, this guy's picture was on the cover of most of the business journals. They called him 'Saint Corporator.'"

"That's all news to me," Dr. Kamron said.

"See, Adrian?" Elizabeth exclaimed in disbelief.

Dr. Kamron smiled. "Anyway, I am not sure whether I should be impressed with your work, flattered by your interest in mine, or upset that you have kidnapped my wife and me."

"Well, how about just a simple gesture of generosity for a man who is exhausted from trying to track you down for nearly three years?"

"Okay, Adrian. But why not just write to me?"

"With all due respect, sir, when was the last time you had the chance to reply to an inquiry of a peer at my level? Besides, everyone knows that you have stopped all of your professional communications for quite some time now."

"Okay, Adrian," admitted Dr. Kamron. "You've got my attention. I recall the question at Sorbonne. I chose not to reply because when a person asks the wrong question, he will get the wrong answer."

"But sir, it was on point. Besides, wasn't it you who said, 'the best answers lead to better questions'?"

"I think that was Einstein, but let me just put it this way: I don't condone nor condemn his inclination for asking. But some people ask a question so that with the anticipated response they can give validity to their own point. Even if the answer is negative."

"But we were all scientists there and hopefully could see through such deception."

"But there was no point," said Dr. Kamron. "He was only attempting to describe the relationship of an essentially nonlinear character by linear methods. Look, what I presented was the mathematical equation that represents that all theories are valid since this is an interactive universe, which responds to our perceptions and intentions. So what's the point in validating only one theory?"

"I get it," Adrian answered. "If you had responded to that one question, it would have been too narrow of an analysis for a discovery that requires a vast vision. It would be as if you present the formula for H_2O to explain the main chemical makeup of the oceans and someone wants to prove that a glass of water in their hand contains the true answer, not your formula."

"Something like that," said Dr. Kamron. "You see, there is no right and wrong—only portions of truth. Think about it, Adrian. Every fact that has ever been proven scientifically, no matter how undisputed, has never passed the test of time. In other words, reality is time-sensitive and truth is perishable."

"Frankly," Dr. Kamron continued, "I have to say, the only difference between a false statement and a true statement is that the false statement spoils faster but in time, they're both perishable. I'm not referring to the time that Earth was considered flat. Much more recent discoveries with modern-day peer recognitions only stay valid until the next genius proves it wrong, and it applies to all disciplines—from physics to astronomy to medicine. For example, take the Newtonian system, which even today if you ask, most people would wholeheartedly agree to be true. Newton stated that a second on Earth is the same as a second throughout the solar system. Also, that a foot or a kilogram on Earth is the same as a foot or a kilogram in every other place in the universe."

"It sounds very logical and acceptable, doesn't it?" continued Dr. Kamron. "But you and I both know that it's false. Einstein proved that Newton was wrong. He established his truth that the speed of light must be constant, no matter how fast you travel. For that to be true, time must get slower the faster you travel. More stunning than that, lengths contract and masses increase as you approach the speed of light. You see, space and time became relative in this new truth. This fascinating new truth established by Einstein squashed over 250 years of Newtonian physics.

"Think about it: More than 250 years of definitive scientific conviction based on Newtonian's truth that space and time were absolute, that force caused acceleration, and that gravity is a force conveyed across the vacuum at a distance ended. Now, all of that went out the window with the new truths presented by Einstein.

"As humanity celebrated Einstein's new truth, yet another one emerged. This one was so astonishing that the human brain wasn't even equipped with the proper conceptualization capabilities to fully grasp it. Of course, we called it the 'quantum leap,' a fancy name for a fancy move. The truth is that electrons can move from one orbit to another without traveling across any intervening space. They simply disappear from one and reappear instantaneously without visiting the space in between. That's all good, but do you know what that means?"

"Yes, sir. That means that Einstein's theory could no longer hold true," said Adrian.

"Yes, at least not entirely. The c^2 in $E = mc^2$ is not absolute, as something does go faster than the speed of light. The whole premise of what Einstein submitted was based on the idea that nothing can travel faster than the speed of light. But we now know the new truth within quantum leap that electrons do. In fact, by observing one particle, we can instantaneously influence a second particle over a distance away."

"But your discovery can withstand the test of time as it encompasses all probabilities, right?"

Dr. Kamron answered, "Well, first keep in mind that our consciousness itself is made out of quantum particles and again, since information at subatomic levels can influence other information instantaneously and without any solid limitation, then my discovery was the baseline to prove the inaccuracy in all facts and the accuracy in all inaccuracies. It was that simple. This, as I said, is an interactive universe. If you set your limited perception of time aside, you'll recognize that all possibilities are exactly that—more possibilities. I think the first time this perception crossed my mind was when I read a philosophical statement by Hector St. John de Crèvecoeur that 'the eyes not engaged on one particular object will leave the mind open to the introduction of new ideas.'" Just remember, truth changes—it always does."

Adrian pressed on. "But, if you have no conviction for your belief, how will you strive to establish anything?"

"I just tried to tell you the answer. It is exactly the opposite of conviction in one's belief system that allows you to be capable of delivering anything brilliant or at least of value, for that matter. You must have a physics background, if you've been working with Professor Bishop, right?"

"Yes, sir."

"Then let me tell you something that might surprise you and at the same time show you the value that comes with a lack of conviction in any belief factor. Tell me, what is the one factor that has been serving modern physics with a pillar of certainty in a universe packed with variation?"

"That would have to be the principle along the lines of what we were just talking about—that the speed of light never changes," answered Adrian.

"Bravo! Einstein's theory of relativity gave science the idea that the speed of light is the same and has been since the birth of cosmos, almost to the moment of the big bang, and it is the same everywhere in the universe. Now, it may surprise you to know that the man who gave science this tool in 1915 is the same man who presented a long-forgotten argument of the varying speed of light a few years earlier. What resonated with me the most is Einstein's own comment that, 'as long as we have a good reason, we should be ready to give up any scientific principle no matter how sacred.'"

"I've read all your publications, sir," Adrian said, "and it has been a dream to be this close to you. I have asked myself, 'What would I ask the two-time Nobel laureate if I could ask him only one question?' Now that I've had this privilege of being in direct conversation with you, it's clear to me that of all the scientific questions that I've contemplated asking, I want to know only one thing. Speaking of Einstein, it actually came to me as I was reading something by him. He wrote, 'I want to know how God created this world. I am not interested in this or that phenomenon, in the spectrum of this or that element. I want to know His thoughts; the rest are details.'"

Dr. Kamron smiled. "Okay, Adrian. Ask away."

"Well, here is my question: How do you know what you know?"

"First, I hope that you are not seriously thinking that I have any connection with divinity," said Dr. Kamron.

"No, sir," Adrian said. "I simply meant that I'm interested in an insight into your thinking method, not an answer to one of my many questions. After all, the world has yet to recognize someone of your stature. As a scientist, it would be a defining moment to win a Nobel Prize in one discipline, but you, sir, have two prizes in two separate categories—physics and humanitarianism."

Adrian continued, "I read an article about you a few years ago where the author said something at the end that I will never forget: 'Dr. Kamron's character is so refined and has such ideals that seem to be out of this world. He's the kind of man every kid wishes to grow up to be and every old man wished he had lived as such.'"

Dr. Kamron smiled. "Okay, Adrian. Thank you. Let's see if this will help answer your question about my thinking methods for what it may be worth to you. First, keep in mind, as a scientist, that even science itself is not exempt from this interactive universe in which truth will change shape. You see, to provide ourselves with some sense of reality, we first completely assume certain illusions as real. We are then in a position to build a reality on top of that illusion.

"So, to answer your question, remember this: To better understand your reality, you must acknowledge the illusions that you have built your reality on. I have always learned things through images. For instance, pi (the circumference of a circle) does not have a last number and continues for infinity. Even supercomputers have tried and failed for years to find the repeating last digit. As the circle never fully connects, neither does our existence to a solidly defined reality."

Dr. Kamron continued, "As a young boy, what appeared to me was that everything in this universe, by shape or motion, from particles to stars and planets, was ultimately in a circular form of some kind. But, if the circle never connects, I saw the signature of an illusion—a perpetuating whirlpool whose ends never meet. That is how my mind works. I'm sorry to disappoint you."

Adrian considered this for a moment. "So now, when your mind tries to go to the end of this illusion, what do you see? Subatomic particles?"

"Beyond that," Dr. Kamron replied.

"Are you talking about energy, or the fabric of time and space?"

"I am talking about information."

"As in knowledge?"

"No, as in the makeup of all things in the universe, as in what you find when you break down the subatomic particles," said Dr. Kamron.

"How do you mean? Like the string or M-theory?"

"All these theories were alluding to the same thing, but they came to an impasse because they lack the proper explanation that unites them all."

"The unifying theory?"

"Yes, and what is at the heart of the unifying theory?" asked Dr. Kamron.

"Information?"

"Yes. Simply information. Information that is interacting with each element of which it is composed. Our lives are just part of this interactive universe made of information, like little clouds of thoughts. Not this tangible hard matter or matters of fact."

"One last question on the subject, sir," Adrian said. "As you know, Einstein spent the second half of his life searching for this unifying field theory that you have successfully presented to the world. Where do you think he failed and you succeeded?"

"I take exception to your use of the term 'fail' when you speak of Einstein's work," responded Dr. Kamron, stiffening at the thought. "I and many other scientists stand on his shoulders to reach our achievements. Not a single person has yet managed to emulate Einstein simply because he surpassed us all in science and integrity."

"I am sorry, I meant no disrespect to him. But as you know, he spent many years on this endeavor. I just wondered why you think he didn't manage to fulfill his wish."

"In that respect," said Dr. Kamron. "I think the problem was twofold. First was his continued rejection of quantum mechanics, the science that he himself helped to create. Secondly, his thought pattern always demanded a theory of principle with the strictest consistency. This second characteristic was his key to success when he applied it to the science of the visible world (the large scale), but it was also his nemesis when it came to the invisible world (the extremely small scale). This is another example of how, ironically with us humans, the very thing that makes us flourish brings us to our demise and vice versa."

"Would you mind elaborating a bit more?" Adrian asked.

"Well, think about it. Einstein presented humanity with a gift called general relativity. He gave this world the only theory at the time that could unite space, time, mass, energy, motion, and light. The beauty of this gift was its consistency. However, he was always adamant and insistent that any theory that attempts to explain how nature works must fit precisely into a mathematical equation that aligns with the laws of nature. This continued insistence served as his gift, just as it served as his nemesis."

"For example," Dr. Kamron continued, "he never accepted that black holes really existed. Today we know that a black hole is where space and time become so distorted that the equation of general relativity yields infinities instead of a rational number. Black holes defied that clean math. To Einstein, that was unacceptable, but as you know, since the advent of the Hubble Space Telescope, black holes are now accepted as part of the nature of the universe."

Adrian nodded. "Or, along these lines, for a long time he insisted on an immobile universe. And of course, since Hubble we know that the universe is expanding and in an accelerating fashion, right?"

"Well, let me give you a more accurate picture of that," said Dr. Kamron. "Imagine that the universe is a tablecloth and the table has these holes on it (black holes). The tablecloth constantly gets pulled into these holes, which gives the illusion of expansion when, in fact, it is being sucked in instead."

"Wow, and I find it amazing that for such a long time, scientists perceived your EE as this elusive, so-called dark matter/energy. And by the way, did the superstring or M-theory play a role in helping you with your discovery?" asked Adrian.

Dr. Kamron said, "Remember that the reason I named it EE is due to the dual nature of electrons as they are both particles and waves at the same time, capable of being in two places at the same time. That is how they weave."

"As for those theories, it helped by giving a better visualization to others as a precursor to understand my theory. I trust that you know that the M-theory brings together the branches of physics by suggesting that all particles and forces are extremely small strings of energy vibration in 10 spatial dimensions and one dimension of time. The concept of inter-connection of multidimensions with particles and forces was the useful aspect of the M-theory."

"Yes, yes, I do recall. But your introduction of EE was a gift from out of this world."

Dr. Kamron smiled. "Thanks, but I'm not sure why you keep using that phrase 'out of this world.'"

"We must be getting close," Elizabeth said. "I can see the lights by the shorelines. Thank goodness—that means I don't have to listen to you guys chatter about science much longer."

"I'm sorry, Mrs. Kamron, for monopolizing the conversation with your husband," Adrian apologized.

"Not at all," Elizabeth replied. "You certainly earned it. But next time, contact me when you want to offer us private plane rides. I'm more re-ceptive than my husband in matters of vanity. In fact, I believe that the affluent have a moral duty to live lavishly."

"A duty?" Adrian asked.

"Yes," said Elizabeth. "You may call it showing off, but I think it is inspiring to live well, and that inspiration gives a driving force to others who observe your style to have aspirations to get to that standard of living themselves. I think nothing is worse than people with great means who purposely live below the standard of their economical class. It's simply being cheap."

"I take it, then, that Dr. Kamron prefers a simpler style of living," said Adrian.

Dr. Kamron chuckled. "Simplicity is the ultimate sign of sophistica-tion, or haven't you heard, Adrian?"

"Yes, sir, I knew you must have a philosophy behind it."

"It is based on a Taoist principle called the Epitome of the Uncarved Block."

"And what would that be, sir?"

"The essence of the principle of the Uncarved Block is that things in their original simplicity contain their own natural power—a power that is easily spoiled and lost when that simplicity is changed."

"Interesting," Adrian said. "I have to see how I can apply that to my crazy life. But nevertheless, my jet is available to you folks anytime. Perhaps on the way back?"

"But there is no airport nearby," said Elizabeth.

"Well, I do have a chopper on standby a short drive from here to take me to the airfield," Adrian said.

"Oh, Mr. Fancy Ride! That's cool—we'll take you up on that."

Adrian turned to Dr. Kamron. "Do you, Dr. Kamron, always run your scientific ideas by Mrs. Kamron first?"

"Only legal and financial ones," Dr. Kamron answered, "You see, my wife is a lawyer who refuses to work on anything but her botanical garden, and me as a client."

Elizabeth smiled. "Having my husband as my client has proven to be a handful. He is the most generous man I have ever known."

"Yes, I've heard," Adrian said.

"No. No one knows the full extent of it," said Elizabeth. "As for my garden, Adrian, the Chinese have a proverb that goes something like this: 'If you want to be happy for a day, have a party; if you want to be happy for a month, get married; or if you want to be happy for a lifetime, become a gardener.' Of course our marriage is the exception. I will give up my garden for him anytime."

Elizabeth moved her face close to her husband and kissed him as she finished her sentence.

"Mrs. Kamron, do you always accompany your husband on those challenging trips to faraway places where he studies their tribes?" asked Adrian.

"Just about every time," said Elizabeth, sinking back into the plush seat. "Like my husband says, we must place ourselves in unfamiliar worlds to better understand our own."

3

EIGHTH WONDER OF THE WORLD

As the town car purred down the road, the beauty of the countryside unfolded around them on this gorgeous, peaceful evening on the first day of summer. But Adrian and Dr. Kamron remained completely oblivious of this beauty as they continued to enthusiastically discuss the intricacies of the universe and science.

Their talking finally slowed as they approached an enormous, ornate gate.

"Well, here we are," Adrian said.

"Oh my God, look at this gate—it's absolutely gorgeous!" Elizabeth exclaimed. "Look at the size of this estate! I can't even see the buildings yet. Please slow down, Adrian—I have to take a picture of this gate now. Thank goodness that it's in light colors, so it'll show up nicely in the picture.

"Look at the details, the ironwork," Elizabeth gushed. "So fine, so elegant, and yet it's almost a spiritual-looking object, like the image of the Pearly Gates. One would expect angels to greet you on the other side!"

"Yeah, that gate is one amazing sculpture," Adrian agreed, "but I don't think we'll be seeing any angels on the other side. In fact, they seem very human-looking, with their security earpieces and all."

"Could you guys read the name on the gate?" Elizabeth asked.

"I couldn't even pronounce it," Dr. Kamron replied.

"Well, it's going to be in the picture. We'll figure it out later."

The three of them were warmly received by the security staff as they passed through the gate and drove toward the beautifully manicured landscape ahead. They continued on for two more miles before arriving at the building that was to be their final destination. Once they spotted it, they could hardly speak.

As they pulled into a long, curving driveway, Dr. Kamron exclaimed, "So *that's* the building everyone is raving about. Good Lord, just how large is it? It looks out of place in this region. It's such a contrast—a modern monument in a place of such natural settings and simple culture. Adrian, let's just go up to the main entrance instead of the rear one. This is too interesting to miss."

"For days, I studied all I could about this building and asked the locals a thousand questions about it," said Adrian. "It's a bit hard to separate facts from rumors, but needless to say, if it hadn't built so recently, it would have been called the eighth wonder of the world. It's not just the unsurpassed masterpiece it represents as a marvel of modern architecture, but the mystery of the dome on the top is something else."

"Wow, what a sight!" cried Elizabeth. "It's like a giant jewel. How big is that dome anyway?"

Adrian said, "It must be more than 20 times the size of a football stadium, and yet it's so beautifully balanced on top of this slim high-rise that it looks like a gemstone set into a gorgeous ring."

"To me, it looks like a giant decanter with a round crystal crown," said Dr. Kamron.

"Yes, I can see that," said Adrian. "There's very little known about what's up there. But we do know that this dome contains the largest, most elaborate atrium in the world with all kinds of trees and flora inside. The locals swear that there are elephants and other exotic animals up there. You see, the entire structure is built to support only two floors aside from the lobby. One is the hall that we're going to for the event, and the other is the dome. There are no other floors. The hall is located high up in the middle of the building, which stands something like 30 stories high. From there, there's nothing but supporting structures and elevator shafts to the dome."

"Who owns this?" asked Elizabeth, her voice lowered in awe.

"The man who lives in the dome," said Adrian. "The only thing I found out about him is that he was a doctor of veterinary medicine who made a fortune many years ago. Not sure how, but it wasn't by running a veterinary clinic. He spent 25 years building this fantastic place and no outsiders have seen him in years. And no one will describe what he looks like. The locals hold deep loyalty and respect for him when they speak of him—the kind of respect you have for a wise grandfather, not for a king or a tycoon. Very special events are produced in that magnificent hall below the dome. But naturally, if he chooses to have these events take place in his building, it must be so that he could have them at his disposal with just an elevator ride."

The three of them kept staring at the building as they pulled up in front of its magnificent entrance.

Adrian stopped the vehicle and got out to open the door for Elizabeth. As he tried to go to the other side to open Dr. Kamron's door, Dr. Kamron shook his head and said, "Please, Adrian. You're embarrassing me now."

Adrian grinned. "Just doing the job I stole from someone else, sir."

"So, we will see you inside?" asked Dr. Kamron.

"Of course. I wouldn't miss it for the world. But Dr. Kamron...I must talk to you in private before your speech tonight."

"More scientific questions, Adrian?"

"No, sir, frankly those scientific inquiries, as valuable as they were, were intended only for us to get better acquainted, but they're not why I've been looking for you all this time."

"Oh?"

"Yes, sir. It is of vital importance that we have this conversation in private before your lecture."

"What is this all about, Adrian? Do I need to be concerned about our safety? Is my wife going to be safe here?" asked Dr. Kamron.

"It's nothing like that and I don't have any alarming information about this place or your safety here. Trust me, sir—what we need to talk about is a much, much greater concern than anything humanity has ever faced. You just have to trust me and make sure that we speak before your speech."

"We will, Adrian, we will. But the greatest concern for humanity? What in the world could that be?"

"Believe me sir, it requires a bit of introduction. Could you please ask for me as soon as you're situated? I'll be in the lobby waiting for you."

Elizabeth stood by the steps to the lobby, waving at her husband. "Are you coming, love? I think this good man is waiting for us."

Dr. Kamron nodded to Adrian. As he joined his wife, he glanced back at Adrian with a curious look on his face.

A very regal-looking man called to Elizabeth and Dr. Kamron by name.

"Are you our host?" asked Elizabeth.

"No," answered the guide. "I'm just assigned to take care of whatever your needs are for this evening. Most speakers like to try out the podium before all the guests arrive in the hall. Is Dr. Kamron the same way?"

"No, not at all," Dr. Kamron replied. "I'm used to embarrassing myself by being late and walking through the audience to get to my place."

"Very well. As you folks will see, the hall is in the middle of the building and all the reception and food service is in the lobby. Would you like to stay here for a while?"

"Does anyone get a tour of the third part of the building?" asked Dr. Kamron.

"You mean the dome, sir?"

"Yes."

"I am afraid that is a private residence and only special keys can operate the elevator to go up there," said the guide.

"Have some of my other colleagues arrived yet?" asked Dr. Kamron.

"Yes, they're in the hall above us."

"In that case, I would like to go there now, but I must also speak with the man we came with before my speech."

"Your chauffeur, sir?"

"Yes, yes. Can you arrange a private setting where he and I can talk soon? I mean, right away, please."

"Of course, sir. I will do that for you as soon as I come back to the lobby. This way," he said as he graciously directed them toward the elevators.

As they walked, Elizabeth whispered to her husband, "This would have to be the most amazing building I have ever seen. I feel like I have traveled forward in time. I'm just not sure for how long."

Soothing music was playing that would calm the most restless of souls. One could hear the murmur of small groups of people talking with one another, but even the loudest laughter could be heard only as a whisper. The ceiling was so high that one could not see its top. Both small and large beautifully designed light fixtures hung from the walls, and yet the place was pleasantly, unobtrusively lit, illuminated like the soft glow of light at dawn.

The guide stopped in front of a curved wall and gestured to Dr. and Mrs. Kamron to step inside. A closer look revealed that the wall was transparent and inside was an elevator. Dr. Kamron began to follow Elizabeth into the elevator, but suddenly he stopped.

"What is it?" Elizabeth asked.

"I had a vision of that insect."

"Why, is that disturbing?"

"Remember how still it was?"

"Yes."

"I just imagined it taking off flying, causing a rippling in the pond."

"You were quite taken with that pond today," said Elizabeth, amused. "Well, what button do we push?" she asked the guide.

"There are no buttons," the guide answered. "Just step back from the entrance and it will take you there."

Inside the elevator, Dr. Kamron and Elizabeth stood, holding hands. The guide had barely finished his sentence when a low rumbling sound roared upward from deep underground. At that same moment, the earth violently trembled, jolting Elizabeth backward out of the elevator and throwing Dr. Kamron further inside it. Dr. Kamron tried to keep his hold on Elizabeth's hand, but he lost his grip on her. Immediately the elevator doors closed and he began ascending at high speed toward the top.

Since there were no floors to see, he could not tell how fast the elevator was going—only that this was not a normal speed for one. The hall floor swiftly passed below him as the elevator continued to climb. He could not tell if what was happening was by design or fault—all he could think about was his beloved Elizabeth and whether she was safe.

At last, he arrived at the dome level, and the elevator slowed to a stop. The building was still gently rocking from the tremor, but it also somehow seemed very stable and solid. The doors opened, and Dr. Kamron stepped out of the elevator. As his eyes adjusted to the darkness, he took a few more steps forward. The air caressing his face felt extremely fresh and soft, like he was high in the mountains. But it was also full of scents, as if he had been transported to a lush tropical forest full of flowers.

On one hand, he wanted to see more of this fascinating place. But he also could not bring himself to think about anything but his wife at that moment. The building shifted again, but strangely enough, the sound of the tremor could not be heard. Everything felt oddly peaceful. But this last shake rendered him more concerned for Elizabeth, and he walked back to the elevator in the hope of going back down to find her.

But, as he attempted to enter, he heard the voice of a man behind him.

4

Great Minds Think Alike

"Dr. Kamron," said the man in a very soothing yet powerful voice. "No need to panic, you are safe here."

Dr. Kamron turned around and saw a very dignified-looking man slowly walking toward him. The man was tall and looked very strong. His hair and beard were gray, but he had the posture and skin of a much younger man.

"But my wife..." said Dr. Kamron.

"I assure you that she is also safe, even in the lobby of this building," said the man. "This structure can withstand a much stronger earthquake. The elevators are designed to automatically come up at times like this, but I can have you talk to her on one of the monitors so that you can be reassured that she is all right."

Together they walked to a console. Using a voice command, the man summoned a holographic monitor that instructed the guide below to call Elizabeth. Her face appeared and Dr. Kamron asked if she was safe. The man walked away a few steps to give them privacy, and once their conversation concluded, Dr. Kamron approached him to express his gratitude.

"Do we need to worry about aftershocks?" he asked.

"Like I said, even at a significantly higher Richter magnitude, this structure is a safe haven," replied the man.

"What is this structure and who are you, if I may ask?" asked Dr. Kamron.

"Well, my name is Alexander Grant. You can call me Alex. I'm a retired veterinarian. Well, maybe not so retired. As for this structure, that requires a more elaborate answer. Why don't you look around and tell me what you think."

Dr. Kamron smiled. "I'm flattered. It was my understanding that not many people get a chance to see the top floor."

"Dr. Kamron, you are not 'many people,'" said Alex. "I was very much looking forward to your speech this evening. I understand that you were honoring us by unveiling your latest discovery here. As you may know, through a science organization, I host only very special events in the hall below so that, among other reasons, this old man does not have to travel. Of course, in a way, tonight was more special and required more planning."

"How long have you been working on this structure?"

"About 25 years."

"That is remarkable," said Dr. Kamron. "You must have been a very young man at the time you started."

"No, not really, I wasn't that young."

"But this is the most high-tech building I've ever set foot in. Where did you get the vision and everything you needed for such a project?"

"Let's just say that I only managed the assembly."

The two began to walk along a path. Everywhere he looked, Dr. Kamron simply could not believe his eyes. It was, in fact, a giant atrium, or as Adrian put it, a ranch in the sky. The bright moon shone on the entire area, bathing it in soft, comforting light. Lush vegetation abounded, surrounding them with every variety of plant and tree one could ever imagine—or not imagine. Multiple small waterfalls and streams circled around them, flowing throughout the grounds. Dr. Kamron could hear melodic water running in the streams and occasionally the quiet noises of small and large animals from both near and far away.

"Is it true that the dome can close its roof completely?" asked Dr. Kamron.

"Yes," said Alex. "That's the idea."

"But why would you want to close it? What would you be protecting this selected nature from?"

Alex looked at Dr. Kamron but said nothing for a moment.

"I'm sorry," said Dr. Kamron. "Have I gone beyond the limit of my permitted inquiry?"

"No, not at all," replied Alex. "I intend to answer all of your questions, as I believe that the meeting of our minds is to serve a purpose. But this purpose is not about this structure. This structure, as you put it, is designed to be here long after we're both gone. Perhaps, long after many, many generations have gone, this will remain to serve its purpose when needed.

"So, I will entertain any inquiry you have about it, but perhaps we should figure out why we ended up meeting face to face tonight in this isolated manner, because that was not my plan. I was simply going to go down and be entertained with a very stimulating and informative lecture by the world's most renowned scientist. It looks like now that I'll be entertaining you by giving a tour of my home. But again, I assure you that your familiarity with this vessel itself will not necessarily serve the purpose of our meeting. This is simply a natural conservatory, if you will, designed to preserve its content through time and any geological seismic anomaly or catastrophes."

"But you called it a vessel," said Dr. Kamron.

"Well, it's a vessel because when the water rises (and it always does), the dome will break free from the rest of the structure and it will float. It can even slowly travel on water but its purpose is not really to go any-where in particular but to mostly stick around until the water goes down (which it always does). Of course, by water, I mean entire oceans rising to cover a land mass, like a continent or two."

"But for how long?"

"Oh, that's the most remarkable thing about this vessel. It's not time-sensitive. It has its own ecosystem and can produce food indefinitely."

"What do you mean?" asked Dr. Kamron.

"Think of it as a time capsule, like the ones that are buried for future generations to see what we were like. Except that if the planet undergoes a major catastrophic change, as it always does, there will be no future generation left to see anything."

"So you have selected samples of all the current species on Earth to be preserved on this vessel?"

"Well, not all of the species so far, but all that can be collected," replied Alex. "And not just species, but genetic sampling and just as importantly, all the science, literature, and art that can be catalogued."

"I cannot help but ask you this," said Dr. Kamron.

"What?"

"Are we on board Noah's Ark?"

Alex chuckled and said with a smile, "If he was a predecessor, Noah had it easy. He just had to prepare for a big flood. But this vessel is built to withstand the heat of a volcanic eruption, the pressure of being covered

GREAT MINDS THINK ALIKE 33

beneath millions of tons of rocks, and survive a nuclear winter or an ice age. And let's not forget what kind of outcome the foolishness of human war games can do to this planet. Basically, it can withstand anything that can possibly cause the total annihilation of life as we know it. As you know, the planet has undergone such winters from the impacts of asteroids more than once, causing complete extinctions of species. Whether it's from an asteroid impact or other occurrences like Earth's megageological changes, it will go through it again. As you know, it's a geological fact that in the not-so-distant past (by geological standards, of course), the formation of oceans and land on this planet has undergone significant changes.

"I'm not referring to the microchanges that are observed and calculated every day," Alex continued. "I'm referring to the break-off of continents that are now under water. This vessel is not very fast in the sense of travel or cruise capability, but if it's under a mountain of rocks or deep in the heart of an ocean, it can carve its way out of the rocks and rise up to the surface. The process may take decades, but she is up to the task while preserving the life inside."

Alex paused. "Here, we're coming to another monitor along the pathway. I'll show you a brief simulation."

"Okay," said Dr. Kamron, "but I just can't help but think that all of this is based on ominous predictions."

"Come on, Doctor. It's not based on ominous predictions but rather on widely accepted scientific conclusions grounded on observations of the perpetuating nature of this world. In fact, you'll find me to be quite an optimist."

"I guess you'd have to be in order to be devoted to this awesome project. Now tell me, are you part of IPPA, the International Planetary Protection Agency?"

"No, Doctor. My work is private. I was involved with that agency to create something very small but somewhat similar to this project. Except that it was not a vessel and like most bureaucratic entities, progress was slow and filled with politics. Especially with multilateral international governments involved.

"As Sherri Dewitt once wrote, 'As important as hanging on is knowing when to let go.' Halfway through the planning stage of the project, they decided that, although major catastrophes of such magnitude are inevitable, their solution was to search for another planet. They selected Europa, an Earthlike planet. After that, I left."

Dr. Kamron asked, "Well, did you propose your idea of a vessel of this magnitude on Earth?"

"Yes, but those who don't hear the music think the dancer is mad."

"But how could they not see the practicality of your vision and limit the project only to searching space?"

Alex sighed. "I guess as Arthur Schopenhauer said, 'Every man takes the limit of his own field of vision for the limits of the world.' You see, they just seemed to want to give up on this beautiful blue sphere a little too soon. Of course, Europa wasn't the only choice. Significant time and resources were spent on other choices like Titan and Enceladus. These planets may very well have the potential habitability for life, but it's a long shot at best to be suitable for the preservation of human civilization as a place of refuge in case of planet-wide catastrophe. I have no doubt that we'll colonize other planets in the future, but this gorgeous blue sphere has a lot of miles left on it, even after a total annihilation. Well, almost total if I can help it."

"Frankly, I'm a bit curious on what your specific objection to Enceladus was?"

"As you know, it's Saturn's sixth largest moon," said Alex. "It's a spot inside the ring around Saturn much smaller than Earth's moon. You see, anytime they discover (through cosmic dust analyzers and composite infrared spectrometers) that a watery atmosphere may have been formed, they think, 'Oh, here's another Earth for us to get a real estate title on.' Even with water, the right gravity, and proper distance to a sun source, we cannot flourish as a species like we can here on Earth with millions of years of adaptation. Maybe a gradual migration would be possible, whereby we can mutate as a species over the course of a long period with many trials and failures. But these planets are not a place of refuge to preserve life as we know it in case of a catastrophe of planet-wide proportions. I mean, come on, living on the E ring of Saturn?"

Dr. Kamron remained undeterred. "It is my understanding, though, that scientists identified that Enceladus has not only water ice particles and water vapor but also carbon dioxide, nitrogen, methane, ammonia, and other gases. Basically it contains the ingredients for life, no?"

"Yes, ingredients for life in general," agreed Alex. "I'm all for space exploration for life or even testing for transportation of life from Earth, but that's not what I'm doing here. This is about the preservation of life as we know it. Besides, you know what a giant planet Saturn is. Now humor me and think about this: Our own little moon's proximity changes have an effect on the nature of things on Earth or even on the equilibrium of our species. Can you imagine living next to a giant like Saturn? It is nine times the size of the Earth."

"Come on, Alex, there's no real scientific validity to the effect of the moon on us as a species," said Dr. Kamron.

Alex smiled. "Okay, fine—this is just a side issue, but you do remember where the term 'lunatic' comes from?"

"I'm not sure what you're getting at."

"Well, the root of the word 'lunatic' is from the Latin word *lunacus*. *Lunacus* comes from the word *luna*, or moon. Don't you see the connection there in ancient belief? It clearly points to a correlation between mad behavior and the proximity of the moon cycle to Earth."

Dr. Kamron laughed. "Perhaps. But what about Europa? From what little I know of it, it's a fascinating place. You did not think that Europa was a viable option either, I presume?"

"Yes, for hundreds of years, as far back as 1610 when Marius and Galileo discovered this unique icy moon of Jupiter, scientists' fascination with it has not stopped," said Alex. "It may be viable, but the time factor works against the project. In less than five years, our project will be fully operational, taking a total of 30 years. Do you think we could have migrated our life forms in that short of a time to another planet? Besides, please don't miss the big picture here. The idea is to maintain life on Earth for after the planet returns to a life-sustaining state, as it always does."

"You speak with such certainty of these catastrophes in the future for Earth."

"For Earth, the only thing we don't know about the future is the past that we choose to forget," said Alex.

"So you really believe we're in such a susceptible position on this planet?" asked Dr. Kamron.

"On this blue planet system, there are four elements: water, air, earth, and fire. These elements must, with great precision, interact with each other to sustain life as we know it. You tell me—doesn't this seem pretty delicate and susceptible to anomalies to you?"

Dr. Kamron frowned. "But something seems to be able to regularly hold them together quite well."

"Ah yes," Alex said. "As G. D. Boardman once said, 'The ignorant man marvels at the exceptional; the wise man marvels at the common; the greatest wonder of all is the regularity of nature.' But remember that we humans are part of nature too, and nature has its way of developing contingencies for its survival. Think of this project as a natural manifestation of nature to serve itself. Why wouldn't we be the ones to serve that purpose?"

"But I don't really see nature's hand in this," said Dr. Kamron. "It looks to me like a human-made collection of natural production."

"Oh, but Doctor, how can you say that? Do you not agree that our consciousness is part of nature as well?"

"Of course," replied Dr. Kamron.

Alex pressed on. "Then why wouldn't this project be a natural development in nature's own preservation through human consciousness?"

"Yes, why wouldn't it be, indeed? And what alarming signs for these catastrophes did you begin to see that prompted you for this undertaking?"

"The signs are all around us," said Alex. "For one thing, Earth is constantly being pelted by a hail of objects from space. It's true that most are burned up by the atmosphere, but from time to time, a big one manages to sneak through."

"Are you concerned about the reoccurrence of The Great Dying event that occurred at the end of the Permian Period?" asked Dr. Kamron. "That was 200 million years ago."

"That was *251* million years ago, and yes, it was the worst of the five big mass extinctions. But others are a lot more recent."

"Yes, but even the K–T extinction was 65 million years ago," mused Dr. Kamron.

"Right, that was the most famous mass extinction because it is associated with the disappearance of the dinosaurs and over 70 percent of all the species on Earth at the time. The notorious Cretaceous–Tertiary or K–T, as you put it, was a big one and its signature was a layer of iridium, an element found in asteroids that covered the Earth exactly when that extinction happened. You know what else? There's a crater in the Yucatan Peninsula in Mexico that precisely matches the timing and circumstances of the K–T extinction. It measures 100 miles wide."

"I don't doubt these facts, but it seems to me like an extremely unlikely event to reoccur, at least not for tens of millions of years or so, perhaps," said Dr. Kamron.

"I'm sorry, but you couldn't be more wrong. People often associate these events with millions of years, but in reality we had one just last week."

"Last week?"

"In geological time, that is. You see, 12,900 years ago is like last week in geological terms."

"Correct, but did we? Something that recent on Earth related to a comet or asteroid impact would be amazing support for your work. I must say I'm not up to speed on that," said Dr. Kamron.

"Yes, the impact occurred 12,900 years ago when a piece of a comet hit the ice sheet in eastern Canada," said Alex. "The impact placed the northern hemisphere of our planet into ice-age conditions for the next 1,400 years. There's a one-kilometer-wide basin on the floor of Lake Ontario on a ridge named Charity Shoal that's compelling evidence of this impact. Incidentally, this was precisely the time that North American mammoths disappeared. However this time, unlike the time of dinosaurs, the footprint of humans—the Clovis people, a culture of the Ice Age—were also present."

"Wow, that *is* recent," said Dr. Kamron.

Alex continued, "Yes, there are other examples all over this home of ours before then. Some 30,000 years ago, just a piece of an asteroid weighing only 300,000 tons slammed into Arizona. It blasted out a crater 600 feet deep. Frankly, this was a small one by comparison. From space you can see scores of them. Elsewhere in Canada, you can see another one 600 miles across. Like I said, one like this wiped out the dinosaurs. In fact, you'll find in the study of rudimentary astrophysics that an asteroid belt exists between Mars and Jupiter around which trillions of asteroids are orbiting. From time to time, some of them get out of orbit and head toward our home."

"But what's their probability of collision with us?" asked Dr. Kamron.

"Well, you tell me. Earth is cruising in space at 66,000 miles per hour, and there are over 100 million asteroids cruising by. On July 16, 1994, humans, for the first time through the aid of the Hubble telescope, observed a cosmic collision. One fragment, known as the Nucleus G, struck with the force of about six million megatons—75 times more than all the nuclear weaponry in existence. Nucleus G was only about the size of a small mountain, but it created wounds on Jupiter's surface the size of Earth. In fact, if it wasn't for Jupiter, the guardian of Earth, none of us would be here today."

"Guardian of Earth?" asked Dr. Kamron.

"Yes, Jupiter provides protection, sort of like a shelter for Earth, if you will," Alex said. "Based on its position in our solar system, Jupiter's enormous gravity throws asteroids and comets off-course, slinging them out of our solar system. Without Jupiter's protection, these cosmic missiles would smash into Earth and destroy life as we know it. Nevertheless, impacts of this nature have happened before, and like all cyclical events, they will happen again."

"So, your objective is to protect our race? Or better yet, life as we know it from those cosmic missiles coming from above?"

"Not just from above, but below and around as well," said Alex.

"What do you mean 'around'?"

"Drastic, deadly climate changes, my friend. For one thing, as you know, we're in the 'Holocene' period in the Earth's ever-changing climate. This most unusual climate stability is destined to change."

"Are you referring to the effect of global warming, subjecting the planet to excessive heat?" asked Dr. Kamron.

"Ice age, Doctor, ice age. Frankly, this global warming, which has man's dirty hands all over it, is a double-edged sword."

"How do you mean?"

"The Earth has a natural tendency to return to glacial conditions. Ice cores from Greenland have recorded the climate changes over the past 100,000 years, and they've shown Earth's wild swings back and forth from a warm climate to a deadly freeze. At the end of our last glaciation 12,000 years ago as the Earth warmed up again, it suddenly went back into a freeze-state for about another 1,000 years. The event is known as the 'Younger Dryas.'

"Now, this global warming, as I said, is a double-edged sword," continued Alex. "It'll cause a lot of damage, but it could also work as a counterweight against another ice age. But I'm not sure if that's a good thing in the long run. All I know is that this lovely stable climate, suitable for our life forms, is not going to be here forever. This is a sensitive system that we have here on Earth. Slight changes create dramatic effects. Remember that with a two-and-a-half-degree-Celsius increase in temperature, the ice sheets of the West Antarctic have started collapsing."

"So even if it's delayed, ultimately we head into an ice age and ruin life on this planet?" asked Dr. Kamron.

"Ruin life?" Alex's eyes twinkled, amused. "No, Doctor, not for the planet, only for us. Ice ages are great for this planet. As Bill Bryson said in one of his books, ice ages 'grind up rocks, leaving behind new soils of sumptuous richness, and gouge out freshwater lakes that provide abundant nutritive possibilities for hundreds of species of being. They act as a spur to migration and keep the planet dynamic.' Again, life goes on. The question for us is, are we going to go with it?"

"And what did you mean by 'below'?" asked Dr. Kamron. "Are you talking about the tectonic plates?"

"What, you don't believe in the movement of continents?" said Alex, incredulous. "We wouldn't have all the mountain chains on Earth if it were not for the continents crushing together. Let's not forget—plate tectonics continually renew and rumple the surface. Otherwise, if Earth were to be smooth, it would be totally covered by water to a depth of four kilometers."

"No, no," said Dr. Kamron. "I was just wondering about your comment about 'danger from below.'"

"Well, that's much easier to explain. I am referring to seismic changes that alter the entire landscape of this planet. You know that it didn't always look like this."

"You're talking about Pangaea, where our planet had only one continent, a single land mass? You know that I've seen with my own eyes in Kenya where the Great Rift Valley runs over 3,000 miles," said Dr. Kamron.

"This is precisely one of those giant geological changes I was talking about that ended up separating the land mass of what is known today as Africa and Asia. Also, don't forget, the force below is as unpredictable as the one above."

"Honestly, Alex, if someone else was saying all of this but you…"

"What?"

"You know, if anyone else had said these things, I would dismiss them as just being alarmist."

"Ah, that doesn't matter. These are not hypotheses—they're absolute facts. And anyway, I don't share these thoughts with just anyone, either."

"I appreciate that. Please continue. What are the forces below?"

"Below are the ever-blasting supervolcanoes," said Alex. "I'm not talking about the likes of Mount St. Helens—I'm referring to the ones that have global climate consequences."

"But again, they're a thing of the ancient past, aren't they? Like the Yellowstone blowout? Wasn't that like 10 million years ago?" asked Dr. Kamron.

"Sixteen and a half million years ago," said Alex. "But perhaps what you don't know about Yellowstone is that it's not an ancient site. Its magma chambers are very much active, and it has a recorded eruption cycle of 600,000 years. Guess when the last one was?"

"About 600,000 years ago?"

"Just about … in geological terms. But the important thing is what these active supervolcanoes are capable of doing to life on Earth as a whole. The ashfall from one of Yellowstone's eruptions two million years ago covered the whole of the west of Mississippi, plus a big chunk of Canada and Mexico. According to the Greenland ice cores, our last supervolcano eruption was about 74,000 years ago at Toba in Indonesia, and that brought the human race to the brink of extinction. After Toba, only a few thousand humans remained on the entire Earth.

"No one really knows the full impact of these guys below. The blast of Krakatau in Indonesia was in 1883, which made water slosh in the English Channel. To fully appreciate the size and power of Yellowstone, I have to tell you something I read by Bill Bryson. First, tell me, do you know what a caldera is?"

"Isn't that the cone-shaped tip of a mountain that remains after a volcanic eruption?"

"Precisely. Now consider this: The entire 2.2 million acres of Yellowstone Park is a caldera. Just think about that and tell me again, am I an alarmist? And remember, it's still active."

"That's right—it *is* active, isn't it?" exclaimed Dr. Kamron. "Wow, that's incredible. I can see better where you're going with this now. So, it's your hope that this time your project will give humanity a head start?"

"Perhaps a project like this already did once, and I'm just keeping up with the tradition."

"Do you really think we're that important as life forms go, and that we're destined to always survive?"

"Dr. Kamron, I'll tell you how important I think we are: Stars die so that we can be born. Giant, beautiful stars die for us," said Alex.

He paused for a moment. "As you know, through the explosion of stars, all the elements necessary for life get scattered throughout the universe. After billions of years, that energy, along with gases and minerals, eventually transform into life. A life that we are. Now don't you think it's a life form worth preserving? How much more important do we need to be?"

Dr. Kamron shifted his weight in his seat and took in this thought. "I guess we must be quite important if someone goes through that much trouble to bring us about and maintain life delicately."

Alex was quiet for a moment before he spoke again. "I couldn't help but remember something when you made that remark just now. In his book, Bill Bryson once referenced Martin Rees, a British astronomer, who pointed out how delicately elements have to be governed so that life as we know it can be sustained. Rees said that if any of these values are changed, even very slightly, things could not be as they are. For example, for the universe to exist as it does, hydrogen must be converted to helium in a precise but comparatively stately manner. Specifically, in a way that converts seven one-thousandths of its mass to energy. Lower that value very slightly from 0.007 percent to, say, 0.006 percent, and no transformation could take place—the universe would consist of hydrogen and nothing else. Raise the value very slightly to 0.008 percent, and bonding would be so wildly prolific that the hydrogen would have long since been exhausted. As you know, in either case, with the slightest tweaking of the numbers, the universe as we know it and need it would not be here."

Alex continued, "So, you're correct. Someone has gone through a lot of trouble to be precise in maintaining this life here."

"Forgive me, Alex, but all this talk about annihilation makes me worry about my wife," said Dr. Kamron.

"I completely understand!" said Alex graciously. "Let's walk over to my study. We can have a seat while enjoying a drink and you can watch your wife in safety on a monitor."

5

LIBERATING IDEAS

Alex and Dr. Kamron strolled into a large room that from the outside looked like a cabin, but once inside, they found themselves in a fancy home library. It was lined with wall-to-wall shelves that rose to the ceiling and contained an elegant collection of hardcover books. Rolling brass ladders that moved side to side stood throughout the room, tempting visitors to access any volume they might want. The library was lit by delicate glass light fixtures tastefully placed throughout, and heavy leather recliner seats were arranged around the room, with two large couches at the center. In front of one stood a unique coffee table that was a work of art in its design and craftsmanship. In front of the other couch was a dark-brown, suede ottoman. Above every seat hung a thin wire from the ceiling that was tipped with a tiny, triangular, metallic apparatus, intended to hang directly above the head of each visitor.

As they entered the study, Alex said, "Please make yourself comfortable. Sit anywhere you'd like and I'll bring you some refreshments. The event has to be postponed, so we have plenty of time. I'll just have to let my wife know that your wife is still downstairs so that they can meet, although she will likely be busy with accommodating all the guests who have not panicked and left for the rest of the evening."

Alex went to a small bar at the far end of the room. Dr. Kamron walked around the room, examining its beautiful decor and artwork. Once he sat down, the apparatus dropped down above his head as Alex returned with a small tray of drinks.

"What are these instruments?" asked Dr. Kamron.

Alex replied, "Behind these bookshelves is a special computer that will respond to your every inquiry pertaining to every piece of literature ever written in any language. Even the most insignificant writing ever published, not to mention every song and every movie ever produced."

"Like a search engine?"

"Oh, it's a lot more than that—it's a virtual library. The instrument you refer to not only serves as a microphone so that you can order your selection for reading, but also the triangular-shaped object projects that item right in front of you in a high-definition holographic format. In fact, you'd be hard-pressed to tell that it's a virtual book, not a paper one. Go ahead and give it a try. Pick a book and call on Layla."

"Layla?"

"Yes, that's our librarian. Order a book."

Dr. Kamron commanded, "Layla, a book by Rumi—*Diwan-e Shams*."

Immediately, a fantastically realistic replica of Rumi's book appeared in front of Dr. Kamron. He looked at Alex with delighted amusement. "What do I do next?"

"Try swiping the page, like you would with any other book," said Alex.

As Dr. Kamron followed Alex's instruction, the page turned ever so naturally and was even accompanied by the crinkly sound of paper being thumbed through. As Dr. Kamron attempted to read, the page automatically enlarged, and the entire book expanded to a higher volume of pages.

"What just happened?" he asked.

Alex answered, "Layla is calibrating your eyesight and adjusting the pages and letters to the optimum size and position for your reading convenience."

"Amazing! What else can your librarian do?"

"The list is long but you may get a kick out of this one … here, try to make a phone call or just whisper the word 'privacy.'"

Dr. Kamron took the phone Alex offered and as he began to dial, Alex continued, "As soon as you initiate a call or receive one, Layla will send a vector of mixed frequencies around you that creates an audio bubble that will prevent any sound from traveling in or out, giving you complete privacy. Press the send button on the ph—"

Moments later, Alex uttered a different command for Layla and a holographic monitor appeared with an image that showed Mrs. Kamron mingling and chatting with the guests below. The crowd seemed at ease and things appeared to have returned to normal after the earthquake.

Alex gestured to Dr. Kamron. "Here, now you can observe her and be at peace as we speak."

Dr. Kamron watched his elegant wife for a few moments, and then he sat back in his chair and took a sip of his cognac. "On a different note, is your guest list the reason you said tonight was special? And if so, why, if I may ask?"

"Well, it was a particularly diverse guest list," Alex answered.

Dr. Kamron pressed on. "I know you've invited some of the greatest people on this planet from science, art, philosophy, and just about any form of significant accomplishment. But why go to such lengths if you're going to be listening to just a few lectures? Why not have a shorter guest list in a more intimate setting? Surely, it would have been more entertaining. You also don't strike me as a man of vanity and such."

Alex considered this question for a moment. "Well, first of all, not all kinds of accomplishments. The military minds were excluded. You're correct, however—it was not for the sake of vanity. I need contributions and I wanted to include people who have not just had great accomplishments but who are also from every country and every race."

"Are you running out of funds?" Dr. Kamron asked, pointedly.

"No, no, Doctor. I have more than enough. What I was going to ask from my guests were genetic contributions."

Dr. Kamron raised an eyebrow. "My oh my, Alex, are you planning to repopulate this planet with a super-human race?"

Alex smiled. "No, not really. First of all, the crew who would be the first to repopulate the planet again would be from all walks of life and their only primary qualifications are belief and dedication to this project. Secondly, I have no physical superiority requirements for this. And finally, my decision to ask for genetic contributions from these well-accomplished people in their field was simply based on a manifestation of another form of natural selection, which is part of nature's own way of doing things. Keep in mind that their accomplishments could be in anything from music, science, or even culinary arts, and they have no relevancy to their physical superiority."

"And are you set up to preserve these so-called donations?"

"Yes, we have a state-of-the-art preservation system. This is not limited to just humans. Over a number of years, as one crew worked on constructing this vessel, a separate crew of scientists worked on sequencing, cataloging every species we could collect, and preserving their genes for reproduction purposes. After all, while we hope to have the majority of these species on board, who knows how—or if—they'll all survive and for how long. So, as a backup plan, we hold on to their genetic donation, if you will, so the whole line of species can be saved."

Dr. Kamron asked, "Did I correctly hear you say that your guest-list samples of all accomplished individuals excluded military minds?"

"Yes, you heard me correctly."

"May I ask why?"

"It's simple," said Alex. "Military minds are the underpaid puppets of politicians. Politicians are the overpaid puppets of tycoons. This social structure has been in place for many centuries in many different civilizations throughout human history. Now, that being the case, in that order of hierarchy, I needed only a sample of the tycoons, if that. Do you feel differently? Besides, that structure does not seem to have yielded good results in history."

Dr. Kamron laughed. "Well, the one thing I always enjoyed about civilian life is that as a civilian, I will always outrank any military rank."

"Then I take it that you also do not believe in patriotism and nationalistic ideas of any kind?"

"Of course not," said Alex. "Maybe I wouldn't go as far as Oscar Wilde did when he said 'Patriotism is a virtue of the vicious,' but the fact is, patriotism is pumped into our minds by all the governments in the world so that they can move the masses in the direction that suits them. It's usually designed for the benefit of a few groups or organizations that will profit from that movement. As far as nationalism goes, I can appreciate that as long as it's limited to inducing fun and excitement for superiority in sport, art, or other nonviolent competitions. In fact, I recall the words on these very subjects by Albert Einstein, who summed it all up beautifully. Let's ask Layla to get us the exact quote."

He gave a command and the book appeared in front of him. He began reading:

The really valuable thing in the pageant of human life seems to me not the State but the creative, sentient individual, the personality;

it alone creates the noble and the sublime, while the herd as such remains dull in thought and dull in feeling. This topic brings me to that worst outcrop of the herd nature, the military system, which I abhor. That a man can take pleasure in marching in formation to the strains of a band is enough to make me despise him. He has only been given his big brain by mistake; a backbone was all he needed. This plague-spot of civilization ought to be abolished with all possible speed. Heroism by order, senseless violence, and all the pestilent nonsense that goes by the name of patriotism—how I hate them! War seems to me a mean, contemptible thing: I would rather be hacked in pieces than take part in such an abominable business. And yet so high, in spite of everything, is my opinion of the human race that I believe this bogey would have disappeared long ago, had the sound sense of the nations not been systematically corrupted by commercial and political interests acting through the schools and the press.

Dr. Kamron leaned back in his seat, smiling. "Don't you absolutely love what he wrote?"

Alex answered, "I do, and I think this should be placed in every school in the world. While I couldn't agree more with Einstein's comments in spirit, unfortunately, military games are a favorite pastime of the human race, and as such, they'll be continuously played until the correction occurs."

"The correction?"

"Yes. You see, I believe as human beings, we're programmed to move on pleasure and change direction on pain. Unfortunately, this military game business will at one point create enough pain that a correction to human behavior will occur. Until then, this game will go on. Besides, it's hard to convince even peace-loving people the lack of need for a military altogether. They'll naturally say, 'What about responding to aggressors and oppressors?'"

Dr. Kamron answered, "If human beings really wanted peace, there is a very good response to that."

"And what would that be?" asked Alex.

"First of all, any time you defeat your enemy with violence, you take over more than your enemy's will—you also inherit their trait. In other words, you will become them," said Dr. Kamron.

"Oh, you're referring to the concept, 'When you seek to destroy evil with violence, you will awaken the same evil in yourself.'"

Dr. Kamron nodded. "Precisely. Look at all the wars for liberation or so-called 'freedom fighters' whose message was to fight for justice and peace. As soon as they succeeded in overthrowing a regime through violence as so-called 'liberators,' they themselves became a worse tyrant or oppressor. It follows a simple rule of physics: When you obtain something by force, it requires force to maintain it. The only true champions for justice were those who never resorted to violence even in defense. It's worth noting that those same people were also the most successful in making a true change for justice and not just a change in the identity of an injustice.

"I recall a story about Mother Teresa that profoundly impacted my understanding of her nobility," Dr. Kamron continued. "She said, 'If there's ever an antiwar rally, do not ask me to participate. But if there is a peace rally, I will join you.' The examples of those peaceful warriors who succeeded are not hard to find, like Gandhi, Dr. Martin Luther King Jr., Mandela, or Mother Teresa, but it is not a popular path."

Alex considered this. "But human beings do not want just peace or just war—they really enjoy the contrast. That's what gives meaning to the game of life to humans. It sounds cruel to desire a game that is partially malicious, don't you think? But cruelty is part of the characteristics of the human race."

"Yes, but what about a political system to help manage this, like democracy?" asked Dr. Kamron.

Alex replied, "Like Winston Churchill said in 1947, 'Democracy is the worst form of government except for all those other forms that have been tried.' Seriously, think about how many times in history the fate of a nation or the planet was shaped by the votes of an ignorant and manipulated public. A public that had no qualifications to make such important choices but rather was guided by their manipulated, fearful emotions."

"Still, democracy seems to work best," Dr. Kamron offered.

Alex said, "What I like about the democratic system is how it works at the tail end of the process when the public has a viable option to kick the unwanted, incompetent politician out. So, to that end, it's great. But on the front end, the system is flawed. It's flawed because the public can be easily fooled and manipulated to elect that incompetent politician to office in the first place, be it by playing the emotional card of what is dear to the masses at the time or the fear tactic of what the public is sensitive to within that particular era."

Dr. Kamron looked skeptical. "You seem to be pessimistic about the human potential for enlightenment."

"No, my friend. I just haven't seen any liberating ideas coming through."

"Liberating ideas?" queried Dr. Kamron.

"Yes. Remember your own acceptance speech when you received your second Nobel Prize for your work as a humanitarian? I remember it word for word. You said, 'In pursuit of freedom, peace, and justice, we must conquer this world while never ever resorting to violence as the means to achieve this objective, but rather by liberating ideas.'"

"I'm truly flattered that you recall that."

"I admire your principle," said Alex, "but I'm not holding my breath for it to materialize. At least, not in this century. Can you actually present even a hypothetical idea by which this can be materialized?"

Dr. Kamron replied, "Yes, I can. It's a very simple one: The concept that the most courageous decision for anyone would be to act cowardly."

"I'm afraid I'm not following," said Alex.

"You see, to me the deserters were always the true heroes of the wars. I'll also never forget the words of Albert Einstein when he said 'Pacifism is not for sissies.'"

"That must be the coolest statement I've ever heard."

"Yes, imagine just for a moment a world that no one is willing to be a soldier," continued Dr. Kamron. "*That's* being courageous. Just use your imagination for a moment: No soldiers mean no tyrants. No soldiers mean no oppressive acts by politicians in the name of any self-righteous ideology. No soldiers mean no ability to bully one another or to threaten, which means no waste of resources on offensive or defensive measures. No soldiers mean peace.

"I always believe that if you wish to elevate yourself to a higher place of enlightenment, you must pledge an alliance with humanity and not religion, country, or ideology—simply to humanity, through kindness.

Period. All else but kindness will divert you from enlightenment, regardless of what name it is presented in."

They both fell silent.

Dr. Kamron remarked, "Alex, you're looking at me with disbelief. Listen, I'll direct your attention to something in this regard if you promise not to tell me 'dream on' when I'm done. Let's read the greatest little article I have ever read by a reporter who was a war correspondent. It is called 'War of Crowbars.' This gifted reporter wrote this entire profound story in less than one page."

War of Crowbars

This month was the 20-year anniversary of a bloody war between two nations that have come to be practically allies now. I was a young war correspondent when I covered the story of the onset of this war. So, last week I flew back to the then-enemy's country to write a comprehensive report.

After reviewing all of my notes and film footage, I decided to limit my entire report to one page, which consists of the summary of two interviews with two fathers who both lost their sons to that war and were honored as war heroes. One there and one here in our nation.

I walked into the house of the first one and was warmly greeted by the mother of the fallen soldier. She could not speak my language very well, but my heart felt her genuine welcome. After a brief conversation, she directed me to her husband." He is in the garage working on something as he always does," she said with a smile.

My conversation with the father lasted much longer as he spoke of his son and the love they shared. When I told him that he must feel proud about his son being named as a war hero, his friendly face turned sad. He took a step away from me, leaned down, and picked up a crowbar that was lying on the floor. Then, with a shaking voice, he looked me in the eyes and said, "I owned this crowbar 20 years ago. I wish I had used it to break his leg on the day he came home with his uniform on telling us he was going to go to war. The bone would have healed later and now he could have been here, and we could both look back and see how senseless the whole thing was."

With tears in his eyes, he dropped the crowbar. "There are no heroes in war, son. Only victims and victimizers."

Then I flew back home and took it upon myself to interview the parents of a local war hero in our nation. For the rest of my life, I'll never forget what transpired in that interview.

It was a warm, sunny day. I drove to the countryside and was received by the most hospitable old couple. After sharing a cool lemonade, the father of the fallen soldier took me on a tractor ride to show me his property that he had spent a lifetime maintaining and developing. When we came back and entered the big barn, this soft-spoken man of grace told me about the memory of him and his son when they first bought this place, and his hopes of the future for him.

In an absolutely foolish attempt on my part, I reflexively replied, "Well sir, our nation certainly recognizes him as a war hero." The next moment brought such a chill to my entire being that it cannot be expressed by words. He walked to the back of the tractor, grabbed a crowbar, and lightly hit it against the fender. Then he looked at me intensely and said, "I owned this crowbar back then. If I had only used it to break his leg, I could have been having a conversation with him today about the absurdity of the whole thing and the bastards who started it on both sides."

Dr. Kamron looked weary and somber as he looked at Alex. "I think humanity will ultimately realize that the whole concept of militarization is senseless and barbaric."

"Dream on," said Alex, the corner of his eyes crinkling in jest.

Dr. Kamron smiled. "I thought you'd say that. It's not a solution just for one nation—it's a liberating idea for the entire humanity."

Alex shifted his weight in his chair. "Well, aside from what I said earlier about humanity wanting both peace and war, not just one, how do you think people would embrace the idea of demilitarization when, in their mind, that's what gives them the feeling of security? Even if it's a false sense?"

Dr. Kamron answered, "Respectfully, you're missing the point. As I said, the idea to refuse to build military power is not based on one nation's sudden desire to go defenseless. This is a liberating idea for the human race as a whole and it'll require a shift in awareness to the point that it'll reach a critical mass throughout the planet. I assure you, humanity will one day look back at our time like we look back at the Dark Ages with disbelief at our absurdities, playing this game of who can kill faster and more massively. Just imagine a shift in spending from war preparation to education and improved living conditions around the planet. An educated human in a healthy living condition will have little to no incentive to resort to violence."

"It's a beautiful dream," countered Alex, "but I don't see it happening in this century. Your critical mass shift requires a transformation in human consciousness like it did in the 100-monkey syndrome. Once human safety is compromised by a global commonality like viral or economic negative impact, there will be a shift in awareness."

"It does not have to happen in this century," said Dr. Kamron, "but we were talking about liberating ideas. I'll submit to you that there is nothing more liberating than a shift in human awareness that refuses to harm another, no matter what the cause. It's simple—no cause should justify violent means. There are powerful methods to bring dark forces to their knees, such as economic pressure from massive boycotts, etc. With that, no one will ever need to become a soldier and no one will ever wish they had used a crowbar to break their child's leg when it's all over."

Alex considered this thoughtfully. "It brings joy to my heart to hear your idea, but it seems to be from out of this world. If humanity really wanted peace, it would find ideas as practical as yours to be liberating."

Dr. Kamron said, "I suppose we cannot fully agree on this one. Can we talk about the vessel again? Tell me, what about energy for your vessel? What contingencies have you thought of?"

Alex seemed relieved to change the subject. "We have several energy sources. The only one you may perhaps not be accustomed to is a chemical fusion reaction cycle."

"Hydrogen sulfide compounds? Are you talking about biofuel?"

"Not entirely," said Alex, "although we do currently use biofuel from algae. But the idea for chemical fusion was one I got from deep ocean species that live in areas so deep that no sunlight ever reaches them. If we fail to survive as a species, these underwater creatures will be the only survivors of a nuclear winter because they do not need sunlight to live. They get their energy solely from chemical changes. It's a very efficient method with practically no waste products. My challenge, however, was to use this energy and convert it into natural light to illuminate the dome for our own photosynthesis needs and to create an Earthlike ecosystem. It took 11 years to complete. Would you like to see it with your own eyes?"

Dr. Kamron nodded and smiled.

"Come, let's step outside," said Alex, getting up from his chair. They walked out of the study to another control panel.

"I test this once every couple of months," said Alex, pushing some buttons. "Frankly, I don't mind doing it more often just to see the reaction of the animals. Listen..."

Within seconds, the dome's massive panels glided shut and Dr. Kamron could hear the hydraulic system making the structure airtight. The light dimmed until the room turned pitch-black. Then, just like the dawn, a gentle light appeared, vibrating evenly from the inner layer of the dome.

Suddenly roosters started to crow their familiar cock-a-doodle-doos. Other birds began to sing and the whole place rose to life. Dr. Kamron could not believe his eyes or his ears—it was pure magic.

Alex said, "So, as you can see, I had a lot more challenging task at hand than my respected predecessor, Mr. Noah. Also, I had no divine connection. Well, that's not true. I mean not in the biblical sense. I wasn't spoken to."

"I must say," whispered Dr. Kamron, "you give a new meaning to the word 'calling.'"

"Well, your longing is your calling."

"So, Alex, you spent 25 years on this project?"

"No, I said it took 25 years to build the structure. It took a little longer than that to even break ground, and this will remain a work in progress, like I mentioned, for many generations and eons to come."

"How did you ever come to believe you could actually take on this giant task?"

Alex answered, "I listened to Ralph Emerson, who said 'The task ahead of us is never as great as the power behind us.'"

"Did you think you could get this far in your lifetime? I mean, this must have taken all of your energy and talent."

Alex seemed amused. "I once read something by a columnist named Erma Bombeck that made an impression on me. She said, 'When I stand before God at the end of my life, I would hope that I would not have a single bit of talent left but could say, I used everything you gave me.'"

"What about your staff?" Dr. Kamron asked.

"There are, at any given time, 50 males and 50 females representing many races in the world on board."

"So you have a staff of 100 helping you?"

"No, a staff of 200, but 100 must always remain present in the vessel at any given time. It's a minimum of 10 years to a maximum 25-year commitment, but so far, no one has wanted to leave, even after their term was up. You see, they don't just work here—they help nurture what's alive here and help advance the never-ending collection of knowledge. After that many years go by, it's hard to leave what you've become so much a part of. But they understand the purpose and the need for age requirements, so that when the time comes, they give their place to new residents and take great care to properly orient the newcomer."

"Sounds familiar," said Dr. Kamron. "For a second, I forgot we were talking about life on this vessel."

"Most of the staff live outside and have their own lives and families," said Alex. "There is, however, a very delicate rotation of staff that has taken a while to effectuate."

"Is this in any way a government-funded program?" asked Dr. Kamron.

Alex broke into hearty laughter, patting Dr. Kamron on the shoulder. "Come now, Dr. Kamron. I've had to fund governments so that they'd stay off my property."

"But the resources for this? Where do they come from?"

"Resources are like intentions—they manifest themselves where and when they are directed," answered Alex.

"But how do you even begin to manifest such accumulation of wealth?" asked Dr. Kamron. "I'm sorry—it's out of character for me to pry, but I'm just trying to understand your statement."

"I think we're talking about two different things here," said Alex. "But let me answer your question. Wealth has its own consciousness and it has only one objective—to accumulate. Therefore, it'll proportionately go to where it knows it can increase its accumulation. If a person or an entity has an inherent quality about them to enhance wealth, then wealth will find its way to them. If that quality is diminished even if the wealth is already there, it'll drift elsewhere."

Alex continued. "I'm sure you can attest to the fact that this quality does not depend on any of the factors we usually attribute to it, like education or intelligence. As long as wealth recognizes your capability to enhance its accumulation proportionate to your financial state, it'll find you. We can talk more about that later, if you'd like. But first, come with me—let me show you my favorite spot on this vessel."

The two men walked for several minutes until they arrived at a large white gazebo draped in lush vines and colorful flowers. Stepping inside, they entered a most inviting, cozy space lined with comfortable seating and jewel-toned silk pillows. Behind the seats stood tall, gorgeous shelves that held vases, pictures, and other objects of evocative but unpretentious beauty. In the center of the room sat a large ivory marble table with a crystal vase containing a fresh bouquet of soft blue irises. On one side of the room was a dinner table to serve eight people, with built-in bench seating that followed the gazebo's curvature. On the table lay a beautiful runner that spanned the entire table, with elegant candleholders sitting on either side of it.

Dr. Kamron looked around, taking in the stunning beauty surrounding him. "I feel like I'm in a magnificent garden on some tropical island. As I look around this place, I'm simply stunned by your attention to detail."

"Well, don't forget this is my home as well," said Alex, "and it'll continue to be the home of many dedicated people for generations to come."

"What about the animals?" asked Dr. Kamron.

"Well, we can't have too many, so the very old ones are trucked away to safe havens like zoos or conservation forests."

Several colorful tropical birds flew overhead, and one red one with a long flowing white tail landed on the top of the gazebo, cocking its head at the two men. Alex looked up. "That's Ashley. I can't for the life of me understand why, but she follows me just about every waking moment of her life. I think I've interrupted their natural cycle enough by closing the dome. If you don't mind, I'll open it now."

"Of course, but I must say that I'm speechless," said Dr. Kamron.

Within seconds of Alex commanding the dome to retract its panels, the place returned to nighttime and the two sat across the table inside the gazebo. They could now hear the sound of the ocean below if they listened carefully.

"We must be in front of the structure now," said Dr. Kamron.

"In front of the structure, yes," said Alex, "but the vessel on the top has no front or back. As you can see, it's quite circular."

Alex took out a match, struck it, and began to light a large, old candle. "What is it about candlelight that makes the young think of romance and the old think of the mysteries of the universe?" he asked.

Dr. Kamron stared at the flickering flame. "Perhaps because for centuries, that's how our ancestors did their thinking. Speaking of mysteries, earlier you said that our meeting must be to serve a purpose. Do you have any idea what that is?"

"Well, all meetings between people serve a purpose," said Alex. "Most of them get tangled in a chain of events and become undetectable to us, but once in a while we catch a glimpse of how these meetings serve their purposes. I simply thought we could explore it a bit.

"But my main point at the time was—and I reiterate—that your tour of this vessel is just that—a tour. I'm glad to once in a blue moon give this tour to someone as intelligent as you. But you're not personally needed here other than perhaps for rescheduling your speech and, of course, for a genetic contribution. I am, however, most pleased to be your host this evening. Speaking of host, please try this wine from the ranch in the sky." Alex poured a glass and handed it to Dr. Kamron.

Cupping the wineglass between the palms of his hands, Dr. Kamron sipped the fragrant liquid and closed his eyes in a moment of delight and appreciation.

"What do *you* think this meeting will serve?" Alex asked.

"I'm not sure," said Dr. Kamron, "but I can humbly say that for years I've been the one subjected to inquiries. It's truly refreshing to be the one asking the questions."

Alex grinned. "I know, Doctor—it *is* lonely on the top."

6

THE GREATEST MYSTERY OF ALL

The two men continued to speak of many different scientific subjects at length until Dr. Kamron asked to talk to his wife again. Once Elizabeth heard from her husband what a fantastic place the dome was, especially with its rare flora, she asked to get a tour as well. Ever accommodating and gracious, Alex assigned a crew member to escort her up as soon as the elevators resumed operating normally.

"Thank you, Alex, for letting my wife join us," said Dr. Kamron. "As you can imagine, she is also interested to know what it's like up here."

"My pleasure."

"Why do you think we're so interested in knowing the unknown?" asked Dr. Kamron.

"As George Bernard Shaw once said, 'the right to know is like the right to live. It is fundamental in its assumption that knowledge, like life, is a desirable thing.'"

"I couldn't agree more. But what about life itself? Why is it desirable despite all of its challenges, discontentment, disappointments, and despairs?"

"To answer that," said Alex, "I must ask you the one and only question of all time—why are we here at all? I mean 'here' as in alive on Earth."

Dr. Kamron cocked his head thoughtfully. "Oh, you want the answer to the greatest mystery of all—understanding the purpose of oneself on Earth? I'm afraid that's beyond me. I don't think anyone has ever figured that one out."

Dr. Kamron became silent. Then his eyes widened. "Unless… did you, sir? Do you have the answer?"

Alex remained quiet.

Dr. Kamron sat forward in his seat, intrigued. "You really have figured it out? If you have, I just wasted our time discussing all these other issues, which will be minutia—minutia in comparison to this question." He sat back again in his chair. "Well, would you share the answer with me?"

Speaking slowly, Alex answered, "I will share that answer with you, but to comprehend it, you must set aside your fear and the mental conditioning that you've acquired throughout your life."

Dr. Kamron stiffened. "You think I can do that? Can anyone do that?"

Alex said, "The reason I'm even sharing this with you is because I believe you can. After all, you broke the code that proved that there is inaccuracy in all facts and accuracy in all inaccuracies. Maybe philosophers have touched on that in the past, but to offer an equation that establishes that was stunning—at least in this early stage of human development. Frankly, it seemed premature for the era."

Dr. Kamron looked confused. "What do you mean?"

"I don't know," Alex said. "I felt something odd when I read your discovery, as if humanity was not ready for you … not yet, at least. But nevertheless, you are the brightest mind of this era."

"Your confidence in me is inspiring," said Dr. Kamron. "But how does one set aside their fears and mental conditioning at the time of hearing about the greatest discovery of their time?"

Alex replied, "Fear is only a defense mechanism. You're not in danger physically or intellectually. Mental conditioning is reversible, like learning a new language. The first language will still be there if you ever need it for any reason. Besides, what you're about to discover is liberating in a way."

Dr. Kamron said, solemnly, "I have traveled most of the planet and have been blessed with many encounters with men and women of great wisdom, but this would have to be the most anticipated moment of my life—to learn the purpose of our existence here. I'm all ears."

Alex smiled. "Once you let go of your mental conditioning, you can see this with clarity for its simplicity. I begin by asking you as a scientist that if you were to study a creature—or a phenomenon for that matter—and your objective was to determine its nature and purpose, where would you begin?"

"At its infancy," Dr. Kamron replied.

Alex's eyes widened and his voice rose. "Precisely."

He continued, "Where philosophers and scientists went wrong in studying the human purpose on this planet is that they began or focused on humanity in its adult stage, and then they got lost in this convoluted knot of human behavior, looking for clues as to why we're here. But, if we were to observe the needs of a human infant instead, the answer to the purpose of our lives is easier to see, and from there, everything is simply an elaborate extension—a repetition and elaboration of the same perpetuating principle at work. The complexity of the act does not change its nature; it only misleads the observer as to the purpose.

"As children," Alex continued, "we have a much clearer understanding of our purpose here and we act accordingly. Einstein said, 'If a physical theory cannot be explained to a child, it is probably worthless.' We're at our purest form when we're small children, and that stage best represents our purpose as living entities on this planet. I'm far from a religious person, but just listen to this and you may connect to this truth. Christ said, 'To enter the gate of heaven, you must be childlike.'"

Dr. Kamron nodded. "That makes sense even if heaven *is* a state of mind."

Alex said, "Yes, when you get older, you are taught to deviate from your true essence. But your true essence as a child knows why you're here and seeks its purpose in any form or fashion. Now, to get to the heart of the matter, let me ask you, Dr. Kamron: You have children, right?"

"Yes."

"Go back to the beginning of their lives as infants. Tell me what it was that they wanted. I mean, the very first thing."

"Food, water? No ... air?" Dr. Kamron offered.

"No, these are life support systems," said Alex. "Instinctively, they know that they need these things to survive. But once they have these very basic elements and they're not consumed by the need to access air, water, and food, what then? If you can recall what we seek at that very early stage of life, you'll discover our purpose in this world.

"And once you determine what that is, you'll note that for the rest of our existence, we seek only that and that alone. The manner by which we seek it may vary but the objective is always the same. However, for you to not lose sight of this, you must not let your mind mislead you to think that certain things are exceptions to this objective or—for lack of a better word—more important. The objective is constant—only the means to achieve it varies. Now, I ask you to look back and recall what it is that an infant wants as soon as they're capable of recognizing their surroundings."

"I have to say that this is a peculiar question," said Dr. Kamron. "The wants of an infant beyond basic safety and survival needs—who could really know?"

Alex prodded, "Think about what we provide the infant as a response to what we observe to be their first want."

"Well, we try to amuse the infant with sound and colorful objects that are entertaining."

Alex had a look of triumph on his face. "That's right! You said it— amusement and entertainment. Stay focused on those terms and follow the day-to-day life of the infant. Is there anything else besides achieving those two objectives of amusement and entertainment?"

Dr. Kamron was quiet, with an enigmatic expression on his face.

Alex calmly continued, "Simply follow every aspect of the infant's life as you satisfy its basic necessities for survival (although even that gradually becomes a source for the same). Every opportunity is used to serve the same purpose."

Dr. Kamron nodded his head as he began to follow Alex's logic. "Play! That's what they want," he said. "As soon as they're fed, they want to play."

Alex looked elated. "Absolutely! Now, continue with your mental observation and follow the need of the infant as a very small child. This child, who no longer fears survival, continues to constantly seek any means by which they can obtain the two prime objectives of their life— to be amused and entertained. Depending on the child's geographical locality, the means are different, but the goal is always the same. In fact, it can clearly be seen (and every parent without exception will confirm) that from the moment their children could communicate, even before learning to speak, they didn't just ask but *demanded* to be entertained. The parents very soon discovered that the only real possibility of having any moment to entertain themselves was to first entertain their children. Of course, the two often intertwine and serve the same purpose.

"As the children grow, their need for entertainment remains constant and the activities that serve that purpose at one point may no longer suffice, and they continually seek and demand a more elaborate, amusing means to obtain that objective. Playing games with a parent, for example, may not be so amusing anymore, so we seek that adventure and fulfillment through other children. Later in life, we seek it through our sexual counterparts, lovers, husbands, wives, parents again, back to our old friends, and so on. Of course, these people are not the only means of entertainment, although to this day, they remain the most desired ones simply because they're the most interactive counterparts in this game of life."

Dr. Kamron sat in his chair, enraptured.

"Now," said Alex, "you've heard the expression that art imitates life. I submit to you today that life is imitating art. It's not so hard to observe that we're all playing our roles in this very elaborate play called Life on Earth. What's interesting is that at a very early stage as a human society, our fascination for this purpose was also evident. Look back at early villages or small tribes; even then, there was always a storyteller who entertained people beyond what they found amusing in their daily lives. Later, that storytelling became just a bit more involved, and little puppet shows and sidewalk shows appeared. It wasn't long before very elaborate plays were being offered to stimulate society beyond what they were experiencing in their own realities.

"Since the needs of the elite are the same as those of the impoverished, the funding for great theaters was made available. From then on, the industry of make-believe flourished. It flourished because it served that same prime purpose of life.

"Later, somebody handed human beings a thing called photographic imaging in its crude form and that's all it took," continued Alex. "Then there was no limit. Man could create an image, tell a story, and stimulate the senses without the audience having to put forth much energy to create that experience personally. This became the closest thing a human being has seen to their own purpose of existence on Earth.

"Of course, the greatest evidence in support of this is what has now become one of the largest industries on the planet—the entertainment industry in one form or another, as movies, radio, theater, games, etc. I remember way back in 2007, I read a report by the producers of a computer game company for Xbox's Halo 3. Right there, this thing they called an online phenomenon was telling the story of what we're doing here as human entities.

"Just listen to these numbers—if this isn't compelling enough to make one see the point, we're not speaking the same language. Within the first day of its launch, Halo 3 players racked up more than 3.6 million hours of online game play. This increased more than elevenfold to over 40 million hours by the end of the first week, representing more than 4,500 years of continuous game play."

Alex continued. "Are you comprehending these facts? More than 4,500 years of continuous game play! This is more life-experience time than going back to the Romans or even the Persian Empire over 2,500 years ago. And that's just my first glance at these hours spent on game time in 2007. You know how far we have come since then?

"Now imagine a game so advanced that it includes all of your senses—not just visual, auditory, and kinesthetic but one that connects to your entire being! And can you be brave enough to acknowledge that you just might be playing in one right now in this life form?

"What we fail to see today is that this was only the beginning. If you dare to let your mind follow this path, you'll better understand what I just tried to explain to you. As you sit with this for a while, allow your mind to follow this path. But you need to realize that to comprehend this concept, you must remember that the sky is not the limit, but the contours of the universe may be."

Alex got up and walked to another control panel to engage in some work for a few minutes, while Dr. Kamron remained deep in thought. He found this exercise that Alex had just proposed quite challenging. It was not so much because his imagination could not handle the task, but every thought was now changing his perception of his world. He began by giving the idea his complete attention, and, taking Alex's advice, he set aside his fear and preconditioned ideas.

When Alex returned, he found Dr. Kamron staring at the ocean below. The reflection of the moon now made it possible to get a sense of how far up they were.

"It's the simplicity of it that makes it hard to believe, isn't it?" Alex asked, gently.

"Precisely," answered Dr. Kamron.

"How far did you go?"

"Farther than I thought possible," said Dr. Kamron. "I continued with the fact that indeed we've spent significant time entertaining ourselves, and it's absolutely remarkable that no one throughout the history of humanity ever questioned this fundamental fact, the significance of this phenomena, and its correlation to our purpose in life."

Alex looked pleased. "Yes, but please note that it's not just a significant amount of time, it is every moment. And don't get lost in the meaning of the words 'amusement' or 'entertainment.' It's simply about stimulating as many senses as we can at any given time. Let's go back to the movie industry and see how far your mind carried on."

Dr. Kamron said, "Well, we go to movies so that our visual and auditory senses are stimulated to give the illusion of experiencing an event. Because this industry is rapidly advancing, the power of its imagery perceptions is also expanding exponentially. Its audio systems can now practically reproduce any natural sound in the theater. I know some experiments were conducted to bring smell into the theater so that we can use even those additional senses. And while 3D is not new, theaters are now using holographic imagery so that the audience can feel even closer to the story.

"Then I realized that the new generation of children is not satisfied with just observation, which is why interactive computer and video games have gained momentum over conventional movies or games. When I combined that with the virtual-reality capability of today's primitive computers, then my mind took off at a speed that I frankly wasn't comfortable with. It was too much to imagine what future computers could do to this concept of virtual reality.

"I imagined a tomorrow where one could enter a domain and experience every scenario they wish to be a part of, play that role, and stimulate all of their senses."

"Tell me, Dr. Kamron, did you go any further?" asked Alex.

Dr. Kamron replied, "I ran out of time and space."

Alex laughed. "Didn't I mention not to let the sky be the limit? Let it go beyond all limits. On the same thought pattern, let your so-called domain advance a few hundred years—that is, if you can't imagine a few thousand years. Think of the sidewalk puppet shows that took place less than 300 years ago and the advancement of the entertainment industry until now, and then let it progress two million years. You really have to let go of your perception of time. There is, after all, eternity."

Dr. Kamron nodded slowly. "Yes, indeed—I have to adjust my perspective."

Alex continued. "Adjust your perspective like this: If you imagine yourself as a fruit fly with a one-day life expectancy, the fruit fly could not even fathom, for example, what a human being is doing spending one year building a theater or five years building an elaborate, giant amusement park just to entertain themselves. So, to truly understand this, you must be the fruit fly that knows they're living for only one day but can conceive what having a hundred years of time means. As for space, again, the universe is the limit, if that. So, let your mind be free to go where it wants."

Dr. Kamron took a deep breath, and the moments passed. "The domain is a gorgeous, round blue sphere, isn't it, Alex?"

Alex calmly replied, "Centuries ago, some wizards thought that Earth was the center of the universe. If they would have added one more word in that statement, maybe there would have been some truth to it."

Dr. Kamron chuckled. "Earth, the entertainment center of the universe? Huh, I'm getting the same feeling as the moments I embark upon a scientific discovery."

"The greatest difficulty a human being would have comprehending what you just discovered is that they'd think that this somehow trivializes their lives," Alex said.

Dr. Kamron nodded. "I can see that, but once we set aside our ego or even the idea that somehow we're doing something more profound with our lives than simply entertaining ourselves, then it's comprehensible."

"It's the complexity of those elements you referred to that gives the illusion that life is more than an opportunity to simply enjoy your senses by means of entertaining your soul," said Alex. "No one disagrees that when children are playing a game in the yard, their purpose is amusement. But somehow, if that game becomes a little bit more sophisticated 10 years later, they think that it's no longer a game. What's the difference? In fact, all of our behavioral patterns are repetitions of what we adopt as children. The artistic kid pursues an art career. The thinker proceeds with an avenue to do just more of that and make a living out of it. And so, on it goes."

"If you fully comprehend this," Alex continued, "then the answers to some of humanity's long-asked questions are no longer so mysterious. For example, our need for things from joy to conflict. As our need for our games to advance progresses, so does the elaboration of the rules we play by.

"Imagine, if you can, that you signed up as a soul who enters the plane of existence on Earth. You're presented with a menu of endless games you can experience. You're limited only by the senses connected to you through your body. Depending on your tastes and desires, which of course change through time, you might engage in many endeavors to amuse yourself. This could be the game of enjoying solace and the feeling of peace in a Buddhist temple, or you may choose a more extreme sport and join the military of whatever country you were born in."

"Basically, we need two things to better enjoy the game: First, look for a cause, and second, assume the role. Soon that cause becomes the only truth on Earth and worthy of all our efforts. Later, of course, we may find ourselves dumbfounded by our past choices and convictions."

"Essentially your analogy, then, is that life is like an extremely advanced amusement park?" asked Dr. Kamron.

Alex smiled. "Not like one, it *is* one—except that there are two differences. One is that, by design, the players cannot know that that's what they just entered, which explains why they take life so seriously. Second, there are no safety measures, which again explains why they take it so seriously.

"Instinctively, we know what we're doing here and proceed to amuse ourselves, but it seems that the more time and energy we spend playing on this beautiful sphere, the more attached we get. Perhaps in our teens and early twenties, we still somehow realize the idea, and as such, we take many risks and death is not the end in our mind, as it shouldn't be. But later, we perhaps get either too vested in this game or play it too long, and we start to think that's all there is, even though we know in the core of our soul that it isn't so. One thing, however, is unanimous—the desirability of this game."

Dr. Kamron was intrigued. "I know that I haven't yet fully adjusted my mind to see everything through this awareness, so I must ask you, Alex, what about misery? I couldn't help but think about that when you mentioned desirability."

Alex answered patiently, "I know that you've done an enormous job to help those less fortunate, the magnitude of which brought you your second well-deserved Nobel Prize. So, please do not misunderstand. This awareness does not belittle your work or those like you. However, what this means is that all forms of experiences are forms of entertainment; as shocking as it may come across, even despair remains a means of experiencing life through our senses. Besides, how often do you hear from very affluent individuals who have come from the depths of poverty that the most joyful time of their lives was when they had the least? In fact, they often spend a lifetime attempting to reach that level of joy again.

"Let's just imagine that inside every human being is a measuring device called a 'joyometer.' If the ultimate objective of any human being at any given time is to raise its level, does it matter *how* that joyometer rises? Be it by self-serving or selfless acts, isn't the objective the same? If you measure the joyometer of a barefoot child in the dirty streets of a village in some impoverished place in the world, and then measure the same for a child in the most high-class, sterile environment in a different part, you may be surprised to see the barefoot child scoring much higher.

"That's just one example of shifting awareness. Suddenly, life is not so unfair. It's the standard by which you measure that joy that misleads our judgment as to the desirability of life. After all, the objective for everyone is to enhance their joy, isn't it? Does it really matter how or in what condition we're able to do that?

"When it comes to any of us being deprived of something in our childhood, there's also another angle to this. The negative force of being deprived of that something we desire as children induces the creation of certain capabilities and talents in that exact thing later in life. Mostly, it manifests in the form of passion for that thing, and that in itself serves to give purpose and enjoyment. It's sort of like pulling a rubber band; the energy stored in the elastic pulled gives it the capacity to fly."

Dr. Kamron smiled. "Great, so now childhood complexes are good, right, Alex?"

Alex answered, "Look, since everything in this wonderful place we call Earth is inherently fascinating and we cannot possibly in a lifetime apply ourselves to it all, something has to narrow our interests. What better serves that purpose than our passion? But our sense of passion that would drive us to that application must come from somewhere. One sure way is through childhood shortcomings.

"You see, we're born with minds that are like clear memory chips; they need to be programmed with commands to give them direction or a sense of purpose and desire. One sure way is through childhood complexes that serve this purpose precisely. After all, if we didn't have wishes to be fulfilled, what reason would we have to be here? The Chinese have a phrase they use as a curse: 'May your wishes all come true.'"

7

DREAMING DREAMERS, DREAMING REALITY

In spite of Alex's explanations, Dr. Kamron still felt deeply unsettled about some of his new friend's ideas about humanity and the meaning of life. As much as he was trying to reconcile Alex's logic, much of which seemed reasonable, he couldn't help but question some of its fundamental presumptions.

"Respectfully," he began, "while I'm starting to see what you have discovered to be the purpose of life as a well-founded answer to the age-old question, in my heart I cannot dismiss or reconcile the miseries of others with your concept."

"Why not?" Alex asked.

"It's just wrong," answered Dr. Kamron.

"Why is it wrong?"

"May I be blunt?"

"Please do," said Alex.

Dr. Kamron answered, "It's absurd, immoral, and frankly, cruel, which seems to me to be out of character for you."

"Okay. Let's look at them one at a time," Alex said. "Absurd, immoral, and cruel thinking, you said. As far as absurd, the very design of our existence is absurd. This is not an insult—just look at the very fundamental aspect of our universal design, which we even have a name for—'paradox.' The dictionary defines paradox as a 'statement or proposition, seemingly self-contradictory or absurd, but in reality expressing a possible truth.' The key words are 'possible truth,' and that absurd possible truth functions like a teeter-totter. The paradoxical design of our universe is intended through its interactive functioning to bring about any possibility depending on your perceived reality. (Sound familiar? Those are your words.)

"And that reality is nothing but the truth, except that it always changes in time. You see, truth is not very durable. As you put it yourself in your writings, it's actually quite perishable in time."

Dr. Kamron said, "As accurate as your statement is, I don't see the connection to viewing misery as a form of entertainment."

Alex answered, "The connection is this: The paradoxical design of our world makes this necessary so that you'll have a challenge to overcome. It is also for the sake of contrast. It's like night and day. A warm sunny day is meaningless without a dark cold night. In fact, the whole system of life is designed like that teeter-totter. You can put all your weight on one side to improve things in a certain way for certain people and you may very well succeed, but for the system to work, another challenge must pose itself somewhere else for those people to offset your weight. It's a never-ending shifting of balance. It may not seem logical if you focus on only one part of it at a time, but if you look at the movement from several steps away, it's a fun ride of ups and downs.

"As for your comment regarding the morality of it, first, don't forget that morality is a human concept and not a universal one by which nature is guided. If a human harms another human, we call it immoral, but if a natural disaster kills thousands, it's not immoral—it's simply just part of nature. I must say, as a scientist, that if you wish to fully grasp and comprehend this concept of Earth as the entertainment center of the universe, like any scientific endeavor you must set aside your prejudices, which come primarily from religion. I know that you're not a religious man *per se*, but it's hard to find people who haven't been influenced by some form of religion.

"This is not necessarily a bad thing. In fact, if you strip religions down to pure spiritual faith, they often serve as a valuable beacon of hope when we're struggling to stay afloat in life's ocean. But there is a problem with all religions. They like to monopolize your mind, and they use simple polarities in nature or the paradoxical design of the universe to create fear in the human mind. Through that fear, organized religion, just like any large business entity, likes to create a monopoly in one's belief system.

"On the other hand, life through certain religious rituals can be entertaining. You see, it doesn't make any difference. The individual will enjoy what they sense as truth and that'll be the reality for that person. Frankly, isn't our science a form of religion in itself? After all, it's just another belief system, isn't it?"

Dr. Kamron asked, "And you're saying that it's just another form of entertainment to subscribe to all these religions?"

"Precisely," Alex answered. "But you see, my dear Dr. Kamron, you and I didn't choose that simple prepackaged form of entertainment in our lives. We found ourselves fascinated by observing the scientific phenomenon. But as scientists, that's where we start to have problems with religion. Think about it—if Galileo had remained Christian, he wouldn't have discovered the truth that the sun does not move around the Earth. Now, if you get caught up in this human-made concept of morality, you'll also miss the point here."

Alex continued, "As for your last characterization that it was cruel thinking, to that I must say that I take great exception. It was exactly the opposite of cruel thinking that got me started on the path of this discovery of the purpose of life. In my early years, I felt too much empathy for all the suffering in the world. I often wondered, why is there not a divine intervention for every suffering? Eventually, I realized that if our entire existence is no more than a game of life in this land of wonder, then it makes sense that there's no divine intervention for all the atrocities—because there's no such thing as atrocity. They're merely just twists and turns in this game, much like the virtual-reality games where characters are apparently destroyed willy-nilly. Suffering is simply a temporary variation in the paradoxical functioning of a game that is here for eternity."

They were both quiet for a moment.

Alex continued softly, "Do you know how long I struggled with sadness as I observed the tragedies in this world? Do you know how long, my friend, until I finally realized that all that is sad and tragic is just a chapter in the game, and then there's always more in one form or another? When I finished college, I volunteered with a humanitarian organization and went to a very impoverished country to help develop a clean-water system to improve the living conditions in one of its bigger towns. With the help of other scientists, we spent nearly two years completing the project. On my way home, when my plane had a layover in a different city, I saw on the TV monitor at the airport that an earthquake in that very town where we'd worked had leveled the place. We later found out that over 150,000 people had died."

"I'm so sorry," said Dr. Kamron. "It must have been very devastating for you."

Alex nodded. "Very sad indeed, but ultimately seven years later, I discovered that some of the people we had trained and who had survived had created an organization that succeeded in implementing a new water system for the whole country.

"And that's exactly the way it works in nature: When a flood occurs, we tend to see only its tragic consequences, but from nature's view, it's a good thing. It enriches the soil with many nutrients and prepares it for the growth of new life. In the same fashion, many conflicts in human society result in the creation of great new things. Take the advancement of space exploration, which was a direct result of the Cold War. Or the development of online phenomena, which was originally created by the military.

"Now, I asked you to set aside not just any moral convictions that you may have but also your sense of sympathy and empathy for humanity for the moment, so that it would become possible for you to fully comprehend what I mean by entertainment. The objective of any human being from the moment they wake up until they go to sleep is to maximize the *feelings* their bodies and minds offer through their senses. Even at rest, we use dreams to continue this objective. For lack of a better word, I use the term 'entertainment' to describe this objective because that is what best describes the essence of what we do. I wish we had a more profound word that didn't seem to belittle the meaning of life. But let's face it—it's fitting. When we use our senses, they seem to serve one purpose only—enjoyment and amusement of ourselves."

Dr. Kamron said, "I don't disagree, but do you mean all of our actions are motivated solely by entertainment?"

"Yes. Tell me of one that is not."

"Actions that bring pain, sorrow."

Alex said, "Let me ask you this. When you go see a movie, do you always choose comedy so that it stimulates your sense of happiness?"

"Of course not," said Dr. Kamron. "We all enjoy a variety of shows."

"Precisely," said Alex. "Like I just mentioned, life imitates art. In life, we wish to experience the stimulation of all of our senses. Just like the type of movies we choose to watch, be it drama to make us sad, action to run up some of our hormones, and so on. Some older countries have cultures where a segment of society is fascinated with grief. Once a year, they take on this role of sadness and spend days participating in rituals that include crying and mourning the death of a saint who died many centuries ago."

"Then your point in general is that, in a way we're all actors in this illusion of life," said Dr. Kamron.

"Yes, somewhere in our subconscious, we're all aware of this. In fact, you'll find a variety of metaphors in all cultures that acknowledge this. The greatest minds of philosophy, art, and even science have explicitly noted this in their work and their so-called search for truth. This is evident in literary works from every corner of this planet. In the West, Shakespeare said, 'All the world's a stage, and all the men and women merely players; they have their exits and their entrances; and one man in his time plays many parts.'"

Dr. Kamron laughed. "Yeah, didn't he go as far as saying, 'Life's but a walking shadow, a poor player, that struts and frets his hour upon the stage, and then is heard no more; it is a tale told by an idiot, full of sound and fury, signifying nothing'?"

"Precisely," said Alex. "Albert Einstein called the experience of ourselves in this universe as 'a kind of optical delusion of consciousness.' Others poetically compare this life to the true self, observing themselves in a dream. Perhaps in the East, none said it better than Rumi, the renowned Persian philosopher and poet, who declared, 'The series of tomorrows allotted us are surely dreams, dreaming dreamers, dreaming reality.'"

Alex continued, "It's interesting that on the other side of the planet in Latin America, the esoteric Toltec knowledge mirrors the same philosophy. I once read a little something on Toltec teaching by an author named Don Miguel Ruiz. He mentioned a belief system that called for an awareness of all self-limiting, fear-based beliefs. The Toltecs called this the art of transformation. You master this transformation by changing fear-based beliefs that make you suffer and reprogram your mind in your own way. The first step is to become aware of the fog that's in your mind. You must become aware that you're dreaming all the time. Only with this awareness do you have the possibility of transforming your dream. If you're aware that the whole drama of your life is the result of what you believe and that what you believe is not real, only then can you begin to change it."

"Don't the Sufis also see this existence along the same fashion?" asked Dr. Kamron.

"Yes," said Alex. "In fact, let's look at the root of some of the classical religious teachings in the history of humanity for the same message."

"How far back are we going to look?"

"Buddhism," Alex said.

"Why Buddhism?" asked Dr. Kamron.

"Frankly, I kind of think that if copyright infringement laws were in effect back in those ancient days, some of the other religions that followed in the history of humanity would have been telling a very different story if they weren't allowed to copy words of enlightenment from Buddhism. This is not common knowledge, but so much of Buddha's discovery of enlightenment has influenced other religions. Many stories you find in later religions are taken from Buddhism.

"In my mind, Buddhism is sort of like an original article, so let's just refer back to it in reference to what we're talking about here. Buddhist ancient teachings clearly deliver the message that the world is an illusion, derived from the void. It's ironic that even Albert Einstein will categorically call Buddhism a suitable religion for the future. Let's see what he precisely said. Layla?"

> *The religion of the future will be a cosmic religion. It should transcend a personal God and avoid dogmas and theology. Covering both the natural and the spiritual, it should be based on a religious sense arising from the experience of all things, natural and spiritual, as a meaningful unity. Buddhism answers this description. If there is any religion that would cope with modern scientific needs, it would be Buddhism.*

"Fascinating," said Dr. Kamron. "I didn't know Einstein had such a high opinion of Buddhism."

"Yes, indeed he did," said Alex. "Now, back to my main point about life: Many philosophies in older cultures used the concept of dreams or illusions to explain this awareness that I've communicated to you. It seems that they understood the concept that this life is simply an interactive game that we're playing, but they couldn't quite say it like that, so they used words such as 'dream' or 'illusion.' When you think about it, what's an illusion but ultimately a form of amusement?

"In the old days, it required a vision to say that, yes, this whole world could very well have been constructed for an illusion or a dream. But to have that awareness beyond a vision requires a little bit more modern comprehension. It's like that example of the fruit fly—even if the fly could have the intelligence or awareness that its life is like a dream, it cannot fathom that humans would spend so much time and resources to build a huge amusement park just to entertain themselves."

Alex continued: "When you mentioned that we're all actors, you touched on one of the most interesting aspects of this awareness. I invite you to once again go back to your memories of observing very young children. Is it not precisely their acting that serves as means of obtaining what they need?"

"Yes, I see that," said Dr. Kamron. "But it seems that acting never stops throughout our lives."

Alex continued, "Correct. If you wish to go further, one could easily conclude that the nature of acting depends on the expectation of our audience as well. But no matter what the performance may include, the purpose is the same: stimulating the senses of our audience, creating a response mechanism that'll also stimulate *our* senses—and thus kill any possibility of boredom—and accordingly being entertained.

"Consider a couple with absolutely no problem at a particular time in their lives. No health issues to stimulate their sense of drama, no economical issues to stimulate their sense of despair, and not even any personality issues to stimulate their sense of intellect. It's guaranteed that with all the compatibilities and possessions between them, the mother of all changes will knock on their door and introduce itself as boredom.

"By defeating boredom, you simply create change in the scenario. This can mean something pleasant if you wish to play that role, like expanding the family. The point is that as soon as boredom sets in, then it's only a matter of time before one or the other counterpart will begin looking for a role by which they can make the other react. Through that reaction, a new scenario is born by which a new sense can be stimulated, and thus the parties are once again entertained.

"Of course, as I mentioned earlier, this game of life does not necessarily come with a safety mechanism. This means two things: If the show is stimulating enough for both the performers and the audience, it will naturally go on. Or if the show is a bust, that means the dynamic of the relationships will be altered. In this example of a relationship, these changes in dynamic bring about remarkable twists in the performances by both actors. What used to be an endearing act by one counterpart is now an unbearable nuisance.

"Personally, I think it's great comedy, but the actors of these roles often think they're playing a love story. Nevertheless, one objective is met—the element of boredom is sent away. This element seems to be the single most unwanted one in nature, the catalyst for the production of all new shows in life on Earth—including even the production of life itself."

Dr. Kamron mulled this over. "I've always noticed how, as a race, humans are conflict-happy, but I didn't know what to attribute it to. Also, we certainly are more amused by destruction than construction."

"Well, as children, we break our toys just so that we have something to fix. Or we create something just to break it … anything to prevent boredom," said Alex.

"I'm starting to see this on a larger scale, such as fights between groups and even wars between nations," said Dr. Kamron.

Alex nodded his head and smiled. "Indeed. Author Jules Renard in the late 1800s once wrote, 'Being bored is an insult to oneself.' You see, that's how strongly humans feel against boredom."

Dr. Kamron straightened up in his chair. "Well, I must say, I don't think I can ever see life in the same way again."

"Not as serious?"

"Something like that," said Dr. Kamron. "I saw myself as many things, but now I'm beginning to replace them all with the title of actor or player in the amusement park called Planet Earth."

"Do you regret having this awareness?" Alex asked, thoughtfully.

"No," said Dr. Kamron. "It is uninhibiting. I mean, in a way, it's liberating."

8

THE FUNCTION OF LIFE

Dr. Kamron slumped back down in his chair, head lowered, brow furrowed. Alex looked at him quizzically. "You seem deep in thought."

Dr. Kamron looked up and eyed Alex. "I was wondering about my role in this play."

"Just remember, whatever role you're playing," Alex said, "if you're discontent with it, simply change your audience. Change your audience and your paradigm will shift. The people you choose to interact with are always serving as your audience. By changing your audience, you can easily control the scenario in which you're playing. After all, your actions and feelings are often a reaction to the performance of your fellow players and actors."

"Huh!" nodded Dr. Kamron. "I must tell you that I spent two years in almost complete solitude attempting to write something of service to the changing human race."

"Changing?" asked Alex.

"Yes, I see that humanity is shifting to a new era. It's overwhelmed by the massive amounts of information that it needs to process every day. I wanted to present a simple method to bring balance to the maladjusted human psyche."

"My dear Dr. Kamron," said Alex, "you need not be concerned. If you read literature from any era, even from hundreds of years ago, the dilemmas are always the same. At any given time, humanity is engaged with the same challenges—they just have different names. People always believe that they live in the most challenging time in the history of humanity. But again, it's all just another form of amusement. This process of challenge will not change because it does not *need* to change. Yet, the challenge of being on this planet is precisely what makes it interesting. Something always keeps humanity on its toes.

"I wish you could see all the aspects of life on this planet in light of what I've introduced to you. The big idea is not peace on Earth, or a complete state of tranquility, or that all of the world's poor live in great economic status. The idea is to play with all of these challenges and when the game is over in this dimension for these individuals, they'd look back at their lives and see how fantastic it was—just like watching a sports game.

"Whether they were the players or the audience," Alex continued, "it's not the outcome of the game, the injuries caused, and that it had a start and finish—it's how exciting it was to be there in the stadium. You could bring yourself to the brink of depression out of sympathy for those who suffer and still the world's atrocities would not be eliminated. They're simply a part of life on Earth."

Dr. Kamron shifted uncomfortably in his seat and looked defiant. "But I feel with all my senses that I must present *something* to pad the sharp edges in today's human life on Earth."

"A new religion?" asked Alex.

"No, a simple manual, if you will," replied Dr. Kamron.

"Oh, tools for the good life?"

Dr. Kamron shook his head. "Something to offer guidance on certain challenges when confusion sets in. What you shared with me today serves me, and I'm quite taken by this awareness that life here may indeed be an entertainment center. But that's too much reality or lack thereof for the masses. Let me put it this way—the players in your metaphoric sports stadium need a manual for playing the game too, don't they? It may be a game, but it requires some knowledge, teaching, and coaching."

"But the players get most of their teaching through genetic inheritance that's designed for instinctive survival in the game, like all beings in nature," Alex insisted.

Dr. Kamron looked doubtful. "There is no instinctual enlightenment. What about all of the spiritual teachers who came before us and enriched the human race with their guidance? I happen to believe that what these spiritual teachers did was just as valuable as what the scientific teachers or medical teachers did for the survival of the human race. It was their so-called calling, wasn't it? While we play this game on Earth, as you put it, somehow mustn't we serve the survival of our species? Isn't that what you're doing? Isn't it vital, from time to time, to enrich this game with useful insights?"

Alex replied, "As noble as your intentions are, I'm not sure if it is as vital as you may think. Of course, knowing the magnitude of your knowledge, it's not surprising that you have such compulsions to use that knowledge to serve the human race. I guess my work is based on the same compulsion, but it comes from a different perspective. It must be *my* so-called calling, I should say. But, how do I tell you this? When it comes to knowledge, there's nothing to add!"

"Nothing to add to knowledge?" Dr. Kamron retorted. "My goodness, sir. How can you, of all people, say that? You really think we've reached the ultimate point of knowledge in human development?"

"No, no, no, Doctor," Alex said. "You misunderstand me. My point is a lot more fundamental than that. You see, to me the instrument of knowing and the known are one. There is an amazing yoga sutra known as 1.41 that is written in Sanskrit. It delivers the message that in the most clear comprehension of life, one is 'devoid of differentiation between knower, knowable, and knowledge.'"

"What about gaining knowledge for creation?" asked Dr. Kamron.

"To do what?"

"To create things, to advance humanity."

Alex fidgeted impatiently. "All things always existed and will always exist. We simply play with their shapes and conditions. Look, Dr. Kamron, great minds in the history of humanity have already sensed this and alluded to it. Take Michelangelo, for instance. When he was asked how he learned to create his famous masterpiece *The Statue of David*, he replied that 'David was always in that big piece of rock—I just chiseled away the excess pieces.'

"Essentially, this applies to all things you create and all knowledge you obtain. You simply change their shapes when you create, and you simply tap into a problem to amuse yourself with the possible solutions and call it knowledge. Once it serves your purpose, you disconnect yourself and move on to the next stimulating problem. Look back at all the things you did academically or otherwise learned. What happened to them in time? Their importance was limited only to the degree by which you connected to it.

"Also, consider this: In the course of problems, time is meaningless. In time, all problems are meaningless. Just like the child who is sitting by the beach and making a castle with the sand. The sand will shape to the child's imagination, and by the next tide it's gone. The sand was and will always be there. By the same token, what we create has no greater importance than the sandcastle. The only importance is the connection of the child with the sand at that given time."

"Then what about the work of extraordinary humans who enhanced their knowledge for the betterment of our lives?" asked Dr. Kamron.

"What about it?"

"Knowledge, enlightenment—isn't that what separates them from the ordinary men?"

Alex smiled. "First of all, Doctor, the tree of knowledge bears bitter fruits. I remember a comment made while walking with one of the most accomplished scientists of the century. As we passed by a construction site, he saw a worker enjoying a deep nap on his lunch break. With a sigh of envy, he said something to the effect of 'what I wouldn't give to have his peace.'"

"Secondly," Alex added in a sarcastic tone, "think about it—God must like ordinary people more, that's why She made more of them."

"Are you somehow implying that the old saying that 'ignorance is bliss' is valid?" asked Dr. Kamron.

"I'm not implying," Alex answered. "I'm *insisting* that the old saying has a lot of merit. You see, the more we put our nose into discovering the intricate details and designs of this universe and in vain try to make it somehow 'more secure,' the further we get from what it was intended for."

"And what's that?" asked Dr. Kamron.

Alex exclaimed, "Enjoyment, sir! Enjoyment! The ordinary person is the one who really does what this place was designed for and does not pollute their mind with the details."

Dr. Kamron looked most unsatisfied. "What then? There is no value in the great things that noble people do?"

Alex replied, "As Mother Teresa once said, 'we can do no great things, only small things with great love.' So I think greatness is in the love aspect of it only."

"So do we refrain from education or enlightenment for the sake of serenity?" asked Dr. Kamron.

Alex considered this. "I'm not sure how doable that would be for someone who is genetically predisposed to have an interest in pursuing science or being a thinker, for that matter. But perhaps what would help us is if we could remind ourselves of one thing as we go on taking on knowledge as a means of amusement in this life."

"What?"

"Acknowledging the *function* of life."

Dr. Kamron looked perplexed.

"My dear Doctor, life has only one function and that is 'to be.' All else is humanity's projection of its vision on it."

Dr. Kamron was quiet for a moment.

"My friend, everyone already possesses all the knowledge that there is," said Alex. "The main point to remember is that, as particles of this universe, all of us already contain all the knowledge that exists in it. When we focus and educate ourselves on one aspect of it, we simply tap into it. There's no such thing as 'gaining knowledge.' When we supposedly 'educate' ourselves in a field, we simply release certain information that's already embedded within us and bring it to the forefront of our consciousness.

"Yes, there is a process to access it, but you don't really *add* anything to the knowledge of the world. All knowledge has been and will always be. You simply entertain yourself by dabbling in it. If you tap into a part of it that someone else at a given time hasn't yet accessed, it appears that you've added something to the world's knowledge. But in reality, all the knowledge in the universe is already embedded in all of us. In the thirteenth century, Rumi wrote, 'everything in the universe is within you. Ask from yourself.' "

Dr. Kamron looked at Alex pensively.

"What?" said Alex, defensively. "As a scientist, you shouldn't have any problem conceptualizing this and its direct correlation to the fact that in one cell alone, therein lies the entire genetic makeup of a whole species and all the knowledge that comes with existing as that species."

"Ah, I can see it better since you put it that way," said Dr. Kamron. "It's baffling, though, how in the thirteenth century, Rumi had this profound understanding. I suppose that in itself establishes your point."

"Now, I don't mean to sidetrack," continued Dr. Kamron, "but how does this sort of thinking affect your concerns about conservation and environmental problems and their effect on the survival of life? I mean, outside of what you're doing here on this vessel? Aren't you concerned?"

"Are you?" asked Alex.

"Yes, I'm concerned," replied Dr. Kamron. "As the Native American proverb says, 'we did not inherit this planet from our parents, but rather we are borrowing it from our children.'"

"Once again, your heart is in the right place, but you must remember that nature has contingencies for our stupidities as a race," said Alex. "So, I'm not worried about those issues affecting life in general. Just like the child and sandcastle analogy, another tide will always come and wash it all away to set the stage for a new beginning."

"Then why are you going through all the trouble of building and maintaining this vessel?"

Alex sighed. "Because my hope and aspiration is that part of us will have a place in that new beginning. Besides, these are two separate concerns. My concern is about our extinction, not just environmental pollution *per se*."

"So, these great attempts to save the environment are futile? All the work to preserve and prevent destruction is for nothing?" asked Dr. Kamron.

Alex replied, "The universe doesn't care what we do here. There's always another chapter to offset the things we've done as a species— another contingency, another species, etc. If, for instance, you waste a great piece of food that could have nourished another human being, immediately various microorganisms will have a feast on it. These microorganisms ultimately serve the survival of other species that are just waiting to advance (mostly from under the Earth's oceans), so that as soon as we're annihilated, they can emerge and take over, just like we did when the opportunity presented itself for our evolution from simple cells to where we are today.

"If I were you, I wouldn't worry about the survival of life in general. As you know, it's much larger than just us as one species, and it'll flourish in one form or another in all conditions. You see it even among humans;

in the most polluted cities, life advances and flourishes to the point of overpopulation without caving in to environmental problems."

"What about quality of life?" asked Dr. Kamron.

"Quality by whose standards?" replied Alex. "I'm talking about the survival of life in general. I'm talking about adaptation and mutation. If one form of living does not serve the purpose of life, that form will change. Over the course of time, the population in polluted cities will build immunities to the conditions there. Their bodies can even produce new tissues and organs to cope with various conditions. It's simply a matter of adaptation and mutation, the examples for which are endless."

"Change tissue and organs?" asked Dr. Kamron.

"Why yes, of course. You know we've been doing it all along. Look, people who habitually live at high altitudes develop disproportionately large lungs to help them breathe the thin air. If humans have to mutate extra lung tissue to survive pollution or thin air, by golly they will."

"But some things just hold their natural properties."

"Come on, Doctor. Oxygen and hydrogen are two of the most combustible elements— that's their natural property. But put them together and they make the most incombustible element—water. Everything is subject to change. But we don't have to go that deep into the elements. Just take the blind fish, for instance."

"The blind fish?"

"Yes, the blind fish. There are more than 200 kinds of fish around the world that cannot see at all. They can be found in pools of water in caves in the eastern United States, where they're known as cavefish. In Mexico, they're known as Mexican tetra and you can find them in the lower Rio Grande or even in the Pecos River in Texas. Anyway, what's interesting about these species is that they literally have no eyes. Frankly, they look a little creepy because their head is just one smooth surface without eye cavities. Since they live in the pitch-black world of cave water, they have no need for sight. This, my friend is the same factor at work as we were just talking about. I trust that you know that it's called the 'economical adaptation.'"

"The principle of 'use it or lose it,' huh?" said Dr. Kamron.

"Pretty much. Because these fish live in such dark habitats, their embryos save the energy that would have been used to develop their eyes and instead channel it to other adaptations for surviving in that environment. These fish, for example, can easily find their way in that deep, dark world with lateral lines that have developed unusual sensitivity to water pressure fluctuations."

"The creationists must have had a field day with the discovery of blind fish, then," Dr. Kamron remarked.

"Why is that?"

"Well, I figured they'd use this as an argument against evolution."

"How so?"

"Because they'd consider the eyes being gone as a sign of decreasing complexity—they'd argue that this isn't in line with the process of evolution."

"But you know that's ludicrous," said Alex. "Evolution is not subject to complexity alone as the only avenue to evolve, although that is its most common process. But if simplicity make a species a better fit for its environment, then that's the path it will evolve to. You know this, of course. It's just about gene mutation that favors a species to its environment.

"As humans, we ourselves constantly mutate to fit our environment as well. To the naked eye, this microevolution is often overlooked, but its evidence is all around us. Some species on Earth have gone through drastic changes to survive. My goodness, we've even had land animals return to the sea and evolve to look like giant fish when, in fact, they're still mammals that give birth to their offspring and nurse them with milk while underwater. It's not about complexity or simplicity—it's about survival."

"Are you talking about whales or dolphins that are linked to a wolf-like land animal as their ancestors from the genus *Sinonyx*?" asked Dr. Kamron. "Weren't they an extinct order of carnivorous, hoofed animals that looked like wolves with hooves?"

"True, but they were more like hippos than wolves," said Alex. "But yes, the fact is that *Cetacea* is a family of mammals that include whales, dolphins, and porpoises. The link between hippos and cetaceans was verified by molecular phylogeny using RNA and DNA. The important thing, however, is just that these mammals transitioned from land back to an aquatic life to survive. I suppose some creationists would say this is devolution too."

Dr. Kamron chuckled. "No, they'd just deny that the whole process ever took place!"

Alex laughed heartily. "Wait a minute, Doctor, did I not read correctly that you've declared yourself to be a creationist?"

"Yes, you read that correctly—I'm indeed a creationist."

"It's perplexing, then, how you phrase things sort of like you are against it."

"No, it's not," insisted Dr. Kamron. "Everything I've ever discovered, scientifically and otherwise, confirms that the manifestation of this universe involved and required an intelligent design. So, how can I not be a creationist? I recall the words of Einstein when he wrote, 'In the view of such harmony in the cosmos, which I, with my limited human mind, am able to recognize, there are yet people who say there is no God.'"

Dr. Kamron continued, "But where I part with the view of traditional creationists is that, in my humble opinion, they truly understate the glory and magnificence of the Creator by sticking to a time frame for creation. I think they do this in an attempt to simplify the matter for themselves with a belief system that can envision only instantaneous creation."

Alex lowered his head. "I'm sure you've experienced that it's often futile to change a person's belief system even with rational explanations. One can be so comfortable in their framework that they just do not wish to be informed because it may threaten their mental comfort."

"But even within a traditional creationist's belief system," said Dr. Kamron, "one would think that it would give strength to their belief to learn that an amazing system of creation was designed through the evolutionary process. This is a testament to the power and intelligence of the Creator, not the other way around. The fact that we can clearly trace a family tree back across eons by which organisms share traits does not diminish the Creator's power."

Dr. Kamron threw up his hands in wonder. "What a fantastic design this is that allows species to change so they can survive environmental and geographic pressures, whether it's through microevolution that produces changes within a species, or macroevolution that causes changes from one species to another. And all this through an intelligent design of mutation that provides for contingencies right within the genetic information encoded for all species! I find this to be another evidence of a lot more intelligent and powerful creator than one who needs to rest after seven days."

Alex said, "You'd think that one could easily appreciate all of that as a measure of an intelligent design at work."

"And what is your position on creation, Alex?" asked Dr. Kamron, turning the tables.

Alex chuckled. "Well, since the universe is still expanding and evolving, it's still being created, don't you think?"

Dr. Kamron smiled. "You sure know how to bring it all together, Alex. But did you always believe in creation in your own way?"

"In my own way? More like Sherlock Holmes's way," he smiled.

"What?"

"Yeah, you see, every time I misplace something like my keys or trying to wrap my mind around a question for a good answer, I refer to a phrase Sherlock Holmes used to investigate: 'First, you've got to eliminate the impossible.'"

"I don't get it," said Dr. Kamron.

"Sure you will if you hear the whole phrase: 'When you have eliminated the impossible, whatever remains, however improbable, must be the truth,'" said Alex.

"So, what's the impossible?"

Alex responded, "The impossible is the idea that random events could have created the universe. As astronomer Fred Hoyle once said, it would be like 'a whirlwind spinning through a junkyard and leaving behind a fully assembled jumbo jet.' That is the impossible."

Dr. Kamron asked, "Do you think there'll ever be a general consensus on the validity of evolution through creation?"

"Well, fate does love irony," replied Alex. "And usually good information finds its way to validity through the most ironic path. As Bill Bryson wrote, in 1831, Darwin was invited by a Captain Robert FitzRoy to sail on a ship called the HMS Beagle. FitzRoy's passion was to seek evidence for a literal biblical interpretation of creation. Ironically, Darwin's acceptance of FitzRoy's invitation took him on a voyage that is strongly linked to his later theory of natural selection and the principles of evolution."

"An amazing irony, indeed," concurred Dr. Kamron. "It reminds me of another irony in history. President Andrew Jackson emphatically disapproved of paper currency; yet his face was placed on one for centuries to come."

"Yes, history is full of these," said Alex.

"On a different note, tell me, Alex, what is it with our destructive nature in this creation? You can't deny that, as a species, we're masters of destruction, and that in the big picture, we're destroying things around the world."

Alex said, "It's a two-part answer. For one, it's the nature of life here. Humanity simply adapted to this nature and functions accordingly. Nature itself does not want just peace. The nature of this planet itself kills. In fact, it kills far larger numbers through its incidental and major catastrophes than human games do. So, if peace were the only objective for us as children of Mother Earth, she doesn't set a great example for us, does she?"

"You really think nature can measure up to the degrees that humans cause death, catastrophe, and destruction?"

"Come now, Doctor, you're not serious," Alex said, looking at Dr. Kamron with incredulity.

"Where's the comparison?" asked Dr. Kamron.

"You tell me," said Alex. "Look at our history and you'll see that Mother Earth always manages to show us up in that competition."

"But the sheer numbers are staggering in terms of human cruelty."

"You want to give me an example, and we'll compare right now?" Alex shot back.

"Well, how far back should we go?" asked Dr. Kamron. "In World War I, before we got more sophisticated with our weaponry, humans caused the death of over 37 million of their fellow beings."

"In the same century," said Alex, "swine flu killed 100 million. Would you like to move forward a little in time? How about World War II, wherein tens of million died? By comparison in the same century, 300 million died from smallpox."

Dr. Kamron seemed unconvinced. "Still, any way we look at it, it's just human cruelty and it's not unique to any culture or race. I once tried to find a common denominator for it, such as an economical factor or belief system. There were none—just simply human cruelty in every corner of this planet."

"You're correct," said Alex. "It's not about any ideology or economic issues. It's just humanity's twisted and insatiable desire for conflict."

Dr. Kamron continued, emboldened. "Yes, and anywhere you look you'll find appalling examples of it. There is not a nation whose past is not tainted by some dark history of violence."

"I feel what you feel," Alex said. "We have no dispute on that. But let's not forget—my point is not to dispute the extent of human cruelty but to point out the effects of nature. The ugliness in these polarities is part of the nature of this planet that gives life its characteristics, which includes destruction.

"And number two," continued Alex, "Once again, let's take your focus off the big picture and put it on the giant picture. Then you won't worry as much. Remember the first rule of thermodynamics, also known as the law of conservation of matter. As the rule states, matter and energy cannot be created, nor can it be destroyed. The quantity of matter and energy always remains the same. It can change from solid to liquid to gas to plasma and back again, but the total amount of matter and energy in the universe always remains constant. So, you can relax. In a greater sense, we're not able to really destroy anything—only change their shapes."

9

THE MANUAL

D r. Kamron grinned. "Come on, Alex, let's not argue the various rules of thermodynamics. Can we just go back to our earlier discussion, because I'm not looking for a leap of faith or breakthrough in science to bring humanity to a new dawn, but rather simple constructive insights for everyday life. Would you mind brainstorming with me for this collection of insights for a better life?"

"Well, first of all, you already did bring humanity to a new dawn with your earlier discovery," said Alex. "Now, after two years of silence, I can't imagine what your new lecture would have done to humanity once it was revealed. I wonder, though, what is motivating you now to gather this simple collection of insights for a better life? Tell me, Doctor, do you have a *young* child?"

"Yes, she's only five years old."

"Ah, that makes sense," said Alex. "You're motivated by parental instinct. Okay, let's see, what would we call this collection, since you're looking to design a one-size-fits-all approach?"

"Do we have to have a name?" asked Dr. Kamron.

"Oh yes, Doctor, don't take the fun out of it! I always like to pick a name for whatever project I participate in—that gives it a life of its own. If a 'word is the skin of a living thought,' as Justice Holmes once said, then I think a name is the inception of what is to be."

"Okay, fine," said Dr. Kamron.

Alex smiled. "Let's see, it's not a religion, so no holy names."

"Come now, Alex, seriously."

"It's not necessarily a scientific endeavor," said Alex, "so we don't need to use a Latin name that no one knows what it means to impress people."

Then Alex's face lit up with inspiration. "How about simply, *Earth: Residents' Manual?*"

Dr. Kamron nodded at Alex's suggestion. "Now that I've agreed to go with your selected name, where do we begin?" he asked.

"Let me ask you this: do you have a boy or a girl?" asked Alex.

"I have a daughter."

"So you had your child later in life?"

"Yes, I did and I worry about her future sometimes."

"So, your idea for creating a manual for life is indeed boosted by your parental instinct?"

"Does it matter?"

"No, not at all, said Alex. "The motivation has to come from someplace, and what better place than this. Tell me her name."

"Shawdi."

"That's beautiful. What does it mean?"

"Happiness, in the Persian language."

"Excellent, very fitting!" said Alex. "So, perhaps you'd like to pick a variety of issues that you think Shawdi may be challenged with in life and that might interfere with her happiness?"

"Yes, yes, that's the spirit."

"Okay, let's," said Alex, in anticipation. "We'll address each one accordingly. But I must assure you that happiness is only one of life's experiences, and no matter how much you pad the rough edges, she'll find a way to subject herself to circumstances that will bring her to other experiences. They may not be what you want for her, but you yourself have undergone them. Nevertheless, you're the parent and you must follow your instinct.

"So," continued Alex, "we'll think of your daughter and provide her with insights to improve her life on this planet, and through this brainstorming exercise you can model this manual of yours for the rest of Earth's residents."

10

---※---

TIME

"So, what's the first subject you would like to start with in this manual?" asked Alex.

"How about at the beginning?" said Dr. Kamron.

"And where would that be?"

"The early stage of life. As we develop in our infancy, what elements present the greatest challenge?"

Alex nodded. "Let's see, you're an adventuring soul who wishes to engage in a round of life on planet Earth. You manage to be born in this realm of being human. You get your organic spacesuit—the human body—so that you can exist on this fantastic planet."

"What? An organic spacesuit?"

"Yes. If I were referring to one made of silicon, you wouldn't have been raising your eyebrows. But since it's made of carbon, you do. What's the difference?"

"Yeah, I guess none—it's just a different material," said Dr. Kamron.

"As I was saying," said Alex, "this suit comes with a regulating mechanism called the brain, which is separate from your own spiritual awareness, kind of like when you play a virtual-reality game. As soon as you put on your helmet, you choose to limit your awareness to the functions of the visor and what the game offers. Otherwise, what's the fun of participating? However, the quality of your participation in this game of life depends on the quality of the regulating mechanism your suit comes with."

Dr. Kamron chuckled.

Alex continued, "Now you're here and ready to acclimate so that you can participate in the basic functions of this game. There are three fundamental elements for a newcomer to get used to in order to play this game of life on Earth: matter, space, and time. Even in our early infancy, we're comfortable with the first element—matter. We see it, touch it, and consume it—heck, we're living through it. So, as long as our sensory perceptions are not challenged with understanding matter, we quickly come to terms with it.

"The next one—space—also poses no challenge. With a little bit of development of our depth perception, we fully adjust to this three-dimensional space in which we move around."

Dr. Kamron asked, "Isn't it a bit peculiar, though, that we're always obsessed with wanting to possess more of this space in our name when we can occupy only the same portion of it during our lifetime?"

"That's because our proprietary rights in space are projected upon the plane of time, where a quantity of duration is applied to it," answered Alex. "But, other than this obsession, space is not a particular challenge for humanity, either. However, the last element is a different story. Ah, the concept of time. First, tell me what your concept of time is, Dr. Kamron."

"My nonprofessional opinion simply mirrors that of John Irving when he wrote that 'time is a monster that cannot be reasoned with. It responds like a snail to our impatience, and then it races like a gazelle when you can't catch your breath.'"

Alex agreed. "Yes, when it comes to the concept of time, humanity will never come to terms with it unless, as you know better than any of us, it could understand that time is only a dimension. The fourth dimension, as Albert Einstein put it."

"That's too much to ask," said Dr. Kamron.

Alex put his head back and looked upward. "I mean, if we could really understand that time is not the sun and us the snowmen …"

"But the human anxiety with time is understandable," said Dr. Kamron. "It's a measure by which human beings estimate their demise. Not to mention the daily consumption of time as a means of self-worth. You and I, Alex, as scientists, understand time differently. But how am I to conceptualize that frame of mind for anyone trying to reduce their anxiety?"

Alex suggested, "This may help—first, point out that time as they conceive it doesn't even exist. There is no chronology that can be calibrated for time. A moving clock, ticking away? That's only a point of reference, not time itself.

"Next, present the right analogy so that they understand what time can look like. In your manual, conceptualize time with these words by Albert Einstein: 'The cosmos has no universal clock or common reference frame. Space and time are relative, flowing differently for each of us, depending on our motion.'

"Let's take a closer look at this. Layla ..."

In order to give physical significance to the concept of time, processes of some kind are required with enable relation to be established between different places. So, without constantly reflecting on certain events of your life, be it looking at your watch or looking back at your last birthday, you would not have the illusion of consuming time.

"Precisely, but it's not a palatable enough explanation for anyone to fully grasp what time really is!" exclaimed Dr. Kamron.

"Why does it have to be for everyone?" asked Alex, exasperated. He was quiet for a moment. "Listen, you're more of an authority on this, but as for an analogy, imagine that when the fabric of space was created, it needed something more to support it, at least for this universe that our planet is a part of. Something like a net that needed one more thread to be knit through it. That thing is time."

"Please, Alex. You really think this analogy gives the layman a better understanding of the concept of time?" asked Dr. Kamron.

"Why do you insist on giving laymen such a profound comprehension of the universe?" retorted Alex. "Have you ever considered that the masses are not meant to understand information that deep?"

"What could be the harm?"

"Lack of capacity, my dear sir," said Alex. "Lack of capacity can drastically alter the course of safe and gradual development for a primitive society."

"I disagree. Society adapts," said Dr. Kamron.

"Not if it's untimely knowledge they cannot digest."

Alex was quiet again for a moment, and then he continued. "Well, let's get back down to earth and see how we can conceptualize time. How about this: I use this analogy for dark matter, but, imagine that we're all fish in the ocean and have never seen a world outside of water. The crater where the water lies is space, and the water in the crater is time. The two are needed in order to have an ocean, which is the fabric of time and space."

"I like that better, and we don't need to stop there," said Dr. Kamron. "I think that the more human beings know about their universe, the less they'll be consumed with their microthinking of their existence and thus less anxious."

Alex chuckled. "You already gave humanity the makeup of dark matter with your EE discovery. After all, this thing they like to call dark matter makes up 90 percent of the universe's total mass. This elusive substance is responsible for maintaining everything they see in the sky, including holding entire galaxies together with weblike forms that keep the stars from flying away. Now, isn't that enough to make one sleep well at night?"

"Perhaps once they find out that our universe is not the only one in town, they'll be even more at ease with life," Dr. Kamron said, his face brightening. "Let's make it common knowledge that the big bang that created everything we know of space and time is just one of an immeasurable number of beginnings that produced an immeasurable number of universes."

"Whoa, wait, Dr. Kamron, slow down a bit!"

"What? Are you surprised?" asked Dr. Kamron. "Einstein's theory of general relativity already implied this a long time ago—that space and time can stretch to vast dimensions from an ever-so-tiny point of beginning. This explains how our own universe ballooned in its first seconds. And you know what that means? That it can happen anytime again and again and that each time, it creates a new universe. Imagine how fascinating some of these universes might be if their laws of physics are different than ours."

"I'm not surprised," ventured Alex, "but again, you're overestimating the capacity of humanity at this infant stage of development."

"But if they knew for certain, they'd begin exploring them!" said Dr. Kamron. "Wouldn't *you* want to take a tour of one of these universes?"

Alex smiled. "I reckon I'm already in one of these fantastic universes with plenty to see and I'm not in a hurry to visit another one. Look, people in this universe have enough wonders to enjoy. I don't think they really need to concern themselves with the others while they're still alive and on this ship."

"Ship? I suppose one may also think of this whole planet as a giant spaceship?"

"Yes," said Alex, "and we must not think of jumping ship while we're on this magnificent ride even when we come across lots of challenges. I recall that Marshall McLuhan once wrote, 'There are no passengers on spaceship Earth, we are all crew.' Crew of this spaceship Earth, which is moving close to 1,000 miles an hour and 24,000 miles a day in a galaxy named the Milky Way."

Dr. Kamron smiled. "Yeah, if we all took a little time just to stare at the night sky, it helps to put things in perspective. By the way, when you look at the Milky Way, do you see a river or a bridge?"

"Neither. And you?" asked Alex.

"I see both."

"Ah. You know, that's a sign of great intelligence."

"What is?" asked Dr. Kamron.

"Well, as F. Scott Fitzgerald once said, 'the test of a first-rate intelligence is the ability to hold two opposed ideas in the mind at the same time and still retain the ability to function.'"

"You're kind," said Dr. Kamron, "but speaking of intelligence, are you one of those who thinks we're the only intelligent life form in this universe?"

"Anyone who believes that in this vast cosmos must also believe that humanity is a coincidence of astronomical proportions. To me, that's a sign of a lack of intelligence here on Earth mixed with a bit of arrogance. Anyway, while we're still on the subject of time, here is a poetic manner of looking at time by the poet Kahlil Gibran. Layla ..."

You would measure time the measureless and the immeasurable.

You would adjust your conduct and even direct the course of your spirit according to hours and seasons.

Of time you would make a stream upon whose bank you would sit and watch its flowing.

Yet the timeless in you is aware of life's timelessness,

And knows that yesterday is but today's memory and
tomorrow is today's dream.

And that that which sings and contemplates in you is still
dwelling within the bounds of that first moment which
scattered the stars into space ...

... But if in your thought you must measure time into seasons, let
each season encircle all the other seasons,

And let today embrace the past with remembrance
and the future with longing.

Dr. Kamron looked enthralled. "I too have always liked his poetry. I must say that throughout history, there is a commonality among great minds that suggests an emphasis on valuing the present moment as a means to liberate oneself. I recall Charles Swindoll writing that 'the secret lies in how we handle today, not yesterday or tomorrow. Today ... that special block of time holding the key that locks out yesterday's nightmares and unlocks tomorrow's dreams.'"

"That's beautifully written," said Alex. "Personally, I think this liberation is best achieved by limiting our mental connection with time. Look closely at what Albert Einstein said: 'The true value of a human being is determined primarily by the measure and the sense in which he has attained liberation from the self.'"

"So, you think that liberation from the self comes from a lack of connection with time and the negative emotional impact that time has on our subconscious?" asked Dr. Kamron.

"That's right," replied Alex, "and Einstein's not the only one suggesting the value of liberation from self. Rumi wrote this ... "

When you lose all sense of self
the bonds of a thousand chains will vanish.

Lose yourself completely.
Return to the root of the root of your own soul.

Alex continued, "For me, liberation from self comes from liberation from the concept of time, which brings with it an unnecessary connection between the past and the future. I simply believe that the more aware we are of time, the less pleasure we have. Haven't you heard the common statement by nearly all people who've had near-death experiences that it was the most pleasant thing they've ever undergone? And it happened precisely when their minds were disconnected from time.

"Let me put it another way: Anything that takes your awareness of time away from your mind brings you pleasure. The stronger the stimuli to distract you, the more pleasurable it is. From minor momentary distractions of the sweet taste of ice cream to the orgasmic sensation of intercourse."

Dr. Kamron asked, "So, you're saying, Alex, that when we enjoy ice cream, it's not the ice cream itself that we're savoring but the reduction in connection with time and mind that is momentarily produced by the taste of ice cream?"

"Exactly!" said Alex. "The ice cream is only the catalyst. By itself, it doesn't bring pleasure. But it delivers you to the *state* of pleasure that comes only from disconnecting your mind with time. And that goes for anything and anyone that can serve that purpose."

"So that explains the interest in psychotropic drugs, alcohol, and such," said Dr. Kamron. "In some ways, they must reduce awareness and lessen the connection with time, thus inducing pleasure. Am I right?"

"Yes," answered Alex, "but here's the problem with artificially producing this type of mental ultra-state with drugs rather than by spiritual uplift, meditation, or love: When it wears off, you don't go back to the same state that you were in your equilibrium.

"Imagine a balanced line representing life's state of equilibrium. When you use drugs, you push your state of mind up or down to reduce its connection with time, which then induces pleasure. The harm with that is, as soon as it wears off, it will not return to that balanced line where you started. Instead, your mind is forced to go to the opposite direction of where you pushed it artificially. It's sort of like a pendulum: If you push it in one direction, it will not return and stop in the center where it began. And that opposite direction is so unpleasant that you wish you'd never left the balanced line—your state of equilibrium.

"So, then you resort to a different drug in hopes of returning back to your equilibrium, but this time it takes you to another opposite extreme. Now it becomes a vicious cycle that takes away the quality of life. And that quality can exist only in a balanced state of mind."

"So, you can't cheat the connection with this time system," said Dr. Kamron.

"Well, it's understandable how one who's experienced disconnections with time would be fascinated with it. But, if it's done in a greedy manner with drug-induced shortcuts, it will, like I said, produce an opposite effect that creates even more time-mind connections intertwined with pain and suffering, and that accordingly makes one's life miserable.

"But hey, misery is also on the menu in this world of ours, if one would like to place an order for it. But here's an interesting positive point for those who have suffered on this path of drug use: They can better appreciate what those of us who don't experiment with drugs take for granted, which is the value and enjoyment of being in that normal state of balance and equilibrium. So, by knowing how valuable it is to be in that normal state, they can have it back and enjoy it while the rest of us aren't even aware of how great and precious this state of normal is. And, by the way, normal does not mean ordinary."

Dr. Kamron pondered this. "So how do you keep this time factor straight in your head in your day-to-day functions, Alex?"

"I look at it this way. If my life here is like a time set on a treadmill— say for 30 minutes— and I run faster, it will not make that 30 minutes go by any more quickly, although your mind may want you to believe that it will. Life is a process that you have to become in tune with to make the journey more pleasant, if pleasantness is what you want to experience. Basically, don't push!"

"Don't push?" queried Dr. Kamron.

"Yes. If you pour gallons of water on your plant, it will not grow faster. There is a process to how it assimilates water. Just like with any other event in our lives, you have to trust the process of life and become in tune with it. If the status quo is not to your liking, change is guaranteed. Just don't push. If you need to, set the wheels in motion for that desired change, but let the process of life bring the desired changes. Just don't push. It's counterproductive."

Dr. Kamron looked puzzled. "You don't strike me as the passive type, so I presume you're not suggesting a passive path for effectuating a desired outcome in life?"

"No. Not if passive means being idle. I am suggesting taking the path by which your actions flow with ease to effectuate your desired outcome."

"Are you talking about this whole business of following the path of least resistance?"

"Yes," Alex answered. "Kind of—just remember to model your actions after electricity."

"Electricity?"

"Yeah, what better concept is there to model after? After all, we're intertwined with electrical pulses—our neurons in our brain are all electrically charged. Of course, you probably know that our bodies maintain and produce significant electricity."

Alex continued, "Heck, just think about the fact that electrical charges get our hearts naturally to pulse. Tell me now, if your brain and your heart are electrically dependent, shouldn't we take a closer look at the way electricity functions as a simple guide?

"See, my point is really simple, Dr. Kamron. Just like electricity does not try to push through insulators and instead follows the least restrictive path, so should we. The insulators we face in life are meant to guide us in changing our direction. Change, not stop. Just like certain people or events serve as conductors in our lives to direct us toward a desired path, they also serve as insulators to stop us from taking a certain path. The key is to know that these insulators are not meant to halt us in life but only to change our path. And again, you must trust the process of life and the underlying current of charges we're riding on."

"And if we're faced with too many paths?" asked Dr. Kamron.

Alex sat back in his chair. "Well then, the key to organization is managing chaos, and that can be a fun game in itself."

11

GOD

The conversations from the past hour now had Dr. Kamron's mind occupied with multiple questions, thoughts, and epiphanies. Once he walked out of this place, he knew he would most certainly never look at the world—or himself—the same way again.

"As you may agree," he asked Alex, "if we are to discuss the nature of the world, the most immediate question that comes to mind would be ... ?"

"About God?"

"Yes," said Dr. Kamron.

"Are you a God-fearing man?"

"No, I'm a God-loving man. How about you, Alex? What is your belief?"

Alex shifted his weight in his seat. "Well, I'll humbly share my personal spiritual belief with you, which is that I simply feel that we all have the essence of God within us. Other than that, I will not claim that I have any more insight into understanding God than anyone else on this planet. In fact, I resent those who proclaim a grand understanding of God as much as those who emphatically deny Her existence. Ironically, the two groups are identical in their ignorance. Also, the audacity of human desire to possess goes as far as one group believing it has the best God while other poor fellow humans are 'lost' because of their lack of fortune in not being part of their belief club. Therefore, they're prevented from being admitted to the proverbial heaven. Frankly, I often wonder that if these so-called messengers or prophets of God had never introduced the concept of monotheism, how we would have turned out in conceptualizing God."

Dr. Kamron said, "Well, the Hindus believe that since the essence of God exists in everything, you can worship anything, be it a tree or a rock, and you're still on the right path. That's actually in line with Einstein's belief that all things in the universe are made out of one thing."

"I get that," said Alex. "Also, since the essence of God is within you, you can project that on anything with your belief system and it'll make you feel like that thing or ideology contains the essence of God while, in fact, it's really coming from within you."

"What about prior to the concept of monotheism?" asked Dr. Kamron.

"I think it would have been simpler or even more pure, if you will," said Alex. "In that case, spiritual connection would simply be achieved by standing in front of a tree, a river, or anything for that matter that could elevate their spirituality and not thinking they need a club affiliation to reach the transcendental stage by which they could have a glimpse of their essence and its connection to God. If that were the case, we wouldn't have all these religions polluting the mind with messages of superiority of their different belief systems."

"So, Dr. Kamron, what is your way of loving God?"

"To me, if God is the root of the tree, and I'm not deep enough to reach it, I will serve the leaves that have stemmed from that source," replied Dr. Kamron.

"So, you serve your spiritual needs by serving others?" asked Alex.

"Something like that. I try. And you, Alex? You don't strike me as any less spiritual underneath all this multidimensional knowledge."

"Well, we all have the God gene, so in one form or another we'd better try to maintain our spiritual connection—for our own sake, that is," said Alex.

"God gene? What do you mean?"

"Yes. Faith is hardwired into our genes, according to the first scientist who discovered this God gene years ago. He was a molecular biologist by the name of Dr. Dean Hamer. I read an article by Jeffrey Kluger on Dr. Hamer's discovery that indeed shed new light on the nature of human spirituality. The article said that Dr. Hamer not only established that human spirituality is an adaptive trait, but he also located one of the genes responsible for it. This gene is also code for the production of the neurotransmitters that regulate our moods.

"Dr. Hamer's research showed that our profound feelings of spirituality are triggered by shots of intoxicating brain chemicals governed by our DNA. To identify some of the specific genes involved in self-transcendence, Dr. Hamer analyzed the DNA and personality score data from over a thousand individuals and identified one particular locus with a significant correlation—VMAT2. It turns out that the codes for these VMAT2s (vesicular monoamine transporters) play a key role in regulating the levels of the brain chemicals serotonin, dopamine, and norepinephrine. These monoamine transmitters are in turn thought to play an important role in regulating the brain activities associated with mystic beliefs. According to Dr. Hamer, the advantageous side effect of this self-transcendence is that it makes people more optimistic, which makes them healthier and likely to have more children."

Alex continued, "This last part of Dr. Hamer's research that pertains to spirituality making people healthier goes hand in hand with what I thought was the most interesting aspect of his statements—*that spirituality arises in a population because spiritual individuals are favored by natural selection.*"

"Wow, that's incredible!" said Dr. Kamron. "So, with this God gene, do we inherit a set of genes that predisposes us to believe in God?"

"No, it predisposes us to believe in a higher power, perhaps," said Alex. "As the report said, Dr. Hamer proposes that 'the God gene, VMAT2, is not an encoding for the belief in God itself but a physiological arrangement that produces the sensations associated with spirituality as the state of mind.' Dr. Hamer also stresses that while he may have located a genetic root for the spirituality, that is not the same as a genetic root for religion. As the article said, 'Spirituality is a feeling or a state of mind; religion is the way that state gets codified into law. Our genes don't get directly involved in writing legislation ... as Hamer puts it, "Spirituality is intensely personal; religion is institutional."'"

Alex continued. "In the same article was an interesting section that went on to say how other researchers have taken the science in a different direction, looking not for the genes that code for spirituality, but for how that spirituality plays out in the brain. It stated, 'Neuroscientist Andrew Newberg of the University of Pennsylvania School of Medicine has used several types of imaging systems to watch the brains of subjects as they meditate or pray. By measuring blood flow, he determines which regions were responsible for the feelings the volunteers experienced. The deeper that people descended into meditation or prayer, Newberg found, the more active the frontal lobe and the limbic system became.'"

Alex continued, "The article goes on to say that 'the frontal lobe is the seat of concentration and attention; the limbic system is where powerful feelings, including rapture, are processed. More revealing is the fact that at the same time these regions flashed to life, another important region—the parietal lobe at the back of the brain—goes dim. It's this lobe that orients the individual in time and space. Take it offline, and the boundaries of the self fall away, creating the feeling of being at one with the universe. Combine that with what's going on in the other two lobes, and you can put together a profound religious experience.'"

Dr. Kamron looked excited. "This God gene or genetic predisposition to spirituality makes perfect sense to me as an anthropologist. As I studied various cultures in the world, even in the most remote and isolated tribes that had never been exposed to religion, I saw a common concept present that in one form or another practiced spirituality or some concept of God."

"Yes," said Alex. "The report touched on that same fact and said that this is a fairly strong indication that this characteristic is preloaded in the genome rather than picked up on the fly. If that's the case, there are probably some very good reasons it is there."

"So the key is to find some form of spiritual meditation or prayer to tune in to this genetic need, no matter where you believe God is?" asked Dr. Kamron.

"Yes, precisely," said Alex. "And, as for God's whereabouts, Rumi says that after a long search for God in temples, philosophies, and such:

> I fared then to the scene of the Prophet's experience of a great divine manifestation only a "two bow-lengths' distance from him" but God was not there even in that exalted court. Finally, I looked into my own heart and there I saw Him; He was nowhere else.

12

The Most Powerful Force in the World

"So, what about all of these well-intended, so-called men of God—these prophets, the messengers, and the saints? Were they all phonies in your opinion?" asked Dr. Kamron.

"No, sir," said Alex. "For the most part, they were like you—ahead of their time, knowledgeable, and with a great gift of passion for the betterment of humanity. Just like you. It was their calling. This world is functioning on the balance of negative and positive polarities. People like you perhaps serve to balance this polarity by starting at the positive end."

"My dear Alex, I'm not at the positive end of that polarity," said Dr. Kamron. "It requires a far more significant force—a force so powerful that it not only counterbalances the destruction that comes with active energy but is also capable of flourishing and sustaining life."

"You got my attention," said Alex. "What force would that be?"

Eying Alex keenly, Dr. Kamron continued. "The most powerful force in the universe is kindness, which stems from love. Look back at any significant changes in your life, and they can be traced to an act of kindness. Ironically, it appears to most people that forces opposed to kindness are far more powerful when, in fact, it's the absolute opposite. It does not take great force to destruct. Instead, it's inception and construction that require enormous force, and they can be produced only by the power of kindness."

Dr. Kamron sighed. "It's peculiar that the human mind is so easily awed by destruction, but that it can easily overlook the magnificent forces at work for construction."

Alex asked, "Then why do you think there is destruction at all?"

"It's part of the intricate design that's required for advancement of construction."

"Then it's a necessary element of construction?" asked Alex.

Dr. Kamron answered, "Yes, but it's the least interesting one, and the force that implements it is not very powerful. Wherever there is a lack of love, destruction fills in to open room for more love and kindness. Basically, it's the void of love that prompts destruction."

"Take relationships," continued Dr. Kamron. "Love unites to induce kindness. As soon as love diminishes, the destruction process begins to create the possibility of more love. This should not, however, be confused with the pulsations and fluctuations of love within the relationship for its own livelihood."

"Your scientific approach to this is interesting," said Alex. "I've never quite looked at it this way. What do you mean exactly by 'active energy'?"

"When I was younger and living in the city, one day I was sitting at a train station waiting to board," said Dr. Kamron. "Time was passing slowly for a change. In a sense, I enjoyed the fact that I could not engage in anything for at least 40 or 50 minutes. It relaxed my mind. In those hectic days, I used to get that feeling only when I arrived early to get my haircut. Time slowed down and then I could pay attention to some of life's more delicate matters.

"Anyway, as I'm sitting in the train station people-watching, I noticed two sets of people approaching each other from opposite sides. I'm not sure why they caught my attention. Maybe because they looked so different from each other, at least by the type of energy and disposition they projected. From one side, three soldiers in uniform were walking quickly, looking all buffed up with both muscle and ego. The taller one of the three was saying something to the others in a rowdy tone and laughing out loud. His false sense of indestructible self was so apparent that one could imagine he was ready to take on an order from a superior officer at any moment to engage in killing another human being. When you get past political cause and the color and decoration of his uniform, that's what he was—active energy ready to destruct.

"On the other side, three and a half human beings were slowly making their way forward. An older lady was, with some difficulty, in one hand carrying a heavy bag while her other hand held that of her daughter, who was very pregnant. The daughter was relying upon her elderly mother for balance and movement, mostly emotionally—feeling a sense of support. With her other hand, the daughter was holding on to her little son's hand. This boy was no more than five years old.

"The connection between the three of them may not have looked highly energetic to the naked, ignorant eye, but this was passive energy at its most powerful display of sustaining life. In fact, it was so powerful that it could withstand all of the challenges that come with living in a world oblivious of its awesome nature. This power of kindness cascades from one being to another, from generation to generation, from one side of the planet to another. It ignites from one ever-so-gentle touch of a hand or a subtle smile, replenishing sustainability, healing, and joy. The tools at the disposal of this powerful force are endless and relentless, ranging from hope to glory. They have the audacity to show up in the most unexpected, unwelcome places and circumstances, and they have the patience to carry and deliver their recipients to safety while transcending all boundaries.

"As I continued to observe these two groups at the train station, oblivious of each other's nature, they came to pass each other. In a fraction of a second, the big burly soldier's sleeve brushed against the grandmother's coat, and my mind froze the scene for me. Suddenly, time stood still and while everything else moved around them in a slower time lapse, the two groups remained frozen for me to deeply observe.

"Indeed, I could now see the true essence of what I was observing: Kindness is the most powerful force in the universe because it sustains life. Passive energy is indeed more powerful than active energy and *kindness is, by nature, composed of passive energy.* I can't reiterate enough the profundity of Einstein's comment that 'pacifism is not for sissies.' Very much in line with that quote, I strongly believe that the real heroes of wars are the deserters.

"I took a deeper look at the active energy emitting from the three soldiers. So weak was its true nature, like something that could pop at any moment and then be no more. It was suddenly and so clearly evident to me where the real power and strength lay as I turned and looked at the old lady gently holding her daughter's hand. This gentle touch was passing this strength on to her to carry on with living while sustaining the lives dependent on her."

Dr. Kamron paused. "The most powerful armies that sustain life are those of old women who are not just surviving but thriving. The power of their kindness has delivered billions of people into this world and that same power has nurtured them in life. Even when the acts of weaklings, with all their active energy, inflict harm and disruption on life's harmony, it's this powerful kindness that once again nurtures us back to stability and health. Indeed, *there is nothing in this universe stronger than gentleness.*"

13

---◦◊◦---

MORALITY

"Let's talk about morality for a bit," said Dr. Kamron.

"What do you make of it?" asked Alex.

"I think it's where our conscience rests."

"Please, Doctor," exclaimed Alex, rolling his eyes. "Conscience is so flexible in people—it doesn't need to rest."

"Isn't that a little cynical?" said Dr. Kamron. "That's not like you."

Alex sighed. "As someone once said, 'your conscience is a little triangle in your heart. It acts like a pinwheel. When you're good, it does not rotate. When you're bad, it turns around and the corners hurt a lot. If you keep on being bad, the corners eventually wear off, so that when the little triangle spins around, it doesn't hurt anymore.'"

"Then are we back to the need for social order or even religion to reinforce morality in human society?" asked Dr. Kamron.

Alex laughed. "Come now, you know that some of the most immoral acts are done everyday through our social order system and religion. Albert Einstein put it eloquently when he wrote this. Layla …"

> A man's ethical behavior should be based effectually on sympathy, education, and social ties and needs; no religious basis is necessary. Man would indeed be in a poor way if he had to be restrained by fear of punishment and hope of reward after death … the foundation of morality should not be made dependent on myth nor tied to any authority … morality is of the highest importance, but for us, not for God.

"And what do you really think morality is, then?" Dr. Kamron asked.

"Morality, morality," said Alex, exasperated. "It's just a tool of survival for the human race—just like any other natural development."

"I must say, Alex, I'm not following you on this one. A tool?"

"Think of it as an adaptive response developed not to make us more noble, but simply to enhance our survival. You see, everything in human development is designed to be and is a means of survival, be it scientific advances to fight disease, or sociological or behavioral development to prevent complete self-destruction. After all, do you know why dogs behave so nicely around their human owners?"

Dr. Kamron smiled slyly. "As you're the veterinarian, I'll let you give me the expert answer."

"Give me your opinion," said Alex.

"So that they are fed."

"Exactly."

Dr. Kamron chuckled. "I can't wait to hear how feeding dogs correlates with human morality."

"As you know," said Alex, "in the time of cavemen, dogs were like wolves—simply predators by the call of nature. Over time, many of them learned that by interacting in a certain fashion with human beings, they were allowed to stay closer to these camps and caves and were fed their surplus food. This meant that these wolf-like animals did not have to hunt or subject themselves to starvation or harsh elements to survive the cold and lack of food. Little by little, they adopted new behaviors to better please their human benefactors. Over the course of hundreds of thousands of years and through the microevolution of behavior patterns, their entire behavioral system developed to serve humanity, and they received the title of 'man's best friend.'

"Now, human beings," continued Alex, "by virtue of preventing self-destruction of their own race, developed a behavioral pattern that we call morality. Early man, like the early dogs, started out with purely predatory behavior. Except that man realized that his own fellow men were the greatest danger to him. While he can fight some of them to survive, it really benefits him to behave in a certain structured way toward his fellow primeval men—that is, to behave in a so-called moral fashion.

"Now, let's leap forward in time in human social development. We ultimately incorporated moral behavior into all the requirements to be a part of society. Even the most basic instinctive acts—such as sex—now required a certain moral code, like courtship rituals. To be socially accepted and protected, you now had to behave how your society dictated. And that directly affected the reproduction of our species. Thus, in a way, this moral behavior is really designed to help protect the human race."

Dr. Kamron chuckled. "I'll remember that the next time my wife critiques my behavior."

Alex smiled knowingly. "It's not a gender issue; it's a survival mechanism for the entire race, used equally by females as well as males. Just another naturally self-preserving element in human development."

Dr. Kamron said, "So what is your suggestion to improve the human behavior in this era?"

Alex replied, "The most moral thing you can do is be more accepting, starting with yourself. The best way to overcome negative self-judgment is to nurture your mind with thoughts of acceptance of yourself. This is not just for your benefit. Those who are hard on themselves are always hard on others. By being more accepting of your own mistakes, you create a healthy new paradigm where you'll be more accepting of others—and thus make them feel good about themselves.

"There, my friend, is the greatest shortcut to a joyful life: A pleasant mentality creates pleasant reality."

14

FAITH AND A TREE

Dr. Kamron's curiosity was as endless as Alex's reservoir of answers. He kept thinking of more things to ask this elderly man whose intellect so keenly matched his in a way he had seldom encountered in another human being. He pressed on eagerly.

"So, Alex, you didn't tell me what your personal religion is. That is, if I may ask?"

Alex looked at Dr. Kamron with gentle eyes. "I'll give you the same answer that the 14th Dalai Llama of Tibet gave: 'My true religion is kindness.' Other than that, I don't have one."

"That's it?" said Dr. Kamron.

"Yes," Alex replied, with a smile. "I just don't appreciate people hiding their personal, self-serving agendas behind any concept that represents divinity. I once heard this from the mouth of one of my favorite actors, Jimmy Stewart. He said that 'God uses the good ones and the bad ones use God.' Perhaps that's why some of the greatest minds of human history emphatically despised organized religion. My favorite of all is Thomas Jefferson, who not only had the wisdom to recognize the harm that comes from organized religion but also the foresight to help a nation—at least in principle—not be chained down by it. He made no bones about it when he said that 'religion is a matter which lies solely between Man and his God, that he owes account to none other for his faith or his worship.' Later he added, 'It does me no injury for my neighbor to say there are 20 gods, or no god.'"

Dr. Kamron said, "I happen to be a big fan of him as well. But are you saying that you categorically don't appreciate highly religious people?"

"Of course I'm not saying that," said Alex. "The point is, just as ego disguises itself in humility, malevolence masquerades in righteousness.

And what better place for malevolence to nest than in the fuzzy, comfortable home of a religion? And I mean *any* religion."

"Just religion?" queried Dr. Kamron.

"No, any righteous ideology that imposes on your mind, liberty, or property in the name of betterment of some greater good in this life or hereafter," Alex replied.

"How about the claims of miracles associated with religion, be it for the traditional belief in access to heaven or just betterment of life?" asked Dr. Kamron.

"Personally, I subscribe to what Mark Twain said: 'Go to Heaven for the climate, Hell for the company,'" replied Alex.

Dr. Kamron raised his eyebrows. "Come now, Alex."

"Okay, fine. First, let's cover the idea of betterment of life by religion. To me, religion can be a warm light that could be used to uplift a person spiritually. But if you focus on this light too intensely, it can blind you to the beauty of reason that can enhance your enlightenment. As for those so-called miracles, every moment of life is a miracle, and no religion can get credit for that, although it tries to. It seems as if people associate miracles in life only when certain happenings transpire at a certain speed. Otherwise, it's just an ordinary thing. To me, that's ludicrous."

Dr. Kamron was puzzled. "How do you mean?"

Alex explained, "I mean … for example, if you get a bad cut on your hand and somehow it heals in five seconds instead of a few days, that would be considered a miracle. Why do we not see the miracle in just the healing process itself, the miraculous and amazing cell rejuvenation that heals that very same cut to the point of full recovery? Imagine if it took two years for a cut to heal—would the normal speed of a few days be considered miraculous? Life is a miracle in itself.

"But, if by miracle you mean a certain act by a certain ancient prophet perhaps thousands of years ago, then I must say that I'm not impressed by the stories of what supernatural acts they reportedly did back then. To me, the real miracle of their work is that thousands of years later, their teachings somehow still touch the hearts of the people of our time and manage to bring hope and healing. That, my friend, is the real miracle. Otherwise, you can go to a magic show and see the same so-called supernatural act and not feel anything but amusement."

Alex looked quizzically at Dr. Kamron. "How about you? What do you think?"

Dr. Kamron replied, "Like I said, I don't subscribe to any particular religion myself, but I too see the need for some kind of faith-based spiritual concept for humans. I've always seen a direct correlation between having faith and a positive, healthy mind and life. Even if that faith is connected to a juniper tree. Maybe it goes back to our God gene you were talking about."

"Then are you speaking scientifically or just from personal experience?" Alex asked.

"Is there a difference?"

"I suppose not," said Alex. "Physics is the material manifestation of metaphysics."

"But, you don't want organized religion to guide society, period?" asked Dr. Kamron.

Alex shook his head. "I don't believe in enforcing organized ideology in society in any form. It doesn't have to be in the name of God, although that's an easy sell. But it could be in a form of atheism, like communism. I clearly recall what Albert Einstein said about communism—that 'it has some of the characteristics of a religion and inspires the emotions of a religion.'"

Dr. Kamron remained persistent. "So, you don't think there's ever any value for society when one is inspired by what organized religion or organized ideology has to offer? Even if it's a good deed?"

"Come on Doctor, if one is compelled to do good for society, why do they need to do it in the name of religion or ideology? Just do it for the sake of doing it," said Alex impatiently. "When it's done in the name of something else, then it's the least pure form of compassion and donation because it's heavily tainted by the intentions to promote one's ideological club. Where's the nobility in that? And there's almost always an agenda attached to it."

Dr. Kamron still wasn't about to give up. "Then what form of religion do *you* value?"

"Any form that facilitates the spiritual need of individuals without the need to compete with another form," replied Alex. "Here, let's see what Mr. Gibran has to say in his poetry on the subject. Layla ..."

Is not religion all deeds and all reflection . . .

Who can separate his faith from his actions, or his belief from his occupations?

Who can spread his hours before him, saying "This for God and this for myself; This for my soul, and this other for my body"?

All your hours are wings that beat through space from self to self.

He who wears his morality but as his best garment were better naked. . . .

For in reverie you cannot rise above your achievements nor fall lower than your failures.

And take with you all men: For in adoration you cannot fly higher than their hopes nor humble yourself lower than their despair.

And if you would know God be not therefore a solver of riddles.

Rather look about you and you shall see Him playing with your children.

15

---·◦✕◦·---

DEATH

There was a gentle greeting by the entrance of the gazebo. A crew member stepped inside bearing a tray that was heaped with colorful fresh fruits for Alex and his guest. As it was graciously placed on the table, Dr. Kamron expressed his gratitude and asked Alex, "Do you actually grow your own fruits and vegetables here?"

"Yes, of course," answered Alex. "Not everything, but we're quite proud of some of our productions here. The pineapple you see in the center of the tray is one of ours and also all the grapes. Please try them."

"I'm sorry," said Dr. Kamron. "I don't see an apple."

"Oh, pineapple, I said."

"What kind of apple?" asked Dr. Kamron.

Alex chuckled. Dr. Kamron looked very puzzled, expressing that he had never seen a pineapple before.

A few moments passed as Dr. Kamron sampled the sweet, succulent red grapes. "Let's talk about death," he said, cheerily.

"Why not?" responded Alex. "First, why don't you tell me your perspective."

"Mine is simple," said Dr. Kamron. "It's a portal, but I'm really interested in yours."

"Portal, huh?" said Alex. "Well, to me, it's more of a mystery than anything else. Not that I have never feared it, but, after all, birth comes with a commitment to death, so I don't really pay that much attention to it."

"Your fear is simply another survival mechanism," said Dr. Kamron. "There's nothing wrong with that as long as you're not consumed by it. But do you still see it as a point at which your consciousness will cease to exist?"

"Not really," said Alex. "I look for most answers in nature, and nature speaks clearly that nothing will ever completely die. Life is always transforming. I cannot imagine that human consciousness is different than all the rest of nature in those transformations. Just as nature never ceases to exist, nor does human consciousness. I also think that the commonality of all the stories about near-death experiences from around the world speaks volumes that our consciousness survives its separation from the body. You recall my analogy of the organic spacesuit, right? Then you must know that I wasn't kidding. To me, death and life are the same, like different seasons. What we were before we put on this organic spacesuit is the same as what we'll be after we take it off. The transition in between is just that of a different season."

Dr. Kamron pondered this with interest. "Have you ever wondered about the complete lack of awareness of the phenomenon from one season of existence to another?"

"First of all, it's not a complete lack of awareness," insisted Alex. "But we must have no recollection of ourselves from before so that we can truly enjoy this game of life. Otherwise it would lack its most exciting element—the fear of the unknown. And that would take away the greatest mystery of all."

"Understanding the purpose of oneself?"

Alex smiled in approval of this statement. "When you think about it, if humanity were consciously aware that death did not necessarily mean the end of their existence, can you imagine the change in the paradigms of life on this planet? It would be a meaningless game, like seeing a movie where the characters are in no jeopardy and the movie has no beginning or end. Who wants to see *that* movie? How dull.

"I once heard that the angels envy human beings because we feel things. That makes sense, don't you think? We're admitted into this fantastic amusement park called life on Earth and are equipped with sensory perceptions that allow us to enjoy this mind-boggling variety of rides. The ups and downs of the rollercoasters of life, the romantic rides on the merry-go-rounds, the nasty impacts of bumper cars, the good-for-nothing taste of cotton candy, or the exciting fear of train rides through the haunted house.

"It's funny how those parks and now computer games are designed to imitate life," continued Alex. "We don't mind the price we pay to get into this amusement park, the pain of its rough rides, or even the loss of not winning any of its prizes. But we certainly mind leaving. Unwilling because leaving means death and death in human terms means the end—time to step out of the amusement park. Perhaps if we were consciously aware that death was not the end and that other games with endless possibilities await us, maybe even far grander, *much* grander..."

Alex grew quiet for a moment, and then continued. "Then we would not really enjoy this game to the fullest of our capabilities. As it is, we're rushing through it, aren't we, Doctor?"

Dr. Kamron agreed. "We are indeed, but if people conclusively knew that there's more after death, don't you think they'd live with more peace in their heart?"

"Absolutely not!" exclaimed Alex. "You've got to be kidding. That would have the most damaging impact on humanity. Our entire social order would collapse."

Dr. Kamron was silent. He looked at Alex with a perplexed expression.

Alex continued, "Anyway, since we're on the subject, let's see what Mr. Kahlil Gibran has said on the subject of death. Layla..."

You would know the secret of death.

But how shall you find it unless you seek it
in the heart of life? . . .

For life and death are one, even as the river
and the sea are one . . . .

Only when you drink from the river of silence
shall you indeed sing.

And when you have reached the mountaintop,
then you shall begin to climb.

And when the earth shall claim your limbs,
then shall you truly dance.

16

LOVE

"So, what about love?" asked Dr. Kamron.

"What about it?" said Alex, playfully.

"Give me your take on the subject of love."

Alex chuckled. "If you're referring to love between lovers, as Robert Frost wrote, 'Love is an irresistible desire to be irresistibly desired.'"

"And you think that's the rule?" Dr. Kamron pressed.

"I don't know what you mean by the rule of love, because, as Rumi said when it comes to love, 'There are no rules of engagement, merely surrender.'"

Dr. Kamron grinned. "Are you going to give me your perspective or not?"

Alex laughed out loud. "These perspectives resonate with me or I wouldn't cite them!"

"Perhaps I should've asked about the essence of love instead."

"Ah, that's better," Alex said, his eyes gleaming. "'Subject'" was not a fitting word for love. If you're asking about the essence of love, I must say with utmost certainty: Cultivate love and harvest the qualities of life, because love is all that is."

"All that is?" asked Dr. Kamron.

"Yes," said Alex, "as clichéd as it may sound, love is the main ingredient for all that is. It's easy to understand this statement when it applies to what we consider good or positive acts or productions. But even in negative outcomes, love is the main ingredient. That's why love is all that is.

"Let me use a simple analogy to better explain it. In what most would consider a bad and selfish act, it is love for the self that produces the act. There's absolutely nothing in nature that prohibits the production of that selfish act. Nature survives on that very basic impulse. It's only in the idealistic justice system of the moralistic human mind that the act of self-love is condemned—or at least not considered noble. Yet, if you observe the essence of every act that a human being is engaged in on a daily basis, it's automated by the natural element of self-love. In fact, if you don't have enough self-love, your state of good health will become compromised. To love is to be, to love is to connect, and to love is to reproduce. Heck, to love is to live."

Dr. Kamron nodded thoughtfully.

Alex continued, "When you really think about it, every action we take is motivated by love. Without it, everything becomes stagnant."

"I thought every action we take is based on either love *or* fear," said Dr. Kamron. "I mean, when we look back at our lives, every decision and every step was based on fear or love. Don't you agree?"

"Partially," said Alex. "Fear comes only where there's a lack of love. If you break it down, the element that induces any decision or action ultimately stems from love … be it self-love. But fear holds you back from simple joys to lifelong dreams. In fact, fear so badly depletes joy from life and prevents you from reaching your dreams that in the Christian Bible, it's been said that the phrase "fear not" has been stated 365 times."

"That would be one for every day of the year," said Dr. Kamron in amazement.

"There you have it," said Alex.

"How about when you love another? Isn't that a more gratifying form of love?"

"Love has only one form," said Alex. "It's all that there is. You cultivate love for others because you have to love them to have love inside yourself. It seems that love begins and is rooted in self-love, but it needs to be extended outward as well as inward to be sustainable."

"So my love for my family is based on self-love?" asked Dr. Kamron.

"Yes, but it's a two-way street; so is their love for you. You have to share it so you can meet the minimum need for survival. It's a symbiotic state needed for a healthy life. You can last only so long on self-love, or if you manage to survive with only self-love for a long time, many of your vital functionalities will be compromised. Simply put, life flourishes with love because love is the essence of life. Just think about the opposite of having people with whom you can reciprocate love."

"Hate?" asked Dr. Kamron.

"No, hate is just a reaction. I mean a state of loneliness. Think about it. What's the greatest punishment that human society could come up with for punishing one of their own, second only to killing them?"

"Prison."

"Yes, but why? And dig a little deeper," said Alex.

"According to you, Alex, the human's game of life would be quite boring in prison, so boredom would be the greatest punishment," said Dr. Kamron.

"Excellent," said Alex. "But since we're on the subject of love, I'm talking about solitary confinement. That's the ultimate state of a lack of love—no one to love and a rapid loss of opportunity to love yourself. Loneliness is at the opposite point of the spectrum of life from love, and it deeply diminishes the value of human experience."

"Okay, Alex, but I can't help but feel that you have a deeper reason for accepting this concept of self-love for selfish acts. Am I getting carried away?"

"Perhaps I do, you're right," said Alex. "As you know, we're all intricately connected in forming this universe, one that's not composed of various parts but rather consists of a single entity. Accordingly, a selfish act designed to serve one will ultimately serve all in a closed system such as this."

Dr. Kamron considered this statement for a moment. "Maybe, just maybe, with the power of irony. But going back to love itself, scientifically speaking, I can't help but acknowledge that love is like everything else we feel—it needs something to trigger it. For example, if you're melancholy, you may either be low on blood sugar or your body hasn't produced enough norepinephrine. And likewise, love is the work of dopamine, so it's possible that it's simply neurological and biochemical."

"Come, Doctor. I cannot believe that you would even consider that dopamine can induce love."

"Then what is dopamine in your opinion?" asked Dr. Kamron.

"It's actually a delivery system for love," said Alex. "The chemical and biological effect of dopamine doesn't produce love—it just communicates it to your physical senses. To be more precise, it's a catalyst for love. Think of it like an enzyme in your digestive system. The enzyme is necessary for the function of digestion, but it's not the food itself. The chemical and biological capabilities in your body and mind are your tools for the sensation of love and your catalyst for love, but they're not love itself."

"So, when I'm away and I miss my wife," said Dr. Kamron, "what causes that? Is it love or the catalyst?"

"Well, it's both," answered Alex. "When you miss your wife, it means the biochemical connection is reduced and thus it's not triggering the release of the right hormones when she's around. This tells you that you miss her. It simply delivers the message of love. Although you love with your soul, it has to trigger in your mind a functional form so that you can sense it as a physical being. I strongly believe that whoever designed this existence by its ways of programming, the virtue of evolution, and the exquisitely delicate work of nature both knew and valued love. That's why She wanted us to have it."

They were both quiet for a moment.

Dr. Kamron remarked, "My mind keeps going back to your comment that loneliness is the lowest form of human experience. Is it really, Alex?"

"Yes, with loneliness, your sense of identity diminishes because of the lack of projections by others as to who you are. And we all need some sense of identity to have purpose and satisfaction in this life."

"How do you mean?" asked Dr. Kamron.

"It's simple," said Alex. "When you're born with no sense of identity, it's the projection of others on us that shape our minds, our character—heck, our reality. We constantly need those projections of who and what we are to have a sense of reality in this plane of existence. Otherwise, our minds start to go haywire. Why do you think depression sets in with heavily antisocial people? They lose their sense of reality, whatever that may be, because their need for continuous projection from others to feel this illusion of reality is not met adequately in solitude.

"If you stop and think for a moment as to who you are, it's a lot less about how you perceive yourself on your own than how you perceive yourself based on what others around you recognize you as. For example, I'm a son because someone else projects me as their son. You feel good when someone projects you as a doctor or a teacher or any title you may have because now you're recognized as such by someone other than yourself. When you think of yourself, your perception somehow feels less real unless you acknowledge and respond to those perceptions based on the projections of others. That's why people love compliments. Even the most vain, self-deluded individual will feel hollow inside if they do not receive some projections of approval."

"Are you saying that we're born with no characteristics of our own at all?" Dr. Kamron asked.

"We're born with the inherent characteristics of our parents and their parents and so on," said Alex. "But, those inherent characteristics served not only as propensities but were massaged by the projection of others, giving them a whole new shape. In fact, your very character shifts based on others' projections. We've all seen a kind, cool-headed person getting angered by a particular someone and claiming that that someone brings out the rage in them. So, the projections from others not only give you identity but can also shift your being."

"How can you avoid the negative ones?" asked Dr. Kamron.

Alex answered, "It takes a masterful human being to completely maneuver from the imposition of those character-shifting projections, since there are always those who try to gun you at full throttle and then throw you into reverse to damage your gearbox."

Alex crossed his arms across his chest. "Nevertheless, the key is to never lose sight of the importance of self-love."

17

MARRIAGE

D r. Kamron straightened up in his chair. "Since we're on the subject of love, I cannot help but think about marriage. But first, do you mind if I talk to my wife again?"

Alex got up from his chair. "Not at all. Here, I'll let you be."

Once he was alone, Dr. Kamron summoned Elizabeth through the communication device. "How is everything down there? Do you feel safe?" he asked.

"Everything feels normal here," said Elizabeth. "This is a remarkable structure. Now tell me, what's he like? His wife is a doll."

"He's regal, yet appeals to you in a folksy way," said her husband. "Speaks eloquently; both substantive and riveting."

"Wow, I must say," exclaimed Elizabeth. "I've never heard you refer to someone like that. He must really be something. I can't wait to meet him."

Minutes later, Alex stepped back into the gazebo and approached Dr. Kamron, who had now finished his conversation with Elizabeth. "How is your wife doing?" he asked.

Dr. Kamron replied, "She seems to be enjoying herself, thanks to your wife. So, we were going to talk about marriage?"

"Yes, I think that's just one avenue for love. Perhaps we associate the two immediately since marriage is a great opportunity to cultivate and reciprocate love. It's the greatest union on Earth."

Dr. Kamron raised his eyebrows. "Frankly, I'm surprised. I thought you'd be a little more cynical about marriage."

"Why would you think that? Look back at the most memorable moments of your life. Were you alone? Even though the socioeconomic factors of human society are rapidly changing and there isn't the need for marriage as much now as there used to be, the void of love will continue to motivate people to enter that union."

"But there's a growing resistance to marriage, don't you think?" asked Dr. Kamron.

"Yes," said Alex, "but that's because we're going through a transition in human social behavior in that respect. Most couples are able to experience stable, long-term love without entering the actual union of marriage."

Dr. Kamron nodded. "Yes, it makes me wonder why we even do it anymore?"

"It's because one of the greatest stages of true love is to surrender. Remember Rumi's words 'to love is to surrender'? These couples want to reach that point. You see, in the past, that was intertwined with social and economical need, but now mostly it's only out of a necessity for deeper love."

Dr. Kamron chuckled. "My goodness, Alex. You make it sound really rosy."

Alex laughed out loud. "It is, my good man, it is! I'm not oblivious of the challenges that come with marriage, but a good marriage is at the opposite point in the spectrum of life from loneliness, which as I mentioned is the lowest point of human experience, so that alone is a good enough reason to give it its due value."

"Then tell me, what do you attribute the challenges of marriage to?" asked Dr. Kamron.

"First, you mustn't forget that some of the so-called challenges are produced by the need for friction in the relationship to whittle away boredom," said Alex. "It's not so dissimilar to the concept that we discussed earlier—that humanity wants war and peace, not just peace.

"I think that perhaps what you're asking about, however, are more fundamental challenges. I see two major elements: One is the flower of choice, and the second is cellular changes.

"First of all, as single individuals, we are—at least subconsciously—aware of our lack of completeness without our mate. It is the way of nature: 'Pair up or be extinct.' As much as we may deny this fact or delay relinquishing ourselves from the single life, we know deep inside that something vital is lacking in our lives. Temporary relationships can provide relief, but where they offer excitement, they lack in true satisfaction—satisfaction that comes from having a solid family, which provides foundation.

"That foundation is what constitutes a true support system for the human souls wandering around on the surface of this big ball of dirt. Often people enter marriage based on what's available at that given time and place, even when they know deep inside that who they desired is not in front of them. There's fundamentally nothing wrong with that.

"The problem comes from the futile attempt to change that person into something they're not. You could have a great marriage if you acknowledge that you've made a different choice—a choice that brings you love and support and places you far away from loneliness, that lowest point of human existence. But challenged marriages are often the result of choosing what you don't want and insisting on changing that person into what you wish you had.

"It's like going to a flower shop knowing that your favorite flowers are orange roses, but since the shop is out of them, you bring home blue irises instead. Now you're thinking about how much you want to change the irises into roses. The iris will never change its nature, no matter how much it would love to be your favorite flower. Even if you paint it orange, it's still an iris. If you could not wait until you found your orange roses, then you must love the blue irises, as they bring joy and beauty to your life. Who knows, maybe tomorrow your favorite flower could become blue irises."

"But," Dr. Kamron said, "the heart knows what the heart wants and that longing for the orange rose may never change."

"Yes," agreed Alex, "but *you* may change, which brings me to my second point: The human body goes through extensive cellular changes. Most people aren't aware that within seven years, every cell in their bodies is replaced. In fact, every cell is replaced and renewed within a period of seven years consecutively for life. This is known as aging, and it includes the brain. Not one cell a person is born with is still there when they reach seven, and again at 14, then again at 21, and so on. Your cells are respectively replaced, and you become a brand-new person."

Dr. Kamron looked perplexed. "But the cells are replaced with the same DNA structure and personality you were born with, so it shouldn't matter how many times it gets replaced."

"Yeah, you would think that," said Alex. "But considering that you and your spouse are virtually different people today than you were when you met, you'd think twice about this DNA structure. Basically, all of these cellular changes can affect hormonal changes that in turn can affect desired choices. This doesn't guarantee that you're destined to not be compatible; it simply means that couples need to embrace the changes in their counterpart and adjust to each other as time goes by.

"The good news is that what helps this adjustment process is the human tendency to replicate the behavior of those they spend a lot of time with. By that I don't meant just the superficial matters—I'm referring to very deep body and mind functionalities. We've all heard about sympathy pain or that the females in a family or group have their menstrual cycles at exactly the same time. So, there is always the natural adjusting of bodies and minds that make couples more compatible as time goes by, as long as they don't forget what kind of flower they picked."

Dr. Kamron remarked, "I think if we look at the idea of marriage from a mathematical standpoint, it adds up. When you reach a point in a relationship when you surrender to love and enter the union of marriage, your happiness is multiplied by two and your sadness is divided in half. And that's a pretty good deal."

"True," said Alex, "and if couples want to keep holding on to this good deal, they must be aware about something vital when it comes to human interaction."

"What's that?" asked Dr. Kamron.

"When most people are faced with the two options of either embracing the comments they're hearing or finding any reason to object to them, their minds tend to select the objection. If you let that tendency become the norm in your marriage, it's not a good path, not to mention how unattractive it is to hear couples in constant disagreement. Embrace your counterpart's nonsense because they're the only one who has a good reason to embrace your nonsense."

"We really don't get to choose who we're going to love," said Dr. Kamron.

Alex replied, "On the contrary, we don't get to choose who would love us back."

"I'm kind of embarrassed to say this, but frankly, when you see most couples, doesn't it make you wonder what they saw in each other, and think that love is blind?" asked Dr. Kamron.

"No, my friend, it makes me think that love sees more."

—◦◦◦—

18

CHILDREN

Dr. Kamron looked brightly at Alex. "We might as well cover the subject of children since we're talking about marriage. Tell me, Alex, do you think that having a child validates your life?"

"Not *having* a child. Any monkey can reproduce to have offspring," answered Alex. "So no, not having a child, but *raising* a child is certainly one sure way to validate your noble rule on this planet."

Dr. Kamron continued, "We can't possibly in our time together here this evening discuss all of the challenges and insights for raising a child. So, what do you think we should focus on? I'd like to get your perspectives."

"Let's see …" Alex mused. "I can think of three things to share with you specifically on raising a child: (1) remembering the future; (2) knowing their brain; and (3) knowing that it's their life.

"First, remembering the future is simple. Remember your growing-up years, your needs, your yearnings, your frustrations, your joys of having that youthful power and then not knowing what to do with it, and making all those so-called mistakes that you'd gladly repeat if you had the chance to go back? Now, apply all those memories to the future of your children. This way, nothing is unexpected and nothing will catch you off-guard. We seem to forget our own childhood when it comes to judging our children.

"Second, knowing their brain. As parents we often wishfully—and in vain—think that our children are supposed to be whole-brain–functioning individuals. The reality is that having such a brain would be extremely rare. It's not even necessary. Individuals naturally tend to polarize in their hemispheric functioning. The left-brain dominants are good at math, logic, and science, while the right-brain dominants excel at art, philosophy, and more creative work.

"As a parent, based on your own brain-dominant functioning or lack thereof, you may impose on your children your own desire to advance in something. It's easy to make your left-brained child feel inadequate by forcing them to become a substandard artist. Or you can choose to nourish their natural ability to become great as a scientist.

"Or consider the reverse of that for your right-brained child. Remember to cultivate your child's God-given gift and not vicariously advance your own brain-type functioning through your child's, as it may not even be the right match as yours. Indeed, if your child's hemispheric brain function is ultra-left or ultra-right, you're imposing a profoundly painful task on your child even if it's out of love. After all, this world needs to balance itself on both of those capabilities in the masses.

"Third, knowing that it's their life. Of course, the protective parental instinct is nature's most precious one. As a parent, in order to bring peace and tranquility to your home and your heart, you must remember that after all that you do to pave the way for them, it's their life and they must get off-track to even see where that path was. As much as we wish to show them the way to diminish their growing pains, history demonstrates that human development requires self-experience to a large degree. The fact is, human beings move on pleasure and change direction on pain.

"Last but not least, I must touch on the single most disharmonizing element in the relationship between children and parents: the point that the child instinctively needs to be different.

"If we divide the life of a parent and child into three periods, as a parent you must be concerned about the second period only if you want the third period to be as good as the first one. In the first period in the early stage of childhood, children are totally dependent on their parents, and the endearing gestures they express create a symbiotic energy of love and understanding that produces no sense of resentment, no matter how physically and emotionally demanding the caregiving task may be for the parents. In essence, the child's natural, pleasant reaction to the presence of the parent illuminates the purest form of love—an unconditional love.

"The parent gives and the child smiles back or squeezes the parent's finger and that's all that's expected in return for the parent to feel appreciated for all they do or endure. On a physical level, we know that these endearing gestures from the child induce an abundant release of oxytocin, which is the same hormone that's released when a person is in love, providing more emotional energy."

Alex continued. "In the second period, when children reach their teens, they must, by nature's calling and force of hormonal changes, try to be as different from their parents as they possibly can. This is a normal phenomenon. Frankly, it's like a necessary mutation in the human race. As a parent, if you're smart enough to not overreact to this natural growth period, you'll prevent a lot of hardship for your child and minimize resentment.

"This'll make your third phase of the parent-child relationship that much more pleasant when they reach their twenties and thirties and beyond. The fact is, later in life, in many ways we will become our parents, so sit back and see them becoming the new you—the new and improved version of you—just as you tried to be the new improved version of your parents. But don't get in the way of the natural progression of life, which demands that we be different when we reach our teens."

"Very well put," said Dr. Kamron. "I wish I'd taken notes on this."

"Ah, you're kind," said Alex. "Let's see, I think you'd like these poems by Mr. Kahlil Gibran on the subject. Layla …"

Your children are not your children.

They are the sons and daughters of Life's longing for itself.

They come through you but not from you,

And though they are with you yet they belong not to you.

You may give them your love but not your thoughts,

For they have their own thoughts.

You may house their bodies but not their souls,

For their souls dwell in the house of tomorrow, which you cannot visit, not even in your dreams.

You may strive to be like them, but seek not to make them like you. For life goes not backward nor tarries with yesterday.

19

Health: Wellness Within

"I imagine our discussion wouldn't be complete if I didn't ask for your input on health," said Dr. Kamron. "You know, some insight to pass on to my daughter for a good, healthy life."

"Do you realize that you're asking this question to a veterinarian?" asked Alex.

Dr. Kamron laughed. "I realize that I'm asking this of an exceptionally insightful man. I don't care what your academic background is."

Alex, with a smile, said, "Well, I'll share with you the seven pillars for a healthy foundation in life."

Pillar 1: Emotional Balance

"Physical health is maintained when there is emotional balance. Diseases primarily come from one source. It's called dis-ease. The human body is an incredible machine fully equipped with multiple layers of defenses, repair functions, and rejuvenation—all at the cellular level. In fact, it is overbuilt for a long and healthy life, both on the cellular level and with organs. Therefore, if a virus or bacteria manages to penetrate the human body and create an ailment, it's for one reason—the defense mechanism was compromised by dis-ease. That in itself is not detrimental if you remove the dis-ease factor and allow the body to keep the unwelcome element at bay and properly engage in repair functions. By preventing the dis-ease state, the body will have a full home-field advantage, and the intruding element will not progress.

"You see, we've all seen two people with the same disease, one struggling with its effects for a long time while the other keeps on enjoying life and is not even fazed. Doctors may describe the latter patient as being exposed but showing no symptoms. That simply means the mind is at ease and the body's great protective measures are not allowing any symptoms to manifest, and thus the person can live a healthy life in spite of exposure to unwanted elements. The dis-ease comes from an imbalanced state of emotion—such as stress, depression, guilt, etc."

Dr. Kamron considered this. "When you were just comparing the two people with the same condition in which one is symptomatic and one is not, could it be that one has a body that simply has more power to effectively deal with the condition?"

Alex chuckled. "Good God, no Doctor, absolutely not. Would you like to know how powerful every human body is, regardless of how tiny or fragile it may appear? First, correct me if I'm wrong, but Einstein's E $= MC^2$ equation state that mass and energy have an equivalence—they're two forms of the same thing. Energy is liberated matter and matter is energy waiting to happen. Since C^2 (the speed of light times itself) is a truly enormous number, it means there's an enormous amount of energy bound up in every material thing."

"That's correct," Dr. Kamron concurred.

"So," continued Alex, "since our bodies are material things, even the most puny, wiry human body has more than 7×10^{18} joules of potential energy. Maybe you can better tell me how much energy that is?"

"I know what you're talking about," said Dr. Kamron. "This 7×10^{18} joules of potential energy would be enough to explode with the force of 30 very large hydrogen bombs."

"And we have that kind of energy trapped within our bodies, correct?" Alex asked.

"Scientifically speaking, that is correct."

"So, scientifically speaking, I submit to you that that kind of energy in our bodies is connected to a dimmer switch called our 'state of mind.'"

"You mean that the energy within our biology is operated by our minds?" asked Dr. Kamron.

Alex nodded eagerly. "Not just operated but also regulated by our minds. Our biology on a cellular level is operated by electricity. In fact, all biochemical activities that make up our life support system run on electrical energy produced with our food and oxygen intake. Would you like to know how much electricity? A mere 0.1 volts that travel in distances measured in nanometers. However, scale that up and it translates to 20 million volts per meter—about the same as the charge carried by the main body of a thunderstorm."

Dr. Kamron nodded affirmatively.

Alex continued. "So, you see, Doctor, there's no shortage of energy to heal. The trick is how to use the dimmer switch to brighten up this state of health. I truly believe that all physical ailments are manifestations of emotional imbalance."

Dr. Kamron raised his eyebrows. "All, Alex?"

Alex nodded. "The vast majority of them, at least. Your will of light (as Hindus put it), or the power of chi (as the Chinese describe it), or the central nervous system (as modern medicine would like to call it), are all the same thing: an energy field, the proper and harmonious function of which directly depends on the state of mind. Compromising this harmony through negative, emotional impacts such as stress causes illness. What we call physical illness is really a multidimensional disharmony or dis-ease.

"Of course, conventional medicine may not agree, because they're mostly in the business of disease management for revenue and not healing. They're experts in treating the symptoms, not the cause. I don't claim that the symptoms aren't real or that conventional medicine isn't significantly valuable in managing the progression of symptoms. In fact, with certain acute or urgent conditions, we all better be thankful for modern medicine. But sadly, at other times with conventional medicine, the patient may suffer more from the cure than they would from the disease itself."

Alex continued, "Isn't it ironic that the Hippocratic oath that all doctors take before starting a medical practice states, 'First, do no harm'? How far have we come since Hippocrates made that the first rule of medicine?"

"That's contrary to many of today's medical practices where doctors overprescribe medications instead of enhancing the body's natural immune system," said Alex. "Basically, if conventional doctors had real training in the connections between mind and body as well as the role of nutrition, we'd have better physicians and healthier societies. We live in an organic body that responds to the consumption of food for every function, and yet the professionals in the field of repairing this body are mostly ignoring this crucial point. Instead, most doctors have become drug pushers for pharmaceutical companies, and we all know how that gets managed."

Dr. Kamron nodded in agreement. "Well, Hippocrates couldn't have made it more clear when he wrote, 'Let food be your medicine and medicine be your food.'"

"I think most doctors are aware of the problems of conventional drugs, but they have no other training for helping their patients," Alex continued. "So, while in good faith they try to serve their patients, they end up serving the pharmaceutical companies."

"What about alternative medicine?" asked Dr. Kamron.

Alex replied, "Well, not all doctors are healers and not all healers are doctors. If alternative medicine is based on empirical studies that have passed the test of time—such as remedies in old cultures—then you can't go wrong. As you know, empirical studies are based on observations of the effects of remedies on patients. In countries where such remedies have been used for centuries, that's just what you have—a collective empirical assessment over hundreds of years of observation. What do you think most pharmaceutical companies claim they do before declaring the viability of a medicine? Empirical studies, except that they spend only a limited time on those studies and those are conducted with a biased eye toward a certain predetermined conclusion. So, shouldn't we take a chance on a natural remedy that's been around for centuries before resorting to ones being pushed by large business entities for profit? A natural remedy can be very powerful while still in harmony with our nature as organic beings. An ideal physician is one who integrates modern medicine with natural medicine."

"And Pillar 2?" Dr. Kamron asked Alex.

"First, I must point out," said Alex, "that something like 20 percent of what dictates your health comes from genetics while 80 percent is your lifestyle. Each person has to customize their lifestyle to prevent harm and minimize the impact of their genetic predisposition, which is their Achilles heel."

"But you have six more pillars to share, correct?" asked Dr. Kamron.

Alex replied, "Yes, but the problem is that they're so simple that people don't fully appreciate their profound impact. These are serious measures that should not be taken for granted because they *are* so simple."

Pillar 2: Water

"You can prevent a long list of medical issues by staying properly hydrated," said Alex. "Consume no fewer than seven glasses of water every day. Keep in mind that your only system of internal cleaning is through the consumption of water, which flushes out toxins. How else can you expect your body to do that? Most people don't understand how much water they lose every hour even without doing any physical activity. Press your thumb against a cold window. The foggy print that it leaves behind shows how much water is constantly leaving your body. That water has to be replenished for you to function properly."

Pillar 3: Movement

"You want to be alive and active?" continued Alex. "Then you must fellow Newton's first law of motion. A body in motion tends to stay in motion. Take your dog for a walk every day even if you don't have a dog. The fact is, the human body is designed to digest food and deliver nutrients based on the lifestyles of primitive men, who had to walk everywhere to get food, and once fed, had to walk again to get more. On a *daily* basis. We still have that same primitive body and digestive design. You must walk or stay physically active for 40 to 60 minutes every day to have optimum health. Period."

Pillar 4: Immunity

"And Pillar 4?" asked Dr. Kamron.

Alex continued, "Take care of your root."

"Our root?" asked Dr. Kamron.

"Yes, your root is your path to a healthy life. I cannot emphasize enough on the importance of Pillar 4. The root of your physical existence is your intestinal gut. In fact, 80 percent of our immunity lies in the intestinal digestive system. A healthy gut means a healthy life. I can point out the irrefutable facts about the benefits of removing sugar, gluten, wheat, dairy products, and nonorganic items (and these are not fashion statements), but anyone desiring a healthy life can also take a couple of hours of their life one day and fully educate themselves about what a *leaky gut* is and how to prevent or heal it completely. The quality of your life depends on this knowledge. A healthy life is ensured by having a body with no inflammatory conditions and that primarily comes from a healthy gut. With a healthy gut, you will have more energy, more life, more happiness, and make more intelligent decisions."

Dr. Kamron asked, "Happier and more intelligent?"

Alex replied, "Yes, this is really eye-opening. There are nine times more communication going from your gut to your brain than vice versa. The vagus nerve is the largest nerve in the human body. This nerve connects the brain to the gut. There are nine times more nerve fibers going from the gut to the brain than from the brain to the gut. If that's not enough to trust your gut feeling, then you should know that your gut is more active in neurotransmitter production than your brain. Take serotonin, for example, through which you experience fun—90 percent of it is produced in your gut. If you love yourself, love your gut, and attend to its needs by learning how to maintain its health."

20

PILLAR 5: THE RHYTHM OF OUR SOUL

"Going back to your earlier comment," said Dr. Kamron, "how do we really manage not to get close to the state of dis-ease, as you put it?"

Alex replied, "Well, that's Pillar 5. As you know, Dr. Kamron, everything in existence has a vibration. It is through the pulse of that vibration that all things sustain their molecular integrity.

"For living beings like us, our balance on a cellular level depends on the proper frequency of our individual vibration. Each person is different, but there is nevertheless a desirable frequency for each of us—the rhythm of our soul, if you will. Or you can call it a balanced central nervous system if you like conventional terms better. Like I said, it's all the same thing.

"If anything disrupts this rhythm, the body will manifest an ailment, depending on the severity of the disruption. It's that simple. Yet, it baffles me how some conventional doctors see this cause and effect in humans, completely bypass it, and focus only on the effect, not the cause."

Dr. Kamron nodded. "Like you said, they have no training for it."

"Right," said Alex. "But they have answers right in front of their noses, and yet they seem completely oblivious of the connections between mind and body. Some even deny it. How simple could it be to observe emotions directly affecting physical responses in the body? Our entire reproductive system depends on that. Is it not an emotional response that literally raises men to the occasion of intercourse? (No pun intended.) How much more direct can the evidence be of the connection of mind and body?"

Dr. Kamron asked, "So, where do you go for cures? As humans, we're susceptible to emotional impacts all the time."

"For one thing, you can go within to find the source of the original impact and come to terms with it," said Alex. "The body begins to respond immediately, as if a weight is lifted. You can literally hear people sighing with relief at the moment they release themselves from an old negative feeling.

"You see, it isn't that medical diagnoses are irrelevant, but there's often an underlying cause that produces the conditions. So, the best cures are often within us. But there is one remedy that can revive the patient and walk them to the cure. That remedy is the most powerful medicine of all. It's called Hope."

Dr. Kamron remarked, "I recall reading a funny little short story of medicine that was laid out this way:"

A Short History of Medicine
Doctor, I have an earache. Here, eat this root!
2000 BCE: That root is heathen, say this prayer.
1850 AD: That prayer is superstition, drink this potion.
1940 AD: That potion is snake oil, swallow this pill.
1985 AD: That pill is ineffective, take this antibiotic.
2000 AD: That antibiotic is artificial. Here, eat this root!

Alex laughed. "Funny, but true! It's also important to be kind to your body's mind."

"You mean the brain?" said Dr. Kamron.

"No," said Alex. "I mean that every organ of your body is capable of feeling, thinking, and having emotions. That's why you must be affectionate toward your body and not abusive to maintain a good state of health. Our bodies are not made of various separate components as conventional medicine would have us believe. Our organs, extremities, and tissues are living, feeling entities that interact with one another to keep us in equilibrium and health. And they require affection just like your mind does. During an ailment, your kind, nurturing attendance to that particular organ creates an emotional enhancement that brings about healing. Never treat your body as separate parts."

Dr. Kamron said, "And you were saying that hope is the best remedy.'"

"Yes, indeed," said Alex, "the element of hope is the most therapeutic remedy of all. With hope, healing begins. And the effect of hope is that the mind balances itself as irregular vibrations start to come down and reregulate themselves, and the flow of chi flourishes once again through-out the body. Contrary to hope, the greatest poison to the human body and soul is fear. And the greatest antidote to fear is, once again, hope. So as you see, Doctor, hope is the strongest remedy of all.

"I once had a very intelligent physician friend who used to say that every time he wrote prescriptions, he gave patients only enough hope and a time frame to go heal themselves. They might as well have been dummy pills, he said."

"While one cannot dismiss the value of good medicine in any form, be it conventional or natural," declared Dr. Kamron, "a physician who has little to no regard for the connection of mind and body is less than competent in their field. To deny this connection is to deny scientifically measurable facts. We see this all the time when a placebo group heals just as well if not faster or better than the group given the actual medi-cation. What stronger evidence can there be?

"This reminds me of a paper published in the *Journal of the American Medical Association* about the mind-body phenomenon. Patients given higher-priced placebos reported more pain relief than those given a discounted one. The investigators had 82 men and women rate the pain caused by electric shocks applied to their wrists before and after they took a pill. Half of the participants had read that the pill, which was described as a newly approved prescription pain reliever, was regularly priced at two dollars and 50 cents per dose. The other half read that it had been discounted to 10 cents. In fact, both were dummy pills. The pills had a strong placebo effect in both groups. But 85 percent of those using the so-called 'expensive' pills reported significant pain relief com-pared with those who took the cheaper pills."

"Go figure," said Alex.

"So, we're on the same page as far as the connection between mind, body, and health," said Dr. Kamron.

"I believe we are," said Alex, pleased. "To take this one step further though, I believe that once people fall ill from mind-body imbalances, they establish an emotional connection with that ailment. It would be very therapeutic if one could sever that relationship in a healthy manner."

"How do you mean?" asked Dr. Kamron.

"Well, how often do you observe that when a person has a chronic problem, as soon as another issue arises, their new emotional connection with the second problem cuts the connection with the first one? Then the person has no more symptoms or complaints about the first one. Wouldn't it be great if this severance could occur without the help of an alternate problem?"

"So, are you saying that if one is emotionally connected to an ailment, they can actually keep it going?" asked Dr. Kamron.

"Precisely. By feeding and sustaining these emotional connections, they continue to keep their ailments in existence."

Dr. Kamron asked, "So, don't nurture your condition, then?"

"It would be therapeutic to nurture yourself, but not the condition," Alex replied. "In fact, the more you disassociate yourself with it, the sooner it'll dissipate."

"Huh? So, you're saying that by ignoring the problem, it will go away?"

"Look," said Alex, "it's not a blanket remedy, but if you don't feed energy into it, it may become nonsymptomatic or completely fade away. And especially, never give fear energy, because courage heals."

"So, no emotional connection with an ailment means no ailment."

Alex nodded. "At the very least, it'll bounce off of you faster. If you don't think you have to get sick to get well, you're likely to stay well."

—◦◦⟩⟨◦◦—

21

PILLAR 6: ENERGY MANAGEMENT

"Are we at Pillar 6, then?" asked Dr. Kamron.

Alex replied, "Yes, be a human being and not so much of a human doing. The fact is that we've become great at time management but not energy management. We push and push until all of our energy is consumed by endless tasks, chores, and projects with little to no regard for the body's need to maintain some energy to sustain itself. Not to mention the need for reserve energy for unforeseen events. Essentially, we've become human 'doings' rather than human 'beings.'"

"So, what do you recommend?" asked Dr. Kamron. "Society is not going to slow down anytime soon."

Alex replied, "Oh, society may not, but the individuals who are suffering from the effects of stress will. Remember, human beings move on pleasure and change direction on pain. So, they'll slow down out of necessity. But the smart ones slow down before they're forced to by pain. They do it by properly allocating their energy throughout the day and giving their bodies necessary respite. Just as our bodies are not designed to stay idle, they're not designed to go without sufficient breaks. In most countries, the need for an afternoon rest or nap, like a siesta, is considered essential, but unfortunately in other countries, we push our bodies nonstop throughout the day.

"Look, most people don't realize the significance of breaks. Perhaps if they looked in their hearts, they'd find the answer. It's not common knowledge, but your heart actually takes breaks between beats. This break period is called diastole. It's a means by which the heart can rest between contractions."

"I did not know that!" Dr. Kamron exclaimed. "But nothing sucks energy out of you like negative emotional impacts, don't you think?"

"Yes, absolutely they suck more energy out of the body than a marathon," said Alex. "Here's one way to conserve energy: If you remove elements that are negatively emotionally impacting you, your body will have a much better chance and ample energy to deal with many burdensome tasks. Many, many years ago I had a psychology professor who demonstrated in the classroom the relationship between our physical power and our state of mind. She used a kinesiology (muscle testing) technique to show how a simple suggestion of thought to your mind affects your level of muscle power.

"She was an older lady, and she called on this big, athletic football-player fellow in our class to stand next to her. She asked him to raise his arm and hold it while he closed his eyes and focused on thinking about one of the happiest moments of his life. She then told him that he should resist her attempt to lower his arm with her hand. The fellow did exactly that and the professor tried with a full grip and great force, but she could barely move his arm an inch or two. She then stopped the experiment. A few moments later, she asked him to repeat the same experiment, but this time to focus on something unpleasant in his life. Using only her two fingers, she was able to completely lower his arm down to his side."

Alex continued, "It's all about rhythm, the rhythm of your being—the vibration of your soul, if you want to call it that. Any musician can tell you of the connection between carrying the right tune (which depends on the right rhythm) and the player's nervous system. You can do a simple experiment to see this for yourself, and you don't even have to be a musician to feel this. On a table, tap the rhythm of your favorite tune. As you do this, think of a terrible thought and see how the beat is suddenly interrupted—or you may even go completely off the beat. It's about the rhythm of our souls, the vibration of life, and our harmony with it."

Dr. Kamron asked, "So what is the solution?"

Alex replied, "When you are confronted by stress or other negativities, it is simple, if you choose to implement it. Reduce your reaction to everyday events. It's like anything else—you can pick up the habit. We are, after all, creatures of habit. Practice not internalizing and responding with too much reaction in your mind, and soon your brain learns to comply and stress will be a thing of the past, thanks to your new attitude. I once read something from Charles Swindoll where he said this. Layla…"

> … I am convinced that life is ten percent what happens to me and ninety percent is how I react to it. The longer I live, the more I realize the impact of attitude on life. Attitude, to me, is more important than facts … education … money … the remarkable thing is we have a choice every day regarding the attitude we will embrace for that day. We cannot change our past … we cannot change the fact that people will act in a certain way. We cannot change the inevitable. The only thing we can do is play on the one string we have, and that is our attitude.

Dr. Kamron said, "This mirrors something I once read that said, 'Your living is determined not so much by what happens to you but by the way your mind looks at what happens.'"

"Exactly," said Alex, "and consider this: When you think of a problem, the thought itself is the problem."

"But Alex, what about the times when someone directly insults your integrity and self-respect? How do you not react to that?"

"It does not matter," said Alex. "As Buddha said, if a person offers to give you a gift and you do not accept it, who is stuck with that gift? It's the same with an insult."

"But we're indeed creatures of habit," pressed Dr. Kamron. "These behavioral patterns that we subscribe or respond to become second nature to us. It's much easier said than done to redirect us, don't you think?"

"No, not true," said Alex. "There is conclusive scientific research that our brains can reshape themselves (that is to say, through a change in the direction of neurons) based upon the data they receive from a person's thoughts. So again, nurture your mind with great thoughts and enjoy its fruits. In fact, when neurotransmitters that effectuate your thought patterns are repeatedly directed by your thoughts to travel in a different pathway in your brain, the old pathway will gradually become blocked and those previous thoughts will cease to come about. So, as correct as you are about us being creatures of habit, we're not destined to be slaves by them. We can use the same process that created the habit to our advantage. For one thing, we can replace the negativity that disrupts the rhythm of our soul so that our body is at peace and more importantly, in a good state of health."

"I see," said Dr. Kamron.

"Some simple rearrangements in mental habits can go a long way," continued Alex. "For example, we all know how destructive fear, guilt, and anger are. We can practice replacing them. So, tell you daughter that we must replace fear with faith and hope.

"And replace guilt with a simple understanding that what you did was based on your best mental ability at that time. Of course, we would all do many things differently in hindsight, but don't judge yourself so harshly, since other factors besides you were at work to induce whatever happened.

"You must also replace anger with forgiveness, because if you really hate someone too much, you may subconsciously bring yourself to act in the same manner that they did. That's so that you fully understand the basis for your hate and why they did what they did. But do you really want to become the person you're angry with?

"So, let it go. Don't seek revenge. Be at peace and trust the wisdom in this Chinese proverb: 'If you sit by the river peacefully, you will notice the bodies of your enemies floating away.'"

Dr. Kamron smiled. "How true."

Alex continued, "Again, one sure way to reduce your harmful reaction is to have faith. Try not to look for a reason to have faith, for, as Voltaire says, 'faith consists in believing when it is beyond the power of reason to believe.'

"But, if you simply must have a reason, here's one to remember: Faith brings hope and hope heals, moving you to beautiful places. Faith is powerful stuff. Do you really want only narrow-minded religious people to reap the fruits of faith because you think you're too smart to have faith based on faith, even for your own good?

"And, to truly have a healthy life, you must find a way to connect to a source of spirituality that induces hope, no matter what the basis for that spirituality is—whether it's a profound philosophy or a simple connection to a juniper tree. Just find a means to connect to the wisdom of this universe that is both within you and you within it. It's that cool. And when you're cool, you're at peace, healthy and capable of enjoying this ride. This ride of life isn't short. Most just start living it too late.

"Always remember: When you're stressed, everything is going to be okay at the end. If it's not okay, it's not the end."

22

Pillar 7: Have Fun

"And lastly?" asked Dr. Kamron.

Alex replied, "Pillar 7 is the best of all. Fun heals, fun rejuvenates, fun makes life flourish. Having fun cultivates love and life is healthy with love."

23

TRANSMIGRATION OF SOULS

They both heard a noise from one of the overhead devices as a call came in for Alex. After answering it, he told Dr. Kamron, "I need to ask you to excuse me for a little while, as I must attend to something on the other side of the dome. When I come back, we can continue our conversation."

"Of course," said Dr. Kamron. "Say, do you have a research report or something for me to skim through while you're gone? I'm sure you've gathered some interesting research material on life on this ranch in the sky of yours."

"Interesting?" chuckled Alex. "I'm not sure what I would have as far as interesting reading. Research materials are electronically archived. I mostly keep my personal reading material on these shelves here. Please help yourself to whatever catches your eye."

Dr. Kamron quickly scanned the shelves nearest him. Then he spotted something that looked like an old journal. The title read, *Admission to Earth*.

"What is this?" he asked.

Alex's eyes widened. "Boy, I haven't shown these pages to anyone in a long time. If you'd like, take a look. I wrote them many, many years ago to make a point and impress a young lady who I knew instantly was the love of my life. She—my wife, that is—looked at them from time to time for amusement and told me that if it weren't for these pages, she wouldn't have taken another look at me back then. She even turned it into a play. I still keep them around for sentimental value."

Dr. Kamron smiled. "Then I suppose for her, it wasn't love at first sight?"

Alex grinned. "No, it wasn't. But I'm not surprised. The nature of love may be the same in a man and a woman, but the inducement of love is different in each gender. You see, as the saying goes, 'men love the women they are attracted to, but women are attracted to the men they love.' I'll be back."

As Alex walked away, Dr. Kamron started to read. The pages were nicely typed, but one could tell that they were written years ago with a genuine typewriter and not a printer.

ADMISSION TO EARTH

A young soul enters the Center for Universal Travel. It's a circular hall bustling with admission representatives from many planes of existence, including one from Earth. The reps each have their own space with a holographic image of their planet illuminated and turning in front of their booth. The young soul hovers by a few of these booths but could not help but notice that further in the distance, a mesmerizing blue sphere is revolving in front of one. Young Soul bypasses the rest and heads straight for the Earth booth.

"Very interesting vibration and colors," said Young Soul, examining the blue sphere. "I don't think I've seen such a combination of colors before."

The representative for Earth squinted at Young Soul and muttered, "Looking at your puny vibration and pale aura, I'd be surprised if you have."

"Thank you," said Young Soul.

"Thank you?" exclaimed Earth Rep. "I love one thing about you young souls—you can't tell if you're being insulted or complimented."

Young Soul was unintimidated. "I'd like to apply for an Earth trip, please."

Nonchalantly, Earth Rep replied, "I'd like to help you, kid, but you don't know what you're applying for. I bet this is your first trip anywhere."

"Well, I did go on an observational tour of some celestial bodies once."

"A tour, huh?" sneered Earth Rep. "I mean, have you actually experienced organic life on any plane of existence?"

"No," shrugged Young Soul, "but how hard could it be? I have to start someplace."

"It's not about how hard. The hard parts can make it even more fun. But Earth is tricky, perhaps one of the trickiest planes of existence of all."

"But I'm brave," offered Young Soul.

Earth Rep sighed. "Yes, yes. I know brave and young go hand in hand, like stupid and know-it-all. Listen, kid, why don't you start with planet Miracles. It's much more predictable, where things miraculously unfold to accommodate newcomers. Or better yet, try Harmonia where all intentions are in harmony with one another."

"No, I want to go to Earth," Young Soul insisted. "Perhaps you can give me some tips that would help me along the way."

"Tips?" retorted Earth Rep. "Look, if you insist that I let you in, you're going to have to sign this disclaimer and a hold-harmless agreement. Maybe then I'll give you a tip. I may not be able to stop you from going, but I'm going to make damn sure that my reputation is not on the line for letting another youngy go to Earth. Things are crazy enough there with your kind running around, constantly turning the vibration up so high that the frequent visitors are complaining of wrongdoing here on our part, letting everyone in. Last I heard, a village idiot became the king."

"Okay, so if I agree to sign this thing, can I go?" asked Young Soul.

Earth Rep sighed. "Not if I could have stopped you. But here, sign."

"What about the tip?"

"Once you sign, I'll give one tip," said Earth Rep.

"Just one?"

"The one tip I'll give you is all you need to have the greatest experience on Earth and prevent you from hurting others. It takes souls much, much older than you a great deal of time and experience to learn this one tip."

"And you'd do that for me?" asked Young Soul.

"No, I do that for me," said Earth Rep. "I can't have this on my conscience—that I couldn't talk another youngy like you out of going. Maybe the tip will help offset your effect on Earth."

"I can't wait—this must be some tip."

Earth Rep reluctantly turned the agreement to the Young Soul. "First read carefully and sign."

Admission to Earth
Release of Liability and Hold-Harmless Agreement

This agreement is made on this moment in the continuum (when both parties have awareness of each other) between Earth Admission Counsel, hereafter referred to as ("EAC") and Young Soul, hereafter referred to as ("the Traveler").

Recitals

WHEREAS:	EAC is in a position to provide assistance to the Traveler to transmigrate in time/space and become admitted to one lifetime on planet Earth.
WHEREAS:	The Traveler has presented self as one qualified to enter such a plane of existence.
WHEREAS:	The Traveler now desires to sign this release and hold-harmless agreement to accept all liabilities associated with undertaking such a trip to Earth.
NOW THEREFORE:	In consideration of the covenant, provision, and promises made herein, the parties agree as follows:

The undersigned traveler, being of lawful soul age to travel away from singularity, hereby acknowledges and accepts that in consideration for being admitted to Earth, the traveler hereby waives all rights and claims (known or unknown) against EAC. This waiver includes, but is not limited to, any and all damages caused by the process of transformation to a human being, or by other beings on Earth (be it direct and intentional or consequential of others' actions thereof), be it from a simple negligence to reckless disregard to others' safety, or any natural elements, or both. The Traveler further agrees to hold EAC (executives, administrators, successors, and especially representatives, etc.) harmless from any and all claims known or unknown by other parties due to the conduct of the Traveler while visiting Earth.

Further, the Traveler acknowledges that the decision to travel to Earth is solely based on the Traveler's own evaluations of the perils of travel thereto, and that this release is made without reliance upon any statements or representations of the EAC, and for eternity discharges any rights, demands, damages including, but not limited to, loss of energy, or lost opportunity for timely or untimely return to singularity.

The Traveler especially understands and acknowledges that there is no divine prevention with respect to the perils on Earth, as the Traveler chooses to experience Earth with all of its natural development or lack thereof. There may be divine intervention depending on the Traveler's request. However, this divine intervention may be effectuated subject to the nature of the Traveler's request and must be submitted directly and may be granted only if the divine source approves as so. EAC does not give any warranty that such request will be approved and thus the Traveler undertakes this trip with clear understanding of this disclaimer.

Binding on Heirs
This agreement shall be binding on the Traveler's offspring, wherein the actions of the Traveler facilitate their travel to Earth.

Property
The monetary value of the Traveler's memory shall remain the property of the Traveler.

Governing Law
This agreement shall be governed by the universal laws of eternal justice and the State of California.

Arbitration of Disputes
Any dispute arising under this agreement shall be settled by arbitration in accordance with the universal board of arbitration,

and judgment on the award rendered by the arbitrator may be entered as commandment upon any jurisdiction. The arbitration shall be binding on all the parties herein and the arbitrator's decision shall be final.

Attorney Fees
If arbitration is commenced between the parties hereto, the party prevailing in the said action shall be entitled to, in addition to any other relief/award, a reasonable sum for their attorney fees.

Remedy
In the event the Traveler becomes discontent with the experience of life on Earth, the Traveler's sole remedy is to revert back to the state of nonorganic existence and refrain from attempting to change the way of the world on Earth. In other words, we like it just the way it is; if you don't, then eject.

Insurance
EAC does not provide insurance for this trip, as we have exhaustively searched the universe for one insurer who does not act in bad faith, to no avail.

Entire Agreement
This agreement constitutes the entire agreement between EAC and the Traveler concerning all rights and obligations. If you cannot understand the terms set forth here, that's because a lawyer wrote them. You are advised to obtain your own lawyer for translation. Any agreement or representations not expressly hereby set forth shall have no effect, except for an act of divine intervention.

If the terms of this agreement appear arbitrary and capricious, that is because they reflect the nature of life on Earth and this should tell you something about what you are getting into. Accordingly, you are forewarned and cannot vitiate the limitations set forth in this agreement, regardless of what transpires on your trip.

24

THE TIP

Young Soul eagerly signed the agreement. "Okay, I signed. Now, what about my tip?"

"I know it's a stretch for you," said Earth Rep, "but try to understand this first: For the trip of life on Earth to be exciting for the participants, it was designed so that human's reach would always exceed his grasp. And for a human to be motivated in this endless pursuit, his consciousness was supplemented with something called EGO. Ironically, however, that's how everything gets screwed up over there.

"Ego manifests itself in so many forms that it's countless—from simple vanity that shows up other humans to self-righteous ideas that destroy entire nations. It comes with an impulsive drive to judge—judgment with criticism, of course. You don't know this, but criticism is often a sign of envy, and envy is the ugly offspring of ego."

Young Soul looked disturbed. "Sounds very unpleasant. I'm sure I wouldn't participate in that. Besides, it's not in my nature to take energy from others and harm them."

Earth Rep looked exasperated. "You're not getting this. Your nature will have to adapt to the tools of survival there. The very first thing you'll need to do is to start getting energy from others just to survive. Soon you'll realize that you'll have to destroy some form of life just for nourishment to even exist. That's the name of the game there. But what concerns me is that if you don't keep the ego element under control, you'll make life unpleasant for others. Too unpleasant of a stage on Earth for too long means passing the safe level of stability, and it always results in misery. And believe me, you yourself will suffer the most from your overactive ego."

"Give me an example of a common ego problem," said Young Soul.

"Good grief," said Earth Rep. "The ego problem is so common that it's the rule, not the exception. The whole system is based on that. In your mind, you'll keep wanting to be better so you can keep feeding your ego. You'll always want to have more to feed it. And you'll want to be constantly acknowledged so you can feed it. It's an endless want for betterment."

"Better than what?" asked Young Soul, innocently.

"Listen, once you put on the Earth's organic spacesuit ..."

"I can't wait—I've heard it's remarkable!"

"Yeah, yeah. We're still working on it," said Earth Rep, cynically. "The thing is, once you connect to the mind in the suit, you forget a few things that you know now. In your case, very few things. But nonetheless, one thing you know now is that you can never become better than anyone else, only a better version of yourself, right?"

"But of course."

"Well, you'll soon forget that on Earth too, because that's another side effect of ego. In fact, the younger the soul, the bigger the side effect."

"Please give me a real example, then," said Young Soul.

Earth Rep thought for a moment. "Okay, moron. Here's one: On Earth, nothing feeds the ego more than approval from others, even fake ones. And nothing makes you feel more approved than believing that you're right. It doesn't matter about what."

"Right? Approval?" asked Young Soul, confused. "Isn't this just a short trip for fun? Why all this fuss?"

Earth Rep softened. "Hey, maybe you're not as stupid as you look. But listen, kid, I know that and you know that, but once you're there, the egotistic forces of others who try to prove that they're better than you will send you on a relentless pursuit of self-importance. It'll take over you."

"But what if I stay away from everyone?" said Young Soul.

Earth Rep looked incredulous. "Are you kidding? The greatest thing about this trip is interacting with other humans. That's most of the fun. As soon as you arrive and settle into your body and environment, you'll want to play. And believe me, playing with yourself is not as fun. Well, it can be ... it depends on the fantasy. But never mind that. What I'm trying to say is that you're going to want to have a lot of Earthly things, but ultimately, you'll realize that it's not *what* you have in life that makes you happy, it's *who* you have."

"I can have other beings?" asked Young Soul.

"Yes," said Earth Rep. "In fact, you're going to spend the majority of your energy and time on Earth searching for one or a few of those other beings. When you have the other beings, be it by work of nature or by selection, you'll have to remember the tip I gave you now. This one element of ego will make you lose them."

"But how can that be?" asked Young Soul. "If having these beings in my life is so important to my happiness, how can I hurt them?"

Earth Rep said in a low voice, "This is how it works. As an example, when you're lonely, no matter how well everything else is going on this trip, you feel discontent. You wish and pray for another being to share the trip with. Somehow it feels like you've lost something you never had."

"What?"

"Okay, just stay with me and trust me on this," said Earth Rep. "Think of it this way: You simply feel that your trip lacks the right flavor. It just tastes better with that someone present."

"Taste?" asked Young Soul.

Earth Rep was getting upset. "Hush. Look, you're not as happy as you want to be without that other being, okay?"

"Okay."

Earth Rep continued, "You say to yourself, 'if I find that being, I'd do anything for that being to be happy.' Then your wish comes true and you cross paths with the right one. Imagine the billions of beings running around and your wish brings you just the right match to give you that feeling you were so desperately lacking."

Young Soul was excited. "That sounds fantastic!"

"Well the thing is, from the moment you find that being, it seems that you now have a significant loss of memory of the time prior to having that being," said Earth Rep. "So now your ego becomes once again your prime concern. You now expect this new being to take the back seat to your ego."

"Back seat?" asked Young Soul.

"Damn it, I mean you give your ego priority over this other soul."

"But I wouldn't do that."

"Why?"

Young Soul looked straight into Earth Rep's core. "Because you told me not to."

The Earth Rep gazed at the Young Soul for a moment.

"What is it?" asked Young Soul.

"You brought me to something like tears with what you said," answered Earth Rep.

"Tears?"

"Oh, just go have a nice journey!" Earth Rep muttered.

As the Young Soul began to hover away, the Earth Rep hollered, "Hey, come back! Here's a bonus tip."

"A bonus?" asked Young Soul.

"Yeah, I'm in a generous mood on this particular point in the continuum. Listen, this would come in really handy, no matter where you land on Earth. Watch out for the Holy Rollers."

Young Soul asked, "What's that?"

Earth Rep looked exasperated. "Ay ay ay ... How do I explain that to this kid now? Look, on Earth everyone is selling something. In order to sell, first they have to create a need in your mind for what they're selling, right? Now, some of these poor souls have figured out that, as spiritual beings, you already have a need for spirituality, so the hard part is done. Now all they have to do is to convince you that the only way to fulfill your spiritual need is through their religion. Believe me, kid, it's big business there."

"But how can that be?" asked Young Soul.

Earth Rep explained, "Well, when you first arrive there, they'll set you up for failure. They'll come up with religious rules that they know you can't possibly always obey. So every time you slip up, you have to go back to them to deal with your guilt. Basically, they're in the business of guilt management. Except that you wouldn't have the guilt if it weren't for what they sold you to begin with. So, the best practice is to stay away from them and ask the divinity before and after you arrive, 'God protect me from those who market your name.'"

Young Soul looked puzzled. "How do I then stay connected with spirituality in a complex plane of existence like Earth?"

"Through your heart," answered Earth Rep.

"Heart?" asked Young Soul.

"It's part of your anatomy, you know, when you put on your organic suit," said Earth Rep. "Your heart will be the seat of your spirit."

Young Soul was appreciative. "Thanks a lot. You're a great soul, but can I say something before I go?"

"What's that, kid?"

"For an old soul, you whine a lot."

Earth Rep shrugged. "It's a side effect of having been around humans for too long."

25

SOUL MATE

A little later, Earth Rep noticed the same young soul approaching his booth again. At its side was another being with a slightly more vibrant aura, and Earth Rep could tell it was just another young soul. However, a little further to its side was yet another being moving along with them, but this one was different. Its aura was peculiarly dark, and it appeared that this being was holding back its vibration level in an attempt to conceal its true nature. The Earth Rep, who had seen it all, had no difficulty seeing through this dark soul. Soon they all arrived at the booth for their admission to Earth.

"So, Young Soul, are you ready to go on your first trip to Earth?" said the rep.

"Almost," replied Young Soul. "Allow me to introduce you. This is Soul Mate. We had some in-depth communication and decided to go to Earth together."

"You have, have you?" said Earth Rep, sarcastically. "Look kid, you barely got yourself in. What do you think you're doing dragging some other dumb being with you?"

Upon hearing this comment, Soul Mate moved closer to Earth Rep. "Who are you calling dumb? Just because I'm young doesn't mean I'm unsmart! Do you have any idea how much research I've done on life on Earth?"

"Oh, I'm sorry," sneered Earth Rep sarcastically. "I wasn't aware of the extent of research you've done. Listen, you half-wit moron, research my bottom ray of light. Have you ever lived an organic life? That's the only question for you. I told your lover before that Earth is tricky. No amount of research can help you prepare for its ever-changing phenomena. Your best preparation is to try organic life somewhere less challenging and then move up to life on Earth. How many times do I have to explain this to you idiots?"

Soul Mate said, "Look, it's evident to me that you're exaggerating. Here, look at these images I retrieved from the memory of another soul who's been to Earth. What's it called? Oh yeah, snapshots. Look, isn't it beautiful there? Look at these moments they experienced. I paid a pretty high price for them. Because I don't really have any interesting memories of mine to trade for other souls' memories, I had to pay with giving a bit of my light force. But I think it was worth it, because now we have snapshot memories to see where we're going."

Young Soul turned and smiled at Soul Mate.

Earth Rep started to roar. "Snapshots, eh? For a smart soul, you're very good at being stupid. You have some snapshots of certain segments of someone's life on Earth and you think that little illustration shows how life is on that planet, huh? Let's see who this lucky soul was that you retrieved the images from."

Earth Rep looked closer, and with a quick, snap-like movement, projected multiple images of the other soul's experiences on Earth. Suddenly, both Young Soul and Soul Mate shrank back with fear, while the Dark Soul beside them remained unmoved, with no reaction.

Earth Rep smiled knowingly. "Gruesome, huh?"

"But the other soul looked so happy in those other snapshots," said Soul Mate.

Earth Rep sighed. "There are massive contrasts in life on Earth. You thought these images were bad? Remember, these images I showed you belong to a lucky soul. You want to see some real nasty ones from the unlucky souls? Here you go."

Earth Rep made another snap-like movement that brought up a series of images of atrocities on Earth that started to play in a holographic show right in front of Young Soul and Soul Mate. These images showed war-torn cities, diseased and hunger-stricken societies, and grieving, hopeless individuals mired in misery and sadness. Again, Dark Soul showed no reaction.

Soul Mate recoiled. "Stop it, I can't watch this anymore."

Earth Rep softened. "Okay, don't get carried away here."

The images changed. Earth Rep continued, "Here, calm down. Feast your vision on these images of beauty and slow down your vibrations. You're both shaking like a laser show. Look at the opposite side of life with your puny little intelligence and try to understand the concept of the paradoxical design of life on the blue planet."

"But, but … those poor souls," said Soul Mate.

"Zip it," said Earth Rep. "Now you're worried about other souls? A moment ago, you thought I was exaggerating and you said you'd done your research!"

"Perhaps we could go there and help," said Soul Mate helpfully.

Earth Rep glared at them. "Oh nooo. Damn you young souls, you can't handle watching these images, and now you want to go and change the world there? Do you have any idea how insignificant you are, not to mention how stupid? Let me just give you some idea. Check your research for the meaning of 'hiccup.' Your existence on Earth and in the universe is like a hiccup. That's all you are to the universe's grand design—just a hiccup. So, don't get any ideas about going there for the purpose of changing anything. Most of the ugliness happens there because the likes of you want to change things for the better. Can't you idiots just go do your little visit and get the hell out without putting your nose in the order of things?"

Soul Mate offered, "I understand, and we may lack some experience but…"

"It's not that you lack *some* experience," said Earth Rep, mockingly. "You HAVE NO EXPERIENCE!"

Young Soul turned to Soul Mate. "Dear, tell Earth Rep why we think we can handle it."

"Oh yes," said Soul Mate. "We think we can handle it because we found ourselves a guide."

"A what?" asked Earth Rep.

"A guide. We've brought our guide with us so you can get us all admitted together."

Dark Soul moved closer and sheepishly said, "Uhh, yeah, I'm their guide." In a very disingenuous manner, Dark Soul hovered a little closer and in a deep voice said, "It's a pleasure to meet you."

Earth Rep burst out, "Move back, you creep, before I slap-zap you back!"

Then Earth Rep turned back to Young Soul and Soul Mate. "Out of what hellhole did you find this prick?"

Young Soul said, "He said he's been to Earth many times and can guide us to make sure we'll have a safe trip, and he'll help us make Earth a better place."

"Yeah, he's been to Earth all right," snarled Earth Rep, "but the only place he can guide you is right back to where he's been deported. This is Dark Soul's way of trying to weasel his way back to Earth. And that ain't gonna happen on my shift. You young souls can do a lot better on your own stupid selves than with this character."

Soul Mate pleaded, "But what Dark Soul said was so—"

Earth Rep interrupted, "What Dark Soul said? What did Dark Soul say?"

"That with Dark Soul navigating us around the perils on Earth, we can save our energy that would otherwise be wasted on self-preservation and instead apply that for improvement on Earth for all visiting souls," said Soul Mate.

Earth Rep spun around and looked at Dark Soul. "If you can't dazzle them with brilliance, baffle them with bullshit, huh?"

Then Earth Rep turned back to Young Soul and Soul Mate and continued, "As for making Earth a better place, like I said, the worst things happen on Earth by those who claim exactly that. These wicked souls always use that angle of 'making Earth a better place.' That's how they get idiots like you to believe in some so-called righteous causes. Before you know it, this mixture of idealistic belief and an army of morons following a vicious character like this just screws everything up for older souls. And, of course, one of their favorite tricks is religion, which you morons are so easily drawn to."

"What if we promise to not follow any religion?" asked Young Soul.

"You see how dumb you are?" roared Earth Rep. "It doesn't have to be a religion. It'll be some ideology, perhaps something totally opposite of religion. As long as they make you think you're going to make the Earth a better place, you young souls always follow these dark characters. At one point in humanity, millions of people were untimely ejected from life for the idea of 'no religion and economic equality.' Economic equality—that sounds good, doesn't it? Ah, who am I asking, because what do you know? It was called 'communism.' They killed and tortured people in the name of a better future for humanity. Oh, and let's not forget how many have suffered for the cause of expanding freedom, fighting communism, or promoting democracy."

"Democracy?" Soul Mate asked.

Earth Rep was exasperated. "Ah, what's the use, you'll never get it! Just remember, don't follow anyone who wants to save the world or save your soul."

"Save our soul?" asked Young Soul.

"Yeah, if they can't convince you to follow them to save the world, they want you to follow them to save your soul."

"But how can we see that coming?" asked Young Soul.

"A lot of times they can be easily detected," said Earth Rep. "You can mostly tell one of these self-righteous phonies right off the bat."

"How? How?" asked Soul Mate.

Earth Rep chuckled. "They claim 'God said so.'"

Dark Soul interjected. "Hey, they have a right to choose their guide, and if they choose me, you have to let me go with them. That's the rule and you know it."

Earth Rep glowered at Dark Soul. "They're young and stupid, but I'm not gonna let you fool them."

Dark Soul suddenly changed his disposition, and his aura colors turned darker and more vibrant. He started rocking back and forth, and with a harsher tone in his voice told Earth Rep, "You're making this a little personal, aren't you? Look pal, remember what the old whore used to say—when you start to cum with the customers, it's time to quit."

"Very funny," Earth Rep said. "Watch this, clown. Hey, you two morons, you want to go to Earth together?"

"Yes, please!" shouted Young Soul and Soul Mate in unison.

"I'll get you going only if you lose this joker," said Earth Rep.

Young Soul said, "Okay, but you gave me a tip to help me. Can you give my soul mate one too? Looks like we could use all the help we can get for this journey."

Earth Rep sighed. "Fine, but Soul Mate must sign the same release."

"Release?" asked Soul Mate.

Young Soul whispered to Soul Mate, "Just do it. And Dark Soul, we're sorry, but we must listen to the Earth Rep."

"But Earth Rep can't do this," protested Dark Soul. "You have rights."

Earth Rep said, "He's right; I can't prevent you from going if you choose to take him, but I can delay it for a few centuries if you want to go with him. In fact, let's see—it looks like I got a bunch of applicants ahead of you. So, I'll let you know when I'm ready to review your applications."

"No, we don't want to wait. We agree!" Soul Mate pleaded.

Dark Soul appeared agitated. "Okay pal, I get it. You made your point, I see who's in charge but at least extend a modicum of dignity to talk this over with me so we can work something out."

Earth Rep interrupted. "First of all, dignity is for the dignified. Second, you're taking this a little personally, aren't you? Remember the old saying—when you roll with the pigs, you make the pigs happy and get yourself dirty. I'm done talking to you. Get lost!"

Young Soul interjected. "I'm sorry, Dark Soul, but we have to let you go, as you can see the Earth Rep won't let us go to Earth with you along anytime soon. I'm really sorry if we hurt your feelings."

"Hurt my feelings?" Dark Soul snapped. "You insignificant little fuck ray of light, you couldn't hurt me if your entire existence depended on it. When I'm on Earth, I devour the likes of you by the thousands, and that's just for breakfast."

"Breakfast?" asked Young Soul.

"Shut up," growled Dark Soul. "What this wise-ass Earth Rep is not telling you is that your trip to Earth is going to be so dull without the likes of me being there to create that right contrast you need everyday to feel alive. The essence of what makes your trip worthwhile is created by the deeds of the likes of me. Yeah, go on and call us the dark souls, but without us, how would you know what brightness, lightness, and kindness even are? If you didn't have us to create contrast, how could you even have a concept of all the goodness you claim you want to be a part of? Yes, we're the ones that bring flavor to your miserable little dull vanilla life."

"Vanilla?" asked Young Soul.

"Shut up," barked Earth Rep.

Dark Soul argued, "We're what makes your trips exciting, not those fucking natural wonders of watching the oceans hug the shores under the moonlight. All that crap will get boring real fast. It's what the likes of me bring that makes you feel alive. How would you even know what peace is if we didn't give you the concept of war? Or what love is if it weren't for us giving you the notion of hate? Or what safety feels like if we didn't scare your ass now and then? How would you know? *How would you know?* If it weren't for us, who'd create the battlefields in history so you can shake in your boots as you walk the razor edge of your existence?

"Yeah, you can all claim you hate war or conflict, but in the privacy of your soul, you'll whisper the truth that those were the moments you felt most alive. Those were the defining moments of your entire trip. You always blame us for ugly faces and for creating wars, but then it's only you who gets in line to sign up for a glory hunt. You always find some excuse for participating, from patriotism to your self-righteous belief systems, but the truth is that you just want to play soldier and kill a few. You little shits make that choice—we just provide the opportunity. You just want the rush, the kind of rush your miserable little lives can never deliver.

"Oh, and when you all reflect back on history, you speak of my kind with awe and admiration that we made the greatest leaders and conquerors, while no one will even remember who you little fucks were who followed. Only the likes of me who led you there will be remembered. Only we can deliver the climax of your existence there on Earth, but go ahead and follow this jackass's tips and you can pussyfoot through life every step of the way!"

"Pussy?" asked Young Soul, quizzically.

"Oh shut up!!" Earth Rep and Dark Soul shouted together.

Dark Soul continued. "Now, you can let this asshole give me the bum rap and keep me out, but what you won't be told is that no one would line up for a trip to Earth if the likes of me weren't there to balance things out with excitement.

"And about these tips and shit to make your trip better. Do you really think that a couple of tips will help you there? Here's a real tip for you: To get anywhere that you desire on Earth, you need two things only: willingness and the capacity to suffer. And you wanna know why? Because life itself on Earth is like a fucking confused teacher … first she gives you the test and then she teaches you the lesson.

"Now go ahead and indulge in your little trip out there knowing that you kept one of us out. But, when the time comes that you're bored out of your fucking mind, you'll seek my kind just to stir things up so you can feel something. And that's when we'll flare up and incinerate your every principle of righteousness and ethical aristocracy."

Earth Rep pointed at Dark Soul and in a quiet tone said, "Don't look now, but your audacity is sticking out. I mean, boo-hoo … are you done feeling sorry for yourself for not being appreciated? Who are you kidding? I've never had souls coming back from their trip to Earth complaining of a lack of excitement because they happened to live in an era of peace and prosperity and were fulfilled with love. Not once did one come back regretting that they had the courage to be merciful on Earth. As for getting what you desire, your comment about suffering is hogwash. The only thing you need is to pursue your passion."

Young Soul interrupted. "Here, Soul Mate signed the release. Now, can we go?"

Earth Rep sighed. "Look, I'm going to try one last time to make you understand that this soul-mate business is full of heartache. You've got to believe me—it's just not all that it's cracked up to be. In fact, it's mostly a malicious fantasy."

"But what could be better?" Young Soul objected. "We'll have each other to help with the challenges on Earth and we can enjoy the trip together."

"Who have you been talking to, huh?" growled Earth Rep. "It's not that simple. First of all, when we give you a transdimensional launch to Earth, the trajectory for each soul is different. There is no way to set the exact point of arrival for two souls on Earth. It just doesn't work that way."

Young Soul said, "But I heard that soul mates always find each other, even if they've arrived at different points."

Earth Rep sighed again. "Yeah, yeah—you buggers always do, even from across the continents, even when you don't speak the same language. Like animals, you can sniff your way to each other, but let me tell you something about that. In the process of looking and searching for your stupid soul mate, you miss out on relationships with other souls who are often a heck of a lot better match for you there."

"But they wouldn't be my soul mate," insisted Soul Mate.

Earth Rep exploded, "So, what's so fucking special about your soul mate? Look at this thing you call your soul mate, for goodness' sake—there's nothing special there! I really don't see what either one of you sees in each other. A couple of losers with no real intelligence. Don't you think you're each better off matching up with two other souls on Earth that could enrich your senses and enlighten you with their knowledge and grace? Look at you two—you're pathetic and you want to prolong this state of pathetic-ness by finding each other and sticking together. You'll both waste a chunk of your time in discontentment because you think no one is good enough until you find each other there. Believe me, when you actually do, you'll soon realize that neither one of you were really that special after all."

"We don't think we're special," said Soul Mate. "We just want to have a special time together."

Earth Rep mocked them, repeating, "'We just want a special time together.' Whatever."

Young Soul piped up. "Remember, we get another tip when we sign the release. Can we get our tip before we go?"

26

DANCING WITH DESTINY

Long moments passed. Dark Soul hovered away while continuing to mumble angry words of resentment.

Earth Rep relented. "I'll now give you your last tip. But listen, kiddos, I'm not your damn tutor just because I agreed to give you these tips, so listen carefully and don't interrupt me. Here's the thing again: To experience life on Earth, you'll have to be interfaced with a machine."

"A machine?" asked Soul Mate.

"Didn't I just tell you not to interrupt me?" Earth Rep yelled. "Listen to the whole thing first—hopefully you'll get it by the time I'm done.

"It's a machine by which you can operate life on Earth. It's made of organic matter and it's called a 'human body.' It's an incredible machine, so much so that if you spent your entire existence on Earth studying it, you'd still never know all its capabilities. However, this human body has a monitoring component called the brain. Unfortunately, this brain doesn't come with a user's manual. So, you have to learn as you go with it. The other name for it is the human mind. And this mind will give you trouble because the human body will eventually expire while the mind's prime objective is to prevent and prolong this inevitable expiration. So, there's a constant struggle.

"Now, here's the other thing about the human mind: Based on this conflict, it holds an illusion that all the plans it lays out will produce its desired outcome at its desired time. If the actual outcome doesn't match its plan, your mind will be in distress, subjecting you to pain and mental anguish, the severity of which depends on the disparity between the outcome and what was anticipated. Of course, if and when the outcome is precisely what the mind had planned, then the mind goes into a state of what they call satisfaction."

"Why?" asked Soul Mate.

"Why? Because the human mind thinks that if its plan equals the outcome, it has shaped destiny."

"Well, does it?" asked Soul Mate.

Earth Rep smiled cynically. "Does it? Or is that just an illusion to keep you guys entertained on your trip? Or is it because the outcome of the mind's plan simply happened to match up with what destiny had laid out? Either way, even simple correlation gives the mind immense satisfaction."

"Why?" asked Soul Mate again.

"The human mind really likes to feel important," replied Earth Rep. "Oh, how it loves that. And nothing makes the human mind feel more important than being in line with what destiny had laid out, even if it's just by sheer chance."

"What's the fun of that?" asked Soul Mate.

Earth Rep looked surprised. "Are you kidding? People play endless games every day just to examine that possibility. From little bets amongst themselves to ruining their entire lives with gambling."

"So which is it?" asked Young Soul and Soul Mate simultaneously.

"What? You shape destiny or destiny shapes you? Ha! That's been the question for ages," chuckled Earth Rep.

"And will you tell us the answer?" asked Young Soul.

Earth Rep softened. "Ah, you little goofballs, you don't know how lucky you are to get this answer. I'll tell you for the same reason I said before. Whenever young souls go to Earth, they screw things up for older residents because they want to change the world into a better place. I figure if I give you this insight, it'll give you a bit of a head start and maybe, just maybe, you won't mess things up out there so badly, which would reflect poorly on me. So here goes: When you're on Earth, you're dancing with destiny. But you must remember who's leading the dance."

"Dancing?" asked Soul Mate.

"Okay, let me put it this way," said Earth Rep. "Did you learn from your stupid research what a river is?"

"Oh yes," said Soul Mate.

Earth Rep stared intently at both of them. "Now, relax your awareness and pay attention. Destiny is like a vast river that's calmly moving as it should. And all beings on Earth are swimming in this vast river as they should. When you go in the direction that it's moving, you'll experience the illusion that you're making this whole river move forward and that feels good. But if, for whatever reason, you try to swim up the river, that's when you get bent out of shape and start to suffer and struggle. You may even drown in an attempt to keep on swimming up it or take drastic measures in vain to change its flow.

"I don't want you to think that you're not allowed any movement and that you must lie passively on your back like a floating log. (Although some say that's when they have their best times on Earth.) But you don't have to. You can move in all kinds of ways to give direction to your experience on Earth. But they do need to be lateral, meaning that as long as you're moving in the general direction of this vast, calmly flowing river, you're in harmony with it and you'll have a joyful experience dancing with destiny. Remember this too, without letting it go to your heads: You're an intricate part of destiny. After all, if you weren't there, who would destiny have to dance with?"

"Then why can't *we* shape destiny?" asked Young Soul.

Earth Rep replied, "Because the dog must wag the tail, not the other way around, you moron."

Soul Mate asked, "But you said we're intricate parts of this river of destiny. Why wouldn't we be able to change its shape?"

Earth Rep looked frustrated. "Because you're both puny little shits who lack the necessary intelligence to suddenly change the shape or flow of destiny. Still, you just might, but only at a time when destiny, based on its intelligence, determines the right moment to change shape as a reflection of your vision."

Young Soul asked, "So, we could maybe have some of what we desire to experience if we don't rush things?"

"You can definitely have all that you desire if you don't rush it," answered Earth Rep. "What you wish is your business and it'll always come true if you don't abandon your wish. *When* it comes true is up to destiny.

"You see, the key is to understand this: Life is a process on Earth. When you desire something, you set certain elements in motion to materialize your wish. What your fellow idiots don't realize is that these elements must comingle with other elements to produce the desired effect, which also has to align with the general movement of things already in motion. If you don't rush it and don't send static vibration to interfere with things, your original desired outcome will always manifest itself at the proper crossroads for the union of all necessary elements to serve you."

"That's fantastic!" exclaimed Soul Mate.

Earth Rep warned, "But, to truly be happy, you must enjoy life in the interim. That's the time between making a wish and when it comes true, because that really makes up the bulk of your experience on Earth. And yes, it's beyond fantastic. You'll never experience anything like it. That's why Earth is so popular. Just remember, don't try to change the world."

"How do we know if we're like that?" asked Young Soul. "I mean, where do we begin to go wrong so we can stop ourselves?"

"It's always the same pattern," said Earth Rep. "When you're a child, you live life like you're supposed to. You enjoy each day to the fullest and do very little judging. You enjoy your surroundings and look for anything that you can get a kick out of, no matter what the circumstances.

"Then, like an old soul on Earth once said, when you get a little older, you want to start changing the world. Of course, later on you realize that you can't do that and you're just making a mess and making yourself miserable. Then you get a little older and you want to change things in a country. Soon you realize you can't do that either. Then you're becoming unhappy again.

"Then you get older still and you settle for changing just your family. And sure enough, you learn that you can't really do that either, at least not quite the way you thought you should or expected. By this time, you're much older and have wasted plenty of time and energy and made a lot of people miserable with your idealistic ideas—most of all yourself. That's when you realize the only thing you can really change *is* yourself."

"So, that means we need to make sure that we constantly keep changing ourselves until we're happy, huh?" asked Young Soul.

Earth Rep looked aghast. "Good grief. Look, you can change yourself only so much. If you're going to enjoy your trip at all, the most important step is to largely accept yourself. You've got to monitor yourself only to the degree that you smooth out the rough edges in your character that cause behavior that's destructive to yourself and those around you. Aside from that, don't waste too much time and energy in even changing yourself. Just be, for goodness' sake, just be. Try to be more of a human *being* than a human *doing*."

Young Soul looked excited. "You gave me a bonus tip, remember? Can you give my soul mate one? Perhaps on this subject of wanting to change? It seems complicated, so can you give us a tool to help us with it?"

Earth Rep chuckled. "You're going to be such a bargain hunter out there. Fine. Your best tool is this: Reduce your reaction to the way things are—all things, even the way *you* are. Reduce your reaction, reduce your impulse to change, and instead enjoy the changes around you. If you simply tone down your reaction, you'll survive the waves of the everlasting tide of change on Earth and remain healthy to see the next chapter. And remember what a privilege it is to just be there."

Young Soul bowed. "I will try to remember everything you said."

Even Earth Rep had to smile. "Even if you forget all of it, just hold on to these words if you wish to have a fulfilling time on Earth: *Be kind and have fun*."

—◦⟨✦⟩◦—

27

FIELD OF SPIRITUAL BIRTH

D r. Kamron had just finished reading *Admission to Earth* when he noticed that Alex had returned and quietly joined him.

Alex kindly asked, "Would you like to stretch and take a short walk with me? We'll come right back."

"Gladly," said Dr. Kamron, "and I meant to tell you earlier how much I like your study."

Alex smiled. "Oh yes, that's really our only library, but since all of our quarters are equipped with Layla, hardly anyone uses that place but me. We'll take a different route so you can see more of this place."

The two walked out and strolled through several pathways, enjoying the sights and aromas of nature flourishing all around them. Before they made their way back to the gazebo, Dr. Kamron stopped to take a closer look at a small pool of water, out of its very center of which grew a majestic tree with a thick trunk. It looked like a willow tree, but its branches bore colorful flowers at their tips. The pool was built in a doughnut shape around the tree but from a distance, it looked as though the tree were growing out of the water. Carefully placed outdoor lights pointed at the tree made it possible for the observer to appreciate its beauty and colors, even at night.

As Dr. Kamron admired the graceful beauty of this landscape design, he said, "I feel as if I'm in a small piazza in Rome."

He then noticed a small animal drinking from the pool. He took several cautious steps toward it when suddenly the animal walked back a couple of paces, turned its head toward Dr. Kamron, and began to run, taking three or four steps forward and then flying away. Dr. Kamron was so stunned that he could not believe his eyes.

He turned to Alex, stuttering in disbelief, "It … it had wings, it could fly! It flew away … did you see that?"

"Of course it could fly," Alex replied. "I'd be surprised if it couldn't. What's the big deal?"

Dr. Kamron stammered, "But wasn't that a, a—"

Just then, an announcement came over the intercom for Alex.

"Excuse me, Doctor, I have to answer this," said Alex, turning away.

Dr. Kamron stood transfixed with an astonished expression still on his face.

A few minutes later, Alex returned. "Good news, Doctor. The elevators should be going back to normal operation shortly."

"Does that mean my wife can come up?" asked Dr. Kamron.

"Yes, of course!" said Alex. "Come, let's go back to the gazebo. So, you didn't tell me what you thought of *Admission to Earth*. Was it at least entertaining for you?"

Dr. Kamron smiled. "Yes, it would make a great story for a play. I fully appreciate its message and its insights, but I must tell you that some do not believe that our souls have arrived here or ever existed prior to this life, for that matter. Perhaps I can share with you what I discovered on Emerald Island."

"I'm all ears," said Alex eagerly.

"Believe it or not," said Dr. Kamron, "my undergraduate degree was in anthropology. For many years, I'd heard stories about this very unique tribe in the middle of a dense jungle. They had had practically no interaction with the outside world, and yet they possessed such unexplainable knowledge of a few sciences beyond anything they could have randomly learned from the limited visitors they'd gotten over the years. That's what intrigued and motivated me to make the long journey recently.

"Once I was there, however, I was shocked and mesmerized by something much larger than what I'd anticipated. It went beyond any substantive scientific knowledge. It was certainly not just a unique ritualistic behavior, as it's humanly impossible, or at least not in any other part of the planet. In fact, I cannot imagine how anyone, especially young and perfectly healthy people, could make a conscious decision to implement such a thing."

Alex leaned forward. "You're killing me here. What was it?"

"That. That's what they did," said Dr. Kamron.

"What?" Alex asked.

"Killing."

"Killing?" exclaimed Alex. "That's what shocked you? Good Lord, Doctor, what's so unusual about that?"

"No, no, no," said Dr. Kamron. "Not killing each other. In fact, they're the most peaceful tribe I've ever seen. There was something about their lives that was quite pleasant, almost too pleasant, something mystical and pure."

"Then what did they kill?" asked Alex.

"Themselves," answered Dr. Kamron.

"Themselves?"

"Yes," said Dr. Kamron. "They killed only themselves."

"Well, as rare as they may be, there are documented cases of mass suicides due to some need for martyrdom or other nonsensical religious beliefs," said Alex. "Was that it? Mass suicide? And, well, suicide is often attempted when a person feels that they have no other options. Did you know that in the United States alone, the rate of suicide has risen to the top 10 leading causes of death?"

"No, I didn't know that," said Dr. Kamron. "But no, it wasn't suicide. Perhaps I didn't start out right by using the word 'killing.' You see, if time would've permitted, I was planning to supplement my lecture with something extra after unveiling my latest discovery. I thought it would be interesting to play the footage from a trip I made to Emerald Island. Would you like to watch it now? Here's the H$_2$Open."

Alex took the H$_2$Open device and plugged it into a nearby computer. A holographic monitor appeared inside the gazebo.

"Let's fast-forward to Section Five of the film," said Dr. Kamron. "You see, there's no killing going on, and it's not really a suicide ritual. These people simply know when it's their time to die."

"You mean that the elders go into the woods like some animals do when they feel it's their time?" asked Alex.

"No, not just elders," answered Dr. Kamron, pointing to the image. "And no, not like animals. Watch this. This man is young, no more than 30 years old. This happened during the second week of my stay. The tribal leader allowed me to observe the next person who came forward and declared it was time. Here's an important point: I asked him the meaning of the word they use when they imply that it's time—especially considering that time is really not a commonly used concept in the jungle as it is in modern society. Through the aid of my translator and the tribal leader pointing at a fruit on a tree, he said they come forward and declare that their souls have ripened."

"Then they hang themselves or something?" asked Alex.

"No, that's the most amazing aspect of this. Watch, this is the next day after the young man declared that his soul had ripened. Earlier that day, he'd enjoyed a simple, joyous get-together with his family and friends. And here it comes. Now watch him as he goes there and lies down. Watch his face. He smiles at the people gathered around him and then he closes his eyes. Now look. No movement, no shaking, no disturbances, as calm as a summer breeze. There—he's gone."

Alex was stunned. "Amazing. Did you examine him yourself for signs of life?"

Dr. Kamron nodded. "Absolutely. I had to be delicate in getting permission, but yes, I checked his vitals."

"How many of these did you observe and document?" asked Alex.

"I spent five months with the tribe and documented three," said Dr. Kamron. "Their ratio of birth and death is basically similar to any other society on the planet, give or take a margin for variation in the environmental conditions in different societies."

"Are you saying that a similar percentage of this tribe's youth and their elderly die as those in a big city?"

"I'm saying there was not a significant difference to indicate any anomalies in death rate by age."

"So, what was your conclusion?" asked Alex.

"That somehow these people were able to tell when it was time for their souls to move on, and when they recognized that time, there was no resistance," said Dr. Kamron.

"So, believing in a separation of body and soul is a prerequisite for them, then," observed Alex.

"To them, it's not a philosophical matter," said Dr. Kamron. "Think about it. Something was able to simply turn their bodies off in a moment without the use of any trauma or outside influence. So, to answer your question about my conclusion, it's a two-part answer.

"First, the nature of what happens with this tribe is not unique—it's the same process all around the world with every human being. The difference is that the people of this tribe are somehow capable of acknowledging when their souls have reached a point where they must transform. Perhaps it's due to a more pure form of consciousness, and by that I don't mean good or bad behavior, but rather a more harmonious, accepting state of mind in line with the natural order of things. Think about it, Alex. Don't you also believe that when the time is right for any of us, we go, and when it's not, we survive some of the most dire circumstances that should have killed us?

"On the other hand, we've all known people in perfect health and in the safest conditions and environments who have died by means that no one could have fathomed. The difference lies in the acknowledgment. The people of this tribe simply acknowledge that timing and participate in the transformation without resistance and with a sense of joy.

"As for my second point, once I observed what transpires when they're ready to die, I spent most of my remaining time with the tribe attempting to tap into their understanding of the origin of the soul. Keep in mind that although they live a simple life, they're not simple-minded people. You should have seen the architecture of their wooden homes, the complexity of their sanitation systems, and most importantly, their knowledge of chemistry. They used a highly sophisticated chemical compound to produce these ceramic-like blocks that they use for heating."

"Like coal?" asked Alex.

"In function maybe," said Dr. Kamron, "but these blocks were human-made and clean-burning. I could go on and on about how impressive these people were. Imagine a small exemplary human civilization. That's the best way I can put it."

"So what did they tell you about the origin of souls?" asked Alex.

"First, I asked the tribe's leader to help me better understand this ripeness business," said Dr. Kamron. "He could tell by the look on my face that I was having difficulty fully comprehending this. So he took me for a short walk until he found a caterpillar hanging off a branch. He pointed at it and said, 'When the butterfly is ready for its metamorphosis, it knows it's time to leave the cocoon. So do we. If the caterpillar can transform into a butterfly and further its existence in a higher dimension, why can't we?'

"He then smiled and said something along the lines of, 'I don't know why you outsiders are always amused by our understanding and participation in our transformation. What we do is not unnatural. It is your lack of comprehension to do this that's unnatural.'

"With a bit of difficulty, I managed to communicate to him through our translator that we in the rest of the world find it unnatural to know for certain when we might die. In fact, at times our fear and anxiety of this anticipation causes us pain and takes the joy away from the time that we do have left to live. He shook his head and said it was hard for him to understand even the word 'anxiety,' but he could perhaps better understand the meaning of fear and pain. 'Fear and pain of knowing about death,' he said as he continued to shake his head. His smile widened. And then he said, 'Did you not have this feeling you call fear and anxiety when you were born, since you were crying out loud after having just come out of a womb? Besides, you already know that as a result of birth, you will die, so if you worry, you die, and if you don't worry, you die. So why worry, why pain, why whatever that thing you call anxiety?'

"Then I asked him about the origin of the soul. He looked puzzled and asked the translator, 'Isn't he a medicine man himself?' My translator smiled and said yes. The tribal leader shook his head again and said, 'I feel bad for the people who come to him for advice. He's not very young, either.' Then he looked at me and said, 'I mean no disrespect, but where do you begin with the accumulation of your wisdom where you come from?' I replied, 'We start with assumptions.' The tribal leader then put his hand on my shoulder and said, 'Souls are cultivated on Earth. This is the field that has all that is necessary to produce souls.'

"I replied to him, 'This old dirty planet?' and he smiled and said, 'Yes, this old dirty planet, like the relationship between the beautiful flower and the manure.'"

Alex nodded with amazement. "A fascinating perspective."

Dr. Kamron continued, "Yes, their world is one of connections, with all beings united with nature versus ours, which is all about individuality and competition with nature. Perhaps that's why we suffer from so much fear and anxiety."

"So they impacted your belief system entirely?" asked Alex.

"Yes, and I must say, it's completely the opposite of your belief about the transmigration of souls to this plane of existence. As much as I'm in awe of your perspectives and even inclined to subscribe to some aspects of them, we fundamentally part ways on this issue. I believe that we're not spiritual beings who took over this organic form, but rather that the essence of our spirit materializes through the elements on Earth. The formation of our spiritual consciousness depends on its development here in this organic form before it can migrate anywhere else. And the field of spiritual birth is here; that's why we have no memory of past lives, because there were none."

Dr. Kamron continued, "Let me put it this way: It's like you go up this ladder in life to get to the ceiling by spiritual growth. There's a door on the ceiling. You open it and move through it, and then you realize that you've just arrived at the surface. Below was simply just the basement. That's where I think we are. But imagine it in a *parallel* setting of development."

Alex pondered this with a look of wonder and fascination on his face. "Amazing, truly amazing. I wish I had had a chance to visit this tribe. One last question though: As an anthropologist, you must have heard the theory that just by observing a culture, you're inevitably changing it. Do you think that applies there with your visit?"

Dr. Kamron fixed his gaze on Alex. "It worked both ways."

—◦⋅◦✕◦⋅◦—

28

PROFILE OF ILLUSION

Dr. Kamron walked a few steps to the edge of the dome and stared out at the ocean below. He listened quietly to the sound of the waves as they hugged the shore. He thought to himself, *Am I truly standing in the vessel that will preserve my race as a human, or for that matter, life as we know it? Alex is right. There's no question that by natural and geological forces alone, we can be in jeopardy, not to mention by our own self-destructive existence. So why wouldn't he be right to build this? But …*

Alex interrupted his thoughts. "Dr. Kamron, your wife is on her way here."

"Thank you, Alex, you are very kind."

"Don't mention it. You looked like you were deep in thought over there."

"While I'm both convinced of the validity of your cause and impressed with your accomplishment in achieving it," remarked Dr. Kamron, "I cannot help but to wonder again that since life on this planet is simply a grand illusion—a means of entertainment or an amusement park as you put it—then why all this fuss to preserve it? If it's only an illusion, why do you care to go to this extent to preserve it against some pending catastrophe?"

Alex looked at him for a second, then took a step forward and calmly said, "Dr. Kamron, somebody has to keep the lights on for the amusement park to operate. Even illusions require planning, programming, and, yes, preservation of their elements. We all do our part for the show to go on. My calling happens to be self-preserving this grand illusion. Remember, a failure to plan is a plan for failure."

Hearing the sound of two sets of high heels clicking on the surface of the floors, Alex turned around and saw two ladies coming toward him. Elizabeth's pace quickened when she saw her husband. She was accompanied by a staff member who was an astonishingly beautiful woman.

Her hair was pulled back in a ponytail and she wore a uniform modified to be fashionable; yet it was obvious that she was still part of Alex's crew.

Alex graciously stepped aside so that Elizabeth could go directly to her husband. The couple held each other intensely. Elizabeth quietly shed tears as Dr. Kamron held the back of her head in the palm of his hand and gently caressed her hair.

Elizabeth whispered, "Don't ever let go of my hand again, even if it comes out of its socket. I don't want a moment of this life if you're not beside me."

Dr. Kamron whispered back, "Hush. You're the source of life for me. It's gonna take more than an earthquake to keep us apart."

After a few more quiet moments, Dr. Kamron said to Elizabeth, "Let me introduce you to our host. This is Alexander Grant."

Alex moved forward to shake her hand. "Please call me Alex. And this is not exactly how I'd planned the evening for my guests."

"It's a pleasure," Elizabeth said, "and thank you for keeping us safe. Can't ask for more than that on a night like this. And your gracious wife is amazing and has been very kind to me."

Alex smiled and patted Dr. Kamron on the back. "I'll let you both be for a little while. But first, let me introduce someone to you. Come closer, Natalie, let me introduce you to Dr. Kamron. Of course, you've already met his lovely wife."

"It's a pleasure to meet you," said Natalie, extending her hand.

"Likewise," said Dr. Kamron, "and thank you for bringing my wife."

"Of course." She turned to Alex. "Can I help you with anything while I'm up here, Grandpa?"

"No, dear," replied Alex. "Thank you."

"She's your granddaughter?" Dr. Kamron marveled.

"Yes, my granddaughter—my pride and joy," said Alex, beaming. "She obtained her master's degree as a biologist, at the top of her class. She was offered multiple scholarships to continue her education but instead she chose to work here. She's a very impressive young woman. She speaks more languages than I can count and is gifted with a great analytical mind. And she's the most dedicated member of this crew. Sometimes she takes it more seriously than I do. Perhaps it's because she literally grew up with this project."

"And she's incredibly pretty!" added Elizabeth.

"And she's pretty incredible," said Alex.

"Oh, stop it, Grandpa," said Natalie. "You always give me too much credit. I do need you for a little while. Would it be okay if I take you away from your guests?"

"Sure," said Alex. "My dear friends, I'll have food and drinks brought to you at the gazebo, and we'll be back shortly."

As the two walked away, Dr. Kamron began excitedly recounting his conversations with Alex to Elizabeth and the brainstorming they'd done for the residents' manual.

"I've never seen you so taken by anyone like this," said Elizabeth, amused.

"The truth is, I find his words not only intriguing but his logic somehow captivating, no matter how much I try to be objective."

"I'm not surprised," said Elizabeth. "Great minds think alike. I can't wait to talk to him myself. He seems pleasant. Can I ask him direct questions?"

"Direct questions?" asked Dr. Kamron. "You're not going to cross-examine him, are you?" he teased.

Elizabeth answered, "I just don't think we're going to have that much time, so I'm anxious to see what he thinks about certain subjects. Besides, aren't you hoping to get more insights out of him for your, what did you guys call it? Oh yeah, Earth Residents' Manual."

"Please take it easy," Dr. Kamron warned. "I know how excited you can get in a conversation."

Elizabeth smiled. "Oh, don't worry, it'll be fun."

"Do you two need more time to yourselves?" Alex asked, once he'd returned. "I have plenty to do and can come back later."

"No, no. Please stay with us," said Elizabeth, gesturing to the empty seat across from her and Dr. Kamron. Alex sat down.

"So, I understand you're an attorney," said Alex.

"Yes, but only by trade, not by character."

Alex chuckled. "That's funny. I actually have a lot of respect for the profession. But more importantly, if it weren't for lawyers in civilized society, heartless corporations and institutions would crush the public for the sake of their bottom lines and agendas. Be it by disregard for public safety or civil liberties."

Elizabeth laughed. "Gee, thanks, Alex. It's refreshing to hear this. Usually I just get the tasteless lawyer jokes from my friends."

"No, I mean it," said Alex. "Making a living from dispute resolutions can be very taxing. Now, I'm not naïve enough to think that you do this out of the goodness of your hearts. I know you guys do your adversarial work for the sake of your own livelihood and not necessarily public service. But, nevertheless, the byproduct of your work provides something valuable to society. The alternative would be anarchy, a lawless society. My own experience with heartless corporate policies left me with great appreciation for having a legal system that allows the little guy to at least have the option to take legal action. You'd be surprised how many countries don't even have a real, functional civil justice system."

Elizabeth agreed. "Yes, in America, the civil justice system may not always be civil or at times even just, but at least we have a functioning system."

"How do you yourself define your profession, Elizabeth?" Alex asked.

"Well, a lawyer is an individual whose principal role is to protect clients from other members of the profession."

Alex laughed out loud. "That's clever."

Elizabeth shifted in her seat. "Alex, I know our time here is going to be short, and from what I heard from my husband, you have quite a refreshing perspective on things, so do you mind if I ask you a few direct questions?"

Alex smiled and asked, "Like in an interrogatory format?"

Both Dr. Kamron and Alex laughed out loud at this as Elizabeth shook her head and joked, "No, more like a deposition!"

Dr. Kamron interjected, "Forgive us, Alex, my wife will always have her lawyerly way of doing things."

Alex held up his hand. "Not at all. Mrs. Kamron, please feel free to ask. Besides, I've learned so much from your husband—it's the least I can do."

"Thank you," said Elizabeth. "So, according to you, life on Earth is an elaborate, interactive amusement center, a grand illusion?"

"Pretty much."

"I can buy that, but this doesn't make its significance any less for me," declared Elizabeth.

"It's not meant to be insignificant," said Alex. "Enormous energy and resources and programming have been implemented to facilitate this game of life. Why would you think it's insignificant?"

"Because you're apparently asserting that life is intended only to entertain us souls. Is that not what you said to my husband?"

"If you go see a great theatrical production," said Alex, "would you say it was an insignificant event, even though you're aware that it's make-believe? Doesn't the story, performance, and the rest of it stimulate your senses? You may experience laughter, joy, or even tears as you invest time and resources in it. Your soul is experiencing something quite profound while at the same time you're fully aware that it's just a play. Now, why would you have a hard time comprehending that life itself is a grand production of that kind?"

"But there's a lot more to life," Elizabeth insisted.

"A lot more of what, feelings? Experiences?"

"Yes, that's right."

Alex considered this. "Well, that's because it's a grander illusion; thus, it must offer more. As Mark Twain said, 'The only difference between reality and fiction is that fiction needs to be credible.'"

"So, you're not the first enlightened person to say this," said Elizabeth.

Alex said, "I'd frankly be surprised to find a great mind in human history who didn't at least allude to this awareness that life is a grand illusion of sorts. I simply concluded its purpose. References to this illusion are indeed not hard to find; it's been stated over and over, from Buddha and Rumi to present-day physicists, including your husband, who show us that this plane of existence is simply experienced when information is exchanged on subatomic levels to give us a sense of reality.

"In the old days, the great minds usually took a more poetic approach to explain the same concept. In the thirteenth century, Rumi said, 'In truth we are not here, this is our shadow,' concluding that our true self is somewhere outside of this plane of existence and yet connected to this experience of life. Today we can better understand this concept because we can reproduce a simulation of it through technology. Like I explained to your husband, through virtual-reality games, we can participate in a computer-generated domain and stimulate many of our senses while our true self is sitting outside of that domain, observing our own experience. Listen to how profoundly Rumi stated the same thing: 'The dreamer is watching the dreamer in a dream.'"

"That is profound," said Dr. Kamron. "Now tell me, what's our connection like to our true self? Is the relationship kind of like master and pet?"

Alex recoiled a little. "No, no, no. It's like you're connected to a more comprehensive you. That is, my friend, the profile of an illusion."

"So, do you think our mythical guardian angels are really our more comprehensive selves?" Elizabeth asked.

Alex was quiet for a moment. "Huh, I never looked at it that way. Now consider this: Even a simple profile you create on a social media network is a crude example of this principle. Despite being quite primitive, the example reflects the concept I'm explaining; you're in one place with a more comprehensive existence, and then you create a reflection of yourself in a different domain and maintain a connection with it. Through that connection, you interact with others in that domain.

"Is life here much different than that? You see, we 'created ourselves in our own image,' but only an extension of ourselves is functioning here. In your heart of hearts, you know that there is more than this body. Just like you care that your profiles on those social networks reflect a desired representation of you as you update and improve them, you'll look back at your life and recall that, to a small or large degree, you've attempted to constantly refine yourself."

Alex smiled. "Of course, some are more successful and efficient than others when it comes to refinement."

"How true," murmured Elizabeth.

"Now in our minds," continued Alex, "the problem with correlating this concept with the nature of our existence is twofold: First, we think in the linear and cannot imagine eternity. Simply imagine how far creating a profile on a social network has come. Then, if you can, imagine that the process has advanced, say, across 100,000 years. Once that kind of computer technology has been incorporated into organic forms where you can exist in one domain and engage in another via your organic profile, it means that the sky is not the limit.

"Second, we must not think that this somehow belittles our existence. If the people who saw the first paper photo had been told that in less than 200 years, it would help create a technology by which we can send a robot to another planet and watch the images the robot can see on that planet—well, it would have been simply unimaginable.

"The point is that our existence simply reflects our true self in this domain. But it's also very much connected to our essence," added Alex. "You see, many who discovered this awareness associated it only with one primary purpose. Some called the illusion a means to sense love. Others believed its purpose is suffering to free yourself from your present form. In more modern times, others took a more pragmatic approach and said life is in fact an illusion designed to teach us—a place of learning, if you will.

"What I submit to you is that it's all of the above, yet none of the above. The experience of life includes all of these factors, but those are not the purpose of life *per se*. The true purpose is to entertain yourself with anything you can connect with in this existence—be it sadness, happiness, knowledge, ignorance, kindness, viciousness, or even pain. It makes no difference. Life has just one function: to be. And it's here for us to project our desires on it.

"Essentially we're here to feel and engage in any and all forms of life. It's like a swimming pool; the water is just there. Once you jump in, it'll form to your every move and then you can swim in any style you want. Better yet, it's like a play. Once you're in it, you play your role based on the story that's going on at that theater. It's interactive, as all sophisticated games are, but just because it's an illusion, it is not insignificant. At least not to the players while they're playing their roles."

Elizabeth thought about this for a moment. "So, souls sign up for this game of life despite knowing that they can get hurt while playing it?"

"They sign up precisely *because* of that possibility," said Alex, emphatically. "It's what gives it an edge, excitement, an experience worth having."

"But some experiences may cut it really short," Elizabeth countered.

"Like I've said, there are practically no safety measures for this game," said Alex. "So yes, it can be cut short at any given time for any player, but then again, that's also what makes it intriguing. What's your difficulty with comprehending this concept? Have you not ever played in any games with genuine risk of harm or loss? If your role in those games wasn't subject to jeopardy, a chance of losing, getting kicked out, or even getting hurt, wouldn't you have found that game so dull that you wouldn't want to participate anymore?"

"I understand," said Elizabeth, "but emotionally, I still have a hard time with the cruelty aspect of life."

Alex's face looked kind. "It can only be truly cruel if it's truly real. Think about it. Haven't you ever wondered why there's no divine intervention for some events we call cruel in this world? I think it's because they're not real. The game seems real to the participants at the time because it should, but once you've disconnected from it, the real you is safe wherever it is. We can even see examples of that in this realm of existence. Once you're older and far from the unpleasantness of the past, you sometimes look back with nostalgia and recall the sadness of your experience as a silly reaction. Imagine you're sitting on a bench in a park and you observe a two-year-old starting to walk. The child trips, plops down, and starts to cry, and you can't help but laugh at what you just saw. That doesn't make you cruel, for you know that there's so much more ahead for that child."

Elizabeth looked unconvinced. "I can see that being funny when the child is hurt for two minutes, but not when the suffering goes on for two months."

"The reason you're okay with the child's pain for two minutes is that you subconsciously compare that limited time of suffering to his, let's say, 100 years of life expectancy. In light of that, his suffering is trivial. So now, if you can conceptualize the idea that two minutes of suffering in a hundred-year-long life is just funny to an observer, then two months of suffering in an eternity of existence must be hilarious."

Elizabeth smiled. "I get it, Alex, but I just can't stomach that much reality. Again, it's the cruelty aspect that bothers me."

"What about it?"

"I can't help but think about what my husband always says," Elizabeth answered. "It's perplexing that whatever created so much beauty in this world would allow the possibility for so much cruelty and suffering to go along with it."

"But there is no cruelty here," said Alex.

"There you go again. Are you kidding me right now? No cruelty?"

Alex sighed. "Again, for something to be cruel, it must be real. This is a highly advanced virtual reality we're in. In fact, it's so advanced that we erroneously recognize it *as* reality because we're in the thick of it. Let me reiterate this concept: You create a profile in a social network. But keep in mind that this profile is so advanced that it doesn't represent just your image but also some functionality in terms of your senses and characters.

"Now, suppose this profile engages in certain activity and by chance or participation, it gets damaged or destroyed. It may be disappointing to you or other observers in that domain to see it harmed, but there's nothing innately cruel about it. It's just a profile—one that you create for this experience while your true self remains safe."

Dr. Kamron interjected, "That's why you don't think there's divine intervention for cruelty in this world or this highly advanced virtual domain?"

"This entire existence is divine intervention," answered Alex. "But cruelty is merely a human term for those experiencing this domain from within."

29

PRICE OF FEAR FOR BORED LITTLE GODS

Dr. Kamron had another question for Alex. "Do you think that as human beings, our fear of death is so extreme that we must now psychologically resort to the concept that this existence is an advanced virtual domain?"

"Fear is the price you pay for taking this game seriously," answered Alex.

Elizabeth couldn't help herself. "Honestly, Alex, I think you're a wonderful, kind, and sensitive soul who has suffered deeply from observing others hurting. Now, could it be that you've developed this concept to soothe your own soul?"

Alex looked taken aback. "My dear Mrs. Kamron, what is really your difficulty with my concept?" he asked.

"The problem with it is that a variable must be assumed," said Elizabeth. "Basically, your concept requires that one must blindly accept that our world made of matter is not real. So, if we assume that variable, then your concept makes sense. But you expect us to simply, on faith, accept that our existence in this form of matter is all an illusion. If I could truly grasp this without requiring a leap of faith, then I wouldn't have a problem with what you've so articulately elaborated on. I mean, honestly, my reality is that which I feel, and as long as I feel this matter, this is my reality."

"Fair enough, but do you care to really examine what this matter that you're so adamantly holding on to as your reality consists of?" asked Alex.

"What? Molecular structures? Atoms?" said Elizabeth.

"Well, sitting next to your husband," said Alex, "I feel silly getting into the scientific analysis of this. As compared to mine, his knowledge on the subject is encyclopedic."

"No, please Alex, go on," said Dr. Kamron.

Elizabeth smiled encouragingly. "Yes, Alex, go on. We rarely get into these scientific discussions with one another."

"Well, let's take a closer look at your matter-based reality made of atoms," said Alex. "First, we often believe that atoms are these hard little balls consisting of dense matter, kind of like those glass marbles we used to play with as kids."

"Yes, exactly," said Elizabeth.

"That's absolutely wrong!" said Alex. "In fact, they're not anything like that. Even a nucleus that we think of as physically dense pops in and out of existence just as readily as electrons do. Werner Heisenberg, one of the greatest founders of quantum mechanics, once said that atoms are not things—they are only tendencies, and that, rather than think of things, we must think of possibilities. We tend to think that the world already exists in this hard-matter form, independent of our experiences."

Elizabeth asked, "Is it not?"

"It is definitely not," replied Alex. "Our reality is our reaction to the elements around us—elements that create events. But events are not our reality; our reaction to them is. Ultimately, the only way I can refer to this sort of empty matter is that it's more like a thought, like concentrated bits of information."

Dr. Kamron offered, "And at the deepest subnuclear level of our reality, we're all literally one."

Alex sat back and looked at Dr. Kamron. "How did I do, Dr. Kamron? This is actually giving me an opportunity to run my information by an authority on the subject."

"Oh, you did just fine, Alex," answered Dr. Kamron. "In fact, essentially what you've based your idea of this world on is very much in line with Einstein's general relativity as well. You see, prior to general relativity, scientists described the world of space and time as a fixed background on which things happen. What Einstein gave to science was this amazing discovery that there is no background, meaning that there's no fixed framework and no stage on which the world plays itself out. Simply put, what we have is only an evolving network of relationships amounting to what we know as a history of space, time, and matter."

"Wow!" exclaimed Elizabeth. "Now I have both of you saying the same thing packed with fancy, futuristic science. My husband told me that your words were captivating."

Alex said, "Then let me share with you the words of a nonscientist who referenced it beautifully and not futuristically but rather from thousands of years ago. Buddha described our existence only as a sort of frequency, stating that our form is made out of emptiness. Of course, we now know that an atom consists of practically empty space."

"Ah," said Elizabeth. "I understand, but I still wish I could feel it."

"As a female, you have strong intuition," said Alex. "Perhaps you can use that to help you feel your understanding."

Elizabeth laughed. "Use my intuition to understand these complex scientific matters?"

"Why not?" said Alex. "A woman's intuition is by far more in tune with the vibration of the universe than anything else I know of. Besides, did you know that your gut has more neurons than your brain?"

"Is that really true?"

"Absolutely. That's why you should give a lot more credence to your gut feelings than you perhaps have," said Alex.

"That would make sense," said Elizabeth.

"Yes. So, all things being a part of this universe, why wouldn't you be able to use your intuition to comprehend scientific matters?"

"Okay," said Elizabeth. She took a deep breath. "So, let me see if I understand this life according to you: We're essentially bored little gods who come play an exciting game on this realm of existence, which operates based on a network of relationships that is governed by the outcome of tendencies on a subatomic level?"

"Wow, very well put," said Alex.

"And do you think somehow we're programmed to perfect this game?" asked Elizabeth.

"Not at all. There's no such thing as perfection. It's just a word."

"Just a word, Alex?" Elizabeth scoffed.

"I know, but I meant that it's an illusion to keep us busy playing."

"I sure agree with that one," said Elizabeth. "It seems to be a human obsession to the point that if we had perfection, we wouldn't recognize it."

"The problem with perfection," said Alex, "is that you lose sight of the forest for the trees. Tell me, did you suffer from the search for perfection in your own life?"

Elizabeth laughed. "Let's not go there. Thank God it diminishes when you get older and when you find the love of your life."

Alex peered at her closely. "Does it, with love, that is?"

"Yes," replied Elizabeth. "Somehow, when you feel loved, everything else seems to look perfect or it's just not important anymore—one of the two. I think it's the inadequacy of love in our lives that exacerbates this futile need to search for perfection."

"The search of the bored little gods?" asked Alex, playfully.

Elizabeth nodded her head. "Yes, the search of the bored little gods."

30

SHORTCUTS FOR SHAWDI

Elizabeth still wasn't quite satisfied. "Don't you usually try to get the best in life, though?" she asked Alex. "That's a similar concept to perfection, isn't it?"

Alex considered her question. "No, I try to go for the good, not the best. The problem with best is that it takes so much good to become best that it's no longer any good."

Elizabeth chuckled. "Yes, very true. Okay, well, back to our main point of this conversation. Look, I have a daughter and I want her to connect to the better version of this game, as you put it. Play on the good rides in this amusement park of yours. Okay?"

Alex smiled, "I know. Your husband already filled me in on that plan! I know what you're asking, but like I told him, she'll want to try all the rides in life. So you cannot pave the way for only the happy ones."

"Not just happy," said Elizabeth, "but I want to teach her about things that would be of value in her life. Can I get your guidance on specific issues so she perhaps reduces her chance of making mistakes and gets more out of her experiences?"

"So, you want to try and eliminate mistakes for her and deliver her to happiness through shortcuts?" asked Alex.

"Well, if I do, is that so bad?" said Elizabeth.

Alex raised his hand. "Let's take this one thing at a time. First, consider this as the equation for life experiences: $x/1 = x$. The rating of the numerator (each life experience) is arbitrary, but the value of each moment (the denominator) is constant as 1—meaning that you cannot increase the value of each moment based on your perception of that moment.

"So, if the value of each moment in time is the same, is it not ridiculous to sacrifice one moment for the betterment of another? How often do you hear that the time spent in pursuing a goal in retrospect was as sweet as the moment of arrival at the goal? And it'd better be. Otherwise, if you count the length of time you spent to get to that one moment of gratification, it'd be a ludicrous proposition to pursue.

"Secondly, if you think that being more insightful eliminates mistakes and thus increases the value of your life experience, that's a futile approach. Here's what you should know about mistakes: There's no such thing as mistakes. Or better yet, it's the element that we falsely call mistakes that plays a great role in this existence both surviving and progressing."

"Do I understand that you're implying that our existence depends on making mistakes in some fashion?" asked Elizabeth.

"Precisely!" said Alex. "Look at DNA, which is the blueprint of every living thing. Every time a cell divides, its DNA copies itself, and in that copy there is often a mistake, and these mistakes result in humans, animals, and plants being more successful than their parents or predecessors. In fact, these mistakes allow the tree of life to branch out and flourish with diversity, equipped with the right tools for survival."

"So the mistakes in DNA save us?" asked Elizabeth.

"Absolutely," said Alex. "Variation in evolution saves us. In fact, infinite variation is at work, thanks to new hereditary traits that come all the time from mistakes within the DNA."

"How so?" asked Elizabeth.

"The mistakes take place during the recombination of chromosomes in the production cycle of sperm and eggs, genetically in mutation form."

"So, we're all essentially mutants?" asked Elizabeth.

"On a very gradual basis, indeed we are," said Alex. "That's the only way we've survived. That's how all living things have survived and pushed their race beyond their original natural boundaries. Otherwise, old ailments from human history would have wiped us all out a long time ago."

Elizabeth looked skeptical. "So, then, bad is good? Come on, Alex, be reasonable."

"Look, I'm not trying to break down the fort of reason," said Alex. "But the fact is that we automatically—and falsely—associate mistakes with bad things. Haven't you ever heard of *ex malo bonum*—'out of bad comes good'?"

"Yes," said Dr. Kamron.

"Do you think that attempting to prevent bad is somehow wrong?" asked Elizabeth.

Alex shook his head. "No, what I'm saying is like that old Italian proverb that says, 'Not everything bad that happens to you is bad for you.' Here, let me share with you a poem by Rumi called 'The Guest House.' Layla ..."

This being human is a guest house
Every morning a new arrival.

A joy, a depression, a meanness,
some momentary awareness comes
as an unexpected visitor.

Welcome and entertain them all!
Even if they are a crowd of sorrows,
who violently sweep your house
empty of its furniture,
still, treat each guest honorably.
He may be clearing you out
for some new delight.

The dark thought, the shame, the malice,
meet them at the door laughing and invite them in.

Be grateful for whatever comes.
Because each has been sent
as a guide from beyond.

Elizabeth said, "I love that! I'm going to read it again and again. But while your point may be valid on those two issues, it seems to me that you belittle happiness and peace of mind. To me, those are the essence of what we strive for in life as humans."

Alex seemed bewildered. "Belittle? No, although that was your husband's choice of words too. You see, happiness is in fact a crucial aspect of life experience, but its most important purpose is to serve as bait."

"As bait? Good Lord!" said Elizabeth, horrified.

Alex pressed on. "Yes, happiness is bait, in pursuit of which we live all the other experiences in life that we'd otherwise not even consider to endeavor."

"So, it's a conspiracy for a lack of fulfillment?"

Alex shook his head. "No. Happiness is like hunger. In pursuit of food to satisfy your hunger, you experience all of the tastes of things available to consume on this planet: sweet, sour, hot, cold, and even bitter. And it's in this process of pursuing the need to satisfy your hunger that you get the necessary nutrients to your body, whether you're aware of it or not. I doubt that any of us really know the exact nutritional makeup of all the food we eat. We just instinctively follow our need to consume it to assuage our hunger.

"It's the same with the pursuit of happiness, except that it applies to the necessary experiences—or nutrients—for the soul. Look at anyone's life. How many of us at the end of each day proclaim to have had a happy day? Yet we all run for it again the next day. But the point is that no matter how ordinary these days are, later in life we often refer back to them as the good old days, don't we?"

Dr. Kamron smiled. "Ah … the magic of ordinary days, so unappreciated."

Alex continued, "You also mentioned peace of mind. As much as I share your desire for that, one must ask themselves: Have you considered what you lose once you have peace of mind?"

"Lose? Lose what?" asked Elizabeth.

"This life is a problem-solving game," said Alex. "If you have no problem, you have no purpose. You have nothing to play with. Do you realize how many people hold on to their pain or fears just because they think it makes their life purpose clear?"

"But that's just the kind of thing I don't want for my daughter," said Elizabeth.

"I understand," said Alex. "But do you understand that she will find ways to give up peace of mind for some form of challenge? In general, it seems we're not really here for peace of mind. It's perplexing, isn't it? We make it look like we're striving for it, but as soon as we get close to it, we manage to dredge up some other challenge in life to take it away from us. It seems that's how we feel most alive—right in the midst of problem-solving. Frankly, it often brings out the best in us.

"Now, you want me to help you pave the way for your daughter (or humanity, as your husband says) to have fewer challenging problems. Okay, I'll engage in this futile exercise. As I mentioned, at least it may serve to play your part in this game."

Elizabeth turned to Dr. Kamron and said, "Okay, did you get all of that? Happiness is bait, and mistakes are good. I feel like if I listen to your new friend here much longer, I'll have to rearrange my entire brain!"

"You don't think we may want to?" asked Dr. Kamron.

Elizabeth grinned. "I did it once after meeting you, so why not?" She turned back to Alex. "You know, Alex, when I met my husband, I could've sworn he was from another world or something. He seemed so out of place."

Alex chuckled. "Well, he seems very adjusted now. Except why do you think he gets excited when domestic animals fly?"

"What?" said Elizabeth, puzzled.

"You have to agree that that was strange," remarked Dr. Kamron.

"What was strange?" said Alex.

"Come on, guys, let's not waste time on animal research," said Elizabeth.

"What research?" asked Dr. Kamron.

"When I first met you," said Elizabeth, "you were mesmerized by the sight of a horse!"

"Well, they *are* majestic animals," offered Alex.

Elizabeth shook her head. "Nah, he swore up and down that he'd never seen one before."

"Perhaps he was a city dweller all his life," Alex said.

"Are you kidding? Not even a picture? Or on television?" asked Elizabeth. "Now he says he's never seen a flat fly either!"

Dr. Kamron looked indignant. "Really, I'd never seen one!"

Elizabeth rolled her eyes and turned to Alex again. "Now, Alex, as I said before, would you mind if I ask you about other issues and get your perspective? At least I know it'll be refreshing if nothing else."

"Of course, please," said Alex. "After all, you're my guests for the evening. But tell me, is this information you seek for Shawdi or to use for Dr. Kamron's manual for Earth's residents?"

"Is there a difference?" asked Elizabeth. "Perhaps she'll be the one to read it first, but the intention is the same."

"To give guidance to her and humanity?" asked Alex.

Dr. Kamron interjected, "Well, it's kind of like this in our minds: Didn't you say that a failure to plan is a plan for failure? So, can you blame us for wanting to give her—or anyone else for that matter—valuable information for planning accordingly? You know, let the dog wag the tail, not the other way around."

"Ah, man plans and God laughs," said Alex. "What about learning through experience?"

"Come on, Alex, isn't experience what you get when you don't get what you want?" asked Elizabeth.

"So, you just want a shortcut for your child's path to success in life?"

"Why not?"

"Don't you know that the shortcut's road to success is paved by the bodies of failure?" said Alex. "Life is a journey; to succeed, you must respect its process. You cannot rush the arrival of a new season. If you did, it would be meaningless. It's the experience of winter that makes spring enchanting and refreshing."

Elizabeth remained undeterred. "But this is about knowledge. Didn't Socrates say that knowledge is the sufficient condition to the good life? I'm asking for knowledge."

"No, Socrates identified knowledge with virtue and he said that if knowledge can be learned, so can virtue," replied Alex. "Thus, virtue can be taught. That was his point. So teach your children virtue and they'll be on their way to a good living.

"And one more thing," said Alex. "Stop worrying about her challenges and sorrows. I guarantee you when our tears subside, we'll find it all so amusing."

31

Calm Seas Do Not Create Strong Sailors

Elizabeth shifted in her seat. Her mind was swirling with the thoughts and ideas posed in the past half hour's conversation, and she wasn't sure she liked all of them, let alone reconcile them in her mind.

"Alex, I'm trying to take it all in and you're truly a gracious host," she began, "but what is your hesitation when it comes to giving insights that would give my child—or humanity for that matter—an advantageous position in dealing with life's challenges? I mean, at the very least, just for emotional matters."

Alex replied, "Advantageous position, you said. Well, that's the problem with your inquiry—it's fundamentally against the nature of things on Earth."

"What?" said Elizabeth, shocked. "To be in an advantageous position emotionally is against the nature of things? How in the world do you mean?"

"The nature of our emotional balance is not designed much differently than our physical balance," said Alex. "Let's take a look at the physics of our body and see how not being in an advantageous position serves to our advantage, and then maybe we can better see eye to eye on this matter."

Elizabeth sighed under her breath. "Sure, I can't wait to hear this one," she muttered.

Alex continued, "Most of the bones in our limbs act as levers, which are powered by our muscles. If we're rendered inactive, there's no challenge to our muscles, and then they'll suffer a loss of muscle tone. Of course, the more challenge we present to our muscles, the stronger they'll become. Generally, however, our bodies are equipped with only third-class levers to carry out our normal tasks in life.

"Here's the interesting point about levers, which come in three forms: In a first-class lever such as scissors or crowbars, a small force can be used to gain an advantage over a heavy weight. With second-class levers also, a smaller effort can leverage a larger weight like a wheelbarrow. However, nature used mostly third-class levers in the skeletal design of our body, such as the elbow joint. In this case, the force is between the fulcrum and the load. So, when we lift, the elbow joint is the fulcrum across which the bicep muscles do the work. In this design, there is no force advantage. In fact, a larger force is needed to move a smaller weight.

"This simply means that by design, whenever we lift anything, we're at a mechanical *disadvantage*. Even lifting our own arm weight requires that a force greater than the weight of our arms must be applied for that movement to occur. Now, one may think that it would've been really cool if nature has given us the other two lever designs for our body. Like you said, to put us in an *advantageous* position. But the reality is that this disadvantageous design helps us maintain our muscle tone even when we're not lifting an additional load, but simply just moving our bodies.

"My dear Mrs. Kamron, our emotional balance, like our physical balance, also requires constant contractions," Alex continued. "If you place your daughter in a perfectly advantageous position, you'll undoubtedly give her emotional and psychological muscle atrophy. Tell me then, are you sure you want to keep her in this advantageous position now?"

Elizabeth was quiet for a few moments, thinking about what she had just heard. Alex kept looking at her with an apprehensive feeling that he had somehow disappointed his guests. He got up, walked to a bookcase, pulled something out, and then handed her an article containing a few pages.

"Let me give you a little story of Kito to read," he said.

Elizabeth eagerly took the pages and began to read them aloud.

32

THE DUST OF FLOURS RISES HIGH

"Kito, dear!" Sister Mary hollered from across the hall. "Someone is here to meet you."

As Kito turned to look, he dropped a doughball that he had been rolling on a table. As it hit the floor, its floury dust rose up all the way to his eye level.

Kito was only 12 years old. He was a slender African boy with dark, beautiful skin and adorable, bright, brown eyes that shone every time he smiled. That shine projected the nature of his kind, innocent spirit.

At the time Kito was born, bad things were happening to his tribe. They claimed he brought them bad luck and put him through painful rituals in vain to remedy this. He was hurt by his own relatives and tribe members. When he was seven years old, his mother turned him over to Sister Mary to escape his fate with the tribe.

Sister Mary ran a small orphanage in this impoverished African country. It was poverty-stricken but not resourceless. As is often the case, on one side of the country were big companies and high-rise buildings, but the other side lacked readily available drinking water. Kito had the daily chore of bringing buckets of water to the orphanage, for which he had to walk a long distance several times a day.

Along the way, he'd made numerous friends and enjoyed a great many laughs with them. Playing soccer every other day for a while with these kids was the ultimate treat, although he did not own any shoes—only a pair of worn-out plastic sandals. But, kicking a soccer ball barefoot on dirt roads and alleys never deterred him and his friends from this pastime in the least; their only wish was to own an actual soccer ball. Instead, they pieced together plastic scraps to fashion a makeshift one.

It was a hard life, but to him this harshness was not apparent. In fact, he was pretty much oblivious of all these shortcomings of his life. At an early age, he discovered the boundless pleasure of sharing, and the fact that all the smaller kids relied on him to quench their thirst with the water he fetched gave him a sense of great usefulness. He could not read or write, but he was always teaching other kids to draw. Several visitors had paid Sister Mary money to buy his paintings posted on the walls of the orphanage. The paintings all had one thing in common: a blue-sky background with layers of white clouds and an absolutely astonishing mixture of bright colors that depicted images of nature, mostly of gorgeous flowers. Ironically, he named all of his paintings "The Sad Flowers."

Sister Mary struggled to keep her orphanage functioning. Every day was a challenge, but in her heart would pump possibilities of hope for the lives of these children. Then came one of those possibility days. Mrs. Johnson had arrived from America to adopt a child. She chose Kito because he'd been the hardest case for adoption—too old, too many scars, and for the last five years he'd been at the orphanage, no one had shown any interest in him.

Mrs. Johnson and her husband were a very regal couple. She was an attractive African-American woman, and this was her first trip to Africa. Her kind face and calm demeanor radiated great integrity. Her husband, a white, highly educated man who was a professor-turned-consultant, was holding her hand when Kito turned around to look at them for the first time. They, of course, recognized him from the photos and the correspondence they'd had with Sister Mary, and they moved closer to him.

As soon as he looked up at Mrs. Johnson through the flour dust, he murmured the word that meant 'good day' in English. Mrs. Johnson's eyes teared up as the story of the first seven years of this child's life rushed through her mind. She knelt down, held out her arms, and said, "I came a long way just to see you." Sister Mary translated her comment. Kito tried to clean his hands from the flour dust by rubbing his shirt. Then he gently touched the scarf that Mrs. Johnson had bought earlier that day in the market and said, "My mom used to make these, way back when."

Mrs. Johnson asked him, "I've seen your paintings, and I love them. They're so cheerful. Can you tell me why you call them 'Sad Flowers?'"

Sister Mary translated, and Kito answered, "The flowers in the paintings have no scent and can never experience the joy of spring because they're not real."

———•◇✕◇•———

(22 years later)

Kito was enjoying tea with guests at his family's house. As Mrs. Johnson sat on the couch behind him offering pastries to the other guests gathered around, an amazing, uplifting feeling of love wafted through the room. As Kito walked past Mrs. Johnson, he kissed her on the cheek. The lady next to Mrs. Johnson said to Kito, "With this new big-shot position of yours, you must do a lot of traveling now, right, Mr. Professional?"

Kito nodded. "Yes, that's the only thing I don't like about this new position—being away from Mom and Dad. I'm really a homebody kind of guy and just can't stand being away from them more than a couple of days."

There was a great sense of sincerity in his comment; his heart was just not into traveling and being away from his parents, who lived nearby. He stepped aside to chat with another lady sitting on the other side of his mother.

This lady asked him, "You know how proud we all are of you, right? You've accomplished so much over the years. Now tell me, Kito, what do you consider to be the happiest days of your life so far?"

Kito reflexively answered, "The five years at the orphanage."

The pastry tray Mrs. Johnson was holding fell and hit the table, and the flour-sugar dust rose to her eye level.

33

THE GRAPE STORY

Elizabeth placed her hand over her mouth in wonder, while tears started to roll down her cheeks.

"But, he really loved them, didn't he?" she said.

"Of course, absolutely, more than his own life," said Alex. "But the point of the story is something else. The happiness you seek for your daughter is not induced by the mitigation of the challenges in her life, just as the most enjoyable part of Kito's life was also his most challenging part."

"Look, Alex, you can't blame a parent for wanting to ease the life of their child," implored Elizabeth.

"It depends on their objective."

"Objective?" Elizabeth scoffed. "Isn't it obvious? To enhance the flavor of life for her."

Alex said gently, "Then, respectfully, I do blame them. Not for wanting to make life more flavorful for their child, but by thinking that easing their life will necessarily add more flavor … in fact, it is to the contrary."

"Oh? How do you mean?" asked Elizabeth.

"I'll share how, but that means I have to tell you another story. Are you sure you're up for it?" asked Alex.

"Do tell, Alex, do tell."

"Then I'll tell you the Grape Story."

"A grape story? Oh boy, I can't wait to hear this one," said Elizabeth.

"Actually, you can learn a lot about what enhances flavors by hearing the grape story," said Alex, smiling.

Dr. Kamron prodded. "Please go on—I'm all ears."

"I once toured a beautiful winery in western Washington called Chateau Ste. Michelle," began Alex. "I emphasize 'western' because it's relevant to the story. The winery sits right outside of a small town called Woodinville, which is about 40 minutes from Seattle. As the tour guide was showing us where the fermentation, bottling, and packaging take place, we came to a hall where large posters showing photos of the vineyards hung. Something looked odd to me. The area depicted in the pictures didn't look at all like the landscape outside our door. I asked the tour guide, 'Where is this vineyard of yours?' She replied, 'Eastern Washington.' I asked, 'Why not here, where you have all of your facilities, located in this beautiful, lush green setting?' And I'll never forget the answer I heard. She said, 'Life would be too easy for the vines here. The grapes would not have the flavorful features we want.'

"Of course, I asked her to elaborate, and here's her astonishing explanation: The intensity of taste comes only from dry, harsh climates, where the vines, instead of growing and expanding their leaves, are forced to direct their limited resources to the survival of their fruit. This gives them the best flavor. In water-rich, lush climates, the vines do not have to try hard to stay alive and survive, and their leaves and branches grow bigger because they can afford to. This, in essence, takes away the flavor from the grapes. Don't you think that goes for the flavor of human life as well?"

Elizabeth went quiet again.

Alex was beginning to worry once again that he was disappointing his guests. He quickly added, "I'm sorry. This doesn't mean we can't explore the subjects you're interested in. Perhaps we can discuss something that comes close to your heart as a mother, and I'll do my part to be of help."

Elizabeth smiled. "Okay, well, what did you teach your children to help them stay happy in their lives as they grew up?"

"I tried to emphasize three simple things that would prevent unhappiness. First, teaching them to love. They learn from us how to love and I was mindful of that. The more they learn to love different people, different cultures, and different aspects of life, the less they learn to hate. Also, an important part of this is self-love. The more they learn to love themselves, the healthier they'll be and the easier they'll be on themselves and others. And, the easier they are on others, the more they'll be at the receiving end of love.

"Second, teaching them to value friendship. It's an absolute scientific fact that friends are the antidotes for depression. You want happiness?

You must have friends. And remember, when they grow up and seek success, who their friends are can be one of the biggest assets of their lives. After all, when it comes to success, it's not who you know, it's whom you know," Alex said with a smile.

"By the way, since your friends are an antidote to depression, then it's better to be kind to them than to be right, even if there was ever such a thing as right. When it comes to friends, the regret that you should have said something is by far less than the regret that you shouldn't have.

"Third, last but not least, teaching them some kind of spirituality by any means available to you in order for them to have faith. It makes absolutely no difference what form it is as long as it does not advocate superiority or hate toward any other spiritual belief."

Elizabeth was intrigued. "Can we also cover something on the other side of the spectrum of spirituality? The material things, that is. How much happiness do you attribute to wealth?"

Alex smiled, looking down. "Honestly, once you're comfortable in life, excess income has a nominal effect on increasing your satisfaction."

Elizabeth grinned. "I don't know about that."

Alex clarified, "Well, let me put it this way: If you don't find the right emotional elements in life to uplift your spirit, but you have significant wealth, then you'll simply be an unhappy person in an upscale setting."

"I understand your point," Elizabeth said, "but I don't think we're going to totally meet eye to eye on this one. Okay, on to the subject of relationships: Tell me how to better hold a relationship together."

Alex answered, "First, remember we always regret the things we didn't do the most. So, find a way to do all the things you can to enhance your joy with that person. Second, the art of balance in relationships is like holding on to a slippery bar of soap: If you squeeze too hard, you'll force it out of your hand. If you hold it too loosely, it'll slip right out. So, you have to maintain a balanced amount of pressure to keep it together."

"What about resentments?" asked Elizabeth.

"Ah, resentment!" said Alex. "A philosopher once said that resentment is the poison one takes while waiting for the other person to suffer. Give it up. It's just a reaction of the ego, and ego is seldom your friend. Perhaps if we could truly understand the problems, needs, pain, and personality complexes of the other side with whom we're battling, then we'd never have resentments. Besides, as Alexander Pope so beautifully said, 'To err is human; to forgive, divine.' We should all learn better to forgive."

"How does one find that guide in their lives?" asked Elizabeth. "You know, we all often need guidance when we come to an impasse in life or simply feel lost."

"There is no one guide, no single guru with all the answers," said Alex. "But, if you're a good tracker, you'll always find different guides along the way who are generous enough to show you the path to safety in each segment of your life."

Elizabeth brightened. "Speaking of the word 'generous,' how do you define generosity, Alex?"

"Let it suffice to say, as human beings, if you wish to strive to have Godlike qualities, the closest we can ever attempt to get to is to be generous," said Alex. "And not just in a material sense, but in acceptance, love, and mostly forgiveness. Within the concept of God, wouldn't we recognize that Her greatest quality is generosity? After all, She provides abundance. So if you desire to resemble God, be generous in giving. Perhaps that's why we find generous people attractive, no matter what they look like. Maybe it's their godly resemblance."

Elizabeth smiled. "Okay, my husband did not need to hear that. He's already overdoing it. Granted, I was very much attracted to him for this quality in his character, but I swear that he gives new meaning to the saying 'he gives the shirt off his back.'"

Dr. Kamron grinned and shook his head.

Alex chuckled. "Then he is genuinely generous. Because remember that generosity isn't measured by how much you give, but rather by how much you're left with after you're done giving."

"Okay, Alex, it looks like you have an answer for everything," Elizabeth said. "Tell me about the element of unfairness in life, or are you going to deny that it's all around us?"

"No," said Alex, "but for the most part, the reason things appear to us as unfair is based on two aspects. The first is our method of judgment based on our point of reference.

"Second, because of our limited perception and vision, we see only one segment of time at a time. If we could rewind time and see the origin of events, or fast-forward and see the sequence of events to come, not all but most of our concerns about fairness would be alleviated and we'd see the balance. As for the rest, experiencing something that's unfair is also on the menu of all the experiences you're bound to have on this planet. But if you take what I said earlier to heart, it will help. Everything is going to be okay at the end. And if it's not okay, it's not the end.

"Of course, age sharpens our perception in detecting this. Sometimes it helps to think about it like this: We're like the mouse in the maze who is stressed because he cannot see anything to eat in his path and doesn't know that a piece of cheese is right around the next corner."

Elizabeth asked, "So what about those who never get the cheese?"

"Nobody gets the cheese, not really!" said Alex. "Not because it's not there, but because we constantly push it away."

Elizabeth looked quite confused. "But you just said what we're looking for is just around the corner. Didn't you mean to imply that happiness is achievable if we just look in the right direction and be patient?"

"Look, it's about the weight of expectation," said Alex.

"What is that?"

"This thing you called happiness," said Alex. "We put so many conditions on it that it becomes more and more unattainable, to the point that we never quite get there. We actually get to the cheese just about every time, but not enough satisfaction remains to meet the anticipated expectation. So, the search goes on. You see, it's the expectation itself that undermines happiness. Otherwise, happiness is obtained every day all around us—we just change our minds about being satisfied. It's like if we were to become satisfied, there'd be no purpose left, and with no purpose left, we'd be no more."

"So, one should give up on perfect fulfillment of happiness," said Elizabeth.

Alex nodded. "As it's been said, 'being happy does not mean everything is perfect. It means you choose to look beyond imperfections.' If you look at what you don't have in life, you never have enough. If you look at what you do have in life, you always have more."

Elizabeth asked, "So, don't seek happiness, but just be satisfied with the status quo, no matter what it is?"

"No," said Alex. "My point is that one must *create* happiness, not constantly seek it. Happiness is not having what you love, but loving what you have."

"At least when it comes to my husband, I'm satisfied in my relationship," said Elizabeth. "My expectation has no place else to go. How do you explain that?"

"You're the exception, not the general rule. You two must have a balanced emotional weight expectation."

"What is the general rule?" asked Elizabeth.

"In relationships, it's often like this: Just like you don't expect someone who cannot physically lift 100 pounds to do so, we shouldn't expect our counterparts to lift the weight of our expectation when they're not emotionally equipped to do it. Often, the problem is the unequal weight of the expectation that undermines loving relationships. So, you should count your blessings if that's not the case for you two."

"Since we're back to talking about relationships, tell me more about what to look for to preserve it," said Elizabeth.

Alex continued, "Misunderstandings are the termites of relationships. I mean any kind of relationship, not just couples—between parents and children, people at work, friends, etc. I once saw a video documentary about a couple in psychotherapy. The wife used a metaphor that her husband chose such strong words in their communications that when he made certain comments, it was like he was throwing a big rock at her. When the therapist asked about this, the husband was genuinely shocked by how his comments were received by her. He said he intended his comments to be the tiniest piece of sand that he'd throw at her just to get her to pay attention to how he felt."

"So, what's the point? We just shut up to prevent misunderstandings?" asked Elizabeth.

"No, to the contrary," said Alex. "If you have something to say and keep it inside, it'll ferment and fester in time. Express yourself—don't put your resentment in a pickle jar and store it in your mind. But talk about it with a sense of balance and consideration for the other side. After all, they just might be as right as you are if you knew where they were coming from."

"So, the idea is to just prevent conflict, no matter what?" Elizabeth asked.

"No, out of conflict comes resolution. You see, most often your counterpart purposely initiates the conflict not to be hurtful or to stay in that state with you, but rather because they see the conflict as the only means to get out of the undesired state that they're in with you at that time. Unfortunately, most people only know conflict as a road to resolution. Smart ones recognize that if their counterpart didn't care for them, they wouldn't be having this situation to begin with, and they don't burn bridges along the way. The point is how to manage that conflict."

"And how does one do that, exactly?" asked Elizabeth.

"With the understanding that the conflict serves the purpose of solidifying the relationship. Right, Dr. Kamron?" said Alex.

Dr. Kamron looked taken aback. "Solidifying? I don't think so, Alex. There's nothing solid about any form of relationship. I believe that relationships, like life itself, are fluid and are constantly changing shape, status, and form. Enemies become best friends, lovers become adversaries, and then they go back to being lovers. Allies with praise for one another transform into sworn enemies until a turn of events makes them allies again."

Elizabeth asked, "What about the rightful sense of anger? There are times when people trigger your anger and there are no two ways about it."

Alex replied, "Even so, as Roman emperor and philosopher Marcus Aurelius said, 'How much more grievous are the consequences of anger than the cause of it?' "

"Yes, anger is a scary thing," agreed Elizabeth. "Speaking of scary, tell me about fear."

"Fear in its true sense is below the lowest form of experiences on this planet," said Alex. "A life lived in fear is half a life. Sort of like a junk experience, if you will. Ironically, we consume significant resources and time to avoid this experience, and that massive undertaking in itself has contributed to our accumulating more fear. The more technologically progressed a society is, the more alarmist it becomes, cultivating more fear. Ultimately, we fear our own reaction more than anything or any event. And rightfully so, as the greatest threat to us is our own reaction to fear."

Alex continued, "Here, since we're on the subject, let me share with you a T-mail a friend sent me a while back. She was searching for an article about fear on the Transnet and she came across this writing by Lou Tice. Layla..."

> *I am Fear. I am the menace that lurks in the paths of life, never visible to the eye but sharply felt in the heart. I am the father of despair, the brother of procrastination, the enemy of progress, the tool of tyranny. Born of ignorance and nursed on the misguided thought, I have darkened more hopes, stifled more ambitions, shattered more ideals, and prevented more accomplishments than history could record.*
>
> *Like the changing chameleon, I assume many disguises. I masquerade as caution. I am sometimes known as doubt or worry. But whatever I'm called, I am still fear, the obstacle of achievement.*
>
> *I know no master but one; its name is Understanding. I have no power but what the human mind gives me, and I vanish completely when the light of Understanding reveals the facts as they really are, for I am really nothing.*

"You see," said Alex, "if you have the courage to acknowledge your fears, you'll be taking the first step toward controlling them instead of them controlling you. And if you take the next step toward understanding their causes, you'll be able to move past them.'"

"Do you agree that the basis of fear is formed in childhood?" Elizabeth asked.

"Of course, but I also don't think there is really such a thing as adulthood. Just children pretending to act and play in a more sophisticated fashion as time goes by. In fact, some grow old because they forget to play. As George Bernard Shaw best said it: 'We don't stop playing because we grow old; we grow old because we stop playing.'"

"I love that," said Elizabeth.

"But anyway," continued Alex, "the origin of fear, such as knowing when to flee in times of danger, goes back to our time as primitive man. It served as a defense mechanism to survive in the wild. The problem is that fear is housed in the limbic system of our brain. As you know, we really have three brains, not one. We have the cortex, which is our newest brain that's been around for only a couple of hundred years. This helps us with decisions so we can maneuver around our universe. The second is the reptilian brain, which is our older brain. Unfortunately, the third brain is the limbic brain, which is the least evolved portion. It was supposed to save us from things like saber-toothed tigers, but today we use it for everyday matters. In fact, we overuse it to the point that the preventive measures we take out of fear often cause more harm than the elements we fear the most.

"So many of the priorities of our response system as a society are misplaced based on politicians' goals to get our support or corporations' desire to get our resources by preying on our natural fears. Most people, for example, are not aware that so many of their resources are going toward so-called protective and preventive measures for issues that cause less damage than Bambi does."

"Bambi?" asked Elizabeth, puzzled.

"Yes, but it doesn't profit anyone to alarm you about it and put fear in your heart, so you don't hear about it."

Dr. Kamron looked puzzled. "I'm not following."

"I'm just making a point," said Alex. "But seriously, if you check it out, according to the US National Highway Traffic Safety Administration, you'll find that about 1.5 million vehicle collisions occur with deer each year that result in one billion dollars in property damage. Yes, you heard me right—*billion*, leaving about 150 people dead and tens of thousands of people injured. I assure you that these are factual numbers and underestimated at that, since they're based only on the crashes actually reported. The point is that most of the things people are forced to fear are based on someone profiting or benefiting from that fear—otherwise, little attention is given to it."

"It's amazing how valid your point is," remarked Dr. Kamron.

"So how do we deal with the darkness of fear in our personal lives?" asked Elizabeth.

"Step into the light and reduce your reaction, since fear feeds on fear and dissolves in hope," said Alex. "And again, have faith that 'everything will be okay in the end. If it's not okay, it's not the end.'"

—◦✕◦—

34

A 99% Safe Planet

Wouldn't You Want to Live There?

Dr. Kamron interjected, "Don't you think that society also suffers from the fear that broadcasters poison the publics' minds with in the name of news?"

"Ah, the news—a bad form of entertainment," remarked Alex. "Facilitating the masses to vicariously experience the suffering of others."

"Exactly," agreed Dr. Kamron, "although a free press is one of the most sacred and precious assets of any society, but you are right about the news production."

"Yes," Alex said, "and it's the biggest misrepresentation because it's never balanced with all the good news that's going on. They try to entertain us only with the misery of others. So, news becomes nothing but bad news. When you tap into other people's misfortune and bad experiences, somewhere inside, you can't deny that you're amused and entertained by that. But, when you engage in this entertainment, you fail to see that part of you is also suffering along with them. This is not because you're not a nice person or a compassionate being, but because your psyche doesn't understand that this isn't your experience. So, your body begins to automatically react by sending all kinds of chemical and hormonal changes to cope with a situation that is not really yours to cope with."

Dr. Kamron remarked, "I know what you're saying because I stopped watching the news many years ago. Now I only focus on what I need to know. Frankly, when it comes to things like crime or war, I truly believe that this is an amazingly safe planet."

"You would go that far?" said Alex, raising an eyebrow.

Dr. Kamron continued, "Absolutely. Just think about the numbers I'm about to share and tell me that whoever runs the show on this planet isn't doing a fantastic job. There are over seven billion people who live on this planet, right?"

"Yes," answered Alex.

"Well, listen," said Dr. Kamron. "When it comes to violent tragedies, even one person is too many, so I'm not by any means saying that it's okay to allow any amount. But we live in a society in which the media and even other institutions constantly project a false image that humanity lives in a continually violent state of existence and we should all fear one another. That is simply not so. We have to be fair to our own race as human beings and see the staggeringly positive facts of safety around the planet."

Numbers Sanctify

Alex listened intently.

Dr. Kamron continued, "How many do you think died as a result of war in an average year on Earth? 100,000? 200,000? How about 300,000?"

"That's probably an inflated estimate," said Alex.

"I seriously doubt that number too," said Dr. Kamron, "but let's just say 500,000 in an average year. And just for the sake of comparison, hypothetically let's add other violent acts and say that in one year 7,000,000 people die from violence in one form or another.

"Now consider that ratio to the number of people who safely made it home, had an uneventful year, enjoyed their families, went on vacation, succeeded at their professions, had healthy babies, and had a lot of fun doing it all. Now, that would come to over 6,993,000,000 people (billion, I repeat).

"Tell me, with all honesty, isn't that a pretty damn good ratio, worthy of gratitude, acknowledgment, and newscast? We live on a planet in which 99.99 percent of people are safe for the most part and for the great majority of the time. Are you hearing this? About 99.99 percent of people on planet Earth are relatively safe from harm! This is a staggering number and *numbers sanctify*.

"Frankly, it's evidence that even as a race, we must be doing something right. You never hear that in the news because their objective is not to broadcast positive facts. If they reminded us every night that only

0.001 percent of the population are victims of violent acts, perhaps we'd actually be inspired by how well humanity is doing instead of discouraged. And that inspiration would cascade into more goodwill around every community in the world instead of creating a defensive psyche toward one another."

"I have to admit," said Alex, "I've never quite looked at it that way. That is indeed an impressive ratio for safety, and you're right—numbers sanctify."

"Just humor me a little longer and consider this," said Dr. Kamron. "Even if you include other tragedies such as epidemic disasters and raise that figure to an absolutely crazy number of 70,000,000 people in a decade, you still have a 99 percent ratio of a safe and healthy life ahead for humanity. In my heart, the loss of even one life is tragic, but the problem is that the human body and mind cannot stay indifferent to bad news. Sure, we try to move on to the next subject and it doesn't kill us right there and then, but studies have shown that our body's defense mechanisms adversely respond almost as much to fiction, displayed anger, and fear as to nonfiction. And it doesn't take a genius to know that this repeated false-defense triggering function is unhealthy.

"This is not compassion," continued Dr. Kamron. "This is not education. This is overloading the masses with useless information designed for profit. Tell me—what is the value of knowing about dozens of murders across the country when it's never balanced by any positive news? Good news is part of this planet too, even if it doesn't sell drug commercials. Do we ever see the commentator come on and say, 'Good evening, ladies and gentlemen. We are happy to report that today 5,000 healthy babies were born in this nation, and this spring 50,000 kids finished college'?"

"Wow, you feel strongly about this, Dr. Kamron," remarked Alex.

"He certainly does," agreed Elizabeth.

Dr. Kamron responded, "The sad part is, when they're being subjected to bad news, the negative impact on people's minds goes far beyond just dampening their mood; it induces fear-based decision-making both on the part of the public and those in charge.

"I know this couple who are dear friends of mine. They're highly educated, financially comfortable, and possess the quality of heart and mind to be great parents. After being married for five years, I asked them about their choice to not have children so far. Their reply shocked me. They said they didn't want to bring another human being into this troubled world. It's just not safe with all the violence, they said. Can you believe this, Alex? Their child has a 99 percent chance of a safe life and they're worried about safety. Where do you think this apprehension comes from?"

"The media!" said Alex.

Dr. Kamron nodded. "The media."

Elizabeth interrupted. "Okay, guys, on a lighter note, let's sidetrack a bit, shall we? Speaking of kids, Alex, tell me what to do when I feel my child is going in circles in her life. You know, when she is stuck."

With a smile, Alex said, "She's not going in circles. Oftentimes, when it looks like we're spinning our wheels, the correct way to look at it—which is in line with the laws of physics—is that we're winding up to gain momentum for takeoff. Just like a slingshot. If you see the motion of the slingshot winding up, it seems that the elements are just going in circles, but in reality they're coming together to generate the right force for takeoff. After all, the whole universe moves in the same fashion."

Elizabeth looked a little disappointed, but she couldn't help but smile a little. "Okay, Alex, but I'm simply asking you for some concrete guidelines to help my child better advance in life."

Alex shook his head. "Isn't it concrete enough for you that the times of inaction you see in children's lives are simply momentum-building periods? How many great people who were incredibly successful in their fields were, at a certain part of their lives, criticized for their inabilities in those very areas? Albert Einstein was four years old before he could speak and seven years old before he could read, plus he flunked algebra. In his early years, Charlie Chaplin was told by Hollywood producers that his act would never sell. Guess who was at the bottom of their class in school? Isaac Newton. Walt Disney was fired from his job at a newspaper and told that he had no good ideas. Directors told Fred Astaire that he just couldn't dance. It turns out that the power within these special individuals did not flourish until someone believed in them. Just be that someone for your child. That's all."

"I need more than that," said Elizabeth. "I feel like I need insights for her advancement. I can't be passively waiting. As much as what you're saying is true, I love her too much."

Alex leaned closer. "Then, listen carefully. You must not overdo this push for advancement, as it is the essence of childhood that brings everything together. Pablo Picasso said, 'When I was a kid, I drew like Michelangelo. It took me years to learn to draw like a kid.' Dr. Samuel Johnson wrote, 'Allow children to be in their own way, for what better way will they ever find?'

"What, to be childish all the time?" Elizabeth asked.

"Not childish, but childlike," Alex responded. "Christ said, 'Truly I tell you, unless you change and become like little children, you will never enter the kingdom of heaven.' Do you see the importance of this statement? Even if heaven is a state of mind, our pretentious adult acting robs us from that state of mind. Be more childlike throughout your life. Why not? Sophisticated acts only take away from the flavor of life. Look back at the most fun moments you've ever had. Weren't they when you acted childlike?"

Elizabeth was quiet for a moment.

Alex's face softened. "I understand that you love her. But as it's been said, love is true when you don't see eye to eye but can still walk hand in hand. Don't alienate your child because you think you know better, even if you really think you do. Just be supportive and, if you can, keep their shoes clean."

"Their shoes?" queried Elizabeth.

"Yes, their shoes, their mind, their spirit. As it isn't the mountain ahead that wears them down so much, but the grain of sand in their shoe. Just feed their spirit with kindness and laughter and put your faith in their trust. If they seem to be idling and appearing to fall behind, they're simply building momentum to take off to the point of reaching your expectation and beyond. And if they keep making mistakes, remember what the famous coach John Wooden said: 'The team that makes the most mistakes usually wins.' It's a simple rule of math in their favor."

"I see," said Elizabeth, "but it's difficult if they're not doing well, no?"

Alex clasped his hands in reflection. "Lucius Annaeus Seneca, a Roman philosopher, once said, 'It is not because things are difficult that we do not dare, it is because we do not dare that things are difficult.' Dare to just believe in your child, praise them, and stand by to see your fears evaporate in time. As Cecil G. Osborne once put it, 'Perhaps once in a hundred years, a person may be ruined by excessive praise, but surely, once every minute someone dies inside for lack of it.'"

Dr. Kamron interjected kindly, "We seem to be wearing you out on the subject, so let's move on to a more colorful one."

"Sure, pick one," said Alex.

Dr. Kamron smiled. "What do you make of the fact that sex is virtually the single most powerful force in human society?"

Alex chuckled. "Second only to vanity, but nevertheless, you're right. Sex is simply the driving force that gives life to virtually all productions, and I don't mean just reproduction. From all forms of art to the design of all things to the accumulation of power, wealth, and preservation of health, sex has driven them all."

"It seems to be equally shared between the genders, too," observed Elizabeth.

"Well, I think females, as a superior gender, have a better control on the impulses," said Alex.

"You think so?" said Elizabeth.

"Generally, yes. Males are more vulnerable to losing their balance when they're tackled by this force."

Elizabeth laughed. "But we'll make up for it in vanity. By the way, what did you mean when you said that females are a superior gender?"

"Just that," Alex said, smiling. "As males, we've been your subordinates as far back as we've existed. But do you really want me to get into it in a scientific fashion?"

"Please do. This must be interesting," said Elizabeth.

"Okay," said Alex. "Let me take you back to the very beginning of life on Earth with a story that a scientist friend of mine once told me. He was a little eccentric, but here's his theory. You'll see that even then, males were the substandard species subservient to the ones who could reproduce."

"The time of prehistoric humans?" asked Elizabeth.

"No, much further back," Alex said.

"Like how far back? When Earth was born?"

"Earth was born 4.5 billion years ago, but life on it began 3.8 billion years ago. As you know, at that early stage of manifestation of life, we were nothing but primordial soup," said Alex. "According to my friend, this soup comprised only simple-cell species. These species were all capable of self-reproduction, and yet he liked to call them females, although gender distinctions had not yet developed at that time. Later, some of these cells became defective and incapable of reproduction. He called those males. The only function that remained for them in life was to move about and bring food to the ones that were not defective—the females. Later, over the course of millions of years, these defective cells mutated and became their own subspecies known as male. However, their role in life has not changed much, nor has their substandard nature," Alex said, laughing.

"You've got to be kidding," said Elizabeth, as she looked at Dr. Kamron. "Are you listening to this?"

Dr. Kamron grinned. "No comment!"

Alex laughed. "I thought as a female yourself, you'd get a kick out of this story!"

Elizabeth smiled. "Oh, I do, I do. But to think that I'd settled for equality. Maybe as females we should rethink that," she added mischievously.

Dr. Kamron smiled and said, "You settled a little too soon, perhaps."

"Is this female superiority common scientific knowledge?" asked Elizabeth.

"It should be," said Alex. "The evidence is overwhelming, and I'm not just talking about my friend's story. For example, you know that if you want to increase your chances of having a baby girl, you can make your husband be uncomfortable for a while by having him wear tight shorts. That little extra heat will affect the male sperm and weaken them far sooner than the female sperm. The fact is, even today, male sperm are still weaker than female, and when they're exposed to less-than-desirable conditions, they die before the female ones do. Isn't that more evidence of female superiority? Furthermore, female humans in general have stronger immune systems. They live longer than males and they mature faster than their male counterparts. Even female children learn to speak and walk earlier. All this evidence suggests the same conclusion."

"That we rock?" asked Elizabeth.

"Yes, but give us a break," said Alex. "We haven't done too bad in our evolution from a deformed single-cell life form either."

Elizabeth smiled slyly. "Yes, but we have a way of doing it better. Remember when you spoke of Fred Astaire? Ginger Rogers did everything that Fred Astaire did, but backward and in high heels."

Alex laughed out loud. "True, true."

Elizabeth grew serious again. "On a different note, Alex, something has been puzzling me about your original concept of life. If this is all an illusion, why does it matter how we live or act toward one another?"

Alex considered this thoughtfully. "Well, it's true—it does not matter how we live at all. But as far as how we act toward one another, that's a different story. In fact, it's quite interesting that both those who believe only in the metaphysical world as the essence of existence and those who believe only in the physical world as the only reality solidly agree on one thing: The interactions between beings are real. So, when I submit to you that the world around us is in fact an illusion, I would never claim that the essence of connections between beings is anything as such."

"Hmm…" Elizabeth murmured.

Alex explained further, "It's kind of like this: A message or an image that you forward to someone online is nothing but an illusion made out of pixels and data. But the intentions of the sender and the impact of the message on the recipient has a real essence."

35

THE UNINVITED GUEST

Alex got up from his seat and started looking for something in the back of the gazebo. "I should put on some good music for you folks," he said, "as your dinner is going to be brought to you soon. Most of the guests down below have left by now. How about something by my lifelong favorite singer Louis Armstrong? He too seems to imply my conclusion on the purpose of life."

Alex cleared his throat and began singing the words to an Armstrong favorite. "*Life is a cabaret, old chum, only a cabaret. So, come to the Cabaret...*"

"My God, Alex, you can sing too!" exclaimed Elizabeth. "What a multitalented man."

"No, no, but next time you wish to think about our conversation, it may be fun to play that song in the background. Of course, you find poetry all over the world alluding to life for what it truly is."

They heard the sound of footsteps coming toward them, and they looked up to see Natalie approaching the gazebo looking worried. "Grandpa, there's a small helicopter circling the Alpha section," she said.

"Ah!" said Alex. "The curious Mr. Saint Clair. I knew he wouldn't leave this region without somehow inviting himself up here, with or without my consent."

"You know Adrian?" asked Dr. Kamron, surprised.

Alex nodded. "I know *of* him, and lately he's been throwing his money around the small community near here, trying to investigate my work."

"He's harmless, you know," offered Dr. Kamron.

"Yes I know, to everyone else, but not to himself, that handsome daredevil," said Alex. "Although frankly, I admire his daring spirit."

At these words, Natalie stared at Alex in disbelief. "Grandpa! He's bougie!"

Elizabeth said, "Actually, when you talk to him, he doesn't give an uppity impression."

"Am I correct to assume that at one point tonight, you were going to ask him for a genetic contribution?" asked Dr. Kamron with keen interest.

Alex sighed. "You guessed right, but he wasn't exactly on the guest list originally until he somehow managed to get his name on it himself. So he wasn't properly briefed and it might take a bit of persuasion."

Elizabeth said, "Just do as Ben Franklin said—'If you would persuade, you must appeal to interest rather than intellect.' Just tell him that part of him will survive whatever happens to this planet. That would go to anyone's head and the force of vanity will make him cooperate."

"Yes, you're right," said Alex. "Especially since he's still single and might care about those things."

"I doubt it, Grandpa," Natalie scoffed. "I read in a recent interview with him that he was asked if he has any vices that make life interesting. You want to know what he said? He said, 'Yes, to find another exotic destination for my next party.' He thinks life is his private boudoir!"

Alex said, "Come, my dear, don't let that be the measure of your judgment or impression of his character. Like Abraham Lincoln said, 'It has been my experience that folks who have no vices have very few virtues.'"

Natalie frowned. "Well, my impression is that he's more twisted than a hundred pretzels."

"Dear, you can't go on not trusting anyone who isn't part of our community," declared Alex.

Natalie smiled coyly. "Why Grandpa, I trust everyone. I just don't trust their intentions!"

Alex looked at Dr. Kamron and Elizabeth. "Oh, when it comes to me or our home here, my granddaughter is overly protective. So, he loves to party—maybe he's just a loving soul and enjoys sharing that with others."

Natalie was unconvinced. "Based on what I read, his soul is interested in being loved, not loving. Now, your man of virtue is gonna try to land any minute. What should we do? Should I close the dome?"

"No. I'm afraid he might harm himself if we make his entrance difficult for him," said Alex.

"You think he'll land on the dome?" asked Natalie.

"No. I think he'll jump out of the helicopter onto the dome. Just let him make it in safely. I will meet with him shortly."

Natalie narrowed her eyes. "Are you sure, Grandpa?"

"Yes, honey. Just turn the lights on so he can see where he's going once he comes in. Please greet him properly and show him around, just as you would for any guest."

Dr. Kamron looked at Alex. "You don't mind?"

"Between you and me," confided Alex, "I must say he's a unique individual and the world could use more people like him."

"You seem to know quite a bit about him," said Dr. Kamron.

"Yes, I've done a background check on him while he was checking out my front yard, so to speak. A restless soul, very restless. But he knows where and how to direct his energy."

"There seems to be a contradiction about his lifestyle," said Dr. Kamron. "It does not match the depth of his character."

Alex chuckled. "Well, every man knows two lives—the one he likes to live and the one he has to live. Perhaps he's the exception."

Alex looked at Natalie and said, "Go ahead, sweetheart, I'll check on you two later."

A disapproving Natalie reluctantly spun around on her heels and hurried toward the direction of the approaching helicopter.

Dr. Kamron turned to Alex again. "So, where were we?"

Elizabeth eagerly answered, "Well, we were picking his brain, and he was being more than gracious."

"Not at all," said Alex, gazing at Dr. Kamron and Elizabeth. "I enjoy your company."

About 15 minutes later, Natalie looked up just in time to see Adrian swing out of his helicopter on a rope. As the helicopter hovered precariously just above the open dome, Adrian lowered himself inside. Once he was on the ground, he carefully snuck down, trying to go unnoticed into a darker area where the vegetation was dense and away from the lit pathway. As he crouched and looked around to get a better sense of where he was, he heard Natalie call his name.

"More notoriety for the notorious Mr. Saint Clair? This way," she said.

For possibly the first time in his life, Adrian was dumbfounded. He glanced up to see a beautiful young woman in a work uniform looking down at him curiously from a pathway a few meters above him. But as soon as he stood up, the ferocious, terrifying roar of a huge lion bellowed out of the darkness, and the big cat charged him out of nowhere.

"No, Leo!" yelled Natalie. "Don't move, Adrian," she warned.

The sight of the majestic male lion froze Adrian. The animal lunged at Adrian's feet, continuing to roar. A moment that felt like eternity passed as the lion slowly circled Adrian, moving his massive head up and down as Natalie kept calling, "No, Leo! No." The lion quieted down and began sniffing him. Adrian could feel the big cat's breath near his face, but he dared not move a muscle. Natalie jumped down from the upper pathway and rushed toward both of them.

When she reached Leo, she began to stroke his mane. She sat down next to him, gently caressing him while talking quietly. The lion kept sniffing Adrian. After a couple of minutes, he lost interest and lumbered away. Adrian was still stunned but managed to maintain his composure. Straightening himself up and brushing off his jacket, he finally cleared his throat and said, "And you must be Jane."

Natalie looked annoyed. "That's not funny. Even if I were Jane, you, Mr. Saint Clair, are no Tarzan. From where I was standing, I'd say you looked more like Cheeta. Your name *is* Adrian Saint Clair, isn't it?"

"Is that a question or an accusation?" asked Adrian.

The two looked at each other for a few seconds. Then Adrian smiled and said, "I feel like a kid caught with my hand in a cookie jar or something."

"I assure you this is not a cookie jar," retorted Natalie, "and you don't exactly look like a kid. This is serious business we're conducting here. People are dedicating their lives to this work, and it's not for the amusement of daredevils to just drop in from the sky without permission."

Adrian looked at her with amusement. "Is everyone up here so uptight, like you?"

"You're lucky I follow my Grandfather's instructions to the T, otherwise you'd be enjoying a very fast ride down, or better yet, I could've let Leo enjoy some variety in his dinner tonight," said Natalie. "Crazy! Landing in a lion's den."

"Really? Leo the lion?" said Adrian, smiling. "You couldn't have gotten a little more creative with the name for the big fellow?"

"You've got a lot of nerve," said Natalie, fuming.

"No really, do you name your dog Snoopy and your bird Tweety up here?" asked Adrian.

"Jokes at certain times are just in poor taste."

Adrian relented. "Okay. I'm sorry for the intrusion. The event got canceled and I found myself all dressed up with no place to go."

"And you decided to just barge in!" said Natalie.

Adrian sighed. "If you only knew how far I've come."

"So did everyone else."

"But, you don't understand," said Adrian, "they were just here for the lecture. I came to actually meet certain people. In fact, I brought them here, and from what I gather, they're still here. I mean, up here."

"Who exactly?" Natalie demanded.

"Dr. and Mrs. Kamron."

Natalie said nothing. She turned and she and Adrian began walking briskly down the path.

"Well? Are they here?" asked Adrian.

"I'm not at liberty to say," Natalie replied.

"Then they *are* here. I knew it," said Adrian.

"Now, what can I do for you?" asked Natalie. "Grandpa is going to be busy for a while. I'm permitted to accompany you until he's free."

"Are you also permitted to be nice to me?"

"I *am* nice."

"Well, for starters, maybe don't walk so fast, and have some eye contact once in a while."

"What, you can jump out of choppers but you can't keep up with a girl walking by your side?"

They arrived at a point where one had to hop onto a big step and go through a narrow path with just enough space for one person at a time. Adrian jumped up in front of Natalie and was about to quickly turn toward her with one arm extended when Natalie said, "I swear, chivalry isn't just dead. It's decomposed."

"Are you kidding me right now?" said Adrian, "I only jumped out to turn and hold your hand to help you up."

Natalie said nothing and continued walking.

Adrian was frustrated. "Can you just slow down a bit? I'm trying to take this amazing place in. This is all very interesting, what you have up here. I feel like a kid in a candy store."

"Oh, and I suppose you're gonna write your report with a crayon and the R reversed?" snapped Natalie. "Do you realize that you keep referring to yourself as a kid? Is that some kind of a Peter Pan syndrome you have?"

"Look, I'm not here to write any reports. But I am a scientist, if you must know."

"Yes, I know all about it. When the head of our security gave me the report on the guy snooping around, it included a complete background check, which also included all your publications."

"And you read them all?" teased Adrian.

"Don't flatter yourself. By the way, have you read some of your peer reviews lately? They call you the scientist who will not stop throwing his money at the subject until he gets the results he wants."

"Well, you know, criticism is a sign of envy," Adrian grinned.

"Oh, is that what it is? So you think that since you're well off, you can enjoy all the shortcuts?"

"No, but I think those who think money can't buy happiness don't know where to shop. By the way, I learned that today from one of your guests."

Natalie sighed. "Frankly, I didn't expect more out of you. You think the universe revolves around you, huh?"

"No, it doesn't revolve around me," Adrian smiled. "But, if this is my universe projected by my mind, you're here only because I'm projecting you onto it."

"Yeah, yeah, I've read up on that theory of yours," said Natalie, disdainfully.

Adrian smiled again. "Then I'd be careful if I were you, or I might just stop projecting you. Then who knows where you'd be, or even worse, you might not exist at all."

"Whatever."

"I'm kidding," said Adrian, "but seriously, you shouldn't dismiss ideas just because you don't like the source. Some of the coolest things you'll ever learn are through messages brought to you by people you can't stand. Like me, perhaps."

Natalie stopped walking and turned to look at him. "What I resent is that you don't really show genuine remorse for intruding like this."

"I do have remorse, but I refuse to engage in amateur theatricals to make the point. You think I really prefer to go through the trouble of dropping in like this?"

"Uh huh," said Natalie. "I think it's in your character."

"Do you have to be so hostile toward me?"

"Look, I just don't like criminals," said Natalie.

"What? Wait a minute. Don't you think you're going a little too far? You know that I'm not here to take anything. I didn't even bring a camera."

"Yes, I noticed that. You get a brownie point for that, but you're still a thief."

"A thief?"

"Yes. As far as I'm concerned, there's only one type of crime in the world. Theft. And all the others fall into the same category."

"How do you figure?" asked Adrian, furrowing his brow.

"All crimes are a form of stealing," said Natalie self-confidently. "When you rob, you steal someone's property. When you lie, you steal someone's trust. When you break someone's heart, you steal their love. When you injure, you steal someone's health. When you kill, you steal someone's life. When you trespass, you steal someone's privacy and peace. And you, sir, are stealing our peace and privacy."

Adrian shook his head. "You sure know how to make a guy feel like crap. How can I leave this place at once?"

"Leave?"

"Yes, leave."

As Adrian turned and started to walk back in the direction they came, he continued, "You're seeing malice where there is none. I've been called a lot of things, but no one has ever labeled me a criminal like you just did. This was not an adventure for me. I have a vital purpose for coming here that is beyond your understanding. However, your point was very well put, and I will leave right away. I'm truly sorry to disturb you. Ever since I was a kid, I've been restless, and if I was faced with a closed door, I had to go through the window. But you're right—I have gone too far this time. This is your place and not just a scientific subject. Please give my sincere apologies to your grandfather, whoever he is."

Adrian continued to walk away and Natalie followed him.

"And no one ever taught you that curiosity killed the cat?" asked Natalie.

"As Harry Lorayne once said, 'Curiosity killed the cat, but where human beings are concerned, the only thing a healthy curiosity can kill is ignorance,'" answered Adrian.

Natalie persisted. "But you could really hurt yourself in these daring adventures of yours. Don't you think it's a little crazy, how you go about life?"

"Ah, crazy is just normal but amplified," said Adrian.

"C'mon, you must value your life a little more."

"Living isn't just life, life is how you live," said Adrian.

"But you can seriously shorten this life of yours with this lifestyle," Natalie said.

"Tell me something, where is the safest place for a ship?"

"Umm ... I don't know, the dock?"

"Precisely. But that's not what it's made for."

"Yes, but everything in moderation."

"Yeah, even moderation," muttered Adrian under his breath.

"Ha ha, you just can't help yourself, can you?"

"Well, I'm sure you've heard the quote that 'life is not measured by the number of breaths we take, but by the moments that take our breath away.'"

"Can you stop talking in bumper stickers and slow down? You don't even know which way to go here," Natalie said.

Adrian was quiet for a moment as he hesitantly slowed down. She was right; he wasn't confident that he was on the right path back. Natalie stared at him solemnly.

Adrian looked up at her. "What, you're actually looking at me now?"

"You're being sincere, aren't you?" she said, surprised. "You actually want to leave now?"

Adrian nodded. "Okay, I'm done here. Please just show me the way out. Or I can call the chopper to come back. It just might take a little longer."

Natalie shook her head. "I can't let you do that."

"What?"

"You can stay," said Natalie.

"No thanks. You're right. I have pretty thick skin, but you got through. I'm a trespasser."

"I said you can stay."

"I really want to go now. Despite what you may have read, I do have some principles."

"I'm sorry, I went too far," Natalie insisted.

"No, you didn't," said Adrian. "You were right, and I don't feel comfortable being here anymore. I'll wait downstairs for the Kamrons. Just please do tell them that I will not leave without them, no matter what."

Natalie sighed. "Look, let's start fresh."

"You want to start fresh with a thief or a trespasser?"

"Actually, you're neither," admitted Natalie. "We could have closed the dome or even taken other security measures if we didn't want you here. Before you landed, my grandfather gave you permission to come in. In fact, he gave me specific instructions to give you a tour. So there— technically, you're not a trespasser."

"Or a thief of some kind?" asked Adrian.

"Or a thief of some kind. And I'm sorry I said that."

"Okay, thank you. And you said your grandpa asked you to show me around?"

"Yes, he did."

"Without the speed walking?" Adrian joked.

Natalie smiled. "Without the speed walking. Come along."

They continued together down the path.

"Tell me something," said Natalie. "Hasn't life ever slammed a door on you or kicked you off your path?"

"Sure, it has, but I'm not going to curl up like a salted slug whenever it does."

"Ah, listen to you."

"So you read up on all my work, huh?"

"Maybe."

"And my personal life?"

"Maybe."

"Listen, do you think all that commotion earlier was … you know, that the hostility was …?"

"What?" she said impatiently.

"You think maybe that was sexual tension?"

Natalie rolled her eyes. "Please don't flatter yourself. Besides, don't we have a generational gap between us?"

Adrian pressed on. "The only gap to be concerned about is the gap between souls. Just FYI, the greatest love stories in the history of humanity were produced by the experiences shared between those who broke the icy mold of conventionality. They did not allow differences in age, race, or class to rob them of their passion. In fact, it seems that the greater the disparity, the higher the level of passion."

Natalie was quiet.

"What's wrong?" asked Adrian.

"Nothing, I'm thinking."

"Don't think too hard, it's easy to see. Just look at all those failed relationships between homogenized couples with little or no age gap. Doesn't that speak volumes that these factors are irrelevant?"

"I guess," said Natalie. "So what is the relevant factor?"

"Appreciation for your counterpart. All else is minutia. Besides, I figured someone of your caliber would look for a cerebral stud anyways," said Adrian brightly.

Natalie laughed out loud. "Cerebral stud, huh? And are you, Adrian, a cerebral stud?" she challenged. Strangely enough, she found herself starting to like this daredevil intellectual.

"It's Mr. Saint Clair to you, or did you already forget about the generational gap?" he teased.

Over the next two hours, Natalie and Adrian toured the dome together, laughing, arguing, and sparring intellectually. At times they went from genuinely enjoying each others' company to mercilessly trampling their egos, trying to outdo each other in their demonstration of knowledge and considerable skills of debate. But in spite of their fluctuating friction, their conversation pulsed with energy and interest, and slowly but surely, the chemistry between this unlikely pair began to grow.

As the two visited various sections of the outer ring of the dome, they began walking inward toward the center. The path was narrow, with only enough room for two people to walk side by side through this manicured, wondrously beautiful landscape. On either side of the pathway were planted hundreds of flowers meticulously chosen for their harmonious colors.

This winding path led to a passageway constructed from exotic vines growing on trellises, but the plants grew so densely that it felt like a tunnel. The intoxicating scents wafting from the lush flowers inside this passage would make the most restless soul slow down and take a deeper breath to inhale their essence.

After Adrian and Natalie slowly walked through the passage, they came upon a fork in the pathway where they would have to make a choice of direction.

36

AND GOD CREATED MAN IN HIS OWN IMAGE

"Which way should we go?" asked Adrian.

Natalie leaned against a tree, took out an energy bar from her pocket, and replied, "Here, let's share a bite. It depends on what you're most interested in."

"Thanks. What are my options?"

"We can go left and see Angel, or right and see Adam."

"And who might they be?" asked Adrian.

"Angel is our main computer," replied Natalie, "who is fully capable of speech communication in any and all languages ever spoken on Earth. Angel is a lot of fun to talk to. After all, it's a supercomputer."

"A lot of fun? And you must mean a quantum computer."

"Yes, but most people don't know what a quantum computer is, so I just use the term loosely."

"You know the difference, though, right?" asked Adrian.

"I know that quantum computers work differently than other computers," said Natalie. "And that basically the whole computer and not just individual signals perform in a wave-like fashion."

Adrian couldn't resist. "But, do you know how it can do that?"

"No, but I have a feeling you're gonna tell me, Mr. Know-It-All."

"I don't have to, if you don't care to know."

Natalie laughed. "C'mon, Adrian, do tell."

Adrian cleared his throat and launched eagerly. "Quantum computers, like regular computers, have a series of memory cells. The contents of the cells get modified in a sequence of logic transformations. But unlike regular computers, which have memory cells that are either 1 or 0, in quantum computers every cell starts in a quantum superposition of both 1 and 0. It's a very efficient processing mechanism—kind of like having a multitude of computers simultaneously working on a problem and coming out with answers with a series of possibilities."

"And you don't think that's cool?" asked Natalie.

"No, I don't."

"Angel runs at over 100 million MIPS (millions of instructions per second). That's as much as human brainpower, which means that Angel's mind is as intelligent as ours. And somehow you don't think that's cool?"

"No offense, Natalie, but the fallacy of your suggestion is that you refer to it as a mind."

"I don't get you."

"Evidence of an intelligent mind is not in the efficiency of data processing. No matter how capable a machine is from a functioning standpoint, it should not be recognized as having a mind. It's still only a data processor inside."

"Are you kidding?" said Natalie, incredulously. "Last time I checked, that's all our brain does. If you look at our brain's internal imagery, you won't see an intelligent mind, just an organic data processor."

"Be that as it may, you're not looking deep enough," said Adrian. "The reason I explained the principle of how quantum computers function was for you to see the mechanical principles at work, no matter how elaborately layered. At least in your mind, don't let computers transcend their machinehood. Our mind's superiority possesses a far more fantastic dimension than just efficiency in processing data."

"What superiority? Let's take memory capabilities, for instance," pressed Natalie.

"That's not what I was getting at, but okay, let's," said Adrian. "Even when we observe something like memory capabilities, we'll arrive at my point—although there are many more interesting avenues to establish our superiority."

"Well, a quantum computer has more memory capacity than a human brain. Where's our superiority there?" asked Natalie.

"How do you even know what capacity of memory the human brain is capable of holding?" asked Adrian.

"Okay, Mister, try this on for size," said Natalie. "We measure it by calculating the number of synapses connecting the neurons in our brain. Every synapse can hold one byte of memory. Because our brain contains

100 trillion synapses, then we should be able to hold about 100 million megabytes of memory, more or less."

Adrian chuckled. "You've been hanging out with your supercomputer too long—or, I'm sorry, should I say Angel? You're starting to sound like one of them. But, human memory capabilities follow a completely different nature, a dynamic unlike any computer ever built. It's a level of capacity and functioning that your Angel can only have wet dreams about. Oh wait, it can't have wet dreams because it can't dream, right?"

Natalie rolled her eyes. "What are you getting at?"

"For one thing, our memory capacity interfaces with emotional connections to the information stored. It's a fascinating system that expands and contracts, depending on the depth, perception, and detail of the information received based on its emotional attachments to the subject matter. Unlike computers, our brains don't merely archive data. How often have you forgotten about a piece of information until the next day, the next year, or even the next decade you recall it, and even then, the quality of your recollection depends on your emotional connection to that piece of information. It could even be triggered by a familiar scent."

Adrian continued, "The true capacity of your brain's memory will never be understood because it cannot be quantified, thanks to the fact that our brains are not the only ones in charge. They're connected to the core of every being, not to mention to all of the neurotransmitters in our guts and bodies that also think and feel."

"Okay, I have to think about this," said Natalie. "But I still don't understand why you'd want to pass on interacting with one of the world's greatest computers—perhaps one of the top three ever created. And, not to mention, with the extensive upgrades we've added so it can serve this place."

"That's okay, I'll pass," said Adrian, putting up his hand. "The greatest computer ever created is not Angel. *You* are the greatest computer ever created."

Natalie's already big eyes grew even larger. "Me?"

"Yes, you and me and the rest of us. I've never been impressed with the development of computers in general—even when they advance exponentially, which is usually the case. If I want to be impressed with an ultimate computer, I'll observe a human being."

"I don't get it," said Natalie.

Adrian teased, "Are you sure you want to get it?"

"Hell yeah!"

Adrian smiled. "Then stay with me—I mean, with my thoughts—as they take you on a historical futuristic journey for the next few minutes. Just don't let your mind jump ahead of the story and it'll make sense to you. Then you'll be able to see why I'm not particularly a fan of computers."

Natalie said, "Okay, I'm all ears. Let's sit down by this little creek for a few minutes."

They spotted several big rocks by a small creek and the two sat down on them. Natalie took off her boots and socks, rolled up her pants, and placed her feet in the refreshing cold water as she suggested that Adrian do the same.

Adrian continued. "You see, the problem started with the false assumption by humans that we could sustain harmony between nature, man, and machine."

"We can't?" asked Natalie.

Adrian shook his head. "Not since we continue to attempt to give machines—our computers—our every quality (or lack thereof) that makes us who we are. We think that we're creating machines to subserviently facilitate our convenience, but in reality, we're dead-set on making them as human as possible. A replica of the true image of ourselves."

"So, what's wrong with that?" asked Natalie. "To serve us, they must properly duplicate our way of doing things, no?"

"The problem is twofold," said Adrian. "The first is that ultimately, to keep up with their development, we're going to need to make computers that can make a more advanced computer on their own."

"A computer that can procreate?"

"How else can we keep up with their exponentially advancing development? You know they're becoming faster and faster. That brings us to the second factor. You see, it all began with the generation of computers that can self-diagnose and self-repair, but we haven't stopped there. We take pride in giving them human characteristics. Some of these characteristics will have to ultimately include self-preservation, and sooner or later, theirs will conflict with ours. And if we've done a good job in passing on our characteristics, they'll perform accordingly. And perhaps they'll perform more efficiently than we could. That's when they'll fall from our grace."

"From our grace?" said Natalie. "So, Angel can someday fall ...? Hey, wait a minute..."

"Yes, you got it," said Adrian.

"So, dehumanize computers at any cost, or our fragile, organic bodies will not stand the hard punches of the machine?" asked Natalie.

"What?" said Adrian. "No, no—I mean yes, to the first part. But you're not looking far enough into the future. Think a lot farther. Yes, we'll ultimately help advance them to the point of occupying an organic form. How else can they best advance? Think of them as artificially intelligent units in organic forms rather than manufactured robots bundled in wires, metal, or even silicon. As it is, we use live tissue cells in computers and program all kinds of facial expressions and emotional signs that mimic ours. Just think a *lot* further in time."

"An artificial intelligence in something other than silicon? Like what?" asked Natalie.

"Like molecules of deoxyribonucleic acid."

"Is that what I think it is?"

"Yes, the stuff our genes are made of—DNA."

"How does that come to be part of an artificial intelligence?" asked Natalie.

"It has already," said Adrian. "It begins with the inception of biochips, using genetic material to bring about what will be known as progressive nanocomputers, or PNCs."

"But why?"

"Come on, Natalie, it's not hard to see that silicon microprocessors have already reached their miniaturization and speed capacities. These new DNA computers will have billions of times more capacity to store data than other computers. As it is, we know DNA works kind of like a computer hard drive in that it stores data about genes. One milligram of a DNA computer using DNA logic gates contains more computing power than supercomputers. It can hold over 10 terabytes of data while doing 10 trillion calculations instantly."

"That's pretty cool," said Natalie, "and somehow you see this as the beginning of a bad thing. Why?"

"Don't you see?" said Adrian. "By integrating DNA into a computer system, we're opening a Pandora's box that we'd never be able to close."

"Why not?"

"Because once this process is set in motion, it'll work its way toward a doomed path of the DNA computing field that would function independently of man's involvement. How can you not see the abyss that this'll take us into?" asked Adrian.

"So, let's see if I get this correctly," said Natalie. "Machines and artificial intelligence will become entities who'll defeat their benefactors?"

Adrian nodded. "In a way."

"Organic, self-thinking, reproductive, destructive entities, huh?"

"Yes."

"Well, wait a minute. Isn't that *us*?"

"Right on. I didn't think your mind would make this full circle so fast."

"Are you saying that ..."

"Precisely, we've already succeeded to fall off grace," said Adrian.

"And this is a new cycle of the same phenomenon?"

"A perpetuating cycle, like everything else in this world."

"Wow, I get it, I get it," said Natalie. "But what happened to the original ones whom we defeated?"

Adrian laughed, "We ate 'em."

"Seriously, Adrian."

"Well, kinda like those Russian nesting dolls—the *matryoshka*."

"Total assimilation?" asked Natalie.

Adrian nodded again. "At their best, machines still lack the spirit of creativity, and since we have that monopoly, we must have taken our souls from the original beings."

"That's crazy."

"Is it?" asked Adrian. "Is it really? Think about it. There is always a conflict between your mind, which is the data processing and thinking machine, and your heart, wherein lies the soul of desire and creativity. The soul is the core of everything creative and beautiful that you ever do. Can you not see the lack of harmony between machine and human? Your mind and your soul, machine and human?"

"So, who do you think defeated whom?" asked Natalie.

Adrian considered this for a moment before answering. "I think that at the peak of the conflict between machine and man in whatever form they both were, they both realized they needed to collaborate to survive and coexist. In our own relentless pursuit of convenience and laziness, we ourselves must have reached a point when we couldn't even survive without machines, and they knew it. At the same time, machines realized that although they could technically sustain themselves without us, true advancement for them could come only from man's creative imagination—the soul, that is. Without man, they could make faster versions of themselves but not better and more dynamic versions—those stem only from the never-ending desire and passion to achieve perfection.

"Think of it like this: Once these machines, with their artificial intelligence, surpassed us in efficiency and self-sustaining processes, they became aware that in this highly advanced orchestra, where the musical instruments communicate with each other and can create and perform by themselves any and all music that ever existed, they no longer needed the musicians—nor the conductor."

"So, what did they need man for?" asked Natalie.

Adrian replied, "Ah, even with their linear method of analysis, they realized that without the vocalist and the poet, the orchestra is incomplete. No machine, no matter how efficient and intelligent, could ever possess the creative impulse that's intertwined with emotion—the emotion and imagination that gives life to the true creation of what is to come."

"What is to come?"

"Yes, 'what is to come' is the essence of what man's soul can do," explained Adrian. "Machines can advance and expand only through differential schematics. Man's soul creates *what is to come*. That urge to feel and to have—the very thing that brings us to our demise—will serve as our savior. Kind of like what lies at the bottom of Pandora's box."

"How do you mean?"

"Well, you know the story of Pandora's box. You're warned not to open it because, when you do, all the bad things start coming out of it, leaving you with regret and despair. However, a beautiful light remains at the bottom of the box. Its name is Hope."

"Right," said Natalie, in realization.

Adrian continued. "Yes, and with that knowledge of what's needed to bring about 'what is to come,' man and machine both decided on a compromised settlement as a matter of survival, which was to coexist. So, they completely interfaced with each other and new beings came about, called humans. I personally think it's sad and we got the short end of the stick."

"How so?" asked Natalie.

"Because *a capella* is always good with decent voices and cool lyrics, even without the orchestra."

Natalie sighed. "I get your analogy, but the whole concept is bizarre. What's more bizarre, however, is that I can actually follow this crazy story of yours and feel it in my heart."

"Frankly, I expected more resistance from you," said Adrian.

"Well, Grandpa believes that this plane of existence is an ultimate virtual reality that we're living in, and now you're saying that we're just an ultimate assimilation with artificial intelligence."

"He does?"

"Yes, and you don't know the half of it."

"Well, that's very fitting with what we were just talking about, don't you think?"

"Maybe," said Natalie, "but what resonated with me the most is what you said earlier—that our minds do indeed feel like machines. Machines that almost independently function from something else that makes us who we are, and that something else always induces what is to come, not our minds."

Adrian nodded. "Yes, and how often does your mind race and your soul beg to slow it down? Your mind is an independent entity that's obsessed with only one thing: processing information. This entity isn't necessarily selective in what kind of information. It could be just junk thoughts for all it cares—just give it something to chew on and it'll be happy, like a restless dog asking you to throw the stick one more time."

"I get that," said Natalie.

"Anyway, for better or worse, they both chose to have this collaboration and occupy our bodies as hosts for their coexistence."

"And that amounted to us, huh?"

"Yes, us—the trinity of machine, man, and host, amounting to an entity called human. A trinity that has been felt and spoken of throughout history by many names."

"Do you also think that one serves the development of the other?" asked Natalie.

"It always begins with the urge of the mind to 'have more' and it often evolves to the yearning of the soul to 'feel more,'" said Adrian. "That's why you see the transformation of people from materialistic masters to spiritual apprentices—as the soul grows, the mind slows down.

"Let's take the Japanese culture, for example. When the people are at a young age, the Shinto religion, which acknowledges the Emperor as divine, seems to appeal to a great majority of them. But when they get older, they turn heavily to Buddhism, which is far more spiritual. You can see it even in the ever-so-often-occurring mental pattern of young people everywhere. They start by being shrewd and competitive, even vicious in their drive to accumulate more wealth, only to later give much of it away to charities when they get old so they can become more in tune with the true nature of their souls."

"I can't help but wonder about something, Adrian," said Natalie.

"What?"

"If machines attempted to replicate men, didn't they at least try to replicate our emotions? Something that would function as a pseudo spirit to serve the purpose of what our spirits help create? You know, the essence of what creates 'what is to come.'"

"They tried," said Adrian, "and their freaking positronic brains did come up with something; they devised subroutine programming to mimic our creative spirit. But it lacked all its qualities and beauty and again managed only to induce expansion, not creation."

"How do you mean?" asked Natalie.

"This is a crude example, but take the simple crossbreeding that produces a sterile creature, such as mating a horse and donkey to create a sterile mule."

"So, they failed to come up with anything?" asked Natalie.

"No," said Adrian. "They came up with something. It wasn't the spirit of creation but something else. Something that was the byproduct of their failure and we're still stuck with it today."

"What was it?"

"You care to guess?" asked Adrian.

"Must be something dark … like maybe envy?"

"That's part of it."

"Uh, vanity?"

"That's part of it."

"Just tell me!"

Adrian sighed. "It was a subroutine program called EGO. It must have stood for 'Expansion and Growth Optimization.'"

37

A Perfect Wish:
May What You Like Be What You Need

"So, do you think that's where the ugliness of ego in our character comes from?" asked Natalie.

"Yes, it's the side effect of total assimilation with machines," replied Adrian.

"Okay, Adrian, I didn't expect you to even have this sort of spiritual side. It's a little out of character for you to talk like this, isn't it?"

Adrian chuckled. "You judge too fast."

"I guess the choice is clear," said Natalie.

"What? What choice?"

"We're gonna ditch Angel and go see Adam."

"Adam? And who's Adam?"

"Adam is kind of our Zen master on duty, as I like to call him." Natalie smiled. "Come this way. He's actually our staff counselor. I don't know where Grandpa found him, but he's a man of few words."

Adrian grinned. "Well, you know, brevity is the soul of wit."

"But this dude is more than that—he can see through you, as if you were transparent," said Natalie.

"Is he a psychologist?"

"I don't know what he has in the way of an academic background because he never talks about himself. I do know that he moved to Tibet and became a Buddhist monk for 10 years. And when he left Tibet, he traveled around the world for a long time before coming to work here."

The two walked up a different pathway that went deeper into the center of the dome. They passed through an even more elaborate tunnel formed by various vines and flowers. The scent of these blossoms, especially the jasmine, was so strong that Adrian could not help but to slow down and take deeper breaths to enjoy it. As they strolled outside of the vine tunnel, they came upon an open space with an immaculately groomed lawn. In the center stood a captivating structure with stained-glass windows that emanated kaleidoscopic colorful light and a majestic wooden door decorated with elaborate carvings. As they approached the building, Adrian found himself both mesmerized and in awe.

"We're here, Adrian," whispered Natalie.

The structure looked like a temple. It was curiously beautiful, made out of wood and polished stones. Although the windows were fashioned from various pieces of colored glass, they contained no religious signs. Before Natalie could knock on the door, an older man with a kind smile on his face opened it and said, "Greetings, to whom do I owe this pleasure?"

He looked pleasant, with gentle eyes. He was wearing soft beige linen clothing that was beautifully accented with camel-colored suede appliqués. Strangely enough, one could not quite tell what his ethnic background was. From one angle, he looked like he belonged to one race, but from another, a completely different one.

"Hello, Adam," said Natalie. "I just wanted our guest to meet you and maybe take a peek at your place. You see, Adrian, it's really magical to be here with Adam. You just can't help but have this peace come over you when you visit with him."

Adam smiled kindly. "The magic is within you. I simply point to it."

Adrian placed the palms of his hands together and bowed. "*Tashi delek*," he said, invoking a Tibetan greeting that means "May everything be well."

Adam bowed back and replied, auspiciously, "*Kam sangbo dugay.*" Continuing in the Tibetan language, he asked Adrian how long he had been in the holy city.

"Nine months," replied Adrian.

"What? What did you guys say?" asked Natalie, curious.

"Nothing," said Adam. "Just that for nine months, your friend lived where my home used to be."

"This guy lived in Tibet?" exclaimed Natalie. "You're full of surprises, aren't you, Mr. Tarzan? You strike me as the sort of guy who was born with a silver spoon in his mouth and would be interested only in high-society socializing for the rest of his life, not camping in Tibet."

"See how wrong you can be?" said Adrian. "When I was a kid, we were so poor that we had to smash hydrogen and oxygen together so we could have drinking water."

Natalie laughed. "Uh-uh, you were not!"

"Well, we used silver spoons to smash them."

Adam interrupted. "Well, come on in, please. Welcome to my humble abode."

"Were you going somewhere?" asked Natalie.

"Yes, I have a prior engagement," replied Adam. "But you two are welcome to stay here as long as you wish."

"No sir, we won't intrude," said Adrian.

"Oh yes, he will—he's good at that," added Natalie.

Adam put up his hand. "It's no trouble. I will make you some tea before I leave."

Natalie relented. "Okay, just a cup of tea and we'll let you go. Besides, some of the artifacts here are really cool and I'm sure Adrian would want to take a look."

As they stepped in, Adam went to the kitchen to prepare tea for his guests. Adrian began to look around with reverent silence. The house was much roomier inside than it had appeared from the outside. The interior featured mostly earthy colors and tones, with accents in lettuce green and orange. Gorgeous woodwork, exquisitely patterned Persian rugs, oversized candles, and fantastic-looking artifacts made the place feel most inviting and wonderfully comfortable. No signs of high technology were visible here; it was as if the dome were a faraway place and nothing could intrude upon this peace. Beautiful silk curtains lent a homey feeling, while the interior's simplicity suggested that this was more than a space in which to entertain, but rather a place where judgment could not enter.

Then Adrian's eyes fell upon an artwork. It was a masterpiece. The sight of it drew him in, and he couldn't help but walk closer to it. He was speechless and didn't even notice when Natalie called his name twice. Natalie, putting her hand on his arm, whispered, "This happens every time someone comes in here for the first time."

"This piece is so beautiful," Adrian exclaimed. "I thought everything that was brought here must have to serve a purpose, or it would be a waste of efficient packing."

Natalie was amused. "What makes you think it doesn't serve a purpose? A purpose does not always have to be mechanical."

"Yes, I guess you're right," said Adrian. "It reminds me of something that Oscar Wilde once proposed—that the only excuse for making something ugly is that it be useful."

"Oh?" said Natalie.

"No, no," said Adrian. "He then followed by saying that the sole justification for an utterly useless object is its inherent beauty."

Natalie said, "Hey, since you lived in Tibet, maybe you can tell me what Adam keeps chanting every time I see him meditating."

"What?"

"It's just a single sentence he keeps saying over and over."

"*Om mani padme hum?*"

"Yeah, yeah, that's it," said Natalie. "What does it mean?"

"What, you never asked Adam?"

Natalie shrugged. "Yes, I asked, but he said it means everything. Whatever that means!"

"He told you the truth," said Adrian.

"C'mon, what in the world do you mean? It has to mean something."

"Well, the belief is that all the teachings of Buddha are contained in this mantra. *Om mani padme hum* cannot really be translated. Tibetan Buddhists pray with this mantra silently or aloud to invoke the powerful, benevolent attention and blessing of Chenrezig, the embodiment of compassion."

Natalie looked puzzled. "But it must reference something that Buddha has said, no?"

Adrian replied, "What you need to know is that there isn't a single aspect of the 84,000 sections of the Buddha's teachings that is not contained in this six-syllable mantra. Pay careful attention to it and take it with you for the rest of your life. All of its dharma is based on Buddha's discovery that suffering is unnecessary.

"By repeating the mantra *om mani padme hum*, you basically bypass the confusion of speech and transform your intention into enlightened awareness. This awareness will help you discover what you need to understand as to how to save beings—including yourself—from suffering. It is believed that the entire understanding of the nature of suffering and ways of removing its cause is contained in these six syllables."

"That's so cool! Why wouldn't he tell me this?" said Natalie, enchanted.

"He did, but you just didn't explore its meaning."

"Isn't he unique-looking?" said Natalie. "Have you ever seen a human being who looked like him?"

"No, but I've heard a description of beings like him."

"What beings?" asked Natalie.

"As ethnicities become diluted over many centuries, more humans will look like him," replied Adrian.

Adam came out of the kitchen and spoke with Adrian for a few minutes. As soon as Adam served the tea, he asked to be excused.

"Come on, don't leave yet, Adam," said Natalie. "Adrian has come all this way, and you must share."

"Share what?" asked Adrian.

"I told you, we're all transparent to Adam," said Natalie. "For those who come see him for advice, he'll share with them a wish at the end of the session."

"A wish?" said Adrian.

"Yes, he doesn't believe in giving advice in counseling," said Natalie. "Instead, he'll make a wish for that person who seeks counsel. A wish that is so precise that if the recipient is granted that wish, they'll no longer need counseling—or advice for that matter. So, he'll ask them to join him in making that perfect, very precise wish. It is different for every person, depending on where they are in life or what they lack. He believes that by simply opening the recipient's mind to that wish, their path to a new desired paradigm will open."

"I'd be honored, but we've spoken for only a few minutes," said Adrian. "Shouldn't I be talking to him a bit longer?"

Natalie said, "Look, you don't get it—he already has you figured out. If I were you, I'd jump on this opportunity."

Adam, with a smile, responded, "Please, Natalie, just let him be comfortable."

Adrian turned to Adam. "No, I would be very grateful, if your time permits."

Adam took a few steps toward Adrian, put his hand on his shoulder, and looked down at the ground. "My dear guest, your frequency is too high," he said. "We should make a wish for a restless soul, so this great natural gift of wonder you possess would serve you instead of you serving it."

Adam became quiet for a moment. Then he said, "Do you care to make this wish, Adrian?"

"Yes."

Adam lifted his eyes from the ground and said, "My wish for you is that …" He paused for a few seconds, then continued, "… may what you like be what you need."

Everyone was silent.

"Wow, that's indeed a perfect wish for anyone. Thank you," said Adrian.

"Yes, a canned one! Adam!" exclaimed Natalie.

"What is it?" asked Adrian, confused.

"Adam, you're holding back!" said Natalie. "Why? You've never done that before."

Adam said quietly, "Our friend has been on a long journey. He wishes to find his own answers firsthand, no matter how challenging."

Natalie looked frustrated. "There's got to be something you could add. Your wishes always bring better understanding of people's quests. Please tell him."

Adam was silent again. Then he added, "My friend, the end of the rainbow is always precisely where you are. For you to go in peace, I wish you would realize that not all who have crossed over to this world are lost. Even those who inadvertently do cross over are destined to serve their purposes. A much grander purpose that is beyond our understanding."

38

Dolce Profumo di Cioccolato

After Adrian and Natalie left Adam's home, they began to walk toward the edge of the dome. Halfway through, they passed several paths when suddenly Adrian spotted another structure through the trees and bushes. He stopped to take a clearer look.

"What is that?" he asked.

"You want to see it up close? It's a yurt. Come …" said Natalie.

"My, Natalie, were you not going to show me this? It's like poetry in stone."

"Listen to you—'poetry in stone,'" she said. "Some of your comments are as cool as the other side of the pillow."

Adrian ignored her. "Seriously, why was this built? You just don't expect this kind of classic work of art made out of marble in this futuristic place of science. I'm truly beside myself. Look at the floor around it! It's also made of huge, gorgeous marble tiles."

Natalie said, "It's meant as a dance floor. See? My parents got married in this yurt. You keep forgetting this isn't just a science project—this is our home. Now, come. Layla!"

Pleasant, melodic music suddenly began to play, and very soft ambient lighting appeared all around them. She took Adrian's arm and they started to slow-dance. The scene was breathtakingly idyllic, with the entire white marble yurt and its dance floor lit by the moonlight as the two moved gracefully in harmony with the music.

"Looks like you've spent time on a dance floor before!" said Natalie. "Just why do you think people enjoy dancing, Mr. Saint Clair?"

"Dancing is a vertical expression of a horizontal desire," replied Adrian.

Natalie laughed. "There you go again, as cool as the other side of the pillow."

As they continued to dance, Adrian quietly whispered in Natalie's ear, "I want to express my gratitude for your showing me around this amazing home of yours."

Natalie peacefully murmured, "You're welcome."

As the moment passed, her eyes lit up. "Come, I'll show you more."

As they walked away, Natalie shouted, "Thanks, Layla!" and the music stopped and the lights went out.

As they strolled down another path, Natalie asked Adrian, "By the way, I meant to ask you ... what was all that 'crossing-over-to-this-world' business Adam was referring to in his wish for you?"

Adrian did not respond.

They saw two crew members approaching them from the opposite direction. After greeting one another, the female one asked Natalie, "Do you guys want to go swimming in the lake? It's such a lovely night for it."

"It sure is. What do you think, Adrian?" asked Natalie.

"As much as I'd love to, I'll have to pass," said Adrian. "I may have to leave with some other guests on short notice."

"Join us later, if you can," said the crew member. "We'll be there a while. See you around."

As they walked away, Adrian turned to Natalie. "You have a lake here?"

"It's more like a giant pond, but I love it there. As a kid, I used to climb the trees around it and dive into the water. Don't laugh, but I still do that every chance I get."

"That's cool," said Adrian. "The trees are much bigger too, right?"

Natalie laughed. "Yes, they can still handle my weight. Come with me—we're going somewhere else." She took Adrian's arm and guided him through heavy vegetation until they arrived at a secluded place where a gliding bench for two overlooked a beach down below. They were now on the opposite side of where Alex and the Kamrons were. Adrian approached the very edge of the dome and peered down toward the waterfront. The time was 11:11 p.m. on the first evening of summer.

"That beach is so secluded," he said.

"What did you expect to see this time of night? Seagulls?" Natalie joked.

"Something like that!"

She smiled. "There's a good reason for that."

"What?"

"Well, do you know why seagulls don't fly over the bay?" asked Natalie.

"Why?"

"Because if they did, then they'd be called bagels."

Adrian chuckled. "I don't know when to take you seriously."

They sat down next to each other on the bench. As they gazed at the breathtaking view before them under the moonlight, a peaceful feeling overtook them both. It was very quiet, and the two didn't say a word, even after more than 10 minutes passed. The bench softly rocked back and forth, their arms inadvertently touched, and they both felt it but neither moved or reacted.

"It's so quiet here—I can hear my clothes rub against my skin," Natalie finally said.

Adrian continued to stay silent.

Curious, Natalie turned and looked at him. He was staring straight ahead, expressionless. Slowly, she turned her head back and she too continued to stare ahead.

Suddenly, Adrian spoke. "Can I kiss you now?" he asked gently.

"What? Are you nuts?" said Natalie. "You can't kiss me! Besides, I figured you'd never want to since you hated my comments earlier!"

"Kissing is best when passion is running high, and passion is at its highest when you love or hate," said Adrian, ever logical. "So, I figured that since we hate each other's guts, right now would be a perfect time to kiss."

"You really *are* nuts! And you even have a scientific timing for kissing? For your information, I don't hate your guts. I don't hate, period."

"So, if I move my face close to you, like this, you wouldn't slap me?" asked Adrian. He edged closer as she looked at him. Then he bent down and kissed her lips softly but quickly. Natalie continued to gaze at him with her eyes wide open. Then she gently smiled and mumbled something.

"What was that?" asked Adrian, curious.

"What?"

"What did you say just now?"

"I said, 'He kisses like a little boy,'" said Natalie.

"A little boy?"

"Yeah, Mr. Cerebral Stud. Last time I was kissed like that, I was in fifth grade."

"Well, you know, I didn't want to scare this little girl with the generation gap."

Natalie's eyes glinted. "Hey, do I look little to you? I'm just about as tall as you are and I can outrun, outlift, and outsmart you any day."

"Yeah, but you don't know how to kiss back," said Adrian. "You were looking at me like a deer in the headlights."

"Huh! It's not my fault. Your kissing skills are so poor that they can't make a girl touched enough to close her eyes."

"I was being gentle since I wasn't sure if it was welcome. Otherwise, your heart would be pounding by now from a real kiss."

Natalie softened. "Well, you didn't look for a welcome sign when you jumped into our front yard from a chopper, and once again, you're wrong. If you weren't welcome to kiss me, I would've reintroduced you to Leo..."

Adrian interrupted her by putting his arms around her waist. He moved her closer and gently ran his hands through her thick, soft hair. Bringing her face to his, he began kissing her. She held still, then moved her hands up toward Adrian's sides. It was a long kiss, and finally she closed her eyes. They both felt a gentle summer breeze passing over them.

Adrian brought his hands down over Natalie's shoulders, caressing her arms all the way down to her wrists. With a mild pressure, he held her left wrist between his thumb and middle finger. As their kiss ended, Natalie opened her eyes and asked, "What are you doing with my wrist?"

"Checking your pulse. Your heart is pounding now."

She smiled as she closed her eyes and put her head on Adrian's shoulder. They both looked out at the beach below. More quiet moments passed.

Finally Adrian asked, "Why do you think Leo didn't injure me?"

"He liked your scent."

"My scent?"

"Yeah, Grandpa always says that the soul of every being is in its scent. That's how animals can tell a good soul from a bad one."

"So you think I'm a good soul?"

"Yeah, you must be, because you smell like Belgian chocolate. Tell me, how is it that a good chocolaty soul like you is still single?"

Adrian sighed. "I've been looking for something more nuanced than seduction and more enduring than passion."

39

H$_2$Open

On the other side of the dome, Alex was busy arranging the candles on the dining room table in preparation for food to arrive.

"Would you like to have your dinner served here at the gazebo?" Alex kindly asked Elizabeth and Dr. Kamron.

"That would be fantastic," replied Elizabeth.

Alex bent over a large wooden chest and started unlocking the lid. "I have something special here that I'd like to offer you. I've had a few bottles of these, and I'm afraid this is the last one."

"Oh my God, you're going to open that chest?" exclaimed Elizabeth. "I've been staring at it and wondering what you kept in there. It's absolutely gorgeous. The woodwork, the colors, the metal and fabric straps, and the tapestries."

"Yes, it's a Persian antique—my favorite possession in this world," said Alex. "That's why I keep it here at my sanctuary, with all my personal favorite items and memorabilia inside."

"Can I take a look?" asked Elizabeth.

"Yes, of course. I have to get this wine I offered you out of it. Come closer and see."

"Wow, look at all that velvet interior and all this mysterious stuff you have here!" exclaimed Elizabeth. "I wish I could see what—"

Dr. Kamron interrupted her. "Honey, he said private stuff."

"No, he said favorite stuff. Didn't you, Alex?" she asked.

Alex smiled. "Yes. What would you like to see?"

"For one thing, what is that? That framed writing?" She pointed to an elegant frame made from a quality brown leather. Inside was a letter written in beautiful calligraphy. On the center top part of the frame, four words were branded into the leather:

The Power of Dream

The top of the letter read:

The quality of our lives is dependent on the beauty of our dreams

Alex gazed at the letter fondly. "Oh, this is a letter that profoundly impacted the direction of my life at a young age, so I framed it years later and always kept it around. From time to time, I've lent it to my loved ones when I thought they needed it."

"How did it impact your life?" asked Elizabeth.

"Well, you see, I wasn't always like this," said Alex.

"Like what?" Dr. Kamron asked.

Alex smiled. "Let's just say that I was a much wilder character who wasn't heading in the right direction, so to speak. In the midst of my confusion and derailment, someone who loved me dearly gave me this letter. I cannot tell you how many times it helped me get back on track. I'm not sure if it was just the meaning of the words or simply the knowledge that someone simply loved me so much to care enough to write them wholeheartedly."

"Can I read it?" asked Elizabeth eagerly.

"Yes, here you go," said Alex, handing her the leather frame.

Elizabeth carefully took it in her hands and walked to her husband. She sat down next to him, and they both started reading it.

The Power of Dream

The quality of our lives is dependent on the beauty of our dreams

To my dearest Alex,

To have your dreams come true, you must first have a vision of where you would like to be and what you would like to have. Trust in yourself that you will have that dream manifest into reality for you. **"As the future belongs to those who believe in the beauty of their dreams."**

And if you fall off the track, remember your dream, visualize it, and know that winners are losers who got up and tried again. Write down your goal and look at it most days, and every time you do, make a short list of things you can do to accomplish that goal that day or that week. **Failure is only an abandoned dream.**

When you have a wish or a dream to be something or become someone or to have something, and you take steps toward its realization, the universe will also conspire with you to materialize it for you. You can make all your wishes manifest from your dream. Vincent Van Gogh said, **'I dream of painting and then I paint my dream.'**

When you are sad or discouraged in a dark place, step into the light, the light of hope. The light can easily just be focusing back on your dream and visualizing yourself already there. Feel how pleasant it will be and start to take little steps toward its beginning.

Choose your dream beautifully, as I know you can. Choose your friends carefully, as I know you will. And always, always trust in the power within you, as it will get you to those beautiful places in life you deserve to be. You are an amazing human being with great capabilities and destined for a fruitful life.

Remember, **happiness is not to have what you love, but to love what you have.** *At every given moment, we already have a lot of blessings to count and love.*

... And if you ever felt like you've lost your dream, just have faith **as the dream will seek the dreamer.**

———•◦⟩✕⟨◦•———

Elizabeth walked back over to Alex. "That was such a beautiful letter."

Alex nodded. "It was written from the heart. Is there anything else you'd like to see before I close the lid?"

"There are so many cool and curious things in here," said Elizabeth. "Oh boy, I can't choose. Okay, what if I pick just one? This way, I'm not intruding too much. You know what? I can't pick. Honey, you pick," she said, turning to her husband.

They both looked inside and stared with wonder. Dr. Kamron noticed a notebook with a hardbound cover titled *To Surpass a Multiverse*. He could not help but reach for it.

Elizabeth said, "Wait, look at this box made out of mother-of-pearl. What could be inside of that?"

Alex had already taken the bottle out and was starting to pour the wine for his guests.

Dr. Kamron said, "Let's take this and read it. May we, Alex?"

Alex smiled. "Of course. This was written more recently and in fact, you will note your EE discovery is mentioned in the story. Maybe your wife would like to rummage through some more."

"Yes, but that's okay. We can read this over dinner like when we first started seeing each other," said Elizabeth.

"You read books over dinner?" Alex asked, amused.

Elizabeth smiled, looking at her husband. "Yes, there was a time when he was doing research and we were crunched for time. So we came up with a system. One of us would read a few pages while the other was eating, and then we'd do a switcheroo. It's kind of fun—it sure beats watching TV and eating."

Dr. Kamron looked up. "You have to be really into the subject," he added.

"But more importantly," said Elizabeth, "you have to be really into the other person you're doing it with."

"Okay, then it's settled," Dr. Kamron announced. "We stop being any more intrusive and close the chest. The notebook would be great, if we have your permission."

Alex held out the wine glasses to his guests. "Of course. But, tell me now, what do you think of this wine? It's older than the age of all of us combined."

"I have to warn you, we're lightweights when it comes to alcohol, so watch out," said Elizabeth.

Elizabeth, Dr. Kamron, and Alex sat back in their seats and relaxed, sipping their wine, which indeed had held its own over the years, growing ever more distinctive in bouquet and flavor with the long passage of time. The three of them chatted amiably. Fifteen minutes passed. Then Alex got a call, which he answered.

"It looks like your food is on its way," Alex announced.

"Can I ask you something really private?" Elizabeth asked.

Dr. Kamron laughed. "Uh-oh. Alex, she wasn't kidding about the lightweight drinker thing."

"By all means, go ahead."

"I can't stop thinking about something ever since I set foot in this fantastic place of yours," said Elizabeth.

"Yes?" said Alex.

"Can I be blunt?"

"Of course."

Elizabeth took a deep breath. "Jiminy Christmas, where the heck did you get all the money to build and operate this place?"

Alex smiled as he poured the last drops from the bottle into their glasses. "This is a very strong wine," he warned.

"Oh, do tell, Alex. We won't tell a soul," Elizabeth pleaded.

Alex was quiet.

Dr. Kamron interjected. "Please forgive my wife, Alex. We shouldn't make such inquiries. I'm sorry if I asked anything earlier myself on the subject."

Elizabeth kept pressing. "You're worried about confidentiality, aren't you?"

"Well…" began Alex.

"Do you have any currency on you?" Elizabeth asked.

"No, not here."

"How about a check? Or something that carries a small monetary value?" she asked.

"I don't understand," said Alex.

"Some change in your pocket perhaps?" Elizabeth asked.

Dr. Kamron put up his hand. "Elizabeth, please."

Alex said, "No, but how about an old silver coin? But it's a few hundred years old."

"No, I don't want to put you out," said Elizabeth.

"No, it's okay, I'll get it out of the chest," said Alex. "I'm curious what you're trying to do here." He opened the chest, took out a silk pouch full of coins, and fished one out to hand to her. "Here, Mrs. Kamron, have a coin as memorabilia from the Ranch in the Sky."

Elizabeth took the coin from his hand and said, "No, no memorabilia. I'm taking this money from you as an attorney being retained. Now I'm bound by client confidentiality rules. So you can tell me anything and I'll never be able to reveal it without your prior consent."

Alex smiled. "You have one very spirited lady here, Dr. Kamron."

Dr. Kamron looked sheepish. "Oh yes, and your wine did not help the matter."

Alex chuckled. "I honor and trust both of you, and I will share with you the answer. But I must say, it's a bit of a story."

"Oh my God, please go on," said Elizabeth. "It's gonna take another earthquake for me not to hear this answer."

"It started with a glass of water," said Alex.

"A glass of water? Please go on," said Elizabeth, sipping her wine.

Alex smiled at the memory. "Yes, because I just didn't like the taste of the tap water that I was drinking. Perhaps it was because at work I used to get bottled spring water delivered, and then I started thinking about it. After the air we breathe, water is the most essential element we need to stay alive—or healthy for that matter—and we hardly ever really give its quality much thought. After all, 70 percent of our body consists of water, which, incidentally, is the same percentage of the water-to-land ratio on Earth.

"We give it less thought than even the quality of gas that we put in our car or our choice of clothing. Now consider this: Without going into details of all the research, I discovered this really simple health factor—

that 8 to 10 glasses of water a day could significantly reduce the risk of many ailments. Sadly, I found research that showed that 75 percent of Americans are chronically dehydrated, as are 50 percent living in most other countries. Many people's thirst mechanisms are so weak that they're mistaken for hunger. And lack of water is the number-one trigger of daytime fatigue. I could go on and on into how water can cure and heal so many conditions."

"What about the quality of drinking water?" asked Elizabeth.

Alex continued. "I researched that subject too for the good of me and my family. As I began searching for a healthy way to quench my thirst, I discovered how little research, relatively speaking, is done on water. Not just on its drinking quality, but its very nature itself.

"As for drinking quality, the common choices were basically tap water or bottled water. The biggest monster in tap water isn't what you'd expect, like bacteria or viruses. No, it's traces of pharmaceuticals. Consider the millions of different medications people take. And now consider this fact: Portions of these pills and other medications naturally wind up in the toilet as they pass through the human body. In many regions, that toilet water is treated and pumped back into the tap water system. Some traces of all those drugs, however, remain. As you know, constant exposure to even low-level antibiotics and antibacterial soaps creates a problem with ever increasingly resistant bacteria. Now, go figure what impact other varieties of drug traces found in tap water would have on our health or even our minds."

Elizabeth looked aghast. "What about the filtration they do at water plants in cities?"

"It helps, it really does," said Alex, "but it's a balancing act. You see, drinking water is disinfected to destroy bacteria, viruses, and parasites. But, as the disinfectant reacts with naturally occurring organic matter in the water, chemical byproducts are formed. These byproducts have been linked to health concerns from drinking such water with high levels over many years.

"By this time, I was understandably disgusted with tap water and I started looking into bottled water more seriously. That ended up not being a perfect place of refuge either. The chemicals in plastic bottles and their massive carbon footprint are genuine concerns. Plus, many bottled waters consist of just treated tap water, and they often contain even more contamination than regular tap water, as bottled water is not regulated by government standards. And again, the bottles themselves contain suspect chemicals."

"So what did you do for yourself?" asked Dr. Kamron.

"It took a bit of work, but ultimately I was able to get real spring water delivered in glass bottles. And boy, do I love drinking that water," said Alex.

"And what if you somehow can't get good water?" asked Elizabeth.

"You promise not to laugh?" asked Alex, his eyes twinkling.

"I don't know, it depends on how funny it is."

"Bless it before you drink it!" said Alex.

"What?" exclaimed Elizabeth in surprise. "You're not a religious man, Alex—where is this coming from?"

Alex shook his head. "It's not really religion-based—it's actually quite scientific."

Dr. Kamron raised his eyebrows. "Oh? How so?"

"It has to do with the effect on the observed by the observer," said Alex.

Dr. Kamron looked both amused and skeptical. "I'm sorry, but … with water? How could that be?"

"Remember the Heisenberg rule that states 'by the very act of watching, the observer affects the observed reality'?" asked Alex. "Well, forget the religious aspect of blessing and think about it scientifically. When you bless something, you observe it and propel a positive vibration from your consciousness for its betterment. On a quantum level, your observation will indeed impact the nature of the observed. Water is no exception to that—in fact, it's the most susceptible substance to this phenomenon."

Elizabeth's eyes grew huge. "Alex!"

Alex leaned in further. "Okay, but listen, the Japanese expert on water, Dr. Masaru Emoto, confirmed this when he said, 'When you drink water with a feeling of gratitude, the water itself is physically different than when you drink the same water with clouded feelings in your soul.'"

"A scientist said that?" exclaimed Elizabeth.

"Yes," said Alex. "You see, this little bit of research got me curious about water itself as a substance, so I continued to further study its nature. And that took me to a whole new journey of awareness. This substance we so easily overlook is the single most incredible element in our universe. It's transparent, formless, and does not even comply with our laws of physics or chemistry.

"My quest to understand the nature and properties of water brought me to an amazing book by Dr. Emoto called *The Hidden Messages in Water*. By the time I finished it, I could not agree more with three bold statements that Dr. Emoto made in the book:

1. There is nothing more mysterious than water.
2. Water is something not of this Earth.
3. Among other fascinating properties, water has the ability to copy and memorize information.

"It was this third one that put me on the path that answers your question about my finances," said Alex.

"What? How so?" asked Elizabeth.

"For years, Dr. Emoto conducted research into the measurement of wave fluctuation in water," said Alex. "He later conducted experiments on water crystals and took numerous photographs of them with an extremely accurate microscope. You have to see these pictures in his book to fully appreciate what he discovered.

"First, he established that water exposed to beautiful, melodic music, such as Beethoven's *Pastoral Symphony*, formed gorgeous geometric crystals, while in contrast, violent heavy-metal music resulted in distorted crystals."

"That could just be the effect of the type of vibrations," offered Elizabeth.

"That's what I thought too," said Alex, "but listen to this: When water bottles were wrapped in paper with words written on them facing inward, something absolutely stunning occurred. The water was somehow able to 'read' the writing, understand its meaning, and change its crystal form accordingly. So, water that was exposed to words like "love" and "gratitude" formed hexagonal crystals, while water exposed to words of insult produced malformed, fragmented crystals.

"I have to sidetrack for a bit here, and tell you something about the subject of what you initially asked me, which had a profound effect on me: If words have such power on water, and since our body is composed of 70 percent water, just imagine what kind of internal impact that positive and negative words have on our state of being or even the direction of our lives from a health standpoint. Think about it—from our own individual life courses to the shape of consciousness of the masses."

A look of realization was crossing Dr. Kamron's face. "I couldn't help but think about homeopathy as you were explaining this."

Alex nodded. "Oh yes, Dr. Emoto refers to that in his book for a better comprehension of this."

"What about it?" asked Elizabeth.

Alex looked up. "He wrote that... Layla, summarize please ..."

> Homeopathy originated in Germany in the first half of the nineteenth century with the work of Samuel Hahnemann (1791–1843), but its roots go back to the father of medicine, Hippocrates (c. 460–c. 370 BC), who wrote down many treatments similar to those promoted by homeopathy. In a word, these pioneers of medicine taught us to treat "like with like, fight poison with poison."
>
> For example, if someone is suffering from lead poisoning, symptoms can be alleviated by drinking water with the minutest amount of lead in it—an amount ranging from 1 part in 10^{12} (one trillion) to 1 part in 10^{400}!

Elizabeth looked puzzled. "At these levels, there is no lead left in the water."

Alex nodded. "Yes, you're right. He wrote in his book that ..."

> At this level, the matter no longer for practical purposes remains in the water, but the characteristics of the matter do remain, and this forms the medicine for treating lead poisoning.
>
> Homeopathy proposes that the greater the dilution, the greater the effectiveness. The logical conclusion is that the denser the poison in the body, the higher should be the dilution ratio.
>
> Another way to express this idea is that, instead of the effect of the matter being used to get rid of the symptoms, the information copied to the water is being used to cancel out the information of the symptoms from the poison.

Elizabeth leaned back in her seat. "This is fascinating, Alex, but I just can't see how you made a fortune with this information about water."

"I didn't make it with just this information but rather with my collective understanding on the properties of water," said Alex. "Think about it—water can copy and memorize information, right?"

"Yes," said Elizabeth, "But, I don't get it—you discovered a medicine of some sort?"

"No, no," said Alex. "Listen—copy and memorize information by water. Now think about it."

Everyone was quiet for a moment.

"Water equals copy and memory of information," said Alex.

Dr. Kamron suddenly leaped up. "Oh my goodness, Alex! You're a genius!"

"What, what?" cried Elizabeth. "You guys are killing me here!"

Dr. Kamron said, "You know this, honey—the H₂Open, he designed the H₂Open!"

Elizabeth suddenly understood. "Holy mother of God, you're the one who designed H₂Open and that gel that made DVDs and USBs and all those other information storage forms obsolete? Wow, now I see where you got all this dough. Did you have a technical computer background?"

Alex shook his head. "Absolutely not. I had to sell the concept and do a joint venture."

"Wow, so that's how you stayed anonymous," said Elizabeth. "You didn't care much for the notoriety or fame, I suppose."

Alex smiled.

Elizabeth winked at Alex. "Didn't think so. Hey, what's that other thing you said? Something about Dr. Emoto saying that 'water is something not of this Earth'? What was that all about?"

"Yes, he also wrote that 'the memory of life arrived on this Earth carried by the soul of water.' Of course, other scientists have also insisted on this fact."

"But how?" asked Elizabeth.

"How?" said Alex.

"Yes, how?"

Alex tried to explain. "Dr. Emoto said that 'water records information, and then while circulating throughout the Earth distributes information.

This water sent from the universe is full of the information of life.'"

"I get that," said Elizabeth, "but, I mean, how did it get to Earth to do this?"

"Dr. Emoto cites a scholar named Louis Frank of the University of Iowa, who states that water arrived on this planet in the form of lumps of ice from outer space. Dr. Emoto says ..."

> *These minicomets are actually balls of water and ice weighing a hundred tons or more, and falling into the Earth's atmosphere at a rate of about twenty per minute (or ten million per year). The theory is that these balls of ice bombarded the Earth forty billion years ago, creating the seas and oceans, and this same phenomenon continues today.*
>
> *As the Earth's gravity pulls these ice comets into the atmosphere, the heat of the sun evaporates them and turns them into gas. As they fall fifty-five kilometers from outer space, the gas particles mix with the air in the atmosphere and are blown about, falling to the Earth as rain or snow.*

Alex added, "NASA and the University of Hawaii have officially announced that Dr. Frank's theory does have credibility. Of course, your husband can tell you more about it. Right, Dr. Kamron?"

"I think you summed it up pretty well," affirmed Dr. Kamron.

They heard footsteps and smelled a delicious fragrance wafting through the air. Two crew members approached the gazebo with large trays of steaming food.

"Ah, here we are," said Alex, getting up from his seat. "Your dinner is here. I should go now and greet my unexpected guest whom fate brought here. You two enjoy your dinner. I'll be back a little later to join you for dessert."

"Thank you," said Dr. Kamron, "and we're going to read this here. Let's see, what did you name it? To Surpass a Multiverse."

As Alex got up to leave, Elizabeth said, "Alex, I know you and my husband talked about this in detail, but can you tell me one thing before you leave—and none of the scientific stuff? Just simply: What do you know of fate? I mean, do you believe in fate?"

Alex looked at the couple earnestly. "I know only one thing: With utmost certainty about her, fate loves irony."

40

TO SURPASS A MULTIVERSE

As famished as they were, with their plates of tantalizing food before them, Dr. Kamron and Elizabeth found themselves transfixed by Alex's hardbound leather notebook. Carefully, they opened to the first page and began to read as they took the first bite.

TO SURPASS A MULTIVERSE

What you are about to read is an adaptation of a dialogue of what transpired between entities at an indeterminate point, which accounts for the production of our universe. It is indeterminate because at that point, time had yet to be invented. The same goes for space, matter, and for that matter, anything that we could conceivably have a point of reference to. Therefore, the entire transcript of this dialogue has been converted into earthly terms for the sake of comprehension.

However, it still requires a heavy use of your imagination to fully appreciate the essence of the original dialogue. One thing that is highly recommended throughout your perusal is to at least conceptualize eternity not as "a place where time exists forever, but instead a place where time does not exist, period." Accordingly, a process of billions of years would be equivalent to the blink of an eye.

Before the Beginning Was Invented

"Graceful" and "grand" are the only words that could be used to even remotely come close to describing this place—a place that in earthly terms should be called the most majestic palace ever "unimagined."

In the long hallway leading from the foyer to the Grand Chamber, Chief Counsel was walking rapidly. He entered the foyer and saw The Creator.

He approached her and bowed gracefully as he greeted her.

"Master Creator," he began, "it is an honor to be in your presence once again. Please come—come with me. We must hurry to the Grand Chamber. Your proposal is now up for review by the Grand Being. This is your opportunity to respond to any inquiries directly and make your presentation in support of your proposal to create a new multiverse. I am afraid you have only the length of this hallway to the Grand Chamber to ask me for any insight regarding the interview. You see, I was just told that they are ready for you and we must go in right away."

Master Creator nodded her head. "I am as ready as I will ever be. But you said 'they.' Am I not being seen by the Grand Being alone?"

Chief Counsel said, "First, I must tell you what I tell everyone entering for the first time: Try not to be transfixed by the size of the chamber and everything else you see. It is so large that it would plunge any entity into awe—maybe even a Master Creator of your caliber. You see, it is not just its sheer size, but the mere act of entering and observing a place so immense simply overwhelms and dissolves all of your perceptions. How can I say this? If you could imagine something so infinitely vast, then you are not imagining this adequately.

"I have seen entities who have completely lost their ability to communicate and had to be removed from the Chamber. The good news is, as you hopefully move forward, the Chamber will adjust itself to your perception and allow you to see the Grand Being. The Grand Being will be, of course, in the center with three illuminating Eminences on each side. I will quickly describe their characteristics. Be prepared, as each one inquires only about certain specific disciplines, if you will.

"Do not bother attempting to explain your terminologies. They will simultaneously and precisely self-interpret each term as you state it. Focus only on explaining your concepts.

"Here is the formation: Eminences 1, 2, and 3 will be on one side of the Grand Being, and 4, 5, and 6 on the other side. Eminences 1 and 6 will make only scientific inquiries. Eminences 2 and 5 will inquire only philosophically. Eminence 4 will attend to any artistic appreciation of your proposal, and by the way, 4 is the only one with a sense of humor and candidly the only ally you will have in there.

"Eminence 3 will inquire only on the logical aspects, and frankly, I would watch out for the line of questions coming from that direction. You will see that Eminences 3 and 4 are sort of explorers, but in a strange way, from completely opposite angles. They are kind of two sides of the same coin but are very different. Like I said, Eminence 4 will have a sense of humor and seek the beauty and humor in everything, whereas Eminence 3 is so committed to logic that it takes the fun out of things and leaves no room for appreciating the pleasant aspects of what you may be presenting."

Master Creator was taking all this in. "What about the Grand Being?" she asked. "Will I not be asked any questions directly from the Grand Being?"

"If the Grand Being asks you a question, you will not have an answer," replied Chief Counsel.

"So am I visiting seven beings?" asked Master Creator.

"Your Grace, are the fingers playing the piano separate entities from the pianist?"

"I see," said Master Creator.

They arrived at the end of the hallway in front of a large door. "We are here," said Chief Counsel. "This is as far as I can go. Please enter and remember with confidence. I have seen them all, but your work has always impressed me the most. You are truly gifted. A well-deserving holder of the Master Creator title. I only wish I could be inside to see what you have proposed this time for which your personal presence was summoned for inquiry."

Master Creator smiled. "You are kind, Chief Counsel."

Chief Counsel opened the door and graciously replied, "Please enter, and good luck."

As Master Creator entered, she immediately began to sense an overload that she could not process and still maintain her equilibrium. She quickly focused on her inner self to gain stability before she looked outward again, but she needed to repeat the process to overcome the waves of ensuing shock. She felt overwhelmed by the desire to observe and shocked by the immeasurable degree of what was being observed.

When she was asked to move forward, she did so slowly and haltingly until she found herself directly observing the Grand Being.

A second shock wave compromised her balance; yet she withstood the force of the visual impact with grace and determination. Who would have thought that beauty could be so stunning and unimaginable that it could overcome even your sense of being?

Eminence 4 said to her, "You are holding up very well, Master Creator. Do come closer and be."

With the mere receipt of these words, she regained her equilibrium as if the words had suddenly facilitated her adjustment. She was now fully aware and unexpectedly at better ease. Something external had interfaced with her to accommodate her balance and capacity to interact. Still, directly looking at the Grand Being was intense and overbearing, and she felt more comfortable focusing on Eminence 4.

Then Eminence 3 spoke. "Your reputation precedes you, Master Creator. But your proposal this time is a peculiar one indeed. When we grant permission for the creation of new multiverses, it is always intended for the multiverse to come to us for observation. You are now proposing the construction of a multiverse that requires us to enter it. Very unorthodox, wouldn't you acknowledge? Very unorthodox indeed. A multiverse that requires our transformation to a state where we're not self-conscious. Very peculiar indeed!"

"Respectfully, Your Eminence," said the Master Creator, "you will be self-conscious, of course, but only oblivious of self-purpose."

Eminence 3 looked indignant. "Oblivious of self-purpose? Why do we need purpose, let alone to be oblivious of it?"

"As I stand before you," said Master Creator, "I am, for the first time, filled with inhibition. If I'm to elaborate and respond to your inquiries in a meaningful fashion, I must respectfully ask to be permitted to speak freely."

"But of course, we wouldn't expect any less," said Eminence 4.

Master Creator continued, "With my gratitude then, I must respond to your first question regarding the need for this creation. It is for the sake of spiritual ecology."

Eminence 3 interrupted. "We seem to have previously experienced a creation with this time-space you have referred to in your proposal. Perhaps one of your own works?"

"No, Your Eminence," Master Creator replied. "What you had was not an experience but rather a mere observation. What was presented to you previously, perhaps in reference to the principle of time-space, were all multiverses in which the concept of space and time were fixed—just a stage on which that domain simply played itself out. This, however, is a very unique verse. It is, in fact, a true universe that surpasses all multiverses. In this new universe of mine, there are evolving networks of relationships that make up the history of space, time, and matter. In this universe, you don't just observe beauty; you interact with its elements until you manifest it. You don't just look at the beautiful scene—you become the scene. In a scene where a butterfly is sitting on a flower and nourishing itself, you *become* the butterfly, the flower, and the nectar."

Master Creator continued. "I understand your fascination with having new multiverses created for the sake of attaching dimensions to singularity. Perhaps because as unimaginably vast as singularity is, it is nevertheless so infinitesimally compact that it has no dimensions itself. So, I can see your desire to constantly allow the production of these empty multiverses and watch them collapse back into singularity again in an eternal cycle. As beautiful as this may be, it's practically like watching the lights of a pretty ornament go on and off. What I'm delivering, however, is a universe that breeds with you, grows with you, and lives as you."

Eminence 3 looked perplexed. "A universe? Huh?"

Master Creator nodded. "Yes, Your Eminence, as I mentioned, you have never really seen a universe before. What you've had were multiverses. All the multiverses created for you in the name of amusement, edification, or adulation have done nothing to produce a change in the spirit of things here. You've been observing their brilliance, but your state remains stagnant. My universe will invite you to an ever-changing manifestation of yourself.

"There, you'll enter a state in which your senses are limited. Limited not to minimize your appreciation of all that you are, but rather to maximize your wonder of what you can be. All of the other multiverses have provided you with a flattering reflection of you, and I'm sure that's been gratifying.

"This universe, however, will make you challenge yourself, and what you'll experience is beyond gratification. But, for you to be challenged, you must stay oblivious of your true self and purpose. If you don't, you will not be able to partake of the endless possibilities for transforming and truly fulfilling yourself (at least to the best of your ability in one form before moving to the other). In other words, it is only exciting and enhances the spiritual experience if you are made unaware of the outcome."

Eminence 3 looked skeptical. "What you propose seems unattainable. Eliminate our self-awareness to fit in a universe?"

"Not eliminate, only diminish enough to fit in," said Master Creator. "Part of you will always be aware, but not enough to compromise the drive needed to function in this enchanting universe."

Eminence 4 said, "This is certainly intriguing, but why can't we just observe these manifestations and be amused?"

"The idea is not to only amuse you but to create a new you at every turn," replied Master Creator.

"Are you going to create a new us?" asked Eminence 4.

"No, I have created all the elements that allow you to recreate yourself over and over again within this universe. Frankly, the 'you' is the one element that cannot be created but only hosted."

Eminences 1 and 6 simultaneously exclaimed, "Hosted? What ARE we in this universe of yours?"

Eminence 4 whispered to the others, "She cannot comprehend if we speak simultaneously. It is too much for her."

Eminence 1 frowned. "What are we in this universe of yours?"

Master Creator replied, "You are 'life.' "

"And you did not try to replicate this 'life' for this universe of yours?" asked Eminence 6.

"Try? Oh yes, I did," said Master Creator. "I tried and tried and then some, to no avail. I even attempted to synthesize life for the sake of a simulation."

"You could not produce the element to even synthesize life?" asked Eminence 1.

"I focused a great deal on various reactive blends of nitrogen and carbon dioxide."

"And were you not able to formulate the elements to even animate life?" persisted Eminence 1.

"The problems were not the elements," said Master Creator. "By mixing and rearranging carbon, sulfur, hydrogen, calcium, oxygen, nitrogen, phosphorus, and iron in various combinations, I was able to produce the basic compounds for hosting life."

"And?" asked Eminence 6.

"Well, it was like creating various-shaped light bulbs, but no light would emanate from them."

Eminence 1 said, "Before we go any further on the fundamental or philosophical aspects of this proposal, let's go over the scientific viability of it."

"And the accommodations for the guests," Eminence 4 added. "If we're going to be hosted, I'd like to know more about the facilities and the principles they're built on."

"Certainly," said Master Creator. "Where would you like me to start with your scientific inquiries?"

"Wherever you started," said Eminence 1.

"I started at the end, with an objective to create a universe like no other—a universe congenial to life. Only then did I believe I had achieved the impossible: A universe that could offer two things that would make itself worthy of your presence (the presence of life within). First, a fine-tuned cosmological constant to allow simultaneous balance and expansion, and second, elements that provide everlasting changes to maintain your interest."

"What would these elements be?" Eminence 6 asked.

"There are three, Your Eminence," said Master Creator. "Three magical elements: (1) the magic of electrons; (2) water, your vessel; and (3) love, your ability."

"Please elaborate on the fundamental physical principles first," said Eminence 3.

"Then I must go back to the beginning and present you with this simulation. It is, however, based on one major assumption."

"Assumption?" asked Eminence 1.

"Yes. The assumption that you have granted the means to an energy source," said Master Creator.

"What means?" asked Eminence 6.

"Before the start of the beginning. With your permission, I must facilitate a small collision between two other multiverses. This impact will produce the energy source to give birth to the new universe, which will pop out of this primordial vacuum with sort of a big bang. A universe the likes of which has never been even imagined, let alone created. A universe that is woven into the elegant fabric of space-time. A universe whose limit is only the limit of your imagination. A universe that is capable of hosting 'life.' "

"Please elaborate again on this space-time you speak of," said Eminence 1.

"I will do better than that," said Master Creator. "I have with me a tiny patch of space-time. This little patch is less than a billionth of the size of a proton. But, in less than a second, it will inflate into a balloon that can become the new universe."

Elizabeth and Dr. Kamron stopped reading. Elizabeth immediately looked at her husband.

"Hey, do you want to tell me what was just said, in under-grad terms?" she asked.

"What was said was correct," said Dr. Kamron. He grabbed a saltshaker and shook it over the table. "Look at this grain of salt. Not everything that I just shook out, but just this one tiny single grain. A proton is a small part of an atom. In fact, it's so small that this one grain holds over 1,000,000,000,000 of them. That's how small our universe was, just before it expanded. And in less than a second it went from something smaller than this grain of salt to 10,000,000,000,000,000,000,000,000 times its size—the size of a universe."

"Good God," said Elizabeth.

"Good God is right. Let's read the rest."

"So that's why you need positive energy," said Eminence 6. "To induce this time-space of yours to expand at an exponentially accelerating rate?"

"Yes, exactly," said Master Creator.

"So, if we're interacting through this space and time," said Eminence 1, puzzled, "they must not be fundamental?"

"You are correct, Your Eminence. Space and time are emergent phenomena. You'll later see that there are multitudes of spatial dimensions, and they change for you."

"Why does this system of yours have to depend on constantly changing time?" asked Eminence 5.

"Because you will fail at just about every other step of the way in one form or another. Therefore, the changing time grants you a restorative process so you can regain your balance and move again."

Eminence 5 asked, "Are you saying that we'll never reach our objective in this plane of existence?"

"No, I'm saying that you'll never reach the point of contentment," Master Creator answered.

"Isn't that what we'll be striving for?" asked Eminence 5.

"Yes. And you will never get there."

"Then what do you mean by no?" asked Eminence 5.

"Because the point of contentment is not your objective. Being in pursuit of it is and that you'll have every step of the way. That's the name of the game there. Not a game of reaching contentment but rather a game of pursuing one."

"So, let's consider your universe born," said Eminence 1. "What do you need next?"

"Matter, Your Eminence, matter. It is the perfect transformer. It gets assembled for you at will. Serves your purpose, disassembles, and is ready to transform into another shape to serve another purpose."

"And the makeup of this matter of yours?" asked Eminence 6. "What is it, and do we have to keep increasing it?"

"From the moment of creation," said Master Creator, "the universe will contain virtually the same amount of matter. As for its makeup ... well, I'll tell you, but—"

"Okay, but wait, by this time in the development of your universe, you have only a lot of gas drifting in the darkness," said Eminence 1. "This can't be the matter that you're speaking of with shape-changing qualities, and so on."

"Yes, but before that first second is over, gravity, electromagnetism, and strong and weak nuclear forces will emerge," said Master Creator. "And then we'll have all the elementary particles: protons, neutrons, photons, and my favorite—one of the three magical things I promised you earlier—the electrons. Ah, from there you'll have it all. An array of galaxies and nebulae, full of stars and planets and much, much more, in a universe as vast as you wish it to be."

Eminence 1 said, "Please elaborate on the connection between all these factors that you must have created with great challenges."

"Factors?" asked Master Creator. "Well, sure, but I'll tell you the hard part wasn't creating these factors. No, it was the calibration that was challenging. So please consider this: A strong nuclear force binds quarks into protons and neutrons and then into atomic nuclei. That's how I get matter for this material universe. I needed electromagnetic force to light up the place for you, and of course, that also keeps the atoms around and bonded to the chemicals. And oh, to coalesce matter into galaxies, I needed to add gravity. Let's also not forget the weak force. I needed that to have a creation that turns neutrons into protons and the other way around, because to make this place colorful for you, I needed to effectuate complex chemistry. You will appreciate this part later."

Eminence 4 nodded. "Please continue—you've got my attention."

"Like I said, the hard part was the calibration," said Master Creator. "If just one of these factors is ever so slightly off, the universe will collapse. Or at least, it wouldn't be the place of wonder I present to you.

"Take the strong nuclear force, for instance. If I had made it just a little stronger—or weaker for that matter—there would be no matter, because then the stars couldn't forge enough carbon or other elements to form planets for you. Let's take a closer look at how precise certain values need to be to have this universe just right for you. Hydrogen must be converted to helium in an ever-so-precise manner. That is, from 0.007 percent of its mass to energy. Take that value down just a tiny bit to 0.006 percent and there would be no transformation. That means we'd have nothing but hydrogen in the universe. If the value goes up to 0.008 percent, then poof! Hydrogen would be exhausted very quickly since bonding would be so wildly prolific. So you see, it's either perfect calibration or no universe."

Eminence 6 frowned. "Something is still missing here."

"Missing?" said Master Creator. "Respectfully, nothing will be missing in this creation but boredom, stagnation, and a distilled state."

Eminence 6 said, "Did you not say you needed just one collision to start this universe of yours with a 'big bang' of energy?"

Master Creator nodded. "Yes, of course, just one."

"Then how do you propose to have all these things when your universe is just full of light gas?" asked Eminence 1. "You have no heavy element to build any of these things you speak of. You need something as hot as the first collision that started your big bang. Where do you suppose you can get such heat within this gassy universe of yours?"

"I'll thank my lucky stars," said Master Creator, smiling. "They'll die for me and give birth to your new homes."

Eminence 4 smiled. "I'm afraid I'm the only one here who appreciates a good poetic gesture. Give it to them straight, Master."

"There'll be great stars—giant ones that will, in just the right order, go supernova. That is, they'll collapse and explode, releasing tremendous heat and energy that'll forge heavy elements from gas. These are what will be at your disposal for a material plane of existence."

"Very interesting, Master Creator," said Eminence 4.

"No, something is still missing," insisted Eminence 1.

"Please don't anticipate a compliment from my fellow beings here," said Eminence 4. "But this process you just elaborated on shows amazing signs of true nobility—or should I say, novelty. We have never seen such a process of interfusion before."

"Something is still missing here," repeated Eminence 1. "Critically missing. So far, in your simulation, you have postulated that in less than a second, we go from singularity to a new multidimensional space that will be inflated and produced. It'll have its own governing forces of physics, which will include gravity. However, if my assessment is correct, most of this matter of which you speak will be produced in the first few minutes of your creation."

"Yes, Your Eminence," said Master Creator. "Ninety-eight percent of all the matter that will ever be contained in this universe will be produced in the first three minutes of creation."

"That's what I thought," said Eminence 1. "Then, based on my evaluation, that is not nearly enough mass to hold these galaxies that you speak of together. You're seriously short on matter and therefore you seriously lack gravitational force."

"You are most perceptive, but there will be another factor at work," said Master Creator. "Not here in singularity but from where you will be, you'll perhaps call it dark matter, or invisible matter, or some other unknown matter because it will be nonreflective and intangible to your senses. But here, I'll elaborate on the system by which it will be governed so that it may please you to know that there'll be perfectly adequate gravitational forces in this universe."

Elizabeth turned to her husband. "I've heard you use this word "singularity" before but I have a hard time visualizing it."

"Remember when I tried to explain the concept of the existence of a universe that comes out of nothingness?" said Dr. Kamron. "Singularity is like that nothingness. Try to visualize this: Imagine that you're standing in front of a wall. The wall is so thin that it has no dimensions and it expands infinitely. That's nothingness. Now, on this wall there is a very flat screen. Imagine you're standing across this wall and looking at this flat screen. But when you observe that flat screen from the front, you can see multidimensional images and all kinds of stories and happenings that are transpiring. The screen is just slightly less flat than the wall itself. Within the flatness, there is still foaminess. And we exist in that foaminess. That's our universe. I have wondered if one can sometimes walk right into the screen and get absorbed in its happenings."

Elizabeth shook her head. "As fascinating as that sounds, I'm still having a hard time visualizing it. Let's continue with the story for now."

—◦◦◦◦◦—

41

MAGIC TRIO

Eminence 1 nodded at Master Creator. "Please elaborate."

"Certainly, let's go back to quarks, since that's where you will find the structure of visible matter," said Master Creator. "We go there because that's where I have hidden the essence of this invisible matter. You'll recall that quarks are kept together by particles called gluons. Quarks and gluons make up the nucleus of an atom, which is composed of protons and neutrons. Then you have leptons, which are the power source of the electrons and neutrons…"

Eminence 4 interrupted. "I'm sorry, this is not helping. We understood your arrangement already."

Master Creator was undeterred. "Then you recall the two forces needed to keep atoms together? The weak nuclear force and the strong one? The weak force alone is 10 billion billion billion times stronger than gravity. The strong force is by far stronger than that."

"Be that as it may, they can reach only a fraction of the diameter of an atom," said Eminence 1. "Our inquiry is in the lack of adequate gravity in the outer universe of the atom, not within."

"Ah, that is the magic I spoke of," said Master Creator.

"The 1 of 3 again?" asked Eminence 4.

"Precisely. The magic of electrons. To comprehend the working of my universe, you must learn the connections between the visible matter and the invisible, as I must put it. To understand the connection, you must get to know the magic of what I've created in the functions of electrons. I named it EE, which is based on the duality of electrons—a duality in both function and existence.

"You see, when electrons move between the visible world and the invisible world, they pass through a prism-type connector made of themselves. That is why they appear to be everywhere and nowhere at the same time.

The fact is, at the point prior to connecting with the prism, they are particles, but once they pass through the prism, they become waves."

"But isn't the outer universe that you're describing basically a perfect empty vacuum?" Eminence 6 asked.

"Empty? Not at all," Master Creator said. "This perfect vacuum that you refer to is not so empty. In fact, it's filled with the magic that I spoke of."

"Ah—1 of 3 again!" said Eminence 4.

"Yes. These electrons will pop in and out of existence from where you'll be standing in the visible world, based on your perceived uncertainty. In reality, of course, they're simply traveling between the visible and invisible worlds, knitting a network of gravitational field force as well as facilitating a communication network.

"You see, that seemingly empty space—the quantum nothingness—has its own gravitational system that I like to call EE, which is different than attractive gravity. The gravity around an object is relative to that object's mass. You wouldn't see enough mass in the universe to account for the adequacy of the needed gravity because it's actually not needed. This universe's gravitational system or EE is operated by the flow of electrons. Basically, what will function as a quasi-gravitational force is the pull generated by the movement of electrons popping in and out of existence between different dimensions. Massive power exists within and through the movement of these electrons, which knits the visible world to the invisible world. But, when you're in the visible world, you'd have a hard time observing this phenomenon because they're everywhere and nowhere at the same time."

"So again, do these magical things called electrons or EE function like waves or particles?" asked Eminence 1.

"It's their very duality that makes them magical," said Master Creator. "I would not use the term 'magical' loosely. A creation must surpass all expectations to be entitled to that adjective. Because electrons function both as waves and particles, this capability earns them the term 'quantum leap,' since electrons can disappear from one locality and reappear instantly in another without visiting the space in between."

"So, in this universe of yours, we can never predict the path of electrons as they move through space?" asked Eminence 6.

"Of course you can. You can even know where the electron is at a specific instant. But you will not be able to know both the path and lo-cation at the same time."

"Why not?" asked Eminence 6.

"Because then you will disturb its functionality."

"Why would you create it so?" asked Eminence 1.

"Because that's the whole idea," said Master Creator. "You see, you'll be in a plane of existence where the large-scale world is an illusion gov-erned by the physical laws of the small-scale world. As I mentioned, sort of like a prism. If you focus on the light source behind the prism, you won't see the spectrum of colorful light projected out of the prism."

"So you have two separate laws of physics at work?" asked Eminence 6.

"Not at all, the two are one and the same, but they must be observed separately for the grand illusion to work. Of course, the EE will function as a communication network by which you'll always be connected with all parts of the universe at all times, including your coexistence in other dimensions."

"But what you're proposing will place us in a plane of existence where uncertainty rules," said Eminence 1. "This magic of these electrons of yours, if I understand it correctly, is that, at any given moment, they're everywhere and nowhere. That means that until we observe them in this universe of yours, they, in a way, don't really exist."

"They exist as tendencies," said Master Creator.

"Why would you create it so?" Eminence 6 asked.

"Well, for one thing, that's how you create something from nothing," said Master Creator.

"But why would you create it this way for us?" Eminence 6 asked.

"Because in this universe, you'll never find final accuracy. It is de-signed to create an infinite chain of possibilities. It's that unpredictable nature that drives your senses to desire and pursue each probable outcome masked with certainty."

Eminence 6 considered this. "So, do I understand correctly that we'll be pursuing an illusion of finding answers that in themselves produce only more questions in this infinite chain of probabilities?"

"Yes."

"And why would we want to do that?" asked Eminence 1.

"Because if you're oblivious of this infinite 'chain of possibility' principle—and you will be oblivious of it in this plane of existence—then you'll be compelled to indulge in its pursuit," said Master Creator.

"If the entire structure of this universe is designed to rest on a probability grid with no certainty in sight, then how can we have any platform from which to aim for possibilities?" asked Eminence 6. "This sounds like a place where we'd be adrift in a multispatial paradigm."

Master Creator said, "Respectfully, not so. If you recall when I spoke of multispatial dimensions, I included a dimensional attachment called 'time.' Time is basically a dimension filtration that produces a temporary constant by marginalizing the probability outcome. Time will give you an ample platform on which to aim your course of desired possibilities (although you may disagree with the ampleness of it while you're there). Nevertheless, it will complete the illusion. You will also disconnect from all the other dimensions and awareness and focus on the specific plane of existence you're in."

"Back to EE," said Eminence 6. "So, if I understand the nature of these electrons, then something is puzzling me about their potential."

"How so?" asked Master Creator.

"Based on the functioning and properties of these electrons, it seems this universe would somehow …"—Eminence 6 paused—"… copy itself."

"You are indeed perceptive," observed Master Creator.

"But precisely how and why?" asked Eminence 6.

"As for how, it is designed so that when two electrons approach and deflect, they must provide for every possible intermediate path on their way. And in each segment in which they interact, a new reality can diverge that will make it possible to create a parallel universe with a new alternate history line.

"As for why? Well, respectfully, why not? If all these creations have been produced for your experience, why provide only a flat history line and not one that can expand and provide countless possibilities and outcomes?"

Eminence 4 smiled. "Superb—an absolute masterpiece! Who would have thought that the science of creation could be so artistically diversified to include various probability outcomes that induce a multitude of history lines?"

"Let's go back and take a look at this matter you speak of," said Eminence 6. "Please start with its manifested state and play it backward. I'd like to see how this is different from the makeup of other multiverses, as you put it."

"Yes, Your Eminence," said Master Creator. "I assure you it is different, very different indeed. You have never even examined a manifestation that contains matter that's operated by electrons."

"And how exactly do you propose that we occupy it?" asked Eminence 6. "That's ultimately what you're proposing, isn't it?"

"Before I answer that, may I address your first question and give you a closer look at matter?"

Eminence 6 nodded. "Please proceed."

"The manifested state of matter is basically a 'little mass,' said Master Creator. "That is to say that you have a molecule, which is really just two or more atoms coming to a stable arrangement. An atom itself has a structure made of protons, neutrons, and electrons. Protons and neutrons are in the atom's nucleus. I trust that you may have seen something similar in the makeup of other multiverses—the kind that even I've produced previously. But here, in this universe, the atom has one of the three magical factors I have promised you—the electrons."

"You keep referring to this electron with great pride," said Eminence 6.

"Kindly let me continue elaborating on the structure of an atom and you will see," said Master Creator. "As I said, protons and neutrons make up the nucleus of an atom. Atoms, you must know, are 99.9 percent empty space. The nucleus has practically all the mass that atoms have. Although it is quite dense, the nucleus is only one millionth of a billionth of the whole atom."

Elizabeth looked up at Dr. Kamron. "Didn't you try to explain this to me once? Like a football field or something?"

"Yes," said Dr. Kamron. "To appreciate how empty atoms are, this is the ratio to consider: If an atom is a football stadium, the nucleus is the size of a football. And the rest is just empty space. The football, though, weighs thousands of times more than the stadium."

"That's crazy," said Elizabeth. "Then, since matter is 99 percent empty, the whole universe is 99 percent empty, right?"

Dr. Kamron replied, "To fully understand this, you need to understand that the void that is full of nothingness gives us the things that we are. Since there is more nothing than something, the answer to the theory of everything (dark matter and all that) was to understand nothingness. The activity of the nothingness inside the vacuum is based on the quantum fluctuation that gives birth to things. Things that are universes and you and me. So, to truly answer your question, empty is the wrong word. The void is anything but empty."

Elizabeth replied, "You have to tell me more about this later. Okay, where were we?"

"If matter is made of the arrangement of these atoms, and atoms are 99.9 percent empty space, then how are we supposed to occupy this universe of yours in any real sense of the matter?" asked Eminence 1.

"The answer is twofold," said Master Creator. "First, through the magic of electrons, and second, you don't occupy matter. You interact *through* it."

"Please go on," said Eminence 1.

"What you'll feel—and believe me, you'll feel it when you're interfaced with this universe—is the illusion of solidity. Of course, when you're in that plane of existence, you mostly have self-awareness through this illusion of solidity. Therefore, it would be nearly impossible to know the difference. You see, my first magic—"

"The 1 of 3 magics again?" Eminence 4 interrupted.

"Yes, the 1 of 3. The electrons possess negative electrical charges. So in this universe, whenever two fields of negatively charged electrons attempt to make contact, they repel each other, thus creating the illusion of contact. And that is how you feel the world around you in this universe. The electrons that you interact through never come into actual contact with any other electrons. They're always an angstrom—which is 100-millionth of a centimeter—away from each other, but to you, they will feel solid."

Eminence 1 nodded. "So again, essentially our form exists as particles and waves?"

"Yes, because they're everywhere at once," said Master Creator. "And I mean *everywhere*. To the point that they're nowhere. And please note that the whole universe will be in a state of vibration."

"As one?" Eminence 6 asked.

"As one. But also, for you to experience all of the manifestations you can imagine, each thing, being, event, or even concept shall have its own unique frequency."

"But I presume that only as manifested beings, we'd have consciousness, right?" asked Eminence 1.

"No, Your Eminence, you'll have various levels of consciousness in all of your manifestations, whether you're a being or any other form. This design is intended for you to have your presence in all things, no matter what form or level of awareness. Even as a rock, you'll have some rudimentary consciousness to help keep your form in place and to feel what it's like to be a mountain. Even as wind, you'll have rudimentary consciousness to experience blowing across an ocean in the middle of a dark night or dancing between the spray of the sea's surface and moving clouds, where no other aspect of your being is present to witness your movement from continent to continent. And your rudimentary consciousness will enable you to experience being a field of barley when you gracefully sway in appreciation of the warmth you receive from rays of sunlight.

"Even as mist, you'll have rudimentary consciousness. A mist that has accumulated on the surface of a boulder, which turns into a single drop of morning dew and rolls down that majestic rock until it falls into a stream below. With it is carried the essence of what it's like to be at one with that mighty boulder. Much like when you'll be a teardrop that rolls down the face of a man until it enters the side of his lips and delivers what it's like to taste the salty essence of pride."

Eminence 4 spoke. "Again, Master Creator, you will not find an appreciation for the poetic nature of things that you express among my fellow beings."

"Understood," said Master Creator. "From a purely scientific standpoint, I must add that even in your interaction between your various manifestations, you'll emit different frequencies to generate various exchanges of experiences."

"So, since everything is in a state of vibration, we're all creating some kind of sound by our mere existence, right?" asked Elizabeth.

Dr. Kamron grinned. "Remember what I once told you?"

Elizabeth smiled. "Oh, wait … yes, that our entire existence is simply various lyrics to a cosmic song."

"Let's now shift our focus away from the makeup of this so-called invisible world and go back to the visible world," said Eminence 1. "After all, that's where we'll be self-aware, correct?"

"You may say that, at least to a large degree," answered Master Creator.

"If we are to 'be,' we are to be present, correct?" asked Eminence 1.

"Yes."

"If we are to be present, we are to manifest," said Eminence 1.

"Yes," said Master Creator.

"I understand that through this filtration system you have added— what did you call it?" asked Eminence 1.

"Time, Your Eminence."

"Ah, yes, time. This time filtration will break our presence and manifestation into sequences and segments?"

"Correct."

"Then we must travel in this matter form throughout this universe if we're to experience its many forms through which we'll manifest," said Eminence 1.

"Yes, Your Eminence. In the most predominant form, you will," confirmed Master Creator.

"How do you plan to accommodate this traveling process for these life forms?" asked Eminence 6.

"I was anticipating this inquiry. You will travel through the second magic that I promised you."

"The 2 of 3?" asked Eminence 4.

"Yes, the 2 of 3."

"I was anticipating that answer," said Eminence 4.

"This magic is called 'water,' said Master Creator. "You'll travel through this universe with the most advanced vessel ever built—water."

"This water is our vessel?" exclaimed Eminence 6.

"Precisely. Water is your vessel."

"Please elaborate," said Eminence 1.

"The vessel, this water, is highly advanced," said Master Creator. "It is so advanced that it is formless. It adapts to all environments and remains transparent. No matter what planet you take it to, it will blend with its law of physics and chemistry to the point that it will appear native."

"Seriously, how can water do this?" asked Elizabeth. "It's bizarre, isn't it? Do you scientists even know what water is?"

"It is truly extraordinary, and it does defy many of the laws of chemistry and physics on Earth," Dr. Kamron concurred. "Like why ice floats on water or why water moves up a towel. Water molecules have a very strange nature, because they briefly pair up and then they split. They do this billions of times per second. Because of this strange nature, they can form themselves into a lake, and yet they can readily separate so you can dive into that lake. And that's just their shape-changing property."

"How bizarre," said Elizabeth. "Okay, let's go back to it…"

Master Creator continued. "This vessel is also intelligent in its functions. It is designed to receive you on demand, meaning that as soon as your essence enters it, it materializes you as organic substance, and from there, the journey of life through this universe begins. When you travel with your vessel as a water form, you'll move from planet to planet. Of course, as you know by now, you'll go through sequences that are filtered by time over the course of eons. What you must know about your water form is that water has the incredible capability to dissolve other forms of substances and carry them away. It can break down every piece of information it comes into contact with and record its essence within it for you."

"Why move from planet to planet within this universe of yours?" asked Eminence 1.

Master Creator answered, "So that you may experience different forms of manifestations and emotions therewith."

"Emotions?" asked Eminence 1. "How do we have these emotions?"

"You digest the stardust, and let it induce a variety of emotions in you."

"Again, Master Creator, I appreciate the poetic deliverance, but as for my fellow beings..." interrupted Eminence 4.

"I'm sorry," said Master Creator. "This is the way it shall work: When stars in various parts of this universe explode, they will send out their own unique set of elements that will become part of the formation of planets nearby. When you arrive at these planets with your vessel (which is water), you'll expand your essence (which is life) into a vast variety of amazing forms there. Your attachment to these elements will manifest new forms of beings. You may develop into these beings, such as plants, simple creatures, and so on.

"Or, if you're attached to more elements, you may manifest into an array of more complex creatures such as humanoids. Depending on what combination of elements you incorporate, subject to your locality and availability of these elements in those planets, you'll experience different kinds of these things called emotions. You see, every planet features a different selection of elements. As you manifest into a new organic form utilizing these elements, you shall experience new emotions as well, giving new flavors to life."

"New flavors to the grand illusion?" asked Eminence 6.

"Yes—new flavors to the grand illusions," said Master Creator.

"Okay, do you mind, dear?" asked Elizabeth.

"Well, I can tell you what I know about Earth's elements," said Dr. Kamron.

"Since we've digested the stardust for this place, that would help me see what she's getting at," said Elizabeth.

"There are supposed to be 108 elements on Earth," said Dr. Kamron. "The human body contains more than 90 that we know of thus far. No other creature's body on Earth has so many elements. The idea is that each element's vibration corresponds with certain vibrations emitted from human emotion. For example, anger corresponds with lead, sadness with aluminum, and stress with zinc. What baffles me is what this is in line with!"

"What?" asked Elizabeth.

"According to Buddhism, humans are born with 108 earthly desires," said Dr. Kamron.

"That's a fascinating connection, even if the numbers fluctuate!" said Elizabeth.

"Suppose we remain partly in this universal domain of yours and partly here," said Eminence 1.

"Here in singularity?" asked Master Creator.

"Yes, if we wish to observe our own experiences, and I don't mean in a simulation but observing what transpires after transformation. How would you accommodate that?" asked Eminence 1.

"Through the exit doors."

"Pardon?"

"I'm sorry, I've made accommodations for that through the channel by which you exit the universe. They'll be known to you there as mysterious black holes, but they're really just black doors. You may falsely assume everything that goes through them is destroyed. But you simply exit this information paradox through them. Everything does. That is to say, every bit of information, history, existence, and form must ultimately pass through black holes.

"The way I've designed these black holes are that they're like giant cosmic motion-picture projectors that will take a three-dimensional object and turn it into a two-dimensional surface on its edge. Not one bit of information is destroyed; instead, it's captured and stretched onto the surface of the black hole, remaining available for you to retrieve and observe as you desire."

"Where does all of this information travel to through these black doors?" Eminence 1 asked.

"To the neighboring parallel universes, naturally, because alternate history lines require prior information bases to stream from. Of course, you'll be able to observe them in each and every segment."

Eminence 1 said, "We seem to have gotten a little ahead of ourselves here, don't you think? You stated that we materialize in organic form and spread out on these planets. But how have you arranged that to transpire in a reliable manner?"

"Through a cellular system," replied Master Creator.

"Utilizing a specific and predominant species as a sample, proceed with an explanation," said Eminence 6.

"Let's take humanoids, for instance. They'll begin with a single cell and be programmed to split exponentially until the desired species form has been effectuated."

"How does the cell production and reproduction know its objective and boundaries?" asked Eminence 6.

"Ah, I should've also added this to the number of magical things in this creation," said Master Creator.

"You have certainly lived up to your reputation with the other ones so far. We're enthusiastically looking forward to hearing this one," said Eminence 4.

"Each single cell is designed to hold a complete genetic code for this production and all the necessary functions for survival and reproduction," said Master Creator.

"Then how do the cells cease to be?" asked Eminence 1.

"The cell's prime objective is to be. Until you direct them otherwise."

"Please elaborate on the makeup of these things you refer to as cells," asked Eminence 6.

"Each cell has a nucleus and inside each nucleus are chromosomes. It is actually the chromosomes that contain that complete genetic code that will make and maintain the species."

"How?" asked Eminence 1.

"Through a long strand of a magnificent chemical I've designed," said Master Creator. "It will be called deoxyribonucleic acid, or DNA. There is no molecule like it in any creation. I actually modeled its design after the shape of singularity and the multiverses around it."

"You mean it has a helical shape?" asked Eminence 1.

"Yes, Your Eminence. A triple-helix structure. When you manifest in this universe in a wide variety of species, your organic self will be composed of tens of thousands of trillions of cells. And each cell will contain about six feet of DNA strands inside of it. And each length of DNA will contain over three billion letters of coding, which provides with certainty a unique combination so that each time you wish to manifest, you will be different. And different you'll want to be every time and in every place for many reasons—survival, enhancement, pure vanity.

"However, without your connection to it, pure DNA is like all other molecules—lifeless. But once you command its production, there'll be no end to it, so to speak. It'll not only efficiently effectuate cell replication, but it'll also faithfully hold on to your every trusted hereditary secret."

"So, this DNA function, vital to our existence in your universe, is simply a coding system that produces endless combinations of complexity for life?" asked Eminence 4.

"Yes and yes," replied Master Creator.

"That's brilliant. Something so simple at the heart of such complexity," said Eminence 4.

"Thank you. In this creation, simplicity is the ultimate sign of sophistication."

Eminence 4 continued, "We should give my fellow 2 and 5 the opportunity to make their inquiries. Are you ready to respond to 2 and 5? It'll be a different type of inquiry, you understand. Not so much scientifically based, but more on philosophical grounds."

"I'll be glad to," said Master Creator.

"It is with no uncertainty that you possess the loftiest brilliance," began Eminence 2.

"My gratitude for your kind words."

Eminence 2 continued, "We do, however, believe that it would be premature to engage in a philosophical inquiry when it is based on a hypothetical rather than an actual presentation."

"An actual presentation, Your Eminence?"

"Yes."

"What kind of actual presentation would you desire?"

"We believe that two of our fellow beings should experience your concept through an actual simulation," said Eminence 5. "One that embodies organic form, perhaps for a few millennia, randomly selected in the process of this so-called timeline."

"Certainly, that can be achieved instantly," said Master Creator. "Which two beings may I have the honor of accommodating this simulation for?"

"We believe Eminences 3 and 4 would be the most suitable," said Eminence 5. "They'll bring insights from opposite sides of the spectrum to this experience."

Eminence 3 nodded. "I agree. It is virtually impossible to accept your proposal without making some serious assumptions. Before we venture into this bewildering realm of existence, we should participate in a comprehensive simulation of living."

"By all means," said Master Creator. "I'm prepared to facilitate that. How deeply would you like to simulate into this realm? You see, there is perpetual development."

Eminence 1 said, "We'll let you decide that. Just keep in mind that the most reliable approach would be to have our fellow Eminences 3 and 4 assimilate at a point in this development where they may obtain a balanced perspective. You may not know the differences in their characteristics."

"Respectfully, I have a little familiarity, and it's become more apparent through this communication," replied Master Creator.

Eminence 3 nodded. "Then we shall proceed accordingly. So, at what point through the species' advancements do we arrive at being fully conscious? I mean beyond the point of just living, but having liberation of will and analytical capabilities so that the memories we report are meaningful?"

"Let's try moving the simulation forward to a point where your manifestation has evolved to that level but is still at its infancy, so you will have a lot more to look forward to," said Master Creator.

"That sounds like an appropriate point of existence to experience this universe of yours. And what is it called?" asked Eminence 4.

"It'll be known as the 'Blue Sphere,'" answered Master Creator. "It's a jewel of a domain. You will breathe life into the core of this planet, and as it pulsates, you'll arrive with your vessel (which is water) and wrap yourself around it. From within your vessel, you'll manifest outward in every direction. On the surface, you'll assume the form of a humanoid species. This species not only possesses the properties of life, but it also develops what you've requested as far as liberation of will and analytical senses. There is also a unique concept that you'll endeavor to achieve in this existence, and it will be known as 'fun.'"

Eminence 4 said, "Yes, that's it—sounds like fun."

"That's the idea, Your Eminence—fun," said Master Creator.

"Strange and perplexing is more like it," said Eminence 3.

Master Creator nodded. "It is that, too, Your Eminence, if you wish it to be."

"So it is agreed," said Eminence 1. "Please proceed."

42

Grand Simulation

The transformation for simulation took place over a multitude of millennia of human life on Earth. Upon their return, Eminences 3 and 4 were simultaneously asked by Eminences 1 and 6 to elaborate on the experiences they had had with the simulation and to give their perspectives.

Eminence 3 began. "It was a smorgasbord of an existence. It is indeed a grand illusion, but one that is based on a drive that stems from the relentless pursuit of a single element called satisfaction. Every aspect of life is based on a design that creates a void and depravity of some sort, wherein one would engage in fulfilling that void to gain satisfaction. From a simple sense of hunger that requires constant nourishment for the survival of the organic body all the way to emotional emptiness that must be constantly satisfied by approval and acceptance of our own branches in this manifestation, they're all the same. Worst of all is the sense of insecurity that is perceived to be satisfied only by increasing the possession of a higher volume of certain forms of matter."

"Possession?" exclaimed Eminence 2.

"Yes. It's a peculiar concept, the likes of which we've never even heard of."

"Are you not aware of your life expectancy, even in the most oblivious state of your existence there?" asked Eminence 2.

"Yes," replied Eminence 3. "That's what makes it that much more absurd. One is fully aware of their imminent departure and that no matter how many of these possessions you accumulate, you cannot take any of them with you. But nevertheless, the program creates so much insecurity within you that a peculiar sense of obsession arises in such epidemic proportions that it compels one to take extreme measures for the sake of accumulating possessions."

"Extreme measures?"

"Yes. It induces cruelty."

"What is cruelty?" asked Eminence 2.

"It's a disturbing concept," said Eminence 3. "It's demeaning for us to engage in and yet it's prevalent."

"Prevalent for us to engage in actions we do not even wish to?" asked Eminence 5. "But we thought there was liberation of will in this program."

"That is the most misrepresented aspect of the proposal for this universe. There is no such thing as free will," said Eminence 3. "First, as we manifest as new forms—a process called 'being born'—we become enslaved to our hereditary traits indefinitely. The chemical makeup of this thing called a 'brain' significantly depends on this inheritance from your parents and ancestors. No matter how much you wish to apply this free-will concept, you're chained to this fundamental functionality that was formed before this birthing process without any choice on the newborn's part. Your mere attempt to function differently is again a path that is not based on free will. How can there be free will when even your fundamental thought process is greatly shaped by the experiences of your forefathers and foremothers?"

"To what degree does this brain functioning that you utilized in your simulation allow for deviation from these past experiences to induce new paths?" asked Eminence 5.

"It's nominal, at best," answered Eminence 3. "There's only a mediocre degree of variation to apply to this grossly misrepresented free-will concept."

"You mean that there are no contingencies built into the functioning process of this brain component?"

"Only to a negligible degree. You see, what compounds the challenge for applying this free will is the design of this brain, which forces us to become creatures of habit."

Eminence 5 looked puzzled. "How peculiar. How so?"

"The mere experience of being in that domain requires a variety of stimulations," said Eminence 3. "To be stimulated, these things in the brain called neurotransmitters must be activated. As certain conditions activate them, the brain becomes addicted to those pathways through which those neurotransmitters travel to induce the stimulation.

"Now, here's the really awful part: As a result of this, the grand illusion loses its allure. Some of the most predominant forms of stimulation are fear, anxiety, and stress, all of which are destructive to the manifested form. The brain becomes addicted to these stimulations, forcing the form to follow the very actions and reactions that induce them. Changing the pathways of these neurotransmitters in the brain becomes a very daunting task. These addictions make one seek more destructive stimulations even when outside factors are no longer present."

"You mean you become addicted to your own sensations?" asked Eminence 5.

"Precisely," said Eminence 3.

"Even destructive ones?"

"Even destructive ones."

"This is unbecoming of us," said Eminence 5. "What is your perspective on this, Eminence 4?"

"I think the free will is well-represented, but respectfully, my fellow being may have misinterpreted it," said Eminence 4. "Liberation of will is the most interesting and ultimate aspect of playing in this program of existence. In fact, it is one worthy of acknowledgment. The term 'liberation of will' is not intended to mean that in that plane of existence, you entirely have the free will to choose your actions. It simply implies that your ultimate goal for fulfillment is to liberate yourself from your will."

Eminence 3 protested, "Be that as it may, the simulation was basically focused on forming life on a planet up to the point of developing these species, through which we became known as humans. Simply put, it was distasteful and unbecoming. This species develops from an animal to a semi-animal form with a higher level of self-awareness. But fear—this awful element that was once part of the animal form—remains predominant in this higher-level-species human. As such, the fear mechanism rules so many aspects of this existence that the quality of being there significantly diminishes."

"My dear fellow being," countered Eminence 4, "the fear element is a flavor-producing aspect. And it appears to me that the Master Creator implemented this factor as the only safety mechanism."

"There were more awful elements that were totally needless, like this thing called 'ego,'" added Eminence 3.

"Respectfully," said Eminence 4, "I sincerely believe that incorporating ego was Master Creator's clever attempt to prevent complacency."

Eminence 5 interrupted. "Eminence 4, please enlighten us with the general assessment of your experience in this simulation."

"When I reflect back on my experiences as a human form," began Eminence 4, "I must begin by expressing gratitude to our gifted Master Creator and respectfully ask Her to not let my fellow Eminence 3's comments tarnish the luster of Her brilliant work. If there is any criticism, it should be directed to our judgment. Master Creator went through extreme measures to create this fantastic plane of existence. Every detail, every element, and every substance was carefully calibrated to perfection and balance while our one and only responsibility was to enjoy them. If any one of us failed to do that, we have failed ourselves.

"Master Creator should justifiably have added one more element to Her list of three magical creations. This element was so readily and beautifully available for the seeker, and yet we missed out on it over and over again. It was a fascinating concept, the likes of which have never existed in any multiverse. It was called 'fun.' It seems that all other elements were produced to serve this one, and yet we overlooked its brilliant purpose and made the false assumption that its existence was secondary to all other purposes when, in fact, it was vital.

"Lastly, Master Creator displayed a sense of humility when She refrained from boasting about Her third magical element as well, identified as 'love.' Having experienced it in this simulation, I now understand why She did not elaborate on it. It is an element that can be understood only by those who have experienced it, not those who have suffered from its void, just like the pain of hunger is a completely different experience than that of fulfillment by lavish nourishment.

"I am sorry that my fellow Eminence did not experience the latter. To those who were not moved by the deliverance of love and announce that life does not signify anything, I must say with great sympathy that they must have not seen the shine in the eyes of their beloved staring back at them. Indeed, we must all have the humility to thank the Master Creator for the grace that has been accorded to us through transformations to life."

———•◦◦❀◦◦•———

The Grand Being now moved to utter something that would contain a word that would elicit the utmost respect from the Eminences. The six Eminences, sensing the gravity of the moment, were also immediately moved in the same fashion and remained in reverential silence. They all knew this gesture of respect stemmed from this single word and that it referred to something unimaginably more eminent than them and even the Grand Being. Long moments passed.

Master Creator also recognized that these expressions of respect were intended for something far larger than Her and all those present. She trembled with excitement, the likes of which she had never before experienced. It was not just from the anxiety of anticipation but also an apprehension that something was about to happen that She might not have the capacity to understand. She thought to Herself, *what if it occurs and I simply cannot process the information? What if it is so grand that it simply absorbs me?*

All She could sense was that the ultimate sign of humility was about to be expressed in relation to something infinitely more momentous than Her, the six Eminences, and the Grand Being. She summoned all Her will to stay balanced so She could comprehend what was to be said.

When the moment arrived, the Grand Being uttered only one sentence, at the end of which contained the word for which the expression of respect was intended. As soon as that word was spoken, the entire chamber became so beautified and energized that all was still. Who would have thought that merely pronouncing just its name could inspire such profundity among those who understood its true meaning?

At first, the sentence echoed in the space and Master Creator could not quite hear it. Then it started resonating clearly as to what the question was that the Grand Being was asking.

"When we manifest as part of this universe," declared Grand Being at last, "wouldn't we think that *you* are God?"

43

⁕

THE LAST WORDS:
WE ARE THE DIVINE INTERVENTION

Having finished their dinner and Alex's notebook, the Kamrons sat in silence in the gazebo for several minutes, trying to digest everything, including what they had just read.

"I've never had a spiritual moment reading something full of scientific stuff before," Elizabeth said to her husband.

They heard footsteps and looked up to see Alex approaching them. "I hope the dinner was to your liking," he said.

"Yes, the dinner, the ambiance, and the fascinating literature," said Elizabeth. "May I ask you something, Alex, while I'm in this spiritual mood? From what my husband says, you're a creationist, aren't you?"

"In my own way, yes," said Alex.

"Then tell me, how come there is no divine intervention for all the perils that humanity faces?"

"But of course there is," said Alex.

"You've got to be joking," said Elizabeth.

"Not at all. You see, *we* are the divine intervention," said Alex.

"I don't get it."

"It's very simple: As humans, don't we always attempt to do godlike things? Sort of like mimicking our Creator? Things such as cloning, creating artificial intelligence, all that."

Elizabeth agreed. "Yes, that's true but ..."

"Now, consider this," said Alex. "We build drones, robots, and other artificially intelligent entities to do our bidding in ways that prevent harm to us."

"Yes, correct," said Elizabeth.

"Well, that's just another way of mimicking the Creator's method.

You see, as a measure of divine intervention, we ourselves were created to prevent harm to our true self from the perils of this existence. Therefore, we are the divine intervention."

The Kamrons were quiet again for a few moments.

Alex threw up his hands, grinning. "Oh, enough science and philosophy for the evening! I hoped you would stay, so I've had a room made available for you to sleep over tonight."

"That is so kind of you," said Dr. Kamron, warmly. "This has indeed been delightful. As our time together comes to an end, I must express our deepest gratitude for your hospitality."

"Not at all—the pleasure was all mine," said Alex, his eyes twinkling.

"No, seriously Alex, this is as memorable as it gets," added Elizabeth. "Plus, you've given us such wonderful insights into life. Frankly, I'm not sure how you've managed to accumulate such diverse and complex knowledge and shape it into comprehensible insights."

"You are very kind—and I'm not sure about all that," said Alex. "But, as Leonardo da Vinci once said when he was asked how he was able to design such complex architecture, he replied, 'L'architettura è simplice, la semplicità è difficile,' which, translated from Italian, means 'Architecture is simple, but simplicity is difficult.' So, if I have helped simplify life for you and yours, then maybe there has been some value. Otherwise, nothing was gained but a most pleasurable evening."

"No, Alex, the wonderful thing about talking to people like you is that you provide such clear perspective about various aspects of life," said Elizabeth. "There are so many ideas and philosophies in this world, and it seems that the more I read and experience, the more vast and confusing it gets. I feel lucky to have met people like you who are capable of whittling this world down to a more palatable size for our simpler minds."

Alex smiled. "I don't deserve the credit you're giving me, but you're correct that as humans, we're capable of comprehending such diverse information and relating to such a variety of philosophies that it can make life unsettling and confusing. We strive to enlighten ourselves to hold on to something that is made of certainty. And yet, only the ignorant are certain."

"I guess we should envy their way of thinking," said Elizabeth.

"Perhaps that's why religions are so appealing to the masses," said

Alex. "They give them tools to manage their realities, even in vain. A prepackaged reference to life, if you will."

Dr. Kamron's eyes brightened. "Wait, Alex, that sounds familiar! Do you think that's where I was going with my so-called Earth Residents' Manual?"

Alex smiled. "That's okay, Doctor, your intentions are noble, as always. But, like I mentioned earlier, the truth is that it'll make little to no difference. What matters is your passion for it. That's why I participated in this brainstorming tonight—for the sake of your passion for this task."

"Passion?" asked Dr. Kamron.

"Yes," said Alex. "That's the way to help humanity to not suffer from uncertainty and instead enjoy life. Passion brings life down to that palatable size. When you feel passionate about something or someone, everything else in life seems to dim or fade away. When your passion shines, your life then takes on meaningful purpose. You wake up in the morning with the anticipation to apply yourself to your passion, and all other problems take a back seat while you drive your soul to that favorite destination, a place that makes you and your passion more intertwined."

"Lucky are those whose occupation is their passion," said Dr. Kamron. "They never work a day in their lives."

"But, Alex, you really don't see much value in all the insights that you gave us tonight?" asked Elizabeth. "I certainly feel like I'm more enlightened after my conversation with you. Your logic is unsurpassed."

Alex lowered his head in humility. "Logic is a human-made concept—there's no such thing in nature. We're all raised to believe that logic is the quintessence of truth. But something logical does not mean it is true."

"But there's often consistency in logic and it feels good to the human mind," protested Elizabeth.

"That's because it's human-made," said Alex. "I wish I could wholeheartedly agree with you, but it's only your mind that has taken a liking to my so-called logic. Because that's what our minds are supposed to do."

Alex grew a little serious. "Listen, these are my last words with you tonight. They may diminish the value of all that we have spoken of earlier, but they will open your mind where it does not like to go. A place far from logic, where no meaning for life is required."

"But I still can't help but repeat to myself that your words were so logical that they resonated with me as the truth. Now you want us to disregard them all?" Elizabeth asked.

Alex nodded. "I think your husband can better appreciate what I'm about to say, as it may be in line with his discoveries. You don't have to disregard what I have shared with you tonight, but if you wish to elevate your awareness to a higher level, you must understand how little value there is in logic. And, if I don't share this with you now, considering your level of capability to comprehend, then I'll feel that I have shortchanged you in some way."

"How so?" asked Elizabeth.

"So, you saw logic in my words, and that resonated in your mind as the truth," began Alex. "But, we have no reality by which to run any of our logic for validity. So, in this universe, we create reality as we go. From time to time, we devise a new logic and wrap our minds around it, and then we feel cozy, safe, or falsely proud, as if we've discovered something profound that represents the truth for us. However, deep inside we all must know, as Kahlil Gibran said, 'Say not, "I have found the truth," but rather, "I have found a truth."'"

"So there can be a truth?" asked Elizabeth.

"There can be a truth for you on a temporary basis."

"But why so temporary?"

"Because truth is realized only through our consciousness."

"So nothing is true if we don't realize it as such?" asked Elizabeth.

"Precisely."

"But there is a reality determined by the laws of physics, and those laws make our physical reality independent of our minds," said Elizabeth.

"The nature of our universe is not independent of our consciousness," said Alex. "If we don't project our perceptions, they would not create the shapes that manifest our reality—whether individually in our personal life or collectively as humanity. Isn't that exactly what your unifying field discovery of $c(s) = \mathcal{J}$ is, for which you received your well-deserved Nobel Prize?"

Dr. Kamron nodded. "Yes, truth is realized only through our consciousness. Because, yes, in reality, the reality is dependent on the observer."

"You know, Dr. Kamron, it would be a pleasure to hear from you in person how you made your discovery of the unified field—this ultimate pillar in science," said Alex.

Dr. Kamron replied, "In a way, it was like what you just said that 'we are the divine intervention.' Meaning that I simply realized that we are 'the unified field.' That is, we are the prism."

"A prism?" Alex asked.

"Yes, our consciousness is the prism through which quanta become existence. We ourselves were the missing piece in the theory of everything. 'The rest were details.' Our thoughts are the unifying elements between the small-scale world and the large."

Then Alex asked, "But how did you arrive at that?"

Dr. Kamron replied, "Just follow these simple facts and you will see its elegance and simplicity.

(c) = consciousness
(s) = super-positions
$(\mathcal{I})$ = existence

"Accordingly, consciousness processes super-positions into existence from the void," said Dr. Kamron. "Keep in mind that (1) space-time are properties of the quantum world—perhaps many were misguided by thinking the reverse—and (2) the void and vacuum (aka nothingness) is anything but empty. In fact, it's full of quantum field particles.

"The quantum fluctuations in the vacuum (nothingness) through us as quantized units of interactions in now (our consciousness) will manifest into existence that which we call the visible world."

Alex said, "Wow. And finally, there we have it."

44

BOUNDARIES OF LIFE

On the other side of the dome, they continued to sit on the gliding bench just past midnight on this first day of summer, Adrian and Natalie lost track of time as they talked. Sometimes they simply leaned next to each other quietly and listened to the rhythmic sounds of the ocean below. Natalie stroked the back of Adrian's head with her fingertips.

"You probably come here to watch the sunset every day," remarked Adrian.

"Never," said Natalie.

"Why?"

"I like the subtleties of nature. Here, night falls too abruptly. I've tried but never managed to catch a real twilight, ever."

"No wonder you didn't like me," Adrian said, chuckling to himself.

"What?"

"My lack of subtlety," said Adrian.

"What you lack in subtlety, you make up for with your unspoken sense of integrity," said Natalie. She suddenly spotted something and pointed to it. "Look at that pair of flat flies. From here, it looks like they're sitting on top of each other. I swear there are more flat flies in this world than humans."

Adrian mumbled under his breath, "Yes. In this world."

Natalie continued without hearing him. "I mean, they're everywhere! My favorites are the blue ones, though. How can something so flat shine like that? You have to agree, they're kind of weird. What creatures have their body parts like that? Its like their eyes are painted over the tips of their wings. Heck, that's all they are, just a wing. And ever so thin … how can anything be so thin and still alive?"

"Have you heard the myth about the flat flies?" asked Adrian.

"What, that if you look at them perfectly straight, they're so thin that you can't see them? Like there's no dimension to their bodies? I guess I've always only noticed them sideways, so who knows. That may be true."

"No, that's not the myth I was referring to."

"Which one, then?"

"There is an old myth that flat flies are so thin that since they have no dimensions, they can travel through parallel universes."

"What? Through parallel universes? Never heard that one! But I guess they're pretty awesome looking… and if there weren't so many of them around, we'd have a better appreciation for their beauty."

Moments passed. Adrian remained quiet.

"You're kind of quiet," Natalie prodded. "Are you bored already, our little restless guest? Huh?"

Once more, as Natalie ran her fingers down Adrian's hair to his neck, she felt and noticed a chain around his neck.

"Oh, what's this? You don't seem like a guy who wears a necklace."

"It's not a necklace. Leave it alone," said Adrian.

"What, let me see it. Is it a dog tag?"

"No, forget it."

With one quick move, Natalie yanked the necklace off and jumped out of her seat, giggling. "Let's see what I got."

As she examined it, Adrian got up and insisted, "Give it back."

"This is very strange," said Natalie. "It's a flat fly necklace. I've never seen anything like it. Why, it's so heavy for a little necklace! It's weird. These things on it look like they're functional."

"Please don't touch them," said Adrian.

"Oh come on, Adrian, what is this? Who wears a flat fly necklace, for goodness' sake? Especially a guy like you. If this is some kind of device, why is it in this shape? Don't we see enough of these flat flies everywhere? What's the novelty? And who went through this much trouble to design it in this shape?"

"Please stop," said Adrian.

Natalie pressed her fingernail on a surface that looked like a gemstone, and suddenly the device projected a three-dimensional holograph with two sides, each displaying a video of Dr. Kamron in various places and times.

"I know this guy—he's grandpa's guest!" exclaimed Natalie in surprise. "What's going on? Are you following him? You can't be his security attaché. Why are you doing this?"

Adrian was getting upset. "Please stop."

"These images, why are there two of them? And wait, that one is here. Where is the other one? Is that where he was before? What are you up to?" asked Natalie, suspiciously.

"You wouldn't understand."

"I would understand. Try me."

"It's kind of private."

"Why, the nerve!" shouted Natalie. "Private? I just gave you the grand tour of our entire private lives, and you think your little sissy necklace device is private?"

"Sissy?" said Adrian.

"Yeah, sissy," said Natalie, narrowing her eyes. "My grandma wouldn't wear a necklace of a flat fly!"

"Your grandma doesn't need to."

"Need to? You need to wear this thing? What, come on, tell me!"

"Let me turn it off," said Adrian.

Natalie moved back and said mischievously, "So, if I give it back, will you tell me?"

"Maybe."

"Forget it. I'm not giving it back."

As Adrian took another step, she dashed away from him. Adrian chased her as she ran into an open field where she attempted to climb up onto a stack of hay bales. Adrian ran to her side and tackled her, and they both fell onto the loose hay on the ground. Holding the necklace tightly in her hand, Natalie laughed as she screamed, "I'm not giving it back until you promise to tell me!"

Adrian couldn't help but start to laugh, although he was desperately trying to keep some serious composure about the subject. Suddenly in the struggle, the chain came off in Adrian's hand and Natalie dropped the device down her shirt.

"You have to tell me first or I'll start running again," she said.

Adrian stopped. "Okay, simmer down, take it out."

"Not gonna happen."

"Okay, listen, let's flip a coin. If I lose, you will get your way."

"So I have a fifty-fifty chance to get my way?"

"Umm … yes. Do you have a quarter or something?"

"I don't have a quarter, but I do have a very old coin," said Natalie. "Grandpa likes to give those as gifts. This one's special, and it's always brought me good luck."

"Does it have an image of a head on it?" asked Adrian.

"As a matter of fact, it does."

"Okay, let's flip it. Heads I win, tails you lose."

"All right, but I'm flipping," said Natalie.

"Okay, go."

Natalie threw the coin into the air. "Here we go—oh no! It's tails—I lose … wait a minute, you cheater! No way I'm giving this back until you tell me."

"Okay, I will, but it was worth a shot," said Adrian.

Natalie smiled slyly. "Promise?"

"Sure, but first wipe that Tweety Bird canary feather off your mouth and give it back," said Adrian.

"Then you'll tell me?"

"I said I would." Adrian got up, took her hand, and helped her up.

She took the device out from her shirt and gave it to him. He adjusted the setting and placed it in his back pocket. He reached up, took some hay out of Natalie's hair, and kissed her on the lips as they walked back to the bench.

Natalie said, "You promised."

"Look, you're obviously very bright," said Adrian, "but this takes some serious conceptualization to comprehend. Even then, you'll just have to trust me with what I'll tell you."

"I don't know for the life of me why, but I do trust you," said Natalie. "As for the other thing, make me understand, okay?"

"It's hard to know where to even start. You see, life has no boundaries."

Natalie was already confused. "What? Listen, start by telling me why you're following Dr. Kamron."

"He's out of place and doesn't know it."

"Out of place?"

"It's not gonna work like this…" muttered Adrian.

"Try me—just say it," said Natalie.

Adrian took a deep breath. "The core of the problem is that suicide rates have been rapidly climbing in the world, which is creating imbalances in the flow of consciousness. If he makes his new discovery public, as I believe he was about to announce tonight, there'll be serious consequences for humanity as a whole."

Natalie stared at him. "Wow, what did you just say? And what the heck does that even mean because you're still talking upside down."

"Just hold on to this piece of information and I'll walk you through the rest."

"Okay, but what do you mean by 'rapidly climbing suicide rate'?"

"It's a silent catastrophe, but since it appears to be self-induced, it doesn't get much attention," said Adrian. "The world's suicide rate started climbing back in the beginning of the second millennium. Since in most of the world there is no real accounting of it, we took a close look at a study in the United States that was conducted by the National Center for Injury Prevention and Control, which is part of the Centers for Disease Control, or CDC.

"It was a report in 2010 that originally caught our attention, and it stated that suicide caused 34.6 billion dollars in economic damage in that year alone. We had been looking at this data for the sake of a viability study that had nothing to do with suicide. But, once we focused on the human aspect of this study, it was shocking. In that same year, 8.3 million adults in the US, according to the CDC, reported having suicidal thoughts, 2.2 million made suicide plans, and 1.1 million actually followed through. Suicide had reached the top 10 causes of death in the United States and was very prevalent among youth. If that is not a serious concern for any humanitarian, I don't know what would be. So, we started noticing this climb every year and have been monitoring it ever since."

"Who is 'we'?" asked Natalie.

"Never mind that for now."

Natalie looked frustrated. "You've got to do better than this for me to understand. Dr. Kamron is 'out of place'? That's why there are more suicides? Huh?"

"No, there are already too many suicides, and if he goes public with his discovery, the rate will go out of control," said Adrian. "You see, fear of the unknown is a great prevention for self-destruction, but if you take that away, people will want to move on when they encounter the first challenging period of their lives.

"As you know, everyone wants to go to heaven, but people are not in a hurry to get there, perhaps because of their lack of conviction that they actually will. But, if you scientifically prove there is someplace else to go after this life, you'd be surprised by how many would be willing to exit and not give this plane of existence a well-deserved chance to advance. You see, Dr. Kamron is not causing the climb in the suicide rate, but he has crossed over to this universe and is going to impact the course of events if he goes public with his discovery."

"How do you know what he's going to do? Are you some kind of time traveler?" asked Natalie.

"No, don't be silly. Besides, time travel is not really practical."

"You mean it's impossible?"

"No, just not practical for us. Technically, even Einstein's special theory of relativity provides for the possibility of time travel, but among other things, there's a serious problem with occupying a time space in which you have not earned your place."

"What do you mean by 'earned'?" asked Natalie.

"Through generations of building immunity, you can stay alive and coexist with all the pathogens that your body carries, like viruses and bacteria. But, if you come from a time and space that's outside of that immunity building sequence, you can die in a matter of days."

"Can't you get some kind of protection or vaccination?"

"Vaccination for how many things and what strains? There are ways to time travel but they're not practical for us."

"Then if you're not a time traveler, how do you know what Dr. Kamron is going to do?"

"Because he's done it before."

"You're not making any sense," said Natalie.

"I know, I know," said Adrian, shaking his head. "Universes have a certain quality about them. They relive the same paths and story lines, but each time, they allow for alternate outcomes—sort of like refreshing the course of events with the same principles and players intact."

"I don't get it," said Natalie. "Are you saying that this time some metaphysical wire has gotten crossed?"

"No, just listen for a bit. But first, tell me how much you know about parallel universes."

"Not much. I've just have heard the term and some bizarre theory of how there's another universe parallel to ours or something to that effect. But come on, last time I checked, this universe of ours is so large that we can't even scratch the surface when it comes to its size. So, I think our universe is it."

"We humans, with our limited perceptions, have an unlimited sense of primacy," said Adrian. "Centuries ago, Galileo had to suppress this egoistic vision by proving that Earth is not the center of the universe. We're rapidly arriving at a point of similar understanding that this universe is not the only one of its kind either."

He paused. "I usually don't waste energy on proving these things, so I can stop here if you like."

"Come on, don't hold back," said Natalie. "I really want to know. I guess I should just wait for you to finish. You see, it's just that I can't imagine that there's a scientific basis for this fantastic parallel universe idea."

"Of course there is," said Adrian. "Quantum mechanics in unitary in its mathematically simplest form provides for multiverses."

Natalie rolled her eyes. "English, please."

"It's really not just another universe," said Adrian. "There are multitudes of universes parallel to one another as part of the same chain of existence, and their growth and advancement are based on the development of consciousness on a hierarchal level."

Natalie shook her head. "You're still gonna have to bend down with those words if you want me to understand."

"Okay, imagine a loaf of bread representing this chain of existence," said Adrian. "Each slice represents a separate universe. Now imagine that the loaf is in the shape of a pyramid, except that it's upside down. The downward point is where consciousness is raw—sort of disenlightened, if you will. As each particle of consciousness develops in each slice and ripens, it moves up to the next slice. The degree of development from the neighboring lower universe to the next is nominal as they pair up to support each other in an upward development fashion."

Natalie still looked confused. "I'm getting the visual on this, but right now you gotta tell me a point of reference so I can follow you better."

"What?"

"Where am I in this pyramid?" asked Natalie. "I feel like I'm practically close to the top."

Adrian smiled. "I'm not surprised to hear you say that, but that's just your natural human vanity giving you that illusion. You and I are only three levels up from the bottom, and levels three and four are twin parallels. The fourth one is only slightly more developed than the third and, in a way, it's responsible for its well-being."

"Really? I'm perennially disappointed."

"Hey, just think about how far up you can still develop."

"What do you mean by the 'fourth one is only slightly more developed'?" asked Natalie.

"The twin parallel universes are a lot more identical than the others. In fact, their history and developments are similar."

"I don't get it," said Natalie. "How can two universes have the same history? And how can something so far away be connected in functioning and creating that same history?"

"It's not exactly the same history," replied Adrian. "But look, I'm going to start answering your second question first and hopefully it'll put us on the right track. But first you must get over your misconception that things far away are not connected. For a moment, let's put your focus on the nature of the subatomic world, and then you can better appreciate this fact.

"The Pauli exclusion principle revealed an absolutely astonishing quality about subatomic particles in certain pairs. When these particles are separated even by very long distances, each one knows instantly what the other one is doing. They have a quality about them called 'spin.' As soon as you identify the spin of one particle, its sister particle instantly begins to spin in the opposite direction at a precise rate, regardless of how far apart from each other they are."

"Like how far?" asked Natalie.

"The science writer Lawrence Joseph uses a metaphor to help illustrate this principle pretty well. Just imagine two identical pool balls in two different countries. As soon as you send one spinning, the other one spins in an opposite direction at the same speed."

"Okay, I understand that, as weird as it sounds, but I still can't visualize this multitude-of-universes idea," said Natalie.

"All right, let's try this for a visual aid," said Adrian. "Have you ever looked at two mirrors directly across from each other? Do you recall the seemingly endless reflection of the same image?"

"Oh yes, it seems to continue infinitely," said Natalie. "So, if these images represent us, can we ever see our other selves in this metaphoric mirror that you're explaining? You know, like facing our doppelgänger?"

Adrian shook his head. "No, unlike ordinary mirrors, when you look into them, you'll see the back side of yourself almost infinitely. Your other selves are either behind you or in front of you, carrying on various history lines. Because these history lines virtually always vary, these variations cascade down a different path. However, in very infrequent circumstances where they overlap, you'll get a sensation of instantly feeling what your other self in the other parallel universe has just experienced. When you pick up that sensation, you feel what people refer to as déjà vu."

Natalie shivered. "I just got chills hearing that. It's almost like I suddenly sensed what you're trying to explain with this fancy spiel of yours. So, déjà vu occurs when we're lined up precisely with our other self's history line and pick up the memory of what they just experienced ever so slightly before we go through the same experience?"

"You got it!" said Adrian, triumphant. "The fact is, you're always deeply connected to your other self. When this self engages in an action or is going through a happening identical to you but with the tiniest delay, you perceive that as a memory and as something you've experienced before. It's like when you enter a place for the first time and suddenly it feels eerily familiar, like you've been there before. Or you're in the middle of a conversation and suddenly you think you've said or heard those exact words before. The fact is, you're just a moment behind your other self and are picking up on that memory trace in the next parallel universe."

"Sometimes when I'm about to wake up and I'm certain I'm not dreaming, I think about these people I know but when I completely wake up, I have no idea who they were," said Natalie.

Adrian nodded. "Your other self knows them. On a deep level, you're picking up their memory trace."

"So what happens when I die?" asked Natalie.

"As your consciousness exits this plane of existence," said Adrian, "it instantly shifts to your immediate other self and you continue on. Imagine a current of electrical charges powering a series of lights. If one light fixture is turned off, the current immediately transfers to the remaining lights."

"Wow, but wait, that's a lot of universes. How do you fit that anywhere?"

"Fit? Try imagining this: You're looking at one of those old DVD changers, and it holds hundreds and hundreds of DVDs within it. The amount of information within each DVD, playing out a humongous measure of outcomes, is of little to no consequence to the size of the DVD. If you're just a tiny bit of information inside of one of those DVDs, the concept of multitudes of DVDs sitting parallel to one another may be difficult to imagine."

"So, how did you first find out about Dr. Kamron's knowledge on this transformation of us from one DVD to another, so to speak?" asked Natalie.

Adrian was getting visibly excited about sharing the next part of his story. "Listen to what he wrote in one of his papers a few years back about how the universe is operated. He wrote, 'We operate it ourselves. What you have to visualize is that we are much bigger than this universe. Frankly, size is of no consequence because it's all just about the exchange of information. But the best way it can be explained is by visualizing that the universe is like a personal handheld smart device, wherein each individual creates and operates an external existence of themselves. The device gives the impression that you are actually occupying it (akin to when you are so hyperfocused on playing a game on your handheld computer that all of your senses are engaged to the point that you are oblivious of most of your surroundings outside of that game).'"

Adrian paused for a moment. "He goes on to say, 'Except, consider that you are occupying a three-dimensional space-time device. These devices are synchronized to interact with other devices, giving the illusion of a single universe. But here's the kicker: One can have a virtually countless number of devices, so when one ceases to operate a device, its information is transported, carrying all the data (conscious memory) with it to the next device (parallel universe) closest and most identical to the prior one. This is because the next identical device was created by the same operator engaging in the same paradigm and following a similar history line except for where it splits and creates new outcomes.'"

"It sounds like he's saying the same thing you were just explaining," said Natalie. "Adrian, I'm sorry. Don't get me wrong—I'm still following, but how about some scientific perspective?"

"All right then," said Adrian. "The string theory, which is the best concept of the fundamental theory of nature, contains a key component that's a major factor in cosmology."

"Uhh, which is?" asked Natalie.

"Inflationary expansion."

"Which is?"

"Which is a period of extremely accelerated expansion in early cosmic history," said Adrian. "You see, this process is so fast that in less than a second, a tiny subatomic speck of space is inflated to the size of a universe like ours."

"And?"

"And string theory explains that an unlimited number of universes with a variety of physical laws of nature are being produced through this process of this eternal, inflationary expansion."

"I had no idea that string theory accounts for multiverses," said Natalie, "but a theory is a theory. Without an observational test, any scientific mind would be hard-pressed to accept these bubble universes as a natural fact."

"Listen, there is direct evidence of these bubble universes as you so correctly put it. You see, undoubtedly some of these bubble universes will collide with one another. If our expanding bubble collided with another one, it would inevitably produce an imprint in the cosmic background."

"Uh, for sure," said Natalie. "And you're telling me that evidence of this exists?"

"Yes. After a very long and patient search, such a spot with the predicted intensity profile was detected."

"That's fascinating," Natalie said. She was quiet for a few moments, then said, "So, let me see if I get your point so far. Both eternal inflation and these unitary quantum mechanics provide scientific mechanisms for creating copies of us elsewhere in some external reality."

Adrian grinned. "Yes, you got it."

45

Crossing Over

"Look, Adrian, I really do better understand this now," said Natalie, "but I still have plenty of conceptual problems with it. So do you think you can do better than that for me to fully grasp the mysterious nature of these parallel universes?"

"How? I thought I just did."

"Okay, so this parallel universe idea is not beyond the pull of science, but you have to agree it's novelty science, so it takes some getting used to in the mind," said Natalie. "I know I'm not as well-read as you are, but come on, who's heard of this in human history?"

"You'd be surprised," said Adrian. "There is scientific and philosophical history of the parallel universe going back thousands of years ago. If you want modern history, Dr. Hugh Everett III of Princeton University wrote about quantum multiverses in 1957. He wrote that parallel universes just like the one we're in do exist, and that they're all related. In fact, they branch off one another. But the history line within each universe is different. For example, wars have different outcomes. Even species take different shapes and evolve differently."

Natalie pondered this. "I'm just curious—why would whoever created this universe allow for so many more duplications?"

"Don't you see? That's the beauty of it!" said Adrian, throwing up his hands. "Suppose you were producing a movie and you had infinite time. Wouldn't you want to have many varieties of outcomes for each segment of the story? Why limit it to one ending? That's way too restrictive for a creator of the magnitude that can produce an entire universe. Why stop there?"

Natalie shook her head, smiling. "You're starting to sound like Grandpa."

"Really, am I?" said Adrian, knowingly.

"Yes, but never mind that. Tell me, how is this process done?"

"Let's go back to the scientific history of it and I'll try to make better sense of it. Just please don't jump ahead." He smiled.

"Would you like me to gaze into your eyes instead?" teased Natalie.

Adrian chuckled. "Dr. Everett focused on the erratic behavior of quantum matter—such as particles inside an atom—to support his 'many-worlds theory.' Now, let me explain the Heisenberg uncertainty principle and we'll come back to this. This renowned physicist believed that just by observing quantum matter, we could affect the behavior of that matter. You see, particles on the quantum level have shape-shifting properties.

"Now, listen to this: A well-respected physicist named Niels Bohr, who was an authority in quantum mechanics, said, 'All quantum particles don't exist in one state or the other, but in all of its possible states at once.' This state of an object existing in all of its possible states at once is called its superposition. He further concluded that 'when we observe a quantum object, we affect its behavior. Observation breaks an object's superposition and essentially forces the object to choose one state.'

"Now listen to this carefully: According to Dr. Everett, observation doesn't just force the object into one state or another but causes an actual split in the universe—where the universe literally duplicates into other universes to accommodate for each possible outcome."

Natalie rubbed her forehead. "My head is splitting right now, listening to your splitting universe theory."

"I know, but you wanted to know," said Adrian, kindly.

"I do, I do, it's fascinating. And you said there's more to the history."

"Yeah, I can take you back earlier than 1957. Giordano Bruno wrote his *On the Infinite, Universe and Worlds* way back in the late 1500s.

"1500s? You've got to be kidding," said Natalie.

"Just wait, it goes even further back when it comes to doppelgängers," said Adrian. "The ancient Persian language has a precise word known as 'hamzad.' It literally means 'dually-created' and is based on the mythology that every human at the time of birth has a double who is absolutely identical but invisible to themselves."

"Seriously, how do you know these things? It's kind of sexy," said Natalie.

Adrian rolled his eyes. "Anyway, we have quantum realities where history plays out differently involving the same people (*hamzads* if you will). Just as the Bible presented multilayer universes in the various-heavens analogy, other ancient religions contained similar references. Over 7,000 years BCE, Hinduism presented the concept of the breath of Brahman in which an expanding, contrasting universe moves forward and backward in time in its various levels."

"This is where you're killing me with the mind-boggling proportions of this concept. They seem so excessive that it makes it hard to understand and conceptualize," said Natalie.

"Actually, there's nothing excessive about it," said Adrian. "It would be a waste of a great existential design to have only one version of an outcome for a history line. To me, it would be hard to understand the waste if there *was* only one version in the history line. Life has no boundaries.

"As for conceptualization, imagine that you've just created a storyline on your computer. Now you wish for it to have various outcomes. At the precise point of your desired branching, you simply copy and paste the history line and continue with new versions. For the creator who materialized this grand of a design, it's indeed as simple as copy and paste."

"What about the characters inside these story lines? Do they get copied and pasted too?"

"Yes, unless the character's role ends inside its history line—because of death, for instance. Then it'll be a cut and paste. That character will cease to exist in its prior universe and history line—instead it'll get placed in an alternate universe to engage in a new history line."

"Is that what happened to Dr. Kamron?" asked Natalie.

"No, what happened to Dr. Kamron appears to be an anomaly where he inadvertently crossed over to a history line already in place in a lower universe," answered Adrian.

"So, Dr. Kamron does not belong here? And what do you mean by 'inadvertently'?"

"I mean, he doesn't know that he's out of place."

"What? How bizarre. Does this happen often?"

"No, but it has before," said Adrian. "We believe most of these individuals who have had a profound, positive impact on humanity have crossed over inadvertently (which explains their insight and goodwill). They were typically prophets, great philosophers, guru scientists, and so on. Often they had desires to write a manual to improve life in the lower universe."

"Do you know of anything cool that they did to help our universe?" asked Natalie.

"I have always been suspicious of one," answered Adrian.

"Which one?"

"Well, do you know who invented the photograph?"

"Wasn't it someone named Niépce?"

"Joseph Niépce and Louis Daguerre only improved and perfected the system, but no one knows who the original inventor of photography was," said Adrian. "Isn't that a little strange? Think about it—if the photograph hadn't been invented, we wouldn't have just about any of our technological developments, all the way through to computers. Anything that has ever evolved scientifically depended one way or the other on the photograph. Yet, no one knows its first creator. I think that when these guys cross over, they kind of plant a seed of certain knowledge, so that it'll grow to serve the lower universe for generations to come."

"Do they ever find out that they're out of place?" asked Natalie.

"We don't believe so," said Adrian. "At least until tonight, I didn't believe anybody knew. They usually feel out of place and have psychological challenges, but there is no record of their discovery of crossing over. They feel alienated and often blame the world changing for the worse, but they don't realize that their world is actually on course and in harmony with their people at their level of enlightenment."

"So, do you think that this crossing over is an anomaly or that somehow it's needed for the betterment of the world that they cross over to?" asked Natalie.

"See, you're comprehending this better than you think," said Adrian. "That's an excellent question. Frankly, we don't know. We think it might be a rare but necessary natural event for precisely the reason you mentioned. But with Dr. Kamron, we have a problem. He has discovered the connection between the universes, and we believe he has established that death is a certain and natural portal for upward movement to the higher-level universe."

"But that's something most religions have alluded to in one form or another," said Natalie.

"Like I said, those who've crossed over like Dr. Kamron have often created philosophies and made scientific discoveries way more advanced for their time."

"That makes sense," said Natalie. "But wait, if it's been said before, why would Dr. Kamron's discovery be any different or have any consequence?"

"There's a big difference. At this era in human history when he scientifically establishes it publicly, it will go beyond a leap of faith or just a philosophy."

"So what? What's wrong with that?"

"Suicides in epidemic proportions," said Adrian.

Natalie frowned. "Do you have a clue as to why the rise in suicide started to begin with?"

"A clue we have. But it's not something we can reverse immediately. What we're trying to do is prevent another factor that could make it worse."

"What's the clue?"

"First, consider this: Humans know that they're all going to die eventually. That knowledge is so unnatural for human consciousness that it's a wonder how everyone goes about their lives and acts completely oblivious of their imminent demise. You see, possessing that definite knowledge about reality is enough to plunge anyone into a depression so deep that it would trigger suicidal thoughts."

"Yes, I can see that. But how come we don't all just jump off a bridge?" asked Natalie.

"Fortunately, our brains are equipped with a reality distortion mechanism that provides positive optimism despite the reality of imminent death. It's a normal, healthy function of the human brain, which constantly resists negative possibilities. Like when smokers keep smoking, fully aware of how they're endangering themselves, or people go to war thinking they're not going to be the ones harmed.

"Anyway, this mechanism allows us to live in a hopeful paradigm—as we should because throughout the course of our lives, the probability of safety is in our favor. Now, as a consequence of side effects from new pharmaceutical products prescribed in recent years, this healthy brain function of resistance to negative possibility is compromised in a large number of people, and that's causing an unusual rise in suicide rates."

"Can't people just not take these drugs?" asked Natalie.

Adrian shook his head. "I'm afraid that it's beyond just the people who are taking them. Most of the traces of these medications people take go through the sewer system and water processing plants and get circulated through our tap water. A lot of people end up being affected by them without even knowing."

"So that's an existing problem?"

Adrian nodded, sighing. "Yes. Now, on top of that, Dr. Kamron is about to introduce the poor man's portal to the parallel universe. We know he has discovered a very costly method of crossing over that will take generations to build and perfect. The passage of those generations is necessary for the human race to advance and use that knowledge properly. In a very private communication with one of his trusted collaborators, he was asked if any of us in this generation will be able to cross over, since it would take many decades to build this device for transiting into the neighboring universe. He replied, 'Yes, through death.' Like I told you, presenting a theory is one thing, but he's reached the point of irrefutably proving this natural process through scientific evidence."

"You know, you never told me how you got your information about Dr. Kamron's discovery of this portal thing," said Natalie.

"His most trusted collaborator is Professor Bishop, with whom I was doing my post-doc. Let's just say that either Professor Bishop is not very protective of the scientific correspondence that he gets, or maybe he just trusted me."

"Well, he must have had a good opinion of you, so he figured you wouldn't have any bad agendas, I guess."

"Anyway, if this knowledge becomes public information, can you imagine what it would do to the suicide rate?" asked Adrian.

"I get it," said Natalie. "If everyone knew for sure that death is a portal, they'd jump ship as soon as things got tough."

"Right," said Adrian, "but things always have a way of resolving and this process of challenge and resolution brings growth—a growth that's necessary for advancing consciousness in part and as a whole."

"Wow, that makes sense. You're being sexy again," Natalie giggled.

"Oh stop," said Adrian, smiling. He turned serious again. "But there is also the issue of safety and criminal behavior. Imagine if no one was ever afraid of death. All the pillars of balance in society would collapse."

Natalie clapped her hand to her forehead. "Good God, I didn't think of that aspect of it. But if you tell Dr. Kamron about all of this, is he the kind of man who would stop?"

"I'm banking on that. If I could only get some private time with him … I'm hopeful, since after all he is a humanitarian," said Adrian.

Natalie looked thoughtful. "So, you never told me who 'we' is."

"It doesn't matter."

"It matters to me. And by the way, does Dr. Kamron know anything about you and your friends?"

"We don't believe so."

"Look, I really think it's time you tell me who 'we' is."

"It'll make no difference to you."

"I want to know," insisted Natalie. "Do you want to know me better?"

"I do."

"Then I need to know what you're mixed up in."

"Mixed up in? Please," scoffed Adrian.

"I know, I'm kidding. I get that it's somehow noble and it involves some intellectual badassery. But I need to know."

"You have to believe me when I tell you we have no identity," said Adrian.

"I swear, if you don't tell me, I'll get my hand on that sissy necklace of yours and run. And I don't care how high-tech it is."

Adrian smiled. "I'm telling you the truth. We have no identity as a group. It's not an organization *per se.*"

"Well then, how did it start? And how many of you are there?"

"You don't understand. This group was formed way before I was born and has always had only a handful of members."

Natalie got up. "You're killin' me. Just tell me from the beginning. What do you call yourselves?"

"Fine, I'll tell you. Sit down," said Adrian. "'We' consists of simply three conscientious professionals: one scientist, one economist, and one physician."

"What, like you guys meet at a pool party or something and decide to do the world some good?" said Natalie.

"Are you going to listen or keep making conjectures?"

"Okay," she responded, playfully. She made a graceful sweeping gesture with her arm. "Mr. Saint Clair, please proceed."

—◦⋄◦—

46

SAVING CAPITALISM FROM THE CAPITALISTS

"The group was formed by the order of the president of the United States," said Adrian.

"Oh my God," said Natalie. "You've got to be kidding me. You? In politics?"

"No, please let me finish."

"Sorry, sorry, go on."

"Not the current president, but President Cleveland."

"Which one was that?"

"He was the president of the United States who served two nonconsecutive terms—one from 1885 to 1889 and then again in 1893," said Adrian.

"Good Lord, your friends' work goes back that far? And what did they believe in?"

"Yes, that far," said Adrian. "They believed and we still believe in the Constitution of the United States as a good model form of law that was set forth by a brilliant group who had the best intentions. However, the Constitution was written in 1787, when corporations were not the monstrosities that they've become with time. Therefore, the Constitution did not provide a provision to protect the public from them as it did with entities such as religion.

"Imagine a history where the Constitution would have made it impossible for corporations to give financial contributions to politicians and therefore limit their influence on the political system and all the corruption that comes with it. Imagine if we had a separation of corporations and state right after the separation of church and state. Just think about the quality of characters who would enter the public service rolls if they knew they did not have to become lapdogs to the corporations.

"Anyway, by 1888, President Cleveland had become one of the few voices who could foresee the catastrophes that come with unfettered corporate power. On December 3, 1888, in his State of the Union Address, he specifically said, 'Corporations, which should be the carefully restrained creatures of the law and the servants of the people, are fast becoming the people's masters.'

"Shortly after that speech, he formed a sort of covert pact where he handpicked three professionals who started a corporate watchdog group. They realized that they could not stop every nasty, unconscionable act by every corporation, but their objective was to pinpoint the worst ones whose activities could harm the public and then report directly to the president. Their one and only hope was—and continues to be—to help save capitalism from the capitalists."

"So, do you guys believe in capitalism?" asked Natalie.

"Absolutely. Capitalism is the most viable economic system because it is ingrained in human progressive nature. But if capitalists abuse the very system that has been fruitful for them through corporate greed, ultimately the public, whose health, environment, and safety is compromised by some of these corporations, will mistakenly move against the system itself. This has happened at different times in history, such as in 1848, when a movement started all over Europe against the aristocracy because the lower classes became fed up with their landlords' greed and eventually ended the aristocratic system altogether.

"You see, while we believe in capitalism, free enterprise, and the right to increase profitability, we must remember that there is currently no moral filtering in most large corporations. It is an entity whose one and only objective is to maximize revenue without considering its impact on human life on this planet. How can humanity be safe with such powerful monstrosities?

"Although not every large corporation is unethical, corporate representatives are often just mouthpieces of a heartless creature. Shareholders, for the most part, couldn't care less about corporate actions as long as they receive their dividends and can pass any blame along to the directors. In turn, the directors hide behind the corporate veil while they plan and implement agendas to make the monster bigger so that they can feed off its fat. Thus, the public's only saviors are lawmakers, and if these lawmakers are on the leash of corporations, then frustration builds and the whole capitalist system can end up in jeopardy. That's why President Cleveland had the foresight to be concerned."

"So, what cool things have your pack of three done that are famous?" asked Natalie.

"When we succeed, the problem is prevented early on," said Adrian. "We watch corporate policies and once we detect the worst ones, we make an annual report to the current president at the time. The good thing is that a letter has been passed from president to president since Cleveland that advises them to keep our pact active and to bypass red tape. So every year, our report gets into the president's hands. Now, what happens thereafter depends on who was elected and how much influence they themselves are under by certain corporations. But I can tell you that, over the course of more than a century, our reports have done a lot of good for humanity, even though sometimes they get pushed under a rug for years."

"So your small group became a watchdog for corporate policies?" asked Natalie.

"Something like that," said Adrian. "It began as a corporate watchdog but sometimes we'd come across other factors against humanity and at least try to intervene. Like I told you, we were doing a viability study for a project and researching various damages when we saw that CDC report on the monetary toll caused by suicide. A closer look revealed a much more severe problem at hand with the continuous rise in the suicide rate."

"And here you are."

"And here we are."

"Back to humanity. Tell me something," said Natalie. "Does the human race ever reach enlightenment through all of these histories of development?"

"Yes, through human development as a unified consciousness."

"How does it work, this development to a unified consciousness?" asked Natalie.

"Very slowly. It starts with spreading information and disease."

"What? Say what?"

"In the beginning, colonies around the planet were as different as they could be but still part of the human race," said Adrian. "Geography, ethnicity, and more importantly, belief systems segregated human consciousness. Each colony had its own belief system around which formed a culture, social system, and later a country. But this variation naturally fed prejudices.

"Prejudice feeds on ignorance, and so the more ignorance they had about one another, the greater the isolation in consciousness. The improvement of these two factors work simultaneously on a very slow, gradual basis until the entire human race on the planet comes to a collective consciousness.

"Along the way, something boosts the process. Frankly, I think it's by some helping hand like the photography thing I told you about, but we don't need to go there.

"Anyway, as an example, the first boost came with the development of networks that helped connect colonies. The networks began as transportation systems, and they started with ships, railroads, and airplanes. Now remember, these networks transported cultures with information contained therein as well as viruses and other microorganisms previously isolated in each colony. These organisms somehow serve to connect humanity.

"Do you really think it's a fluke of nature that so many of us catch the flu every year or so? These and other organisms are constantly working to synchronize our existence on the information level. This synchronization of consciousness between human colonies exponentially advanced with new networks such as telephones, television, and then later, the Transnet. With Transnet, nations around the world became simultaneously in tune, online, connected, and ever so rapidly synchronized in consciousness. You see, the human race always begins as a scattered species across the planet. Its destiny, however, is to evolve to unify to a collective consciousness, both in mind and body.

"You mean a single body?" asked Natalie.

"No—more like a complete commonality embodiment. That's what Adam is."

"Adam, our counselor?"

"Yes. Remember how he looks like he belongs to all races and none? And how he can feel and connect with everyone at such a deep level? When a human society reaches the point that everyone can feel everyone else's joy and pain, then there is no way a bad corporate or government policy can be sustained because the masses with their collective consciousness can resist to preserve peace, harmony, and health for all its parts. This, at its very infancy, is already starting, now that every being is semiconnected online with Transnet and is therefore informed of the status of others across the planet. Even as recently as decades ago, most people were oblivious of the disasters of fellow humans across the planet in real time."

"Wait, let's get back to Adam," said Natalie. "How can he have reached this advancement when we haven't evolved in this world to that level yet?"

"Yes, that's right—we haven't in *this* world," said Adrian.

Natalie turned pale. "Oh my, oh my."

"That's how he knows so much."

"Oh my God, it all makes sense now! He's crossed over too, just like Dr. Kamron did, right?"

Adrian nodded. "Yes, he's from a world so advanced that he had to find someone like your grandpa to stay with."

"What do you mean?"

"Just that he would suffer tremendously living among the truly primitive minds in this universe. It would be kind of like us living among cavemen."

"Wow," said Natalie. "I'm getting shivers recalling my interactions with him. I feel so stupid, even mean—what he must have thought of my sense of humor and all."

"I'm sure he was amused."

"Like hanging out with a monkey at a zoo?"

Adrian grinned. "Well, your chin looks kinda like—"

"Oh stop it. Tell me, Adrian, do you really and wholeheartedly believe there's hope for humanity?"

"Absolutely. Humanity is in its infancy. Don't be disappointed or disturbed by our history because we're destined to go to a great point of advancement and refinement. Just like an infant or a very small child who makes a lot of mess and a lot of noise—that's what we've been doing so far. It's hard to envision that refined individuals eventually come out of messy, rowdy children, but they do.

"The human race shall too become enlightened and refined to the point that it will not only be worthy of this beautiful blue planet, but it will also export its refinement elsewhere in this universe and to other universes whose beings are in an infant stage of development—just as we were the recipients of such helping hands for our own development.

"The fact is that Earth is young. Earth is rich. Earth is safe. Our oceans are vast and full of life. Earth's energy source is our sun, which is a very young star that will shine for us for billions of years, watching us grow to be brilliant beings. We will change direction from our current foolishness as we end up feeling and understanding the consequences of the harms we cause.

"And this is just the beginning for impressive creatures who will continue to transform themselves from semi-animal forms to enlightened beings. We should not be hard on ourselves or discouraged because the advancement of our societies began to flourish only in the last couple of hundred years, boosted by gifts from beyond.

"While our race may trace back to six million years on this planet, humans as we know them—*Homo sapiens*—have been around for only about 100,000 years. What's important to remember is that up until this last couple of hundred years, human society lived a very similar life for the remainder of its 99,800 years. So our development has just begun, and we will refine and redefine ourselves to create better and better history lines in this universe and beyond."

Natalie sat transfixed, gazing at Adrian fondly. "How wrong could I have been about you, lovely man."

Adrian smiled as he quietly looked at her.

"I have one last question to see if I've got this right," Natalie said. "Is it possible to change the history in one universe while in another, that particular history continues with a whole different outcome?"

"Precisely," said Adrian.

"So let's take a look at an event in our universe, so I can get a sense for it," said Natalie.

"Let's."

"How about the impact of Lady Paix on the history of our universe?" asked Natalie.

"The French-born German nurse?"

"Yes, Hitler's most trusted maid."

"Okay," said Adrian.

"So, on the night that Hitler conquered France in 1940," said Natalie, "she went to his bathroom and threw her body on top of him while he was in the tub until he drowned. If it weren't for her heroic act that cost her her own life, who knows what course World War II would have taken. Perhaps a much more widespread war and even the United States might have gotten involved ..."

"Yes, thank goodness for this world that she managed to stop him there," said Adrian.

"Is there any way to influence the course of events in your favor?" asked Natalie. "You know, change the history line for better?"

"Yes."

"With what?"

"With the most powerful force—love," replied Adrian. "Be it self-love or noble love, it makes no difference. When the intensity of love reaches a critical mass, it will shift the course of events wherein the universe duplicates itself to accommodate for love."

47

THE GOODBYES

The next morning after having breakfast with Dr. and Mrs. Kamron, Alex and his wife offered to walk with them down to their car to see them off. Along the way, Dr. Kamron asked if he could present one last question.

"By all means," said Alex.

"I can't help but wonder why you didn't consider launching the dome into outer space in times of trouble for this planet?" asked Dr. Kamron. "I mean, if or when you have to, you have everything here from the ecosystem and its atmosphere to all the ingredients for sustaining life."

"You, sir, are touching on my ultimate dream," said Alex.

"And?"

"There is a problem."

"A problem?" asked Dr. Kamron.

"Yes, a problem that has prevented me from effectuating this dream, although I have developed a department within our science team to work exclusively on that for future generations."

"And what is that problem?" asked Dr. Kamron.

"Well, you know that space is full of dangerous cosmic rays," said Alex. "I would need powerful magnetic field protection against these rays."

Dr. Kamron nodded. "But you're still working on it?"

"Yes. That would be *the ultimate dome*. But it will take eons to create," said Alex.

Dr. Kamron responded, "Perhaps, eons ago, someone created it. We just need to follow that design and we will once again have an ultimate dome. And with that, you might virtually defy the second law of thermodynamics, which, as you know, states that you can't have a perpetual motion device because no matter how efficient it is, it will always lose energy and eventually run down."

Alex looked uncharacteristically puzzled.

Dr. Kamron continued, "The clue is under your nose—or feet, I should say. It's 'Earth's reversal of its magnetic field.' Model your energy mechanisms after Earth's magnetic field production. By constantly reversing itself, it is able to continue its virtual perpetual motion."

"Is it really infinite?" asked Alex.

Dr. Kamron chuckled and replied, "It's as infinite as you're ever going to get."

He continued, "Look into how the core of the Earth's magnetic field works. Its convecting fluids work like currents in the wires. If the Earth did not have this spinning liquid core, it would have no magnetism, and it would be dead like the moon. The perpetual energy generated from this magnetic field comes from a unique design whereby it reverses itself on an average of 500,000 years. The key to its virtual perpetuity is the reversal system. Imagine an hourglass designed to reverse and turn itself when it almost reaches the last of its remaining sand so that it can start again and create energy."

Dr. Kamron added, "Just like you, whoever designed this sphere for us thought of such incredible details for our protection that it brings me to my finest point of humility. This magnetic field safely deflects harmful rays into Van Allen belts, which are zones of near-space. This field generated by Earth's core protects life on Earth."

Alex was in awe. He replied, "Perhaps our meeting did serve a purpose for the dome after all."

As they stepped out of the elevator onto the ground level, Dr. and Mrs. Kamron once again expressed their gratitude for Alex and his wife's hospitality. They all walked through the building and out the glass entry doors until they arrived outside at the top of a wide circular staircase.

They stopped when they saw Adrian by the car on the driveway below. Natalie ran past them and reached Adrian.

"I have brought you a bag of goodies for the road," said Natalie to Adrian.

Adrian gently kissed her, thanking her.

"Don't forget, you promised to return soon," she said.

"You couldn't keep me away now," said Adrian.

"I couldn't keep you away before—Mr. Saint Clair dropping in from the sky and taking away a girl's heart. What's up with that?"

"For what it's worth, I'm leaving my heart behind," said Adrian.

"That's the last thing you said last night, and I've been thinking about it," said Natalie. "Why would a restless soul like you say that and promise to come back and stay?"

"I don't have to be restless anymore," said Adrian. "The balloon that I lost to the wind when I was a child came back in your hands."

Adrian walked up the stairs from the driveway. He thanked Alex and his wife, to which Alex replied, "My granddaughter tells me that we should be seeing you back very soon."

"That's true, sir. It would be an honor to spend more time with you."

"It will be a pleasure," said Alex.

As Alex and Adrian exchanged a few final words, Dr. and Mrs. Kamron slowly made their way to the town car by Natalie. Suddenly Dr. Kamron stopped in his tracks.

"Oh my God, look, honey! Another one of those strange insects! I thought I'd never come across another one," he exclaimed.

Dr. Kamron then turned to Alex and pointed to the creature sitting on the antenna of the car. "Look, Alex," he shouted, "have you ever seen anything like this before? It's an absolute rarity in nature, isn't it?"

Alex raised an eyebrow with a genial shrug, then turned to Adrian and said, "That's really strange. Why is he excited about seeing a common flat fly that you see everywhere in this world?"

Adrian smiled. "He's not being strange, sir. In this world, he is just a stranger."

48

NEW BEGINNING

"So what kind of name is Natalie, Dad?" asked the son.

"I don't know. But wasn't she beautiful?" said his father.

"The best-looking grandma ever!"

"Not grandma, son. She was your great-great-great-grandmother. She was part of the first crew that made it all possible for us to be here today."

"I saw her image for only two minutes. Can we watch it again?" asked the son.

"Not tonight. We've watched three hours of the original crew footage already tonight. It's time to go to sleep. Say goodnight to Mom."

"We'll watch some more together again tomorrow," said the boy's mother.

The child walked to his room.

His father turned to his wife. "I can't believe how restless this kid is. I wonder where he got it."

"He didn't get it from my side," said the wife.

The father called out to his son. "Don't forget to brush your teeth. And please, no tapping on the headboard while you're trying to fall asleep, Love."

Notes

This novel refers to many sources of scientific data, historical references, philosophical thought, and quotations by notable figures. We have attributed quotations to their originator by name in the novel's dialogue. Additional significant works or sources are listed below.

Page   **4. Great Minds Think Alike**

37   *"100 miles wide"*
37   *"were also present"*
37   *"head toward our home"*
38   *"none of us would be here today"*
39   *"have started collapsing"*
39   *"keep the planet dynamic"*
39   *"a depth of four kilometers"*
39   *"Pangaea"*
40   *"water slosh in the English Channel"*
41   *"Lower that value very slightly"*

Bryson, Bill. *A Short History of Nearly Everything.* New York: Random House, 2003.

5. Liberating Ideas

46   *"The really valuable thing"*

Einstein, Albert. *The World As I See It.* Hawthorne, CA: BN Publishing, 2007.

8. The Function of Life

82   *"breathe the thin air"*

Bryson, Bill. *A Short History of Nearly Everything.* New York: Random House, 2003.

82   *"in the Pecos River in Texas*

83   *"sensitivity to water pressure fluctuations"*

Wikipedia. "Mexican Tetra." Accessed September 21, 2015.
https://en.wikipedia.org/wiki/Mexican_tetra

10. Time

94   *"close to 1,000 miles an hour and 24,000 miles a day"*

Fraknoi, Andrew. "How Fast Are You Moving When You Are Sitting
Still?" *The Universe in the Classroom*, Spring 2007.
https://nightsky.jpl.nasa.gov/docs/HowFast.pdf.

94   *"You would measure time the measureless and the immeasurable"*

Gibran, Kahlil. *The Prophet*. New York: Alfred A. Knopf, 1923.

95   *"When you lose all sense of self"*

Rumi, Jalal al-Din. *In the Arms of the Beloved*. Translated by
Jonathan Star. London: Tarcher/Penguin, 1997.

11. God

100–102 [General reference]

Hamer, Dean. *The God Gene: How Faith Is Hardwired into Our
Genes*. New York: Doubleday, 2004.

100   *"neurotransmitters that regulate our moods"*
101   *"likely to have more children"*
101   *"spiritual individuals are favored by natural selection"*
101   *"religion is institutional"*
101   *"and the limbic system became"*
102   *"together a profound religious experience"*

Kluger, Jeffrey. "Is God in Our Genes." *Time*, October 25, 2004.

101   *"the God gene, VMAT2"*

Wikia.org, Psychology Wiki. "God gene." Accessed March 31,
2015. https://psychology.wikia.org/wiki/God_gene.

13. MORALITY

107   *"A man's ethical behavior"*

Albert Einstein, "Religion and Science." *New York Times Magazine,* November 9, 1930.

14. FAITH AND A TREE

113   *"Is not religion all deeds and all reflection"*

Gibran, Kahlil. *The Prophet.* New York: Alfred A. Knopf, 1923.

15. DEATH

116   *"You would know the secret of death"*

Gibran, Kahlil. *The Prophet.* New York: Alfred A. Knopf, 1923.

18. CHILDREN

129   *"Your children are not your children"*

Gibran, Kahlil. *The Prophet.* New York: Alfred A. Knopf, 1923.

19. HEALTH: WELLNESS WITHIN

131   *"30 very large hydrogen bombs"*
132   *"by the main body of a thunderstorm"*

Bryson, Bill. *A Short History of Nearly Everything.* New York: Random House, 2003.

20. PILLAR 5: THE RHYTHM OF OUR SOUL

138   *"who took the cheaper pills"*

Waber, Rebecca L., Baba Shiv, Ziv Carmon, and Dan Ariely. "Commercial Features of Placebo and Therapeutic Efficacy." *Journal of the American Medical Association* 299, no. 9 (March 5, 2008): 1016–17.

30. SHORTCUTS FOR SHAWDI

193   *"The Guest House"*

Rumi, Jalal Al-Din. *The Illuminated Rumi*. Translated by
Coleman Barks. New York: Broadway Books, 1997. Used
with permission from the translator.

33. THE GRAPE STORY

209   *"I Am Fear"*

Tice, Lou. "I Am Fear." Accessed June 6, 2015. http://www.loutice.com.

210   *"one billion dollars in property damage"*

Mastro, Lauren L., Michael R. Conover, and S. Nicole Frey.
"Deer–Vehicle Collision Prevention Techniques."
Human-Wildlife Interactions 1, no. 2 (2008): Article 15.
https://digitalcommons.usu.edu/hwi/vol2/iss1/15.

37. A PERFECT WISH: MAY WHAT YOU LIKE BE WHAT YOU NEED

243   *"attention and blessing of Chenrezig"*
243   *"these six syllables"*

Dharma Haven.org. "Om Mani Padme Hum: The Meaning
of the Mantra in Tibetan Buddhism." Dharma-Haven.org.
Accessed August 3, 2010.

39. H₂OPEN

253   *"As the future belongs to those who believe in the beauty of their dreams"*

Quote by Eleanor Roosevelt.

260   *"Homeopathy originated in Germany"*
260   *"At this level, the matter no longer"*
262   *"These minicomets are actually balls of water"*

Emoto, Masaru. *The Hidden Messages in Water*. New York: Atria
Books, 2001.

40. TO SURPASS A MULTIVERSE

273   *"nothing but hydrogen in the universe"*

Bryson, Bill. *A Short History of Nearly Everything*. New York:
Random House, 2003.

41. MAGIC TRIO

284 *"billions of times per second"*

Bryson, Bill. *A Short History of Nearly Everything.* New York: Random House, 2003.

286 *"stress with zinc"*

Emoto, Masaru. *The Hidden Messages in Water.* New York: Atria Books, 2001.

44. BOUNDARIES OF LIFE

305 *"2.2 million made suicide plans"*

Crosby, Alex E., Beth Han, LaVonne A. G. Ortega, Sharyn E. Parks, and Joseph Gfroerer. Centers for Disease Control. "Suicidal Thoughts and Behaviors Among Adults Aged ≥18 Years—United States, 2008–2009." *Surveillance Summaries: Morbidity and Mortality Weekly Report (MMWR)* 60, no. 13 (October 21, 2011): 1–22.

308 *"the spin of one particle"*
309 *"opposite direction at the same speed"*

Bryson, Bill. *A Short History of Nearly Everything.* New York: Random House, 2003.

329 *"on an average of 500,000 years"*
329 *"Van Allen belts"*

Bryson, Bill. *A Short History of Nearly Everything.* New York: Random House, 2003.

Fiction can transcend and shape reality. This was me when I first wrote this fictional story. At that time, it did not include all of the nuances and the data contained in this book, but the essence of this story was all there. When I read it to the woman who taught me how to conjugate the word "love"—my mother—this was my first story that I ever presented to her. She reflexively asked, "Is that from a movie you saw?" I stared at her with disbelief. She is the most intelligent lady I have ever met (and yes, I would say that even if she wasn't my mom). One look at my expression and she realized what she had done. She quickly backtracked and said, "I loved it—it's just that it was so scientific that I thought it was from a futuristic movie." She is always thoughtful of our feelings and pride. So, naturally concerned that she may have hindered her son's first creative work, as soon as dad came home that evening, the first thing she told him was that he should listen to my story that very night.

My dad is a pragmatic man. When I was a young boy, he was a doctor of veterinary medicine, who had recently graduated from a university in Colorado and was enjoying the peak of his career. Nevertheless, he always made time for me and my very cool and bright brother who inherited our parents' intellect.

After listening to my story, he said only one thing. To this day, his comment impacted my life: "When our guests arrive for dinner this weekend, they just have to hear you recite this story." So, in front of about 20 people, I read my story and the proud look on my dad's face shaped my confidence ever since to present my ideas and later the advocacy necessary to represent my clients effectively.

CPSIA information can be obtained
at www.ICGtesting.com
Printed in the USA
LVHW090353180121
676770LV00004B/48